DRUM
INTO
SILENCE

Tor Books by Jo Clayton

DRUM
INTO
SILENCE

JO CLAYTON
and
KEVIN ANDREW MURPHY

TOR®

A TOM DOHERTY ASSOCIATES BOOK
New York

DRUM INTO SILENCE

A Tor Book
Published by Tom Doherty Associates, LLC
175 Fifth Avenue
New York, NY 10010

www.tor.com

Tor® is a registered trademark of Tom Doherty Associates, LLC.

ISBN: 0-312-86120-6

First Edition: December 2002

Printed in the United States of America

0 9 8 7 6 5 4 3 2 1

Acknowledgments

Finishing Jo's book has been an amazing experience and I have many people to thank.

First, Katharine "Kit" Kerr, Jo's literary executor and one of my oldest friends. Thanks for asking me, Kit, and thanks for all the support as I worked on this and so many other books.

Likewise, thanks to Howard Kerr, for all his comments and support, and thanks to Fran Zandonella, one of Jo's oldest fans and my oldest friends, for reading, comments and moral support.

Likewise, thanks to my editor, Debbie Notkin, for her fine edits and understanding when I ran late, and to all the fine folk at Tor working with her.

Thanks also to Jo's agent (and mine, for this book), Elizabeth Pomada, for all her help and encouragement.

Thanks also to my mother, Christine Murphy, for her support as I worked on this and other books.

But finally, most of all, thanks to Jo. We talked of working on a book together, and now we have. I hope this is the way you would have finished it yourself. I'm glad I played muse to you back when you were starting work on *Wild Magic*, at that party when we first met and I made you laugh, only finding later that you'd transmuted my silly joke about eccentric magicians and yodeling daggers into the Wrytstrike. Your humor was wry and subtle, and you had the final jest. Halfway through revisions, I realized what story the Parable of the Braysha Boy had been recast from, and I could hardly stop my laughter. I wanted to call you and tell you and thank you.

But I couldn't. So I'll just have to do it here. Thank you, Jo, for being friend and muse and so many other things. And for making me laugh.

Kevin Andrew Murphy

North

NYDD'S

Vale of the Mountains
Caerfynnon
Prenpool

Ellars Farm
Cyfareth
Carcalon
Tyst

The Halsianel Sea

Cypresta

FA

TILKO

KALE
Mage's Tower

Lim Ashir
in the
Aygirsade
Aile
Kuvvel

Yosun

The Continent of

NORDOMON

cMitchell '96

GLANDAIR

VIKAWAID

Finger
Lakes
Kingakun University
Lake
Mizukor

Banyakor

Idainamin

Higamin
Nishamin

CHUSINKAYAN

SEMMERTA
ISLANDS

Mionach

DOMAIN
EOLAIS

DOMAIN
PLANDA

Palanar River

DOMAIN
MIONN

Fasalla

Teyas Brota

The Continent of
SAFFROA

CMitchell '96

DRUM
INTO
SILENCE

Beginning the Pursuit of the White Bird

By the secret calendar of the Watchers, events dating from the 1st day of Seimis, the seventh month in the 739th year since the last Settling.

{ 1 }

A ragged, pain-filled cry drilled through Breith's sleep and woke him from the chaotic images that had been haunting his dreams since he stumbled through the Membrane between the worlds and found himself walking slopes where he'd spent so many hours watching Cymel and chattering with her about a thousand thousand things. Friend in a way no one else had ever been. Her voice echoed in that cry and brought him half-leaping, half-falling from bed; he went running down the stairs and out of Ellar's Tower.

In the patch of feathery, gray-white ash by what had been the kitchen of the farmhouse, he stumbled over a scatter of bodies someone had dropped there, caught his balance before he fell onto the most distorted of them — Ellar's mutilated corpse.

Though Ellar's limbs were twisted, wrenched from their

sockets, and his torso disfigured by cuts and bruises, his face was almost untouched. Despite the thick windy darkness of the night, Breith recognized him immediately. He dropped to his knees, smoothed the matted gray hair back off the man's face. "Dead. Prophet! Cymel must be half-crazy. I heard her. I know I did." He crawled to the next sprawled form. A woman. "Cymel?" He moved his fingers across her face. "No." He was surer than before that it was her voice that had wakened him, but this wasn't her. He scrambled round the corpse, drew his hand back hastily as it landed on a belly and startled a groan out of the sleeper. Man? "I think I . . ."

A bubbling, moaning cry jerked his head up.

At the top of a crumbling tor rising behind the line of fire-withered trees that marked the edge of the home-ground of the farm, the White Bird spread her wings and began shifting from foot to foot, her body swaying and jerking; she extended her long limber neck, her beak stabbing into the darkness, her throat pulsing as she repeated the call. She was getting ready to fly.

"*Mela!*" Breith bounded to his feet and raced toward the trees. "W*ait!*"

The bird grew more agitated; she snapped her wings back, pulled them forward in increasingly vigorous strokes, the wind she generated buffeting him as he lurched up the brittle, unstable scree. "Mela . . ." he called more softly, trying to calm her. "It's me, Breith, wait, don't move, it's Breith, don't . . ."

The bird sobbed again, then powered herself into the air — fleeing his touch with a fear that cut at him like knives. He leapt and caught hold of what felt like a knot of feathers. It shifted under his hand and he fell back to the tor clutching some long black hairs and a clasp woven from thin leather thongs—one of the ties that Cymel used to bind off her braids.

She didn't look back, just kept fleeing north, no hesitation in the sweep of those great white wings. He scowled after her, uncertain what he should do. Follow her? No. Not now. Kaxon and his wealmen would be here soon as it was light. If they weren't already on their way. Ryn Kaxon, the would-be Bigman, was jumpy as a hot-tail skink. If what Breith'd picked up from wealmen gossip was true, Kaxon wanted Ellar's land so bad he'd mow the meadows with his teeth if he had to. All he needed was an excuse to take before the Tyrn's Court. "Got to clean the ground before I give it to him." Breith eased himself around, nearly fell as a fragment of rock turned under his foot. "Ahhh! So I'm stuck here for now." He cautiously shifted his weight to his other foot, looked over his shoulder.

The White Bird had vanished among the clouds. "I'll be seeing you, Mela. Sooner than you think." He closed his fingers about the hair clasp, felt it grow warm against his skin. "Yes. Sooner than you think."

His immediate problem was what to do about the folk she'd brought to him; the dead might be safe from Kaxon and his ambitions, but their presence meant trouble if Breith left them where they lay. They gave away too much—maybe not to Kaxon; he was an ignorant man with no feel for Pneuma, but the men running him were much more dangerous. And there was always the Nyddys Mage. And what about the others? The sleepers?

He glanced to the east—no light showing yet, but dampness, coolness hanging in the air, and he could feel the dawn wind lifting, dropping, lifting again. Day was coming faster than he liked. Even if Kaxon had missed the White Bird—a stroke of luck Breith didn't expect—the wealmen and the cofflegang working the farm for him would be on the road soon, heading up the mountain.

Moving as fast as he could in the thick, humid darkness, Breith hauled the sleepers inside the Tower, laying them out on the stone flags of the entryway. But when he got to Ellar and the horribly mutilated stranger clinging to him, he hesitated. He didn't know what the death of Cymel's father might do to the magic sustaining and protecting the Tower. "Do I have a choice? That's the worst of this whole mess. There's always a choice, but you never know the consequences until you've stepped in it so deep. . . ."

Glad he couldn't see much but twisted outlines, wishing his nose was as blocked as his eyes, he hoisted the awkward burden to his shoulder and staggered into the Tower.

As he folded the arms of the unknown man across his battered chest and started winding the body in a sheet off one of the beds, he could sense the Tower approving his actions—which felt decidedly odd—so he stopped worrying about the spells that protected it and him. Something else was going on here, something he couldn't get in focus . . . it was like a fish of some sort swimming at the edge of his blind spot, a faint vibration that he could never be sure he wasn't imagining. Cymel might know, but she was gone. Ellar was dead. And he didn't dare trust anyone else. Not on Glandair.

No threat. More a sense of waiting. Breith shrugged and went on with his unpleasant but necessary work.

Once Ellar and his companion were shrouded and ready for burial, he carried them into the dark earth-scented cellar. When the wealmen were gone for the night and wouldn't hear the sounds of his laboring, he'd pry up some of the flags and bury the dead. He lifted his head, stood very still as he heard a rooster crow. That would have to wait. He still had to do something with the sleepers. The Tower attracted Kaxon like a sore tooth; he hovered round it, kept trying to peer through the dusty, vine-covered windows. Breith moved his aching shoulders, groaned as a wave of fatigue washed over him.

One more chore, then I can rest.

He dropped to his knees, groped among the dense shadows until he found one of the sleepers. Grunting under the weight, he eased the body over his shoulder and got to his feet.

After he left the last sleeper on a dusty, cobwebby bed in a room filled with the thick gloom of the predawn darkness, he stumbled up the stairs to the bedroom he'd taken for himself. Yawning, struggling to keep his eyes open, he poured water in a basin, then dropped on the edge of the bed, shaky knees giving way before a tsunami of fatigue, a weariness of mind and body that overwhelmed him. He was asleep before he'd more than lifted his hand from his thigh, intending to strip off the filthy nightshirt and wash away at least the top layers of sweat, ash and stench.

Breith gulped down the last swallow of tea in the mug; it was bitter and barely lukewarm, but he was clean again, rested, and that murky fluid gave him a jolt of energy that brought a twisty smile to his face. With a snap of his fingers, he lit a pale witchlight, and with it floating a few inches above his head, went to see just who it was Cymel had dropped on him.

Lyanz.

"Why am I not surprised?" What this was all about, shielding that man from the Mages and everything else. Didn't matter who else got maimed, murdered or driven off from home and family, the Hero had to be protected. And he was more beautiful than ever. He looked like one of the Prophet's Messengers laid out like that on the bed, his golden hair in a tangled halo about his golden face.

"I'd like to see you try to survive being a slave; bet you wouldn't even get out of the House, let alone escape and get away from the Hounds like I did."

Fiercely glad that Cymel wasn't here to spend her time hanging over the Hero, fluttering like a female colo at the peak of her season—a thought that made his stomach burn and churn—he pulled the door shut and climbed to the next landing.

Amhar.

"I thought I knew you." Scribe and Walker. He wheeled and went to stare out the window, scowling at the faint shadows of the wealmen reaping winter rye from a meadow higher up the mountain. She didn't have to wait for thin places in the Membrane to step across from Iomard to Glandair. Just because she'd been born with a womb and he hadn't. He remembered his lessons with her and felt anger burn hotter in him. "Prophet! Why'd Mela bring you? What happened? Where were you? What are you doing here?"

The third sleeper startled him. That street thief Talgryf. Lyanz's friend, though Cymel knew him too. A long, skinny type who could squeeze into a crack in a wall and come out the other side with room to spare. He looked strange away from city streets, and Breith couldn't think of any reason why he should have left his natural territory. Or why Cymel had dumped him here with the others. All the same questions, the same nonanswers.

Breith scratched at his chin. If he walked out on these folk and went after Cymel, his father would look at him like he was a worm. Lower than a worm. But if he found someone better to take over? The anger and frustration burning in his belly cooled as he grinned down at the unsuspecting sleeper.

Yes. Dump this on him. Gryf. Breith's grin widened. This is his world and he knows its secret ways and he'll hate like fury having to run the Hero and Amhar. He reached down, took hold of the thief's shoulder and gave it a good shake.

Talgryf pulled away from him, muttered and wriggled around, working his face into the dusty pillow, his eyes squeezed into agitated crescents as he struggled not to wake.

"Gryf!" Breith shook him again. "Shift tinn!"

Talgryf blinked. For a moment he lay staring up at Breith, then he whirled over, bucked himself out of bed and was nearly to the door before Breith had time to snap his fingers and weave a stopweb into the opening.

"Calm down, man. It's not me who's apt to chew you up and spit you out. This is Ellar's Farm and it was Cymel who brought you here. Dunno why. She didn't stick around long enough to say."

Talgryf circled warily away from the blocked door, scowling at Breith who'd hitched a hip on the windowsill and sat there with his arms crossed, his head resting against the window glass. "Who seated you, Tyrn?"

"Hunh! Neither of us had a say in how we got here."

Eyes fixed on the doorway, Talgryf stood shaking his arms, loosening the joints. "You're not going to dump this mess on me."

"Sure I am. Ellar's dead and Cymel's tied up in a spell she can't get loose from. Can you work Pneuma? I can. So I'm heading out soon's I can to find her and break her loose." He straightened, let his arms fall to his sides. "The Hero's here. Still sleeping. You know the smugglers and their ships; you can take care of those two idiots in a dozen ways I couldn't. You can get him off Nyddys and across Faiscar and keep him alive while you're doing it. And you know cursed well you've got to do it." He shrugged. "Besides, isn't Lyanz a friend of yours?"

He wiped away the stopweb and headed for the door, talking as he moved. "There's food of sorts in the kitchen. Dry wood, so no smoke. We can make tea and wake the others up, then get to some planning. Have to keep heads down. There's wealmen working out there and worse. They suspect we're in here, we've got big trouble."

Gryf joined him on the stairs, his narrow dark face still closed up, a cold, smoldering anger like thunder at the back of his eyes. "Why not just stay till they get tired of us?"

"Because the Settling has started and there's no stopping it. You want to end up alive when this business finishes, you get our Hero to the Empty Place before the Mages manage to kill him." Breith waved at the bedroom doors. "Amhar's there. Lyanz is off the next landing down. You want to wake them, be my guest."

Breith filled the kettle and started water heating for tea, then he unwrapped one of the small round cheeses and handed it to Gryf to slice. "This stuff, it's Ellar's supplies. You want to hunker down and trust the Tower's spells to keep you out of the kak flying round out there, you can do it. Up to you what you do."

The kettle started to thrum and rattle on the burner. Talgryf finally unstiffened enough to help set out the meal, then carried the tray into the dust-ridden gloom of the lower hall.

Breith wrapped a hand about the bail of the kettle, his palm protected from the heat by a quilted pad. The pad was singed in spots and he disliked touching it, but it was better than acquiring burn blisters. "So," he said, as Talgryf came back into the kitchen, "what happened? Why did Cymel haul you here?" He tapped a measure of tea leaves into a strainer and poured boiling water through it into a large pot with a glaze of blue crackling.

"The Mages, all of them, they came after Laz." Talgryf shrugged, his face immobile, his eyes gone dull. "Not just them either. Raiders. The bloody gwarts that have been hitting settlements and slaughtering everything that draws breath. Likely no one left alive in the Vale."

"Hmp. I see." He filled a mug, pushed it across the table to Talgryf. "How likely is it we'll have Mages on our necks come morning?"

"Dunno." Gryf sipped at the tea, his face hard as a doorpost. "Like you said, you're the one knows magic." He took another sip. "So how you get here? You Walk like Amhar?"

Breith grimaced. "Walking only works if you have a womb." He poured himself a mug of tea as well, watched it spill over, didn't care, set the pot back on the table. "Can't Walk. Just ran into a spot of Pneuma Luck—ran through a hole in the Membrane from Iomard to here."

"Pneuma Luck, eh?" Gryf grimaced over the edge of his mug. "Round here we call that Tyrn's Luck. Or Hero's Luck. Not the sorta thing ordinary folk kin count on, Dyf Tanew and the Hag smilin' at the same time." He sipped a bit more tea. "Most folk it happens to once in their life, if that. After that . . . pffft! 'T's gone. Guess I used mine, Cymel savin' me from the Mages. Looks like you used yours too."

Breith thought back to the slavers of Ascal. "Guess so."

Gryf unwrapped another of the cheeses and carved it up into small fat wedges, laying them out on the crinkled white paper. "Best to make your own luck and alternate plans, that's what we say in the Bothrin. Only type who can count on Hero's Luck more than once is a Hero, and those come by only once every Settling." He offered a couple pieces to Breith. " 'Sides, I 'spect it all evens out anyway. Laz may have the Luck of ten Tyrns, but we don't have every Mage on two worlds chasing after us neither."

Breith took a long moment choosing between the virtually identical wedges, in the end deciding that it didn't matter and just taking the nearest. "Don't we?"

Talgryf popped the other wedge in his mouth. "Guess we do, so long as we're with Laz," he said around the mouthful, then gave Breith a sharp look. "Or are you another Hero? Got one for Iomard to go along with Glandair?"

Breith looked at the cheese, smooth and white with bits of nut and dried figs in the center, but didn't have the stomach for it. "No, just a Companion, same as you." He set the wedge aside with the others, untouched.

"For now." Gryf glanced around nervously. "Like I said, can't count on Hero's Luck if you're not a Hero. 'T's like the Hag—sweet milk one minute, chews you up and spits you out the next." He waved one hand, gesturing to nothing in particular but agitation. "Watchers are all dead. Used all their Tyrn's Luck finding the Hero."

"Had to, I guess. Only way to save the world. Both of them."

Gryf nodded. "Guess so. Guess it's up to us now." He sighed. "Only hope enough of that Luck will rub off Laz to save us. Wouldn't mind a spot of Tyrn's Luck once this is all over and done with."

"Hopefully for the better."

Gryf shrugged. "If it ends up for the worse, neither of us'll be in a position to complain. Best with you findin' Mela; she saved me, an' I hope she ain't used up her Tyrn's Luck yet."

Breith decided he liked Gryf. "Thanks. Best to you too, getting those two to the Empty Place."

Talgryf snorted. "Not going to count on Hero's Luck. Be nice if it happens, but better to count on good old Bothrin planning. Make your own Luck." He raised the mug and took a long sip of tea, contemplative. "Know anything that might help?"

Breith thought about it for a moment. "Hmph. You'll find maps in Ellar's workroom; that's up at the top of the Tower. From what I've seen, it's all Broony land east of here, mostly open ground and easy travel—except you'd better be careful to keep clear of Broony landguards. Which I expect you know better than I do. Me, I'm heading out round moonset. To-night."

[2]

Deep beneath the Temple of Dyf Tanew in the heart of Tyst, the silver lines of a hexagram glimmered uncertainly for a moment, then steadied to a pale, bluish glow. Pale flesh oozed through the stone flags, slowly yet with a certain in-evitability, until the naked body of the Nyddys Mage lay in-side the lines, solidifying into his normal state.

For nearly a full watch nothing more happened.

A finger twitched; a meager muscle spasmed along the back of a calf.

A groan fluttered thin, bluish lips.

A second groan. A line of drool leaking from the corner of his mouth, crawling across his face to drip on the floor.

For several more moments the Mage's body twitched and shuddered, then Oerfel pushed himself up and sat with his shoulders hunched, his head resting on arms braced on knees. Damp cold from the stone flags struck up through his buttocks; his teeth ached, his head ached, the migraine worse than he'd ever known it. He started to get to his feet, then folded his arms across his ribs, shuddered and retched, spew-ing vomit over his arms and knees; a few of the drops hit the hot silver lines and boiled into a miasma that eddied about his trembling body, the sporadic gusts of stench that blew into his face waking new waves of nausea. White jags sliced through the auras that rippled like water in front of his face and stabbed into his eyes until all he could see was that hard, cruel whiteness. The air he sucked in seemed devoid of vigor. . . .

[3]

Mahara glanced out the flap of his tent. Though the night was just beginning, the half-moon floated low above the peaks of the Ascarns, its pale glow fluctuating as the high winds blew wisps of ragged cloud across its face.

The clouds were thicker overhead, blocking most of the starlight, turning the night thick and black, so black that even the sharpest eyes had trouble seeing more than a step ahead. The sentries that walked their circuits through the tents of the siege army camped about Kar Markaz carried lantern poles to light their patrol routes, the red-gold fire of the wicks like lightning bugs crossing and crisscrossing the ground of the encampment. The walled city had its own complement of red-gold dots—braziers scattered along the walls with the catchfires meant to blow the coals under the oil pots into flame should the Kale army show signs of imminent attack.

Mahara followed the War Wizards from his tent and stood watching them walk off, their robes shimmering with sparks of color as the light that streamed from the opening left by the drawn-back door flap moved about the silk threads, jewels, and miniature mirrors of the elaborate embroidery that announced what they were. His mouth twisted briefly into a tight smile. Those robes were a boast of a power that none of them had paid the true price for. He knew the price and he knew the reward that paying it was going to bring him. Soon.

He shifted his gaze to the walls and the braziers whose

catchfires' red-gold dots drew the outline of the city on the thick black of the clouds. His lips curled in the same tight, triumphant smile as a quick count of fires on the nearest wall told him that the number of braziers had been reduced by half; fuel had to be running low. He rubbed at his nose. Inside those walls were the last defenders of High Tilk—the Farmyn, the remnant of his army and the portion of the population who for one reason or another hadn't had time or opportunity to run for the hills. And the Farmyn's sole War Wizard, a slippery, clever, unusually proficient practitioner, capable of out-thinking or out-playing any two of Kale's own War Wizards, but he was an ancient man with diminished energies. He tired rapidly, needed long rest periods between his strikes, and could be blocked with relative ease from any direct access to the Pneuma Flow; he needed the sparks from the catchfires to light the fuel laid beneath the oil cauldrons. Despite all his weaknesses, though, the Wizard's War Dance had kept them out of Kar Markaz much longer than Mahara had expected and had made its capture considerably more costly in men, supplies and time than the Mage had at first estimated.

He glanced at the sky, reading easily enough the turbulent Pneuma above him, despite the heavy layer of clouds. The Third Prince would be in Camp soon and this tedious waiting would be over. Once again his eyes dropped to the fire-dotted outline of the Citadel. Not that he'd let the days slide away unused. Hudoleth was going to bang her delicate nose against some surprises when she marched her army into Nikawaid. He stamped a broad, high-arched foot against the cold dirt and opened his mouth wide in a soundless shout of triumph.

[4]

Hudoleth closed her eyes, opened and closed her hands.

She reached out to a small hexagonal table that almost touched her hip and took up two crystals with faint blue glows deep inside them. Deliberately not looking at the image reflected there, she stood swaying before the immaterial analog of a full-length mirror, a magical object she had just created from a hoard of crystallized Pneuma.

What came next was always difficult for her, but there was no way she could avoid it.

THE IMAGE IN THE MIRROR: *An ancient hag, thin white hair straggling about a face plowed with wrinkles like rough furrows, everything about it—except those wrinkles—as sharp as a newly honed knife blade, especially the nose and chin. Skin dry as old leather, flaking away with every change of expression. Meager body dressed in a gown that dropped from shoulders like dress hangers carved from the rib bones of sharks.*

The woman who cast that image was a version of the Hag at the brink of middle age, beautiful still, though the forerunners of the wrinkles were visible in the creamy gold of her Myndyar skin. Her mouth twisted with distaste and resentment; she hated having to confront her fate—if she survived long enough, the time would come when the flood current of aging would be too strong for her to turn aside, when that ravaged face she saw in the mirror would be her only face.

The need for the renewal rite had come on her much sooner than usual. The failed attempt to snatch the Hero from the hands of the Watchers had drained her of much of her Pneuma-buttressed youth; she'd burned up still more energy as she extended her reach deeper into Nikawaid, moving her influence closer and closer to Mahara's perimeters, working silently, subtly through scores of surrogates to take control of the land that the Mage Mahara was planning to invade. Once she had that control, she could lay traps and destroy her greatest enemy, win the prize of prizes — control of the Pneuma of two worlds — the power that would make her greater than all the gods of Glandair and Iomard combined. And in that greatness lay the key to her deepest desires, to the safety she had fought for from the moment of her birth; she could defeat for eternity the Hag in the Mirror and there would be no one left who could tell her NO and make it stick.

Hudoleth drew in a long slow breath, held it for a few moments, then let the air trickle out as she forced herself to open her eyes and confront the ancient face, that withered, fleshless form. Lifting the crystals above her head, she began the rite that would return her youth to her. "Wa' ka," she chanted in the ancient tongue, the speech of the Dream-time. . . .

Wa' ka, lohon ah
Q'i manteenan soodu oh

She stamped a foot, swayed, began a slow circle dance, the crystals glowing brilliantly blue as she waved them above her head.

Ah' ka, eenees q'nay
Fey el do q'man atrodu oh

[5]

Rinchay Matan, Shaman of the Dmar Spyonk, a clan come forth out of the Grasslands to take the Promised Lakelands, sat atop a low hill at the edge of the Field of Final Killing. Her uncle the Pai-gor was dead, cut to rags by the soldiers of the Emperor. The children of her body were slaughtered along with most of her kin, her herds were scattered, her wagon and her tents were reduced to cinders and ash. Now she watched her god shrivel and fade like paper touched with fire.

Kamkajar the Merciful and All-Mighty, the Parter of the Seasons, who scattered the seeds of life with His golden right hand and reaped them with the scythe in His black left hand, Kamkajar, God of the Grasslands, halted before the battered remnants of the Grass Clan horde and stood with His arms outstretched, rays of red light welling from His fingertips, reaching from horizon to horizon.

The rays wavered and dimmed, faded to nothing. Tears gathering in His ice-colored eyes, the god lifted his face to the heavens. With a cry that filled the sky curve, He vanished and His Alaeshin vanished with Him.

[6]

A flimsy shield of no-see pulled round him, Breith slipped away from the Tower and slid into the scrub and bracken that grew in vigorous profusion between the fields and the dusty dirt road. It was hard going, but safer by far than a road thick with clumps of wealmen trudging back to the bunkhouses where Ryn Kaxon housed them. It'd been a long day that started too soon with the alarums generated by the appearance of the White Bird.

By the time Breith reached the point where the River Road split into three lanes, one going south, one north, and one east to the shore of the Halsianel Sea, he was more exhausted than he expected to be. The straps of his pack cut into his shoulders and his boots had already rubbed blisters on his heel.

He found a hiding place near the point where the road divided—the center of a storm tangle where a silkwood tree had been uprooted. A small thicket of silkwood saplings had grown up around the matted roots and a heap of boulders. He worked his way deep into the thicket and lay there listening to the grunting monosyllables of the weary hands passing by a few feet away from him.

As he lay in the clammy dampness, he was startled to see the owner of the Livery Stable at the River Landing driving a small herd of swayback ponies. He couldn't remember noticing her up the mountain before this. Her son rode behind her with a string of silent rivermen tied to a rope coffle, the control rope whipped about the horn of his saddle. One of the smaller forms stumbled, but the shaggy skeletal figure beside him caught hold of his shoulder and steadied him before the liveryboy had time to react.

Irritated, the boy gave a hard jerk on the rope; the bonded rivermen expected the reaction, rode the rope and trudged on in silence. Cursing under his breath, with a nervous glance to his mother, who gave no sign of having heard, he spat into the muddy ditch at the side of the road. "Gonna be raining afore we get home, Ma. Tildee here, she been sneezing in threes. You know what that means. Why's Ryn Kaxon so antsy about Ellar's Farm? Who's he think's hangin round there?"

"Less you talk 'bout that, better off we all are."

"Ma, 's better I know what to keep shut about." His voice was high and shrill, cutting through the whine of the wind and the clip-clop of the ponies' hooves. Once again he twitched the rope, sniggering when he saw another of the bondsmen stumble. "And if you thinkin' 'bout them here, they don't talk to no one except maybe each other. And mostly not."

Breith stretched out on the damp grass and leaves, worms of damp black mud crawling into his clothes, wet leaves blowing into his face. He'd heard all this before, grumbling gossip from wealmen farmhands eating their meager midday meals. The hobbled rivermen working off their sentences kept their silence and went on working; Kaxon might have rented them from the stablewoman, but he wasn't going to waste coin feeding them.

"That're *Ellar's* Farm up slope, not the Badger's land. That're what itching at him. He wants it."

Breith yawned, rubbed at his eyes. "Move it," he whispered. "Clear the road so I can get going again."

The old woman snapped her longwhip by the ear of a mare who'd slowed and started toward the grass-filled ditch. "Look and learn. The Witchman's land, it'd give Ooshai Kaxo enough stretts to make a Broony. He're tired of folk Rynning him. Wants the Broon brow knuckle. Say he catches the right game hanging round there. Say the Tyrn looks at Kaxon's catch and is happy to see it. When the Tyrn's happy, so's our Kaxon. 'Cause he gets his stretts and his Broony." She moved her shoulders in irritable circles. "Why do you think I been letting him have the ponies at cost and that lot you got there for a kalk a head when I could get double with a bit of looking about? He'll be our Broon and you know what that means. So you keep your mouth shut and jump when he says hop."

When road and river were at last empty of travelers, Breith crawled stiffly from his nest and sat on a lump of rock beside the road. Fingers deft from all the years he'd spent building ship models, he lined his boots with the thick soft leaves of the silkwood trees. Then he gathered all the silkwood pods he could find, filling his pockets with them.

A long, bone-cracking stretch and a yawn, then he began walking north on the trail of the White Bird. He had a suspicion that this was going to be a long chase, but also a grim determination to be there in the end. He was only just beginning to realize just how important Cymel was to him and how much he was willing to do to keep her in his life.

2

Flight

By the calendar of the Domains of Iomard, events starting on the 17th Ekhtos, the eighth month of the Iomardi year 6536, the 723rd year since the last Corruption.

[1]

"Breith!" Malart looked harried and worn; his green eye was bleached almost to a light silver, while the brown one was the color of dark beer. "Where are you?"

"Glandair, Da. What happened, first I go over the wall at the Chaletat then I sort of bump into one of those weak spots in the Membrane and before I know what's happening, here I am. Going to find Cymel, among other things. How are Mam and Mum?"

"Breith, what's wrong?"

"Nothing, Da. Why?"

"Because you don't talk like an illiterate ladesman unless you're playing some kind of game."

"Oh." Breith chewed on his lip. "Well, I've had a bit of a problem with the Glandair Mages. Ellar's dead. Cymel is spelled, don't know if she did it herself or one of the Mages did it to her. The Hero has started on his trek, but I'm not going with him, not until I find Cymel and shake her loose from that spell. What's happening in Valla? You look terrible. And what's happened to Mam and Mum?"

Malart drew his hand across his face. "Valla Murloch is under siege, Bré. The Army of Purification hasn't managed to take the Port yet, but I'm afraid it won't be long before they do. Your mam . . . well, you know her. Nothing and no one is going to shift her away from here as long as Urfa House is still standing. Your mum and I . . . well, we can't do that. Once Radayam has Valla, we're dead. Corysiam is finding us passage out while there's still time; we're thinking about a ship from Ascal. Not that we really have much of a choice."

"Da! Doesn't matter what their reputation, every Ascal captain is a slaver."

Malart smiled tiredly. "We know, Bré. It's just that we prefer slave chains to a brain burn."

Breith closed his hands into fists. He didn't know what to do. . . . "Ahhh. I've got it. Look, Da, you don't need to fool with Ascal. Get Corysiam to Bridge the two of you to Glandair and you can stay in Ellar's Tower. You and mum will be safe—and Mam Fori if you can talk her into it. All you'd have to do would be sit quietly and take a bit of care and wait for the Settling to be over."

His father shook his head. "Bré, we can't run like we're tickbirds laying eggs in ouzoets' nests. Your mum and I mean to do everything we can to stop the Domains—not just stop them, but turn them back—but first we have to get out of Valla and find a place where we have room to work. And that has to be somewhere on Iomard. You know your mum's Gift. Well, she's Seen a way . . . maybe. . . ."

"Then let me help. Tell Corysiam to Bridge me back to Iomard."

"NO!"

"No? What's wrong with me?"

"Breith, get the Hero to the Empty Place." There was a passionate force in Malart's words. "Find Cymel if you have to, but above all get Lyanz to the Empty Place. Help? You'll save us all!"

The deep conviction in his father's face and voice woke an answering heat in Breith and an equally strong belief that his father was right. He lifted his hand, the tips of his fingers resting for a moment over Malart's as he accepted his father's blessing. Then he finished the sign that closed the Window and got to his feet. Cymel first, then Lyanz. Work to do and no time to laze about.

[2]

Shaken by the rasping cough she hadn't been able to throw off for days now, Corysiam signaled Old Neech to open the gate, then leaned against the wall and fought to regain her breath.

Radayam had seized all shipping on the river and was sending a constant stream of smoke boats into Valla Murloch. Anything that could be made to float she ordered stuffed with anything that would produce stench and thick, clinging smoke—wet and moldy bedding straw; fresh droppings from horses, tribufs, cayochs and other beasts traveling with the army; stinkweed, algae and dead fish. Pneuma burnpods were sunk into the heart of these loads and triggered when the first houses of Valla Murloch came into sight. Great billowing poufs of smoke merged into a gray pall that hung over the city and leached at the spirits of those trying to defend it. The Traiolyns couldn't strike at Valla Murloch as directly as they had the other cities of the Eastern Confluence because there was too much power in the hands of the Valla Trade Houses—not all that much difference between Householders like Faobran and any of the Traiolyns ruling a Domain—and the various ruling Councils of that city, but Radayam was proving adept at finding inventive ways to abrade away that power.

[3]

Scribe Archivist Slionn breathed a sigh of relief as her count confirmed that the shadow of an old woman slipping through the gate marked the last of the book-bearers on tonight's run. She waited till another shadow touched the bearer's arm and led her away, then she gave the signal herself for Old Neech to shut the gate.

With Faobran's consent Malart had arranged to take into Urfa House the Scribes at the Repository who secretly belonged to the Valla Murloch branch of Corysiam's History Runda and to provide a hidden space to hold the more important—and dangerous—of the books and records from the Repository. The Rundanar had already brought enough material to fill to capacity several of the lowest basements and storage caves.

Each book-bearer knew what would happen if enforcers from any of the three Councils caught her doing this smuggling, but though all of them were often afraid, they were also contented with their choice. They were the daughters of two traditions, the new born from the old and completing it.

Slionn labored with pride and determination, feeling the same satisfaction as her workers, though when she was tired and depressed, as she was tonight, she sometimes yearned for the old times when all she had to do was rub protective wax into the book covers and mend torn pages. She sighed, then followed her ears into the heavy shadow clinging to the wall.

She found Corysiam crouched with her arms folded tight

across her breasts, coughing weakly and spitting gobs of pale phlegm on the ground.

"Prophet!" Slionn muscled the younger woman onto her feet and began walking her toward the house. ". . . acting like a fool. If you kill yourself, Radayam and her lot have beat you and hurt us. Just hurt us, mind you, not stopped us. You aren't that important and you'd better get that through that mop of fuzz you call hair."

A chuckle came from the darkness ahead of them and Malart stepped from shadow into starlight.

[4]

A snore broke in half as the hard fingers that gripped Corysiam's shoulder shook her out of a heavy sleep. She jerked upright before she was fully awake, then pressed the heels of her hands against her eyes as a spate of dizziness started her swaying from right to left. "Wha . . ."

"Sorry, Cory." Faobran's voice sounded hoarse and tired. "I'd let you sleep yourself out, but there's no time. Did you find a ship?"

Corysiam pressed harder against her eyes, as if she were trying to force light into her laboring brain, then she sighed and dropped her hands. "No. Ah! Is there some water handy? My mouth is so dry I can hardly talk."

"No?" As Faobran pushed a half-full glass against Corysiam's palm, the Scribe could feel the woman's fingers tremble. "The Army of Purification is getting set to attack. Probably tomorrow afternoon."

Corysiam gulped at the water, sat cupping the glass against her stomach. "No one I'd trust with a crippled fryher. The best of them are in the names you gave me of those captains who have dealt fairly with you—I say best because they might be wary enough of you to treat your Seyls better than they would otherwise. I'll add my weight with the Scribes. We keep our business to ourselves so he won't actually know how little that means. My own choice is Bryheris and his *Kelai Maree*—mostly because he'll be leaving on the sundowner tide so he'll be long gone by dawn tomorrow."

"Bryheris. I don't know. . . ." Faobran spoke very slowly, her eyes narrowed. "He's slick. In our dealings he's been as honest as most, but . . . hm . . . more than once I've smelled resentment on him. Could be he'd do me a deliberate injury if he felt he could get away with it." She sighed. "On the other hand, he doesn't take chances with his ship or with his crew. And the others are no better. With the choice so limited . . . well, Yasa isn't helpless and she'll have Malart with her."

[5]

Impressive in the smoky gray glass of her Pneuma-drenched armor, her longsword across her back and the short, stabbing sword at her side, Faobran came rapidly into the room, crossed to Yasayl. She hugged her sisterwife hard, her eyes glittering with the tears she'd never let fall.

When she finally let go, she stepped back and looked around. "Where's Malart?"

"Here." Malart came in and dropped two packs on the floor beside Yasayl. "I've stripped out everything but blankets, rope, some tools and a bit of canvas, food, water, soap, mending things and some changes of clothing. Any cash we have we'll carry in our belts and boots. And we don't bring it out until we get where we're going. I've just heard from Breith."

"How is he?"

"*Where* is he?"

"Fine. Glandair. He stumbled through the Membrane." Malart pulled his hand across his eyes. "You know that's going to happen more and more as the Corruption approaches finality. He didn't say much about what he was doing, but I think he was being chased by someone, and it was a lucky accident he found the weak spot." Without further comment, he passed on Breith's idea about sanctuary on Glandair and his answer to his son.

Her lips trembling, Faobran smiled. "He has a good heart, but he's still so young and he doesn't understand a lot of things." She sobered. "And, I'm afraid, has a hard time ahead of him learning about impossible choices."

She hugged Malart, drew her hand tenderly down the side of his face. "I regret nothing, my Seyl. *Nothing.*" The last word was said with a terrible fierceness as if she wanted to be absolutely sure that he understood all that it meant.

Finally she drew away from them. In the doorway she looked over her shoulder. "I have to go with the troops and I won't see you again before you leave. If you go and die on me, I'll find your corpses and haunt you through the rest of your come-back lives. You hear me?"

[6]

Old Neech stood by the narrow opening in the front gate. He offered his hand to Malart with a complicated grunt that might have been words though even years of habit couldn't untangle the sounds.

Malart grinned, but shook the hand. "Watch over them all," he murmured. "We'll be back when we can."

After another strangled grunt and a tightening of his calloused hand, Neech stepped aside.

The first out were the dark-clad Rundanara Scribes; they vanished swiftly into the heavy darkness pooled at the base of the House walls. They were acting as peripheral guards, shuttling along parallel walkways, maintaining no contact with

Malart and Yasayl. They moved at random speeds, passing and repassing each other, circling round, doing their best to make sure the refugees had a free run to the waterfront.

Next out were a band of the older girls from Urfa House; the enforcers of the Riverine Council often used adolescent girls as spies, girls from poor families, unaffiliated and often filled with a simmering resentment of the Merchant Houses. The Urfa girls would be the quickest to spot these and point them out to other Watchers, then to work out a route that would let them keep a tighter watch on the spies without being spotted themselves.

A feral dog pack went trotting past, adding the huff-chuff of their breathing and the click-scrape of their claws to the whistle and rattle of the night wind as it lifted leaf and grass fragments from the unpaved, packed earth of the Riverway. A moment later the steady drone of these background noises was broken by the wheep-wheep of a night thwar.

"Clear," Corysiam whispered. She touched Malart's shoulder. "Go."

Yasayl drew in a wavery breath, tightened her grip on Malart's sleeve. Visions dealing with the events whirling round her had been fragmentary and infrequent, but what she'd puzzled out disturbed her. The things she'd seen and heard were so stupid and so ignorant that they seemed to have lost any connection with reality; those who ranted passionately about purity had to be deliberately shutting themselves off from any true perception of the measure of humankind, making themselves blinder than she had ever been by their rejection of all that didn't agree with their theories and systems.

She accompanied Malart with grim determination and fear, for she had not been outside the House without her staff and a pair of servant guides since the accident that had blinded her. Because the blindness would instantly identify her to anyone watching, she couldn't use her staff. She had never felt so vulnerable before, or so useless.

[7]

Thador saw shadows come pouring through the slight opening in the front gate and knew that something was finally
happening in the House across the road. The shadows melted
into the darkness, but she didn't move. They weren't her target.

Two more figures slipped through the opening, so heavily
cloaked that she could tell little about them. They were walking close together and each of them carried a large backpack.
One of them had to be the blind woman Yasayl, but both
had staffs lashed to the backpacks. Their postures provided
no clue as to who was leading whom.

Thador's hand dropped to the upper curve of the short-
bow clipped to her belt. She could try for both of them but
in this murky light, if she took out the blind woman, the man
had a good chance of getting away and Mirrialta would be
furious with her.

No. Best to follow and make sure.

As she ghosted after the bulky pair of shadows, the streets
and walkways were filling with the despairing and the dregs
among the refugees from the Riverine cities already destroyed
by the Army of Purification. Yells from the living, screams
and silence from the dying and the dead. Every doorway had
its cluster of sleepers, with armed watchers standing guard.
Even this late there were children everywhere — running and
playing, crying, laughing — not from joy or even transitory
happiness, a laughter more akin to a spell they were chanting
to protect themselves and their families.

Since the Siege had begun, the natural order of the city
had been coming apart.

There were spit-and-scratch fights between the lesser
among the Sighted women, male punching matches and/or
duels and the occasional riot where everybody was fighting

everybody. And rapes. Even a Sighted woman was prey. And the victim was always killed so the perpetrator couldn't be identified.

Thador found it both easy and very difficult to follow the shadow pair through the chaos in the streets. She didn't have to conceal her movements because the refugees did that for her, but if she took her eyes off Malart and Yasayl for an instant, chances were they'd disappear immediately. Already she'd lost them several times and had spent frantic moments trying to relocate them, playing a guess as if it were fact, lucky each time so far.

Smells. Rotting seaweed, dead fish, barrels of salt meat, bales of rawhide. They were leaving Valla Murloch. On a ship.

Tonight.

Thador turned away, moving considerably faster than she had before. She wanted to get ahead of them if she could. Chancy. She could lose them. No way to know which ship they were heading for . . . no . . . that's not right . . . had to be a ship leaving tonight . . . they wouldn't want to wait around for Prophet knows who to land on them . . . couldn't be that many ships ready to sail . . .

She shuddered as the freshening wind blew around her, immersing her in the mix of stenches that meant ocean shore, a smell she loathed, a smell underlined by the voices around her, corrupt with the slippery croak of Ascalese trade tongue. Prophet!

Small boats were one thing. She could stay in sight of land where she could swim ashore if the boat turned treacherous. An ocean-goer meant constant vomiting, weakness and a terror that she couldn't show, but which would never end until she walked ashore again.

She shuddered. With luck she could set up an ambush and get Malart before he was out of reach. Once he was on the ship, she'd have to face Mirrialta's anger with no answers ready.

Or follow him onboard.

[8]

As Malart tacked up his piece of canvas as a combination privacy shield and shelter from the cold, Yasayl used the tip of her staff to acquaint herself with the square of deck they'd been given for living space. It was a premium place because they had the mast at one end and could use that as a support for the canvas and as an anchor for their packs. They would sleep and eat there for the whole time they were on the ship; having the mast as an extra amenity would make living in that cramped area a lot more comfortable.

She took blankets from the pack and spread them on the planks, using push-pins and a tack hammer to pin them into place as if they were a carpet she were laying instead of just a thickness of wool to cushion her bones against the unyielding planks.

Malart came round the canvas shield and stood leaning on the mast. When he spoke, she could hear the smile in his voice. "Home from home?"

She punched his knee with her free hand. "Why not?"

He dropped onto his heels, touched her shoulder. "Don't expect too much, Yasa. We're going to be cold, wet and hungry for a long long time and we'll both miss sleep until we're groggy with need. I wish Bryheris had a cabin left even if it cost more than the ship."

Her lips firmed into a bitter line. After a minute, she said, "He did. But not for us."

"You're sure?"

"Mar! You're asking me?"

"Why didn't you say something before?"

"Because I was keeping my face toward him and shaming him into giving us the next best available. If I made him angry, he'd have thrown us off the ship. Waste of my time and his."

"Ah. I should have known."

3

Visions

By the secret calendar of the Watchers, events dating from the 2nd and 3rd of Seimis, the seventh month of the 739th Glandairic year since the last Settling.

{ 1 }

Brother Kyo, formerly Kyodal Kurrin of Kurrin House, of the High Merchants of Nikawaid, sat on the floor of the inner shrine, his mind as tranquil as his surroundings, and almost as ordered. Three grapefruits were positioned before the candles on the altar, their golden cheeks tinged with pink, symbolizing health and harmony. A stick of senswa incense was angled slantwise in the simple ashwood burner to the right, releasing a delicate plume of musky smoke. Opposite it, a waterglobe held a school of tiny fish, their bodies almost invisible but for the skeletons and jots of glowing azure and fuschia. They hung suspended like his thoughts — aware of their surroundings, but at rest.

He polished the round icon of Marath Alaesh with silkrush oil and the sleeve of his old yellow robe until the Alaesh's hunched form glowed with the candlelight. All except for one stubborn spot, which Kyo buffed until the icon, slippery with oil, popped out of his hand and went bowling across the wooden slats.

Kyo almost broke his vow of silence right then and there, but all that came forth from his unused vocal chords was a dry rasp as he lunged after the orb-Alaesh to stop the desecration, watching in horror as it bounced on the uneven boards, then began to jig about as unpredictably as a drunken frog as the knee, or foot, or slightly raised hand of the blessed Maratha contacted slats. Kyo's fingers briefly contacted the wood of the icon, but this only gave it more impetus, the ball-god picking up speed and spinning around the altar in a dervish dance until it became quite apparent that the icon was not reacting to the accidental desecration in the normal way, but rather in some way miraculous, especially once the image of Marath Alaesh unfolded, changing from the Alaesh in His humble meditative pose to Maratha Alaesh in His laughing aspect, upright, mouth wide with glee, hands lifting the hem of His robe as He ran around the altar like a child playing Finjin Finjin Catch the Ball, giggling all the while, a sound like wooden birdcalls, hee-hee-hee.

Brother Kyo came to a stop as he suddenly realized he was no longer chasing a runaway icon but an incarnation of the god Himself. Marath Alaesh, however, was still in His laughing aspect, now dancing from one foot to the other with mirth and pointing one hand at Kyodal's face and the expression he knew he now must wear. Brother Kyo dropped into a low obeisance until he felt the wooden hand of the idol knock three times on his shaved head, making him realize that while reverence was appropriate, the Alaesh wished him to pay attention.

He looked, seeing the wooden icon smiling and animate before him, but silent except for an occasional giggle. Then Marath Alaesh held His left hand up in the unbroken circle, the sacred mudhra that signified filial piety.

Kyodal took his god's meaning. His own father had been lost at sea and had not yet received a proper burial. He signed back with the secret signs of the monks that he would go to the beaches and search them for his father's bones, and when he found them, he would burn them so that the spirit could go free.

Marath Alaesh shook His head.

Brother Kyo signed back quickly. *My father is alive?*

Marath Alaesh shook His head again and held His right index finger to His cheekbone in the attitude of sorrow. He then held His hand up in the mudhra of the sacred crane, signifying Responsibility.

I must return to the Kurrin Merchant House?

The icon shrugged and waffled one hand, still in the attitude of the Laughing Alaesh. The wooden hand then formed the mudhra of filial piety again, but held it lower, twinned with the crane mudhra of Responsibility, held up by the eye in the attitude of Regret.

Brother Kyo signed back. *I must aid my brother Lyanz?*

The icon laughed, holding up one hand in the mudhra of Perfection, then made the blessing sign of Marath with the secret turn that meant, *All depends upon this.*

Like a hedgehog then, the idol folded itself up and rolled to fetch up against Kyodal's feet, once more just a smooth ball of carved wood glittering in the light of the candles.

Yet the smudge was gone.

[2]

Oerfel opened his eyes, slowly, warily, but at some moment in that endless crawl of moments, the migraine's agonies had muted to a dull ache. He could think again, though the things drifting into his mind were not pleasant to contemplate. Concentrating fiercely, he forced himself onto his feet and lurched to the workbench set along one wall.

"Made it." He stood a moment, swaying and a little dizzy, clutching at the edge of the bench. "Now clean yourself, man. You stink." Though he had to stop repeatedly and hold tight to the bench until an attack of vertigo passed over, he managed to fill a basin with tepid water and shake a washrag loose from the pile he kept in one of the holes of a waspnest filer he'd bolted to the wall behind the bench. He moistened the rag and began washing away the vomit. By working his mouth and swallowing repeatedly he managed to avoid a second hurl.

"That miserable scrap of a girl—Hag suck her bones clean!" Even in his deepest withdrawal, when he was a knot of earth nearly indistinguishable from the earth about him, he'd felt her go. She'd fled Nyddys and was somewhere on the Mainland. Now that he was fully himself once more, here in his workroom beneath the Temple, he felt her absence more intensely than before, felt it in every bone of his cold and battered body.

And the Hero was also gone. The final gathering of the Companions was beginning. From now on, they'd stay as close to that boy as ticks on a cernot. Oerfel shook the rag over the basin, carefully not looking at it, focusing instead on the triteness of the figure he'd used. Tsah! *Ticks on a cernot.* A wealman drunk on yesterday's doolybrew could find a more spirited phrase. My mind has gone to mush.

He swished the rag through the dirty water and dabbed at his arms. As a sudden thought struck him, his hands stilled and his thin mouth twitched into a smile that exploded into guffaws that bounced off the walls and filled the room with echoes as he visualized Hudoleth screaming with frustration when the girl walked through her traps as if they weren't there. Gasping and clutching at his middle, he shouted, "You don't know what's coming at you, you haven't a clue, not a clue clue *clue!*"

He sobered as his head started to throb again, dropped the washcloth back in the water. "Even when that chidophid is nowhere around, she harms me." His breath coming too quickly, black discs wheeling through the watery aura that hung before his eyes, he turned slowly and flattened his back against the workbench, cursing his stupidity as he waited for the attack to fade. Like an earthquake, the worst of his migraines usually had aftershocks, but he never remembered this or prepared for them, never caught hold of the triggering sentiments and forced them away from him.

Like that girl.

Cyfareth was responsible for creating her. Cyfareth University and that maverick Pneuma researcher whom the University tolerated—no! Encouraged. Mole, he called himself and mole he was, digging into the Pneuma as if it were garden dirt. No respect for scholarship, none for the millennia of experience and danger suffered by Mages and their apprentices.

Mole. Creating—shaping—patterning—whatever. Turning that girl into another like him. I should have realized what was going on and dealt with him, but oh no, I had to wait for that Siofray Mage to do my work for me.

Oerfel groaned, pressed the heels of his hands hard against his eyes. "T'teeth! Discipline yourself, Mage! Cold and calm. Plan, don't rant like some crazy old Gossip with rats in her head."

Destroy Cyfareth.

Raid its archives, carry off its research for his own uses and burn the buildings to ash and cinders.

Destroy the Scholar-Watchers. Take their land and their money, seal them to a Broony as wealmen or mine slaves, ring them with laws that would curtail their activities until they were left without purpose. Take their children from them as soon as the cubs are weaned. Make teaching those children to read and figure a crime against the state, punishable by seven years of indentured service for each offense.

"Two generations. That's all it would take. Two generations and there wouldn't be any Watchers, just ignorant animals grubbing in the dust." Oerfel turned his arms so he could inspect them. Most of the fouling was gone and the water in the basin was so filthy that to continue washing with it would be adding dirt rather than taking it away. "Prudence, Mage. Two generations, yes, but you don't want to pull the tops and leave the roots intact. You'll need to turn round the scope and watch the Watchers for the third generation and the fourth. Then maybe you can relax and catch your breath. A few atypical fanatics can always wriggle out of any net. Hag be praised, the stragglers are likely to be small, foolish losers nobody pays any attention to. Easy to deal with."

He carried the basin to the drain and poured it carefully through the grid.

"And I can't do any of this till Anrydd sits in the Seat."

Isel might loathe the Watchers and hate Cyfareth, but he was truly his father's son when it came to greed. He would never destroy *anything* he saw as part of his own heritage.

Oerfel stroked the tips of his fingers delicately across his eyelids. "So. Second step. I have to get back to my rooms. Look for Anrydd. See what he's doing." He shuddered. "What messes he's stepped in. Gods! What messes." He looked down at his arms, at the gooseflesh stippling the pale skin. "I'm cold. It's freezing in here. What time is it?" He stared at a blurred blue sign on the back of his left wrist. The rag had smeared and washed away some of it, but there was enough left to enable his Sight. "Night. After moonset. Starting to snow. Ahh, finally the Lady favors me. Don't waste the gift, O Mage. Get dressed and out of here."

He circled the basin and walked unsteadily toward the closets built into the end wall. He kept clean robes in there, wool longstockings, and a pair of worn sandals, whatever he'd need for emergencies like this.

[3]

The Third Prince arrived with considerably less panoply and fanfare than was usually his wont, though the forest fire likely had something to do with this. The smoke roiled and built into the air, coil upon coil, merging with and becoming indistinguishable from the misty convolutions of the Dark Wyrm of the Earth, the Chthonic god of Tilkos, its eyes blazing with the light of the fires below and the molten heat of the earth even deeper within, a choking miasma looping over Mahara's forces, who in the far reaches of their pennantry merged with the emerald and crimson scales of Rueth, the Serpent of Kale above.

The Farmyn's old War Wizard, with even more craft and guile than Mahara had given him credit for, had strategically set fire to the Royal Grove of High Tilk, giving power to his magic and fire to his god. It was a desperation gambit — the Tilk considered the parkland, if not sacred, at least a source of national pride — but pride, as with every other vanity, was fuel for the fire, and all could burn to save the city. Victory for Kale, if it came at all, would be costly and pyrrhic.

The old Wizard had cannily waited until the wind was pointed directly at the Kale army, then harnessed the power of his own catchfires to whip it into a frenzy, sealing the whole with a Pneuma-knot of astonishing complexity, twisted and riddled in with the coils of the god of Tilkos, and Mahara did not have time to unknot it, to trace the labyrinthine pathways of the Pneuma-working, before the force of the fire—natural fire, whipped by Pneuma-charged winds—consumed the forces of Kale.

Instead, Mahara erected rude shields and crude bulwarks from raw Pnuema to hold off the rush of the flames. Fire clashed against Pneuma, licking at the solid nothingness like the flames behind the windows of an isinglass screen, stopping the rush and blunting the heat before it could escape the firebox. Yet this did little to halt the smoke, billowing up and over and around the cracks, and the tinder ash that flew with the wind, setting spots of the Kale tents and pennants alight.

Damn the old man! Mahara ground his teeth. If only he were back at his Tower, thick with its dust and the debris and detritus of ages of sorcery. There would doubtless be some spell in one of the ancient scrolls and mouldering tomes left by his predecessors, the ones in the lower room, crumbling to dust with the weight of years and the volumes penned since. Perhaps something by Sitoon Kaa, or Burgu or Faraza, or even Muedafi Keyn. The spell-knot had the feel of something old, if not ancient, an antiquated twist to the weavings of the Pneuma, like a scrolled flourish from an ancient Scribe's pen at the close of some forgotten document, and Mahara was certain that if he could just read the writings of the Mages who had come before him, he'd find that the knot-wind was the signature trick of some old school of War Wizards, long ago unriddled by the Mages before him, and as such, abandoned by all but the old, the clever, and the desperate.

It had, in fact, the feel of a taunt. *Let's see if you know this one, you young upstart!*

Mahara didn't know it, and ground his teeth in fury, seeing to the retreat of the army at the same time as watching Prince Zulam's retinue, much diminished, come rushing to meet them, running from . . . something else. Damn the old bastard! May the Hag tat lace with his entrails and wear it for a shawl! Mahara realized with a cold certainty that the fire of the Royal Grove was not just a taunt, it was a distraction — at the same time as the ancient War Wizard had set the true fire and the Pneuma-winds to blow smoke over the main armies of Kale, he'd aimed a volley of Wizard-strikes directly at Zulam's retinue as they made their way to join them. His friend was rushing to him, not as reinforcements, but for protection, the smoke and fire encircling them along with the coils of the Chthonic god around the Serpent of Kale. The wind was blowing in a vortex, hot ash and Pneuma-fire both catching the grass on all sides and burning it inwards as the Dark Wyrm caught them in its coils and began to squeeze.

Curse the old Wizard! May the Hag drag the bastard down to Her black garden and feast on his balls! Pick Her teeth with his rib-bones, then take his member and use it to floss! Mahara couldn't think of a torture fitting enough, and didn't have time — the riddle-knot was taunt and distraction both, like the barbed and beribboned fan a war dancer waved in one hand while she coiled a whip strike behind her back, and in the time he'd taken examining the lace-subtle patterns of the Pneuma-weaving, the War Wizard had lashed out with his second strike and caught them in his noose.

Strangulation alone, however, was not enough for the old man. Mahara sensed it then, another Wizard-strike, aimed straight at the Third Prince, the blazing eyes of the Dark Wyrm of Tilkos focused on him as well, a mirror and a lens for the Farmyn's malice. With a cry of rage, Mahara snapped his hand back, deflecting the force of the spell with a shield of raw Pneuma. It was a weak magic as such things went, easily countered, and pitiful compared to the Power of a Mage, yet deadly all the same. Pitiful but deadly, like a bee slipped through the chink of a visor slot to sting a warrior in the eye.

And still the smoke came, and the flames, and the coils and the primordial hunger of the Wyrm of Tilkos as the old Wizard used the Royal Grove as the catchfire to power his Wizard-strikes.

Fire rained down around them, gold-crimson as the belly scales of the god of Kale with which it mixed, mocking them, their god thrashing about them in a mist of pain, as Mahara contracted his Mage-shields to protect himself and Prince Zulam. Not fifty feet away, a column of flame came from above and immolated a man where he stood, leaving naught but metal and twisted ashes in its wake. What's more, that man had been the Zulam's standard bearer—a taunt, a blow and a deliberate insult all at once.

"Mahara!" screamed the Third Prince, abandoning his palanquin as it crashed to the dirt, the slaves who were his bearers diving headlong for the ground as a flamebolt came down before them. "Do something!" Gasping and stumbling, his arm held over his head as if that pathetic gesture could somehow save him, Zulam ran toward him.

Mahara gnashed his teeth—he was doing something. He was being beaten by a War Wizard ten times his age and a fraction of his Power, who relied on nothing more than craft, guile, and War Dances so antiquated that the younger War Wizards would likely think of them as quaint.

Yet there was nothing quaint in the flaming death raining down around them, or in the cries of the dead and dying, and the ash-choked screams of the men and horses as they ran in panic through the smoke, trampling each other till the ground ran red with blood and the Serpent of Kale screamed in pain.

Then the Third Prince was upon him, screaming in his face, his shock and desperation giving voice to his god. "Do something! Do something! Do something, Mage—I command it!"

Mahara glared, a hot rage kindling in him to rival the great catchfire before them. The soldiers ran and screamed, as useless and self-deadly as their panicked horses, and even Mahara's own War Wizards either made pathetic toe-shufflings and hesitant gestures at the sky, or else stood there slackjawed and amazed at the quaint old death being rained down upon them, as if the Hag had arrived to show them how to suck eggs. Useless!

For pride, if nothing else, Mahara would have to do something more effective, though what he wanted to do now more than anything was simply slap the Third Prince. Yet instead, he only bowed his most solemn and courtly bow, tasting the irony on his tongue as he spoke the words: "As you command, O Prince. To my tent. We will be safe there."

A lie, or at least an inexactitude. Zulam looked as if he did not believe it, but was not about to question any offer of a refuge, no matter how dubious. At least inside the tent those without Magesight would not see the doom aimed at their heads. "Lead on."

Mahara nodded and swept his way back to his tent, banishing the smoke from it with a wave of his hand, and with the other parrying the continued rain of Wizard-strikes. It wasn't hard, but it was distracting, like continually shooing at a bee buzzing at one's ear. But this bee bore a measure of poison, tiny and insignificant by itself, but deadly when delivered in sufficient amounts, and multiplied to a thousand times to one sensitized to the venom of the sting by past mischance. If he did not find the means to swat it once and for all, it could mean his death, as surely as the fire-coils of the Wyrm of Tilkos would burn and choke and crush them.

Mahara reached beneath the dragon-embroidered cloth that covered his war table—a gift from the Third Prince at the start of this campaign—and pulled forth the cases that held the Mage Drums, starting with the one he had made himself, the Drum Sitoon Kaa, stretched from the tattooed skin of his master the night he had murdered him and taken his place as Mage of Kale.

He gestured to Prince Zulam. "Silence!" then added as an afterthought, "My liege."

He caressed the skin of the dead old man, the Mage who had taken him in off the streets, fed him, and nurtured the hunger inside until it rose up and consumed him. Rather like the Wizard-strikes of the War Wizard of High Tilk might do with Mahara if he did not act quickly.

He stroked the skin of the drumhead, feeling the oily texture of Mage-skin massaged with man-fat till it glowed, of the sinews from the old man's legs and arms holding the drumskin taut over the frame woven from his own bones. The Mage Sitoon Kaa had been old and brittle at the end and Mahara had had to test at least five ribs of his old master before he found a set that would hold, stretched and reinforced with a cross-joist formed by the Mage's femurs crossed together and lashed with the sinews of the man's neck to give it voice.

Mahara gestured again to the Third Prince for silence, deflecting as he did another strike from the War Wizard, and took out the beater, smooth and double-ended, made from the ulna of Sitoon Kaa's right forearm, the arm he had used to focus much of his magic and harness the Pneuma, as well as, on occasion, to beat the backside of Mahara when he was young and disobedient.

There was a pleasing symmetry in it. The beater become the beaten, furnishing the instrument to beat his own backside in time with the rhythm. Mahara began to twirl the bone in his hand, striking the skin of the Drum Sitoon Kaa, and bringing forth a voice that only he could hear.

Master, I have need of your aid.

The drum pounded back, echoing his dead master's voice

in the confines of his head. **Why should I aid you, ungrateful wretch? I brought you in, I fed you, I clothed you, I taught you, and what thanks do I get in return?**

The same thanks you gave your master. The same he gave his master before him, and she gave her master before her. The thanks for a lesson of Power well taught and immortality, of a sort. Mahara paused, letting his message sink in. *The same thanks I have not yet been given, and have no chance as of yet to give, for I am young, and have not taken an apprentice, and so have no one to betray me and give me the immortality that you and the other Mage Drums all share. If I perish here, you all will perish and be forgotten with me.*

There was a silence in the tent but for the repetitive echo of the drumskin and the labored fear of the Third Prince's breathing. **Very well,** said the voice in his head. **Ask.**

An old War Wizard has spun an intricate Pneuma-Knot that threatens to consume me. It bears the feel of something ancient, as a pattern traced from a scroll or sprung from a talisman-brand heated in the fire. Do you know it, and do you know how to unweave it?

Show me the tracery.

Mahara spun the pattern then, an image-echo like the partial whorls of a smudged thumbprint, of the force he could feel operating behind the Pneuma-wind.

There was a longer drum-silence, thick with the fear of the Third Prince and the continued rain of Pneuma-fire from the Farmyn's War Wizard. **I am unfamiliar with this, student,** said the voice of Sitoon Kaa at last. **Were it clearer, perhaps I might solve it. However, the stylings have the feel of something from the era of Faraza or Muedafi Keyn. Ask them next.**

Mahara had time for nothing more than rushed formality. *My thanks, Master.* With that, he threw the Mage Drum back in its case, taking forth the Drum Muedafi Keyn, the second of the Great Mage Drums of Kale. O *Ancient Grandfather,* he Pneuma-thought as he pounded the drumskin with its knucklebone flail, *we have need.*

Muedafi Keyn had none of the anger of Sitoon Kaa, his magics having been taken from him at the end of life, at his request, so as to preserve them, murder by a technicality, suicide in all but deed. As his successor the Mage Faraza had penned, when asked to select the manner of his own death, the Mage Muedafi Keyn had answered simply, "Surprise me."

He was similarly succinct now. **Show us, Grand-heir.**

Mahara did then, opening himself to the trapped spirit of Muedafi Keyn, showing the Pneuma-Knot, the flame strikes, the coiling of the gods, the Dark Wyrm of the Earth constricting and suffocating the Serpent and the army of Kale.

The Drum Muedafi Keyn beat, considering, then at last the old voice spoke in his head: **I have theories, but nothing concrete, and nothing that you need. I suggest you try my daughter, Faraza. She is clever, and if she has not seen this knot, she may still give you the keys to unworking it, and thereby saving all of us.** A pause. **Or else she won't, and we're doomed, but oh well. It happens.**

Mahara grimaced. **My thanks.** He put the drum away, and took out the skin of Muedafi Keyn's daughter, Faraza, the only patricide of all the murderous Mages of Kale, and the only one to do it at the Mage's request.

The tattoos upon the skin of the Drum Faraza were somewhat more elegant and delicate than the others, but no less powerful for all that. Like Hudoleth of Chusinkayan, Faraza had been a beauty in her day, and had cut the Mage marks to accentuate that, not detract. Her beater was her skull itself, delicate and fine, fastened atop a femur with the jaw left free to clack and click as a second source of percussion.

O *Drum Faraza,* Mahara intoned in thought as he beat the skin of the woman's drum, *our line has need.*

For what? came the response as Mahara pounded the drum, causing the woman's jaw to clack.

For the answer to a riddle, a riddle that threatens us all. Mahara showed her then, showed her the same as he had her father, and the skull began to laugh, the drumskin vibrating in sympathy.

That? Is that it? Is that all?

To Mahara's mind, it was certainly more than enough. But he kept the beat of the drum courtly, measured, rather than smacking the skull on the ground a few times, which he would rather do. *Yes, O Wise Faraza. That is it. Now quickly, tell me the solution to this riddle, before we all perish.*

The Drum Faraza and her striker click-clack-laughed again. **There is no solution, Mage. No solution save time. What you have shown me is a Death Knot.**

Then are we doomed?

Faraza laughed again. **Only if you are so foolish as to drop your shields. This riddle-knot is a false riddle. There is no solution. But to create it, the War Wizard has spent his own life as the catchfire. When it dies, he dies.**

And the wind?

The wind and the fire are one. Hold your shields, Mage, and extend them as far as you dare to save whatever part of your army you need. Simply weather the storm. Your enemies will be without any defenses save mortal ones once the fire has died and the War Wizard along with it.

Mahara felt bile rising in his throat at the galling trick the old War Wizard had played, and grim satisfaction at knowing his enemy would soon be dead. *My thanks for your wisdom, O Drum Faraza. . . .*

You are entirely welcome, O Mage Mahara. I look forward to hearing wisdom from you at some time in the future. . . .

Mahara threw the Drum Faraza back in her case, waving

away another of the dying War Wizard's Pneuma-strikes and crystalizing a shield of Pneuma-ice about the tent. He hoped that it had hurt when Burgu had plunged the knife into the bitch's heart.

[4]

The Emperor slid his eyes slyly around to Hudoleth, dark irises glistening like the tar that oozed up in the pools of Burning Land Park. He was a short, slight man on the far side of middle age, bald except for a strip of gray fuzz that went from ear to ear; he had heavy pouches under his eyes, deep furrows running from his nostrils around the corners of a full-lipped mouth. He liked to pretend that he was a simple man of the people, a poet and philosopher, his Power only lent him by his god Ancestor, Tayo Sugreta, and by the collective will of the people. Away from the Court and its rigid rules, he wore farmer's sandals and a frayed silk robe that had once been part of his formal attire but had gone soft and nearly transparent from age and repeated washings. Here within the walls of the Inner Chambers he waved off the formal address of the Court, insisting on the casual converse of men sitting in a teahouse, chatting about the tedious events of their mundane lives.

He was growing restless, bored with the teasing of the succubi. Despite the control Hudoleth had established over his will, he had a core of stubbornness that she couldn't touch. No matter how cleverly she maneuvered, that core resisted her. It kept her installed here in the Palace, away from her house and the workrooms where she kept the philosophical instruments she'd devised and constructed with her own hands, away from her collection of birds and mirrors. Kept her here under the eyes of the Niosul who'd become used to her presence but still didn't trust her. His magic sniffers were intensely loyal to the Emperor and their presence limited the amount of force she could use to control him and the Pneuma she could bend to other uses.

Restless.

A banal mind but not a stupid one, she reminded herself. Never make that mistake, woman. A mind capable of sudden, sharp deductions. An instinctive assessment of what he saw, a skill honed by decades of practice, perhaps even a trait inborn in an inbred family who'd reigned here for millennia. A skill that kept his Imperial buttocks planted firmly on the throne. I should have realized he'd see me renewed and understand instantly what this meant. And want it for himself. Gods!

His eyes slid round to her again, flicked away immediately.

Hudoleth knelt before the writing desk, her shoulders bent in submission, anger crawling like fire through her veins. Anger at herself. My fault for letting this happen—stupid, stupid. Forgetting to replace used-up vigor. Not thinking. I could have managed this so he didn't notice anything, taking off a few years each time I did the rite. Maybe I'd have had to pull back from Nikawaid, let my agents go passive for a few tennights, but timing isn't that critical right now. Mahara has to finish off Tilkos and that will take months. No. I was afraid of the Hag and I didn't think. Afraid!

The Emperor hadn't yet worked up sufficient resolution to discard the mask of the simple farmer-poet that had become so much a part of him that pulling it off would be like ripping his skin away. And he hadn't dredged up enough courage to confront her and insist that she bring back his youth and the vigor that had graced that youth. But he would do both. Soon.

Put it off for today. Somehow. I need time to think. Distract him. Firedemons? No. He's bored with them and I don't want to waste the last of their usefulness. The war? Yes . . .

blood and suffering and death . . . those should still hold their charms. . . .

She curved her back into a deeper bow, the long fall of her hair smooth and glistening as black water, concealing her face and the set of her shoulders, pooling on the mirror laid on the floor in front of her knees. For several heartbeats she maintained that position while she turned a rosary of crystal beads through her fingers, the glassy surfaces sliding like water across her skin, each bead calling up a stanza of the chant that created an analog of the floor mirror and hung it flat against the wall across from the desk where the Emperor was writing. "O Belovéd of Sugreta, may I show you the final triumph of your Grand Army and the destruction of the Grass Clans?"

[5]

The land shook. Cracks jagged across dry, matted grass and weeds. Dust rose in yellow-white puffs.

On three adjacent hilltops, reduced to shadows half seen in the dust, Rinchay's sister Shamans sat in furious and fearful silence, watching as the last of their clans and kin fell to the swords, lances and slicing warshoes of the Myndyar army and its warhorses.

Rinchay Matan rose slowly to her feet. She stumbled a few steps before she managed to straighten her spine and push her shoulders back, stumbled again as a tiny, twisted, black monstrosity that had once been a little god appeared suddenly beside her, dragged its claws through the flesh of her calf. When she kept walking with no sign that she had noticed the pain or the blood oozing down her leg, it screeched at her, then ran clumsily downhill, its head twisted around so it could keep red eye-slits fixed on her.

Slowly, uncertainly, she lifted a hand and kneaded the nape of her neck.

Betrayal.

The Sending that brought the clans to this place was born of the Liar.

Her eyes flicked briefly toward the place where Kamkajar had stood a moment before. Another Sending of the Liar or a God Befooled?

The little-god-changed dropped to its belly and crawled toward her through the tangled, sun-dried grass, chittering angrily, but she ignored it.

Used. I was used.

Goat. Leading clans and kin to the slaughter ground.

Her shame turned to despair as cold as the blizzards that blew across the grass.

I have lost the right to wear the Shaman's Shawl.

She took the fringed leather triangle from her shoulders and held it out, the pain of her loss slicing through her. Finally she forced her fingers open, dropped the Dmar Shawl into a crumpled wad at her feet.

Shoulders rounded, head hanging in shame and distress, she left the hilltop and walked slowly downslope.

Groaning and creaking, the land moved under her feet. The earth shared her pain, shared the grief of her sister Shamans. It did not comfort her. Her guilt was greater than theirs, her shame deeper and more true.

"Who?" she sang. The word was drowned in the noises from the dying war—the squeals of the horses, the clang of harness and armor, the screams of the dying, the clash of sword against sword, the distorted laughter and harsh squeals of the monstrosities that once had been little gods, those personified bits of Pneuma that as the Settling progressed were mutating from a mixture of pest and joke to ugly manifestations of resentment, abuse and hostility.

"Why?" she sang and pushed at the war sounds, struggling to mute them so she could think.

"What must I do?" she sang, though she knew she'd get no answer.

She reached level ground and stood red-eyed and weeping in tangles of sun-cured grass and aggregations of broken stone, clouds of yellow-white dust swirling about her, obscuring everything more than a few paces away.

A Myndyar soldier lunged from the murk.

They saw each other at almost the same moment. She stood unmoving, waiting for death. His mouth stretched in a soundless scream; he swiped at her with his saber.

The mutant godlet leaped from a tuft of grass, sank needle teeth into the warhorse's leg; the beast screamed, reared and stumbled. The tip of the sword tore into the muscle at the end of Rinchay's shoulder, ripping loose a flap of skin, drawing from her a rush of blood that dwindled to a trickle half a breath later. The tiny grotesque scrabbled up the saddle leathers and leaped at the warrior's head.

Swaying, dizzy with shock, Rinchay closed her hand tight about the wound but made no other attempt to stanch the flow or bandage the wound, merely watched as blood seeped slowly between her fingers.

The warrior wrenched the godlet off his face, then gaped at his hand as the thing he'd caught melted through his fingers. Still staring at his hand, he shifted in the saddle, lifted the reins; the horse shuddered, then went limping into the swirl of dust.

A mask of sweat spread across Rinchay's face and she howled her grief. Her guilt was too great. The Odyggas would not accept her—death guides, they stood between her and the dark waters and would not let them carry her earth soul to the Gathering.

The remnant of the war split around her, the fighters ignoring her as if she were of as little importance as the poufs of dry yellow dust kicked up by the dancing hooves of the warhorses, the dragging feet of the exhausted soldiers. More Myndyar fighters followed the first over the hillocks, killing her sister Shamans as they went past, silencing the last mourners for the dead and dying Grass Clans. Ignoring her as if she were already a ghost.

The chill of despair in Rinchay Matan transformed itself. Despair became rage.

Passivity became a drive to act, a need to *do* so great that the tiny hairs along her spine and on her arms snapped erect with the force that flowed into them.

She spread her arms to the sky and to the ailing, impotent god who lurked there until He gathered enough vitality to take form once more and stride across the grass as Kamkajar the Parter of Seasons. "Fear me," she cried.

Fear me, Soul Eater!
My eyes of fire will force you from your hole.
Betrayer
Mother of Lies
I will find you.

Her voice merged with the clash of swords, the screams of the dying, but in her ears the words of the oath were as clean and sharp as if she stood in a circle of silence.

Hear me, Soul Eater!
My iron tongue will shape this oath:
My iron nose will sniff you out.
You cannot hide or rest.
Betrayer.
Puppet Master.
My iron nails will rip your heart

> *From out your breast*
> *And squeeze*
> *Until you scream*
> *Until you beg for death.*

Bitterness fell on her from the broken knots, the fear-shattered pattern that had been her god—bitterness and an acceptance of her oath. And from the Odyggas came acceptance and on the wind of their breath a promise. Urgency filled her with unexpected strength—the God, the Guides, her Kindred Dead bleeding themselves into her until she was more than she had been, more than she would be again.

> *Fear me, Soul Eater!*
> *Betrayer.*
> *Puppet Master.*
> *My iron hands will repay*
> *God mockery and spilled kin blood*
> *My iron nails will carve with small delay*
> *DEATH*
> *DEATH*
> *and yet again*
> *DEATH*
> *Into your traitorous flesh.*
> *What I have writ*
> *That will I do.*
> *The treachery will be repaid.*
> *The Liar will die.*

The last word cracked and rose to a squeal that was sharp enough to slice a thought in half; it grew louder and louder as Rinchay Matan drove it back at the suffering god and out toward the force still unknown who had launched this war and spilled the blood of kin and kind. On and on it went, like the rings that formed and spread when a stone was tossed into still water. At last she could do no more. The shout died and she stood in expanding rings of silence.

When the trembling was gone from her body, she turned her face to the north and began walking, ignoring the tiny monstrosity that skittered in circles about her feet, at times screeching at her, at other times buzzing to itself. She needed shelter, a house or barn left half-burnt, a root cellar, even an overturned wagon—any place that would let her rest and dream her way to discovering the traces of the Liar.

"Liar," she whispered. "If you sleep, I will hear your breathing, I will find your bed. Liar, do not sleep. I will taste your dreams, I will walk your dreamlands, I will eat your heart. . . ."

[6]

Breith yawned and pushed up from the pile of half-rotted burlap sacks he'd used as a bed when the gleam along the eastern horizon gave warning that the night was nearly over. Luck had set this woodcutter's shack in the right place at the right time and he'd accepted the gift with tired gratitude.

The shack was empty except for those rags and the heaps of bark fragments scattered about the beaten earth of the floor. The walls had been green wood when the shack was built, hacked from trunks split down the middle, the crude shakes also, everything pegged together with a certain slap-dash skill that had kept the structure intact long after it had been abandoned.

Breith washed in the tiny stream outside the shack, ate a lazy breakfast of bread, cheese and honey, washed down with the clean cold water from the stream. When he was finished, he patted a yawn, then took out Cymel's hair clasp and examined it.

Even without calling on Pneuma he could feel a weak tug on his fingers. He grinned, pleased at the implications of this. "You didn't really want to lose me, did you, Mela?"

After loosening two of the thongs, he managed to tie the talisman securely about his throat; for a moment he stared at nothing, covering the clasp with one hand, feeling the warmth and liveliness in the mix of leather and hair, then he tucked it inside his shirt and smoothed it down so the low bump was nearly invisible. He leaned against the creaking planks, his hand still resting over the lump.

"Mela. . . ." He moved the tip of his finger round and round over the woven thongs; when he spoke, it was as if he spoke to Cymel. "I've got to see if I can reach my father now. My family should know I'm alive and well and I'll be a lot happier if I *know* they're not locked up or booted out of our house. Last time I had news from home things were getting nasty."

A tree rat ran down the trunk of a silkwood sapling, stopped abruptly as it saw the young man sitting with his back against the wall of the shack. Its whiskers twitched wildly; its beady black eyes darted about as if they were marbles in a game of Wild Boys.

Breith snapped his thumb against his middle finger and laughed as the little rat jumped the rest of the way to the ground and vanished instantly beneath the carpet of dead leaves left over from last autumn. He patted the clasp a last time. "There it is. Game's over. Time I went to work. Pay attention and you might learn something." He laughed aloud as he felt a sudden coldness strike inward from the clasp. "Can't duck the truth, quack quack."

4

The Usurpation War *or* Oerfel's Progress Across Nyddys Begins

By the secret calendar of the Watchers, events dating from the 7th day of Seimis, the seventh month of the 739th year since the last Settling.

[1]

Near sundown on the fifth day after Breith left the Tower and went chasing after Cymel, Talgryf stood at the window that let daylight touch the topmost landing of the stairway and gazed out through the vine-darkened glass, watching the wealmen farmhands gather in the trampled snow and start trudging down the road, heading for their bunkhouses and the supper waiting for them. In the bedroom below him Amhar and Lyanz were wound round each other in sweaty passion—as they'd been more often than not since they'd wakened from the shock trance and found themselves in the Tower.

Hero's Luck, that's what it was. Whatever Laz needed, the gods just dropped in his lap. Need an escort to the Vale? Watchers would find him, against all odds, and take him to safety, no matter how many died along the way. Need to leave the Vale, now that it was no longer safe? Mela would shape the Pneuma and Bridge everyone to the safety of her childhood home, never mind the fact that her mind wasn't healed right and she got changed into a fat white bird for her trouble. Mela maiming herself to save his gilded ass inconvenient for the Hero's plans? No trouble; the gods would open up a hole in the Membrane between worlds and Breith would slip through right to the Tower, right where he was needed, as slick as a melon seed spat through the Hag's gapped teeth to hit Dyf Tanew in the eye. Hero's Luck, nothing more. With Breith chasing after Mela now, the Hero didn't have to concern himself with anything save Amhar and the thickness of Ellar's mattress.

Gryf was annoyed with them and growing more irritated every day. There was work to do, no time to do it in, but Lyanz had dropped his responsibilities and hit the sheets as if nothing else mattered. Amhar acquiesced in all of this, so infatuated with Laz that she forgot all her training, everything she was meant to do. Kaxon's wealmen, the strings of convicts he rented from the liverywoman to do the muckiest of the work, the farmer who came twice a week to see that everything was done right, these men with no grand destinies and without personal stake in Ellar's Farm—they worked the fields and tended the stock despite snow, rain and chill winds, despite vicious attacks from little gods turned into monstrosities, despite quakes that shook the slopes, opening cracks in the earth wide enough to swallow a workhorse. Though they complained and refused to hurry themselves, they never stopped working. But Lyanz who was meant to save two worlds lazed about and pleased himself like some pretty Broonson without the wit or judgment of a flatworm.

Talgryf dragged his thumb down the thick, green-tinted glass, drawing a line through the condensation on the inside surface. The snow had stopped for the moment, but the clouds still hung low overhead and the fall might start again any moment. Of course the wealmen had a powerful argument for their diligence blowing into their faces with every puff of wind; they were landless farmhands loosely tied to the local Broonies and let out to work for Free Farmers in exchange for a wintering, shifting the cost of that provision from the Broon to the Free Farmer. Winter. The smell of it was everywhere. If they didn't get the crops harvested and stowed, that provision would be meager and more than one of them would starve. He flattened his hand against the icy glass of the windowpane, pulled it quickly away and thrust it up his sleeve. T'teeth! Shoulda left before the snow started coming. Mage won't have to hunt down the Hero, we'll all be froze to the ground ready to pluck.

Amhar and Lyanz! Tchah!

Sometimes they made him feel like a ghost. When he tried to remind them why they were here, they pretended that they didn't hear a word; sometimes they seemed not to see him, though he was standing in front of them.

Five days since Breith left.

Five days!

That was enough patience. More than enough.

He tapped his forefinger on the stone sill. Get the backpacks loaded. Middle finger. Get the tool belts ready, weapons, hardware. Ring finger. Provisions, ground sheets and blankets. Little finger. Boot their butts out of here even if it meant getting them so mad at him they forgot where they were and chased him out of the Tower. He licked his lips. He'd seen them sparring. They might half-kill him before they calmed down enough to hear what he was yelling at them. Cursing Breith for dumping this on him, he turned from the window and sauntered from the room, in no hurry to set up the drubbing that might be waiting for him.

·   ·   ·

During the next several hours he collected food and spare clothing for the three of them, hauling it from closets and storerooms and dumping it on the floor of the reception hall in lumpy, disorganized heaps splayed out across the flags until the place looked more like the Bothrin Market than where someone was actually living. When he first saw the resemblance, he had to hold onto the rail until he could will away the tears that threatened to spill over and turn him into a blubbering mess. Two months ago, when none of this had happened and he was still at the Vale, he'd got a Scribe-written letter from his stepmother; it said his father was still clinging to life, but tending him was getting impossible since she had to work to keep a roof over the family, so she might have to try the Dying House the Sisters ran even if she had to drag him there with him cursing her the whole way. Don't get mad at me, she said. I just can't do any more, Gryf. You've always been good to me, don't stop now.

Two months ago. He'd thought about going back, but he hadn't even tried. Dyf Tanew give his father peace. Talgryf dragged his sleeve across his eyes, readjusted the blanket bundle and went running down the stairs. He couldn't help resenting his stepmother and feel a corrosive fury at what she was doing to his father, an anger he knew was partly directed at himself. He'd thought about going home to Tyst but he hadn't even made the effort. Just as well if you think about it. The past is finished. I can't change it and blubbering's a waste of time.

Lyanz caught hold of the bannister and leaned over it, sweeping an arm in a wide circle. "What's all this?"

Gryf dropped the load he was carrying onto one of the smaller piles. "Laundry. Marching supplies."

His scowl deepening, Lyanz walked down the rest of the flight. "You keep picking at us every chance you get. What's going on?"

"You want to fix supper or sort through the piles?"

"Why should I do either?"

The arrogance in the voice tightened Talgryf's mouth into a thin line. "If you expect me to keep on playing chambermaid, think again. You're able and intelligent enough. You want to be comfortable? Work for it."

Amhar came yawning round the curve of the stairs. When she saw the two glaring at each other, she ran a hand through her hair. "Not again. The pair of you are worse than half-grown tribufs butting heads over some obscure patch of gravel."

Gryf shrugged. "I'll be in the kitchen. Up to you where you go from here."

Talgryf set a kettle on a burner to heat water for tea. He was furious. Nothing had changed. He'd grown up in the Bothrin and knew what it meant to be to treated like a dimwit who'd walk off with anything not nailed down, an unpredictable animal liable to bite and kick if you got too close. His father had taught him that the dimwittedness was on the other side of the divide, that he should enjoy fooling them and take pride in the skills that nobody knew he had, but sometimes it was hard to remember that. He was a thief — a good one and pleased by that, the best in generations at the family's trade.

He'd thought Lyanz was his friend. What he'd done here came out of that friendship, not because he was paid or forced to do it. And it hurt more than he'd anticipated when he discovered how wrong he'd been about Lyanz's understanding of their relationship.

More than a dozen times during the last five days he'd been ready to quit the struggle and go off on his own, but at each of these low points he would recall Cymel's pleas and Ellar's kindnesses along with the urgency in Breith's voice when he spoke about the Hero's Quest and the death of two worlds—his own death—if Lyanz didn't get to the Empty Place. Though he was still angry and hurt, he jammed down his anger and his impatience and he endured.

Well, today was the day he stopped enduring bad treatment and laziness; if he couldn't pry the Hero loose from his comfortable life in the Tower, there was no longer any point to his presence here. The game was lost and he'd better hunt himself a hidehole deep enough to let him survive as long as Glandair held together.

If he could just get the fool moving! Somehow the Hero had to be smuggled off Nyddys and landed . . . hm . . . landed on the south coast of Faiscar. What Cymel said when she was talking, not squawking. Weird. He wondered for a moment how far Breith had got tracking her, shook his head to settle his thoughts on a useful track.

Faiscar. He scowled at the condensation collecting on the tin kettle, the drops forming, sliding in long wet curves down its sides. All he knew about Faiscar were his father's stories and a name or two—smugglers operating out of Lo Phreomo, a harbor town near the border between Faiscar and Kale. He scratched at the back of his neck, easing an itch where some bug had bit him. Getting there was going to be more trouble than dodging Klendo the Fat when the guard got your scent hot in his snogger.

Lyanz the Pure could slice your head off between one breath and the next as long as it was some sort of sword fight, but he didn't want to know about weasel tricks and ankle biting, ambushes and drop pits, smoke fingers, blow pipes, knockout drops and dream dust, the tricks that really saved your life. Swords just got you killed.

Hero stuff out of songs. Hmp! *I don't sing.*

Killed. Cymel got a spooky look on her face when she talked about the Hero's Quest. He doesn't know, she said. I don't think he could do it if he truly realized what was going to happen to him . . . or maybe he could and that's why he *is* the Hero.

T'teeth! *I wish she were here.* With two of us doing the driving, we'd be halfway to the coast by now.

Gryf pumped more water from the well in the corner of the kitchen and filled the hot water cavity in the stove, laid a fire under it and started bathwater heating. That pair would need baths after this afternoon's orgy. This was supposed to be a secret departure . . . he grinned at the memory of Hot-to-trot Maggie and the packs of dogs that would follow her around Tyst when it got to be too long since her last bath. Put Lyanz and long, tall Amhar in Maggie's place, what a howl that'd be — toothsome twosome-driven buggy by the amorous noses of hounds.

Puffs of steam popped from the spout of the kettle and it rattled on the burner supports. He made two big pots of tea, then peeled slices of dried meat and tuber from Ellar's storage packets and dumped them in a pan with water and some herbs he'd collected from the forest.

Probably the last hot meal for months to come. Best make it a good one. Hm. Voices in the hall. Amhar trying to sound judicious, Lyanz getting more and more frustrated and angry. Gryf snorted. Just because she's telling him things he don't want to hear. Hang round staring at each other much longer and we'll all be climbing the walls. Or out for blood.

Whistling softly he finished arranging the meal, then went to call them to eat.

Gryf pushed his chair back and got to his feet. He stood with his hands clasped behind him, his eyes moving from one face to the other. "We're leaving tonight," he said. "Laz, when you got to Nyddys, you didn't know katch about snow and cold but you been through plenty of winters since. Seimis. First Snow. You know what that means. One thing— we don't start now, we don't get across the Halsianel." He lifted a fork, tapped it on the table for a moment, then looked up.

"We're bound to get chased on one Broony Road or another when we start the scramble for Nordomon. We gonna take all of Seimis and maybe some of Wythamis to reach the sea. Season of Storms, Laz. Amhar. No ships will be leaving any of the Marshtowns from the ninth till the twenty-third Wythamis; we get there, we don't go nowhere." He raked a hand through his hair. "We hunt us out a hidehole, curl up and let the Mages whistle for us. Which means we've lost the game. Minute we stick our heads up come spring, Tyrn lands on us. I tell you this, we got to reach the coast before the Marshtowns shut down for the winter."

Amhar flattened her hands on the tabletop and fixed her eyes on a reddened hangnail. After a quick glance at her and a short, exasperated sigh, Talgryf focused all his forces on Lyanz. The Scribe was in love with the Myndyar, so distracted and upset by what she knew about the Hero's Fate that she'd do just about anything to postpone the moment when it began acting on him.

Face flushed with anger, eyes narrowed, Lyanz snapped, "Who died and made you Tyrn?"

"You want the truth?"

"What?"

"It was *you*, Hero. You're supposed to be leading us, but you turned yourself into a coney with the hots and forgot what you were." Gryf bounded to his feet. "You want to lead, *lead!* Tanew knows I don't want the job of booting you off your butt and out the door. But I'll do it if I have to. Ellar died defending you. Think about that. And think about Cymel.

Lost her father, lost her lover, even lost her shape so maybe she's forgot she's more than a fat white bird. All for you." The accusation in the thief's voice brought a darker flush to Lyanz's face and a sudden shudder.

Gryf collected his plate and tea mug. In the door to the kitchen, he turned and spoke. "One way or another, I'm out of here tonight."

[2]

Clouds cast a dense gloom across the land, a darkness that intensified as the layers thickened between Glandair and the moon and the streams of stars that flowed in milky extravagance across the black bowl of the night sky.

Ghosting along the white sand of East Argotikal Road the travelers were smoke-edged silhouettes, shadow legs flickering, their knapsacks shaping them into humpbacked trolls. Now that they were out of the higher mountains, most of the last snowfall had melted, just a few irregular patches of white where an overhang of foliage sheltered a section of the ground. The same chill that preserved the snow blew in the wind that crept into the interstices of their clothing.

Talgryf fumed at the stupidity of making targets of themselves like that but he kept an impassive face and a silent tongue. Sooner or later—probably sooner if Lyanz refused to listen to him or Amhar—Gamekeepers or Landrates from the Broonies of the Argotika would bring their bands of wealmen and throw a ring around them. He was ready to save himself, but the others would likely end in chains or dead.

A sudden sharp pain hit just below his shoulder blades— something in his pack, poking through the canvas.

Cursing under his breath, he slipped out of a shoulder strap, pulled the pack around in front of him and jerked the flap open.

Tiny red eyes glared up at him.

Chittering and shrieking, a monstrous, misshapen little god scurried up the leather and leaped at him, claws extended.

Talgryf gasped, jerked his head back and slapped at the little god, swatting it away, the angular, insectoid body hard and prickly against his palm.

The silence that came after the slap swelled with spite and a rage so thick it burned Gryf's nose. He turned slowly, scanning the road and the thorn hedges for the little god who had stirred up this minor hazard. Listening for whatever the god's hurry-scurry commotion might have brought searching for it.

Nothing. Only the usual noises of the night.

Annoyed and impatient, Gryf swung the pack around, settled it against his back and started on, trotting to catch up with the others. When he was two paces behind Amhar, he dropped to a steady walk, his eyes on the ground, his mind ranging ahead, focusing on what he knew about the coastal marshes that lay between the Broonies and the sea.

The Halsianel Sea was a long finger of saltwater, thicker at the middle—The Knuckle—than at each end. Though the sea was wider and more troubled at the Knuckle, this was where most of the smugglers based in the Bog Towns, as well as the pirates, poachers and legitimate traders with transient posts in the larger towns, all took to the water. It seldom snowed here and even the smaller, shallower harbors seldom froze, though sometimes they acquired ice rims and the occasional floe.

The east coast of Nyddys was a rambling, tangled water maze mostly unmapped and impossible for the Tyrn's coastguard to police. The Guard ran spies in the largest of the Bog Towns, set up ambushes and pounced on targeted ships as they poked their noses from the reeds and salt swamps, but for the most part the patrolling cutters ignored traffic heading into the Maze; once they reached the Shallows, the runaways, thieves, fugitives, smugglers and pirates who lived in or visited the hundreds of Bog Towns, which appeared and disappeared among the reeds with the flimsy fragility of dream cities, were safe from interference.

Even the Tyrn's tax-collectors left the Maze alone.

Talgryf's father had known a great many smuggler captains and high-trade Fences in these towns, and as he lay slowly dying, he'd recorded that knowledge in four notebooks filled with his sprawling, spidery handwriting—names and notes meant to reinforce what Lider had told his son during the trips the two of them had made to the Maze, when his illness had just begun to eat at his strength.

Talgryf belonged to a line of thieves whose origins vanished in the mists of history, passing back through Settling after Settling for as long as Glandair had existed. These lists, along with the introductions that Lider had arranged with his Sources of Convenience, were the most important assets of the Family Business—the means by which the Head of Household got rid of those trifles of worth that the Family acquired that were too hot to hold and too valuable for him to dispose of on the waterfront at Tyst or Dadeny.

The Trivon Tangle. That's where he planned to take Laz and Amhar. The grandest of all the Bog Towns.

Lushly leafy towers growing soft grass green, hard glassy emerald towers among the dripping and drooping vines, the wide-spreading canopy throwing opaque green shadows across the murky water. Deep water, wide silent streams where ocean goers could slide up to Pole Trees like cats rubbing against trousered legs, drop their anchors, and discharge cargo with little more than a whisper of sound. Where dark figures swaddled in cloaks and masks climbed into keel boats, rowed away from shore and vanished into shadow, Nyddys knowing them no longer.

Us, Gryf thought. If I can get us there.

Walk into the sun's face and keep on walking. What his father said.

He scraped his hand across his face. T'tears! Keep on walking is right. I remember when me 'n Da came this way. Took us till the cat fell dead even if it was high summer. His eyes stung as his memories came flooding back, golden days, fresh meat roasting on improvised spits, yams in the ashes. Or maybe fish dipped in cornflour, broiled over charcoal. Wild onions fried with cheese and bread. Tea boiled so strong you had to slap it down to keep it in the cup. In a way he was grateful for the change in seasons. Winter was hard even in the Maze. Good enough. The struggle would keep his mind off times it was best not to remember.

The Trivon Tangle.

The House of the Spider.

It'd be a good day when he could relax into his city self and acquire merit with the skill of his bargaining.

Unfortunately, he still had to get Lyanz and Amhar safely across two-thirds of the width of the Nyddys before they reached this safety, part of it by the road they were on now, part of it through the warded woodlands of the Broonies—and all of it dangerous.

Talgryf drifted toward the side of the road. The Hero's mistakes kept him wincing and put knots in his innards.

Look at that eeth! Walking down the middle of the road as if he owned the sand under his boots.

Lyanz had moved closer to Amhar. His hand was on the back of her neck. He was smiling at her and rubbing her nape; as Gryf watched, astounded, he bent over and gave the place where a halo of short dark gold hair escaped from her braid a quick light kiss. Amhar trembled; her body shouted to Gryf that all her long years of training were for that moment wiped from her head.

Neither one of them were paying any attention to the road or the snow-packed ditches running along both sides of it, or the deep shadows around the hedges that fenced the fields beyond. Anything could be lurking there.

Talgryf shook his head. It was like watching a slow disaster. The young Scribe's fierce determination to avoid embarrassing her lover meant that Gryf couldn't count on her backing if he tried to tell Lyanz what an eeth he was making of himself, that he might get them all killed if he didn't pull himself together. That he should start using his head instead of listening all the time to the jubilee capers of his jizzy slowworm. She would stop Gryf any way she could no matter what was happening around them. That made him very very nervous.

Once again he drifted closer to the side of the road, listening intently for sounds behind the hedgerows. The Broony Landrates posted sentries at the paddocks and Broony Gamekeepers patrolled the fields and plantings looking for poachers and thieves — and the children of the wealmen who worked the land; as destructive to the crops as vermin and even better at avoiding traps.

The flush fading from her face as her training reasserted itself, Amhar pulled away from Lyanz and glanced back at Talgryf. When she saw where he was walking, a frown darkened her face. She didn't like the criticism implied by his hugging the shadows at the side of the road, but she also knew that he was right. For a moment she struggled with the contradiction, then she slipped her hand within the circle of Lyanz's arm and leaned against him.

Slowly, subtly shifting her weight, she eased him from the center of the road over to the more difficult travel at the side. By the time the moon rested on the peaks of the mountains rising behind them, they were walking in the grass on the ditchbank, lost in shadow, footsteps muffled.

Hero's Luck happened when the pink glow in the east announced the approach of dawn. The lefthand hedgerow opened up at the edge of a hayfield, swung away from the road in a half circle of grass, gravel and sand with an irregular line of haymows set up under the wide, shallow canopy of a grove of sundew trees, their waxy leaves stiff as cardboard and still green though the smell in the air told Talgryf that the first snowfall was closer than he'd expected.

At the deepest point of the incurve he saw a horse shed, its thatch buried under a heavy growth of dark green moss, beside it a three-sided lean-to with rakes, scythes and other implements hanging on wall pegs, forks and twine bundles, folds of canvas piled up on ancient, dusty shelves.

This was one of the Wayfarer Turnouts that a long-ago Tyrn had squeezed out of the Council of Broons. No matter what they'd done to annoy one of the Broons, travelers were permitted to camp here undisturbed, free from Broon Law for as long as the Time of Sanctuary persisted.

Talgryf tapped Amhar's arm, jerked his head at the Turnout. "Luck," he said. "Gives us three days when nobody can touch us. No Broon, anyway. Broony Law doesn't run here."

Amhar drew in a long breath, glanced at Lyanz's scowling face, then at the luminous sand of the road as it curved round the outside of the grassy space and vanished into the darkness cast by the resumption of the thorn hedge. "They could sit out there and wait."

Talgryf brushed a clump of sweaty hair off his face. "They could."

Lyanz was standing in the middle of the road, hands on hips, eyes narrowed as he examined the way ahead.

"Which is why we need to keep heads down so the locals don't see any reason for hanging about." Gryf resettled the pack. "But we gotta rest sometime and this is a better place than most. We can sleep warm and safe. No one's gonna search the mows or dig through the hedges. The Turnout is Watcher-Warded and anyone who starts twisting the Rules will get a warp in his own guts that he won't shed for a lot longer than he wants." He gathered himself, jumped lightly across a shallow ditch filled with sundried grass. "So what're you waiting for?"

After a quick, cold meal, Gryf crawled under the canvas tied down over one of the mows, made himself a comfortable nest in the hay.

Lyanz had claimed first watch, sunup till mid-morning, but even he couldn't make a mess of something so simple; all he had to do was watch out for poachers and a wealman or two footing it in from the hills and if any came, make sure they didn't see him, Amhar or Talgryf.

Gryf curled on his side, yawned, shoved a knot of straw under his head for a pillow. Last he'd seen of Amhar, she was perched in the crotch of a sundew tree, starlight running silver along the polished pallor of her staff; she'd been given second watch—mid-morning till a span past noon—but couldn't rest without setting herself up as a hidden reinforcement should her lover run into trouble. And she'd persuaded Lyanz to give Talgryf the last and most dangerous watch, the hours when it was most likely that travelers would be using this place for an overnight stay before they moved on to the Broony Halstead. Gryf had kept his face impassive when he heard the result of her whispers, but under that mask he sagged with relief. He trusted himself a lot more than either of his companions.

[3]

Oerfel wiped the scry mirror and took up its fine parchment case, but he didn't tuck the mirror away; he set the case on the table, laid the mirror beside it and tilted his chair back, balancing it on the two hind legs. He stretched out his long thin body, resting his heels on the seat of the chair across from him. Tired and already suffering from an overload of images and data, he had too much to think about, anxieties building for the coherence of plans easier to conceive when he hadn't known all he knew now. If he missed some small detail, with things so unsettled, that might be enough to bring down the structure he was building.

Small detail. That was one of the problems. The Changing of the Mistress was not a small detail. Oerfel wasn't particularly interested in adding to his memory another example of the varied ceremonies Isel used to dismiss his mistresses. They showed the methodical cast of the Tyrn's mind and his amazing ability to hold a good number of contradictory views in his head without making that head itch, but he'd seen enough already to have a detailed impression of Isel's thought/action habits. Unfortunately, there was a lot more involved than that.

Oerfel let the chair's front legs crash down, then he edged it around so he could look out the window and let the hypnotic flow of high clouds bring ease to his thinking.

Anrydd's raids were like hot wires against Isel's skin, making the Tyrn squirm at every repetition, and this small fact alone brought Oerfel pleasure. The last raid at the largest of the iron mines had resulted in the destruction of the smelter and the slaughter of some of Isel's most knowledgeable ironworkers. Mules, rolling stock, even the miners were a big loss.

This was not only the largest mine, it was also held by a Broony traditionally at odds with the Seat and any Tyrn who planted his fundament on it, and the Broony was blaming Isel for what had happened because he was responsible for peace and order throughout all Nyddys; they were telling friend and foe that he should have stomped those raiders flat after their first depredations. Why were they allowed to run free killing and looting wherever they chose? Who was leading them? Were the Tyrn's men taking bribes to look the other way?

Oerfel smiled, glad that he no longer had to tend as Secretary to the paperwork this would generate, merely sit and watch Isel deal with the chaos engendered by Anrydd's raid on this particular Broony, which allowed him to savor the point of all this destruction, a wealthy and powerful clan turned from neutrals to enemies — unless Isel dipped into the treasury and came up with the coin to finance repairs and replace lost income. Oerfel glanced into the mirror and watched Isel wince with what looked like the pain of his own worst migraines as the Tyrn signed the exchequer's authorization.

Of course the Tyrn's spies knew about Anrydd and the schemes swirling around him, as did the Broons, though they didn't much care who was Tyrn so long as their own Power remained secure. And Isel was gaining a fair overview of the growing disaffection in the country. But the only one who seemed to have even a glimpse of the whole scope of the plan was Isel himself.

His spymasters and guard captains listened with grave attention and wise noddings to the Tyrn's rants about conspiracy and an organized uprising aimed at the Seat, but his speculations and extrapolations, while disconcertingly accurate to Oerfel's mind, were a bit too farfetched for the Tyrn's advisors. As soon as they were out of the Tyrn's presence, they shrugged, waggled fingers at their temples, wiped imaginary tears from their eyes, silently agreeing that it was sad to see such a mighty mind fallen so low.

In his sampling scrys, Oerfel watched those hypocritical displays and the condescending grimaces afterward, his thin lips curling into a taut, smug smile. I've fooled you all and I'll continue fooling you till you hang for your folly or bleed out on the battlefield.

Of course, the spymasters had to acknowledge Anrydd's involvement in the raids—there was too much evidence to disregard—but they saw him as no more than a bastard repudiated by his putative but no longer complacent father, kicked from wealth and privilege to poverty, which was enough to turn anyone sour. Especially a son of the former Tyrn who had inherited Dengyn's temper and his pride.

Fools. Blind fools.

As Anrydd's raids grew bolder and more destructive, Isel became increasingly frustrated, and Oerfel watched with pleasure as the Tyrn became unable to find a sympathetic ear that wasn't paid to be so. Even his wife, Afankaya, discounted his fears, snorting with scorn, proclaiming with her customary firmness that the Line had held the Seat for nearly a thousand years and it wasn't about to fall to some ragtail juvenile, a would-be warchief of a puny gang of bumbling brigands.

More fool she.

Isel's wife was an intelligent woman and he counted more on her than on his spies and sycophants for an accurate reading of the Court's emotional temperature and a feel for the loyalty of the Broons; she was right more often than the spies were and she wasn't afraid to tell him hard news—but she did have her blind spots. Afankaya had nothing but contempt for the lower classes, denying them the intelligence and will to work out complicated plots.

Oerfel knew better, as did Isel.

To cover those areas where his wife's arrogance—and ignorance—left him vulnerable, he searched through the middle and lower classes for a woman who would have the sort of insight he needed. Because of his own limitations and those of the women he found, he was continually changing mistresses, something that went against his nature and made him uncomfortable, but he knew what he needed and had enough cold iron in his spine to do what was necessary to keep himself steady on the Tyrn's Seat.

Oerfel was one of the few who understood what the Tyrn was doing and he kept a careful watch to make sure that Isel was continually disappointed in his choices, a task that was more time-consuming than one might think since the Tyrn's procurers had refined their practices till as many as three out of five of the candidates had both the intelligence and information Isel required. Oerfel cast a glamour over two or three of the women under consideration, enhanced their wit, slipped a steely glimmer into their eyes that hinted of quickness of intellect and a clever, acerbic view of life—qualities that faded soon after the Tyrn had made his choice and established the woman in the room-set of the official mistress. Then he watched with sour satisfaction as once again Isel found the woman unable to give him what he wanted and needed.

Isel was getting ready to change bed partners again. Oerfel sighed. He'd have to keep an eye on the parade as the Tyrn's procurers went in search of replacements. He scowled at the scry mirror, reached over and tapped the silver rim that enclosed the glass. "More work for the weary. Why don't you give it up, fool? You're not stupid. You have to know that you'll never find the right person because you're looking in the wrong places." He rubbed the tips of his fingers gently around his temple, his weariness casting a blur across his eyes. "You want someone to tell you why outcasts in the mountains are turning political and raiding for Power rather than for gold. And you're not going to find her, Hag curse you. Never. Not now. Not ever."

Oerfel groaned, slid from the chair and went to fetch pillows from his narrow bed. He tossed a pillow on the seat of the empty chair across the table, arranged a second pillow on the slats of the chair he'd been sitting in, kicked off his shoes and settled his feet on a padded footrest. After he'd once again focused his eyes on the thready clouds high overhead, he brooded over the choices that confronted him. He could repeat what he'd already done a handful of times. That was uncomplicated and effective. But so static! Simply preserving things as they had been got him nowhere.

A while later he blinked, pursed his lips, nodded. Yes. I can use that. Word gets round that Isel's looking for a new bedwarmer. Then it seems he's settled on some respectable girl. Young girl. Very young girl, very respectable. Hm. Get the Rumor men ready to ride. Have to start the whispers moving, Dadeny to Tyst. Rabble Shouters. Call them out . . . they'll need boltholes . . . especially Prufexic . . . Dadeny will be too hot for him soon as he opens his mouth . . . Isel won't tolerate that kind of nipping at his ankles . . .

Hm. A daughter of the middle class?

Someone's prize. Pride and joy. Road to climbing the social ladder.

Someone whose importance won't be apparent till it's too late for him to arrange a cover.

Trader? Merchant? Not a Broon's daughter, that's *too* obvious. Daughter out of the Maze?

A possibility, that. The Watermen were quick to take offence and murderous over insults to themselves and their families.

Oerfel shook his head. No resonance outside the coast marshes. I need someone who'll get a caustic and wrathful response from high and low alike. A hot wind of rage against Isel blowing across the land.

Hm. Scholar's daughter? Yes! I've got it! It's perfect. The Varotere. Doctor to the Tyrn's Herds. Veterinarian Prime at University.

Yes! Fallorane Wieranson. His wife is a snob and a

climber. He couldn't care less about his wife's concerns but he adores his daughter and he's been teaching her his secrets as if she were a son and could inherit his place. Anyone that blind to what's acceptable . . .

Ah! Yes yes. Fallorane has a thick web of ties with the Broons. He's bred most of their champion racers and jumpers. And the blue ribbon bulls. And he's a University Scholar—so I start my campaign against Cyfareth. Hit that cursed place hard. Tyrn's own Varotere—tangle Isel deep in that knot . . . whispers . . . sly glances . . . knowing looks . . . Fallorane's daughter is a charmer, sweet and tender as a heap of rose petals. A shame she has to go, but death is the end for us all, and hers will at least be quick.

Oerfel stroked the corner of his mouth, his lips curling into one of his rare unforced smiles. Prufexic will turn himself inside out with that plum to play with—*our Tyrn, our anointed leader, look at him, a degenerate, a monster, he can't even keep his hands off the daughter of one who belongs to his own household. If he won't stop there out of shame and in fear of Tanew's Curse, where will he stop? Your daughter next?*

Still smiling the Mage trimmed a pen, took a scrap of paper from the pile of spoiled documents, turned it over and dipped the pen in the inkwell.

It will start at Broony Mirmyan, he wrote. *Isel bred the Broon's prize mare to his best stallion. Foal due soon. Hmm. Strangler Weed in the foal's larynx?*

A patch growing at Cyfareth, Fallorane studying it.

Use that some way?

Danger of losing foal and mare both . . . Mirmyan will certainly call on Fallorane. . . .

[4]

The foaling stall in the horsebarn at Broony Mirmyan was a seethe of smoke and torchfire . . . wavery shadows of a man shifting through the chaos in a single thread of purpose . . . blackness with sudden interruptions of glitter . . . the liquid crimson of blood turning black in some lights . . . hot steamy flashes of blood spurting in angry arcs . . . the pink sheen of bald heads . . . hairy forearms . . . hands scrubbed raw . . . watery gleam of worn, rubbed leather aprons and the cutaway boots of stablehands.

All this whirling around the mare, the white, violent heart of the stall. The mare screamed, tried to rear, screamed again, staggered and nearly fell.

The Tyrn's own Varotere, a burly man with gray-streaked broom-straw hair and a vigorous ugly face, had been standing with his shoulder pressed against the mare's flanks, his head drawn down between his shoulders — listening with an intensity that seemed powerful enough to drag words from a mute.

Before the second scream died away, Fallorane had the temporary rope slings in place and was shouting for his peculiar aides (the source of much scandal, speculation and jealousy at University and in Carcalon; their loyalty to Fallorane was as absolute as their silence about their own methods and their origins). "Vaudrau, Truk, narrowpacks and all the cheringqus you can find. Oy! Move it!"

A few moments later a foal was on the ground, legs bending into impossible curves, chest heaving futilely as he fought to draw air through weed-blocked passages, a sour sickly smell hovering around him, the smell of might-be death.

Repeated gouts of blood surged out after the foal and threatened to drain the mare. Fallorane Weiranson began working with heedless, headlong speed that should have meant instant disaster but was instead a dance of the hands that merged impossibly different flesh and enigmatic magic into a powerful healspell. He snatched time to glance at the foal. "Towrari, Peltor. Foal. Strangler Weed. Seated deep. Get him over the brazier. Smoke those suckers outta there."

[5]

Isel leaned forward, shifting from foot to foot, peering at what he could see of the colt; every glimpse he got made him angrier at the deadly seed that had somehow crept through the defenses in his herd of young stallions—or into Broon Mirmyan's assemblage of famous mares. As he watched the Varotere and his aides work over mare and foal, however, the edges of his anger dulled and his acquisitiveness woke. The secret to destroying Strangler Weed . . . his hands closed into fists and his eyes glistened. Fallorane and his aides were ripping that deadly web out of the foal and cutting the mare free of the whip ends that kept tearing at her already lacerated flesh. It was not certain yet, but it was starting to seem likely that both foal and mare would survive.

Abruptly Fallorane broke off the rumbling continuo he'd been providing for the chant spells of his twinned assistants; he walked heavily across to Broon Mirmyan and began talking without a greeting. "Clear out the horsebarn except for that pair of mutes you keep round as guards. We will be wanting breakfast in about an hour. The milk of six mares freshly procured. Four fwats of blood whipped into the milk. Two honeycombs. If you don't have honey, molasses will do. Five loaves of bread. One fark of butter. Have it here and ready by the time the sun is fully up."

He turned and walked heavily away, settled himself back into the group and insinuated the continuo thread back into the healchant.

Broon Tichnor gan Mirmyan flushed purple; he took a

hasty step forward, growled as another hand closed about his arm. He nearly struck at the man holding him until he remembered who was standing beside him. When he'd mastered himself and was calm enough to speak, he said, "You let that bucket of 'bort worms talk to you like that?"

"If you want his services, you do. If it bothers you, arrange to have no witnesses." The Tyrn's voice was a whisper like the rustle of a serpent hidden in dry leaves. "A small reminder, my friend. Fallorane is *my* servant. And now that I've seen him defeat Strangler Weed, his value has expanded beyond anything you can afford to pay."

Anger replaced by wariness, Tichnor nodded. "Let's get out of here." After a last glance at the men weaving healmagic round the mare and her foal, he wheeled and stomped toward the door.

A wash of watery gray marked the eastern horizon and what stars were still visible were dim, half-lost in haze. The air had a biting chill; his breath blew white and he could feel the pinch of frost on his ears and nose. Broony Mirmyan was too far south for snow this early in the winter season, but during Isel's journey from Carcalon his coach had labored through two ice storms and he hadn't seen the sun the whole trip. The luminous, white, night-blooming flowers on the wall vines of the various gardens were folding together for the coming day while their pale leaves crept into the shelter of the Morning Shade vines that overlaid them. The cold didn't seem to affect them, even the scatter of tiny ice crystals across the petals. One last burst of fragrance, one last shimmer of luminescence — then the rule of the night dreams would be finished and the prosaic visions of daylight would take over.

As if the Broon felt Isel watching him, he flattened his shoulders and forced the strut back into his short-legged stride. He snarled something at one of his guards, sent the mute running ahead to open a carved, wooden gate set deep in one of the woven wall that circled the outermost of the nested Mirmyan gardens.

Tichnor's guards had been bred for the purpose and were the only individuals he trusted near him armed. They were huge and stolid, with broad curly polls like young bulls and mild brown eyes. These mutes were a product of magic and generations of inbreeding—and one of the things that made Broons like Tichnor abominations in the eyes of a large portion of the population of Nyddys. Unfortunately they were also among Isel's most dependable supporters, so he was forced to expend time and considerable thought to keep them pacified and the rest of Nyddys relatively ignorant about their beliefs and activities.

One of those mutes waited beside the gate to the inner gardens, his lance presented, his eyes mud pools utterly empty of thought. The Morning Shade vines darkened on the walls, their dotted flower pods bouncing at the end of long, spiraling stems. The garish pods dangled in an eccentric halo about the guard's moon face and turned him into an image of Half-a-God, the Trickster Easily Tricked.

Tichnor snarled and trotted over to him, unbuttoning his sleeves and rolling them up to his elbows as he moved. Using both hands he beat a rapid tattoo on the guard's face. "Fool!"

=B . . . but I just. . . . I did what you said,= the mute signed, his fingers stumbling as if they stuttered like a tongue.

"No. You were embellishing." Tichnor looked at his left hand, shook it, stood rubbing it up and down his side.

=B . . . b . . . but when C . . . Crow. . . . = Still flustered and uncertain, his signs ended with a meaningless flutter of his fingers.

"It is his place to embellish. It is yours to be exact. Now

get that gate open. Then you walk ahead of us and see that we don't have to wait when we desire to pass from one garden to the next."

Isel passed through the gate, shivering as the chill air mixed with the somber mood of the dawn as the rising sun put crimson edges on the long shadow that jerked before him, his own shadow, insect-thin, wrinkled and strange.

Sleeves pushed above massive forearms, hands clasped behind him, Tichnor stumped along the raked gravel of the path, scowling morosely at the ground. This night had been hard on both his pride and his possessions. He turned a corner, let out a roar—a mix of rage, grief and despair that stopped the Tyrn in mid-stride and woke the deeply ingrained wariness that his fatigue had deadened.

Isel took a step backward, then another until the hedge bulked between him and the Broon. Ignoring the prick of the short, curved thorns, he peered through a web of trailing branches at the scene unfolding in the footway beyond.

A gap-tooth young man with the Mirmyan nose jutting from the heavy-boned Mirmyan face was kneeling beside the body of a young woman. A very young woman.

She'd been badly beaten before she was strangled; her face was blackened, twisted and deformed, her body a pulpy mess. Isel dragged the back of his hand across his mouth. Despite the mangling of her features, there was something familiar about the girl. Disturbingly familiar. *I know her. Why do I know her? Dressed too richly to be one of the maids, but too poor for a daughter of the Broony.*

The thorns dug into him as he leaned harder against the bushes espaliered against the hollow concrete bricks that walled the footways. *Something about her. I could name her, I swear I could. If the light was just a bit stronger. Not so much shadow where she's lying.*

Isel's breath came louder, harsher; cold fear clutched at

him. He didn't know why. He didn't know how. But his deepest instincts screamed that this was an attack directed against
him. Somehow, someone had laid out a trap for him. The
girl had some connection to him. She was the bait . . . no . . .
not bait . . . she was planned to function as the accuser, the
finger pointing at him.

He flattened his hand against the bricks; the concrete was
cold and rough against his palm. The youth was part of it.
Ostensibly he was the guilty one, but because of who he was,
Tichnor would turn against Isel, would be the first and loudest of his accusers. Not hard to identify the youth. He'd seen
him at the supper before the vigil in the horsebarn, and Isel
knew well enough who he was—Tichnor's youngest, Chamelly Tichnorsson. Stupid, silly, puffed up with the Power of
the Broons and all the control of a young beefer, along with
the muscles of one.

Tichnor's roar froze him in place. The Broon stood with
his hands on his meaty hips, looking grim.

Strangling a girl while the Tyrn was in residence at his
father's Hall was exactly the sort of arrogant stupidity that
would appeal to the floxhead Chamelly, at least to judge from
what he'd said the night before. Putting his father's rants into
action under the Tyrn's nose. He probably thought Tichnor
would be pleased with him.

Isel glanced at the body, frowned. The morning light
struck full on the dead girl's battered face, and he suddenly
recognized her from the supper the night before. Lauresa
Falloranedattar. Fallorane dotes on her; the minute he knows
about this, he'll call Blood Feud on Mirmyan. Mirmyan will
scream foul and point his finger at me. He'll have all the
witnesses he needs to back him up; none of his folk will
naysay him, that'll weaken their words but, enough stories
repeated often enough, people start believing them.

Isel rubbed his thumb along his jawline. This was part of

the conspiracy. He was jumping without data, working on air and shadow, but he knew it to the marrow of his bones. The plotters he'd not been able to find, they'd done this. As a corollary, whatever else he might be guilty of, Mirmyan wasn't in on this. That didn't matter. *I've got to get away from here. Do something public. . . .*

"You!" The Broon scowled at a shapeless darkness stirring in the corner of a deepset doorway. "Come here," he growled.

The shadow got to its feet and crept forward, trembling. She was a thin, shivering serving girl, even younger than Fallorane's daughter.

Isel eased deeper into hedge shadow, backing silently, slowly toward the nearest turn in the footway. That shivering wisp was one of the Mirmyan wealfolk, a witness who could place Chamelly Tichnorsson with the body. She wouldn't, of course. And Tichnor knew it. He also knew wealman gossip. By moonset tomorrow Fallorane would know where his daughter died and how she was found.

Wrinkled, papery lids drooping across frightened eyes, the serving girl passed her tongue across dry lips. "He din' do it," she burst out.

"Yes yes, very loyal." The Broon caught her by the neck, snapped it with a forceful constriction of his long fingers. Casting her aside as casually as a crumple of paper, Tichnor turned to his whimpering son and slapped him across the face, the blow powerful enough to send him sprawling.

"Who was she, fool?"

Chamelly hunched over, shivering and miserable. "Tillni. One of the housemaids."

Tichnor ground his teeth. "You got cheese for a brain? Who gives a curse about a housemaid. The dead girl. Who was she?"

"Oh. I dunno." Chamelly grimaced, dug his fingers into his thick, oily hair. "I think. Hard to say with her face mucked up like that." He put his toe under the dead girl's ribs and lifted her shoulders so he could see her face better. "Nah. Like I said. I dunno."

"Why don't I believe a word of this?"

"I knew you wouldn't believe me. I saw her lying there and I *knew* you'd put it on me. I didn't lay a hand on her, I swear it. Tillni could've told you. Me and her, we were with . . ." He lowered his eyelids, long lashes sweeping with absurd grace across the knobs and juts of his bony face, "Some people. Having a party."

As Tichnor continued to hurl questions at his son, Isel backed cautiously from the scene and as soon as he could, turned into another footway and fled as fast as he could into the house.

When he reached the royal suite, he roused his servants, saw that his Special Guard were in place, had himself bathed and put to bed with a pleasant small supper and a goblet of emerald wine. He couldn't stay there long, though fatigue struck at him the moment he stretched out on the soft mattress and pulled the bed clothes about him. He needed to leave an impression of unhurried undisturbed rest. Wealman gossip could work for him as well as against. These whispers the Broons and their kin wouldn't hear, but the stories would travel like spring fires from one end of Nyddys to the other.

Floating in the rosy light seeping through the silk blinds, soothed by the warmth from steam-heated sheets, propped up on scented pillows, Isel nibbled at a chicken leg to lay down an impression of undisturbed appetite and at the same time contemplated the disaster that had been prepared for him.

Scandal and feud. He swallowed the mouthful of meat, gulped wine to wash it down.

Tichnor would be rampaging around the South Broonies like a bull in must. He considered himself one of the "old school," those worshipers of the Hag who spat on the image of Dyf Tanew, the Man of Sorrows, and were agitating for a return to rule by the ancient caste system set up in the time before History began, when the Worthy Men suckled on the dugs of the Creator Hag and drew the Vis of Power into themselves until they shone with it. In the days that followed, more Vis was stolen as it leaked from the limp dugs while the Creator Hag rested or slept—snatched by warrior and scholar, wizard and merchant in gradually smaller amounts— with the result that the line of obedience was simple and strong. Broon ordered, warrior obeyed, warrior ordered, scholar obeyed, the lesser compelled by the greater, lesser and greater determined by the strength of the Vis-within. By this argument, nothing Chamelly might have done to Lauresa was illegal, immoral, or impossible, since his Vis was so much greater than hers. Might have done. Probably didn't. He hadn't the brains to be part of the plot that was starting to close tighter and tighter round Isel. Tichnor wouldn't settle for the argument from Power and Right. He'd be going for a complete vindication of his son—which meant finding a goat to blame for the child's murder.

It was all too easy to visualize the uproar that would follow Tichnor's accusations. And the discord that would come when Hag worship surfaced once again—something that was bound to happen. Tichnor's personal beliefs almost guaranteed it.

The Tyrn dropped the legbone on the plate. "This business will chew away my support faster than I cleaned that bone." He dug out a wing. "Too bad this isn't your neck, fat man. T'teeth—Hag worship! Not just illegal, but in bad odor with everyone except these idiots with their heads twisted on backwards."

He looked round at the room with its dubious taste, swags of crimson velvet and satin, gilded plaster vinework, more gilt laid over wrought-iron window guards, gauze-fronted niches where servant girls knelt, waiting with mindless patience for whatever orders he might dredge up for them. "Why am I here?"

It wasn't a question, just a petulant complaint. The gauze hangings stirred as the hidden girls turned to watch and wait.

"Whose idea was this, breeding my stallion to that mare?" The hand that held the wing went suddenly still as Isel scowled unseeing at the wall beyond the foot pillars of the bed. "Whose idea. . . ." he whispered. "As far back as that . . . plotting against me . . . no accident. Ahhh! No one believes me. Plotting. . . ."

He finished the wing, gulped down the rest of the wine. "*Va nar o diabors!*" He closed his eyes a moment, fatigue like a wave washing over him. "Enough time laying trail. Time I was away from here. If I could just drop Tichnor and all his brotherkind down a well. . . ."

He swung his legs over the edge of the bed, ignoring the faint noises that came from the watching servants. "He's dumping the body. Yes. Working out how to land the guilt on me. Does he think I don't know what he's up to? Overdosed on Vismilk till he struts like a god?" He looked around him, aware suddenly that he was overlooked by dozens of eyes, even more than when he was home in his room-sets at Carcalon.

Tyrn Isel slid out of bed. "Helgart! Get in here." He stalked across the room and pulled back one of the gauze drapes. "You." He stabbed a forefinger at the crouching woman. "Get the rest of your minions and go back to your quarters."

A tall Rhudyar opened the door and slipped inside. "Sri Tyrn?"

"I'm done here. The colt's born, that's all I need to know. Get your unit and clear out this room." He waved a hand at the woman still crouched in the niche, her back bent in a sharp curve, her brow pressed against the floor. "She doesn't seem to hear me. I want to be out of here before the hour's up. Anyone not ready to march might as well stay here. I don't want to see their lazy faces again."

[6]

Oerfel blew the scene off the scry mirror and slipped it into its parchment case, wishing as he did so that the mirror could reproduce thoughts as well as it did images. He would have given a lot to see inside Isel's mind and know how much he understood about what was going to happen. From his mutterings and other indications, it had taken him less than a dozen breaths to get a fair idea what had happened, who'd done it and what must follow from the death of the girl.

What was dream is now fact. Fallorane's daughter is dead and that is fact; that can't be undone. Now let me loose rumor and watch each account transform the tale.

In a carefully disguised hand, he wrote a brief note to the Courier waiting to ride to the Rabble men, sanded the ink and folded the paper into quarters. "Zazeel, come here."

A street urchin rose from the corner where he'd been crouching and came slowly to the table, his feet dragging, his eyes glazed. He took the note and left, moving faster now that he was carrying out the commands that Oerfel had impressed on him.

"Sweet Rumor, if you had a temple here, I'd gild your image and pour diamonds at your feet." Oerfel chuckled. His plans were moving forward as smoothly as an otter slithering down a mud slide. The Hero had eluded him for the moment, but Nyddys would be in his hands before the spring thaw. Mahara and Hudoleth were already wearing each other down, wasting vitality as they brought more territory and more souls under their control; by the time they were locked in their last battle, he'd be at the peak of his strength and ready to strike.

The windowpanes rattled, the table's legs bumped against the floor. A sudden weakness spread in waves through his body. "Earthquake." He clutched at his ears, closed his eyes and tried to shut out the groaning that came from deep in the earth and played lugubrious hymns in his bone and blood.

5

Death

By the calendar of the Domains of Iomard, events starting on the 22nd Ekhtos, the eighth month of the Iomardi year 6536, the 723rd year since the last Corruption.

[1]

On the fifth morning of that unpleasant voyage, Yasayl woke to the feel of warm liquid seeping into her skirts. She squirmed, trying to make groggy sense of it. "Malart, you've . . ." Her hand brushed down his cheek, only to encounter more warmth and wetness, then a bloody opening, a gash in his throat, and the tangled ends of the wire cutting deep into his neck. The reason for the first wetness suddenly made sense—his sphincters had let go at the moment of death.

Yasayl's pseudo-sight flared alight, the eerie, green-tinted black and white line drawings that her Gift sometimes granted her as a substitute for true sight. The ghost images were on all sides of her, and she left her hand in Malart's blood, searching for the assassin who had killed him, who would strike her, but there was nothing. No one.

Folk lay sleeping, their outlines huddled together for warmth under the ghost-shapes of blankets, just as she had with Malart, or slumped about the deck, clutching cups of morning tea, engrossed in private conversations. The killer could not have gone far, could not have left, but the ship was small. It would be only the work of a minute to walk away, take up a position at the forecastle, pose oneself with a teacup.

Malart was dead. She had been spared. Only one person had seen Malart's death. Besides herself, only one person knew.

Yasayl wanted to scream. She wanted to weep. But more than that, she wanted to know *why*. And she didn't want to lose the touch of Malart, the last of his warmth, even as she felt his flesh grow cold.

Pain gave way to the flat affect of shock. She let her pseudo-sight flow out to encompass the ship, taking a bird's-eye view. She flipped through the faces of one person and another, the harsh green and black outlines, scanning them above and below decks like a rogue's gallery to find the killer of her beloved. But whoever that person was, she'd covered her tracks well and betrayed no sign of her guilt.

At last, the shock began to ebb and the grief set in. Malart had gone fully cold. She touched him. Her fingers stroked and stroked the swollen wound until they were coated with tacky, coagulating blood. His flesh was cold, drained of the vitality that had warmed her, filled her life. The blood glued her fingertips temporarily to each other. They made small ripping sounds when she pulled them apart.

She sobbed suddenly. Then she started the keening that custom and her heart demanded.

[2]

Malart's body was dumped into the ocean. That was the only ceremony he was allowed. Yasayl was permitted to stand beside the rail and wait for the splash. Abandoned there by the crew, she was left to find her own way back to their place.

"Ow! Watch whatcha do with ter steek, ol' crow. Tibby, lad, shove 'er off, huh?" A harsh, nasal voice with the flat, unmodulated syllables that came out of the South Drain section of Valla Murloch, a collection of shanties and filthy lanes, ignorance and rage, a thieves' refuge, the last lighting place of failed ridos who could be bought for a handful of coins and a hot meal. "You. Ol' hag, getcha ugly face outta here. Turns m' gut looking atcha."

Flustered, momentarily disoriented, Yasayl tapped about with the staff, listening with a sudden fierce concentration. If she'd lost her ability to move about . . . When she'd convinced herself that she hadn't mistaken her path, she brushed her fingertips through the film of sweat dripping over her scars. "What . . . what are you doing in my. . . ."

"Your! No such thing." A puff of sour body odor gusted up around Yasayl along with the scratchy slither of thick greasy cloth. Down round her knees something small and hostile was mumbling and muttering and hitting at her, feeble blows she barely felt through the folds of her skirt.

"Gorgo! Shift you lazy bones and get her off our place."

Bony hands closed on her shoulders and sought to turn her away.

She swayed, clenched her teeth to hold back vomit as waves of stale sweat, rotted food droppings and sour beer turned her knees weak while the verbal and physical attacks continued. The man's long thin fingers tightened on her shoulders and a shambling bony body pressed against her.

He rubbed himself against her, a breathy chuckle sawing in her ear.

Fury seized her, bringing with it the pseudo-sight. She raised her staff, cracked the man across the head and dropped him to the deck, swung round and rammed the point of the staff into the belly of the harridan, cutting a curse in half as the woman ran out of air. As a continuation of the same movement, she did a drumroll on the back of the gap-tooth boy and finished the turn using the point of the staff to send the small girl yelping into the crowd of passengers. They paid no more attention to the child than they had to what had gone on before.

Rage still driving her, she levered the unconscious man off her blanket and shouted the wife out of there with a Pneuma-enhanced voice that cut into the head like knives.

Terrified, whining that she was killed, the South Drainer woman caught hold of her limp mate and began dragging him away. After a few steps, the boy oozed reluctantly from the crowd and helped his mother lift and tug at the body of his father.

Yasayl turned slowly, the pseudo-sight still functioning. Some of the eyes fixed on her were frightened, some thoughtful, but most were carefully blank. She wanted to spit in their faces, but stood tall, Pneuma fizzing in an aura about her as the anger that had driven her moments before began draining away. She swung her blind, scarred face from side to side until they were shamed into turning away and leaving her alone.

She lowered herself to the blankets, wrinkling her nose at the smell that the South Drainers had left behind. Hands trembling as her body chilled, she began running her fingers over the blankets and searching out the debris that fed the stink. She found fragments of sardine sandwiches; two limp, wilted onions that felt like rats had gnawed at them; two heavy stone bottles partly filled with raw batta, a cheap, dangerous intoxicant made from whatever slop the stillman found in the gutters of South Drain; a waterskin that still had the hair on it, though clumps fell out each time her fingers brushed over the plump sides; and some ragged bundles that made her skin cringe as she touched the stiff, greasy fabric. She contemplated calling the woman back to retrieve her things, but her anger sparked at the thought. Instead, she simply tossed the things out where others could take or leave them as they chose.

When she had the shelter purged to her satisfaction, the South Drainer smell still lingered, mixed with the raw blood and urine of Malart's death still soaked into her blankets and skirts. She set her back against the mast, drew up her legs and closed her eyes. "Mar," she whispered, but the sense of him was gone. She could think of nothing but her anger at the captain of the ship who let Malart get killed and the squatters try their tricks. Bryheris didn't do a thing to prevent either and she knew with cold certainty that he wasn't about to help her find out the motive for the murder either.

Night brought wind that scoured her nest clean and kept her awake and missing Malart with her body in ways she hadn't realized were possible — missing the warmth of him curled up against her; missing his breath in her hair; missing the sense of him, his goodness, his love, the emotional warmth more subtle but just as necessary as the physical warmth of the body. Toward morning she wept, her sobs hidden by the howl of the wind, the tears freezing to her face.

As the cold gray light strengthened, she used some bottled water to clean her face before she sat up. No one would be allowed to share her grief, especially these people, so closed into their own affairs that they could feel nothing but curiosity or perhaps a kind of prurient intrusiveness.

After she'd combed her hair, she sat once again with her

knees pulled up, her forearms draped over them, the depleted packs as a rest for her back. She stared past her unseen neighbors at the broad white wake the ship was braiding behind it, an image in her head, not in her missing eyes, etched there with the startling clarity her pseudo-sight could sometimes achieve, a wake that thinned and vanished rapidly but contributed more than the snap of the sails and the motion of the deck to her sense of how fast the ship was traveling.

As the morning crept on, what startled her most was the discovery that she had no interest whatsoever in who had killed Malart, but she urgently needed to know why. Her mind and body had somehow chilled around that *why* until she was cold as stone and less feeling. She searched the fragments of image her Gift brought to her, fragments out of the future that were really signs from the past, probing these for the face or name of the person who had done the killing— but only to discover the answer to that *why*. She didn't want revenge, only an answer she could believe.

Late that afternoon she felt men closing around her — Bryheris and three of the crew, sailors whose Pneuma profiles she remembered from Malart's perfunctory funeral. The pseudo-sight was intermittent now, sudden flashes of color-free image, then the familiar darkness. She welcomed that darkness, the sense of shelter she found in it—as if by not-seeing herself or her surroundings, she would herself not be seen.

"Can you stand, Cay Yasayl?" Bryheris, his voice as bland as his face must be at this moment.

"Yes," she said. She didn't move.

"I have made a cabin available. If you'll follow me, I'll get you settled in there now. I want no more such bloody accidents. The assassin might mistrust your hearing, Cay. There

are many legends about the blind and their ears. I am sorry
for the belated realization, but there it is." He mouthed the
words of his speech out of an indifference so deep she felt
bathed in warm, stale saltwater; the body stench of the South
Drainers was a kind of perfume beside this.

"Courteous of you, Captain." *I wonder who you're really
talking to and why. Or are you just playing sea turtle with
your reputation?* "If I don't wish to move?"

"I am desolated to add insult to your injury, Cay, but this
is not a request."

She got to her feet slowly, staggered a little as dizziness
washed over her. But when hands closed about her arms, she
jerked angrily free of them. "Touch me again and I will brew
such misery for you, living won't be worth the trouble it
takes."

The cabin was little more than a closet. The smell em-
bedded in the walls came from decades of broken wind and
body fluids, effluvia from all the ocean crossings the *Kelai
Maree* had made since that distant day when her keel was
laid. A porthole in one wall was sealed shut by dirt and grease.
The only air that got into the cabin came through the slats
that covered the mouths of the several air shafts opening high
up on the four walls.

Two sailors used her blankets to make up one of the cots,
slapping at the straw mattress with a vigor that raised clouds
of dust and even bigger clouds of tiny black biters. The horde
of meager, itchy lives heaved round her, teased at her nose,
and raised welts on her skin.

A third sailor swept out what sounded like large piles of
debris, some paper, some hard lumps that made odd clunking
sounds as they moved across the floor. The slapdash job of
cleaning was quickly done and she was left alone sooner than
she expected, feeling battered.

Before she did anything else, she gave the room a Pneuma firebath, her mouth set in a grim line as she felt the infinitesimal deaths of the biters and the clumsier bedbugs hiding in the straw pallet. The rats in the wall fled before the heat of her converted anger and she let them go. She set alight the dirt and grease sealing the porthole shut, letting it sizzle and stink until the glass popped open and she was rewarded with a breath of fresh air and salt mixed with fine ash and the sound of the ocean waves. When she was done, she wiped the muddied sweat from her face and dropped wearily onto the hinged cot.

After a moment she pulled her boots off and stretched out on the cot. The inside edge of its frame was hinged to the side wall. Through this connection the cot acquired a swaying twisting motion while the two legs of the outer edge of the frame picked up and amplified the up and down movement of the floor. The straw mattress felt harder than the decking and the blankets were not soft enough to impart any ease to her body.

The horsehair pillow smelled of ancient hair oil and harsh lye soap. She pulled the hard lump under her head, wriggled around onto her side and braced against the combination of motions. Now that she had the privacy to grieve, she found that she had no emotion left in her except her need to know WHY.

After a while, she slept.

[3]

For nine days the *Kelai Maree* raced north.

On the tenth day the ship crossed an intangible but agonizing barrier; though no one else on board felt it, Yasayl felt as if she'd passed through a ring of fire—fire that shocked awake her pseudo-sight.

She pressed her face to the open porthole of the cabin that had become her prison, breathing in the fresh air and ocean sounds. As the ship moved along, her solarized pseudo-vision showed her the blanched outline of a small rocky island, then a cluster of islands, then a long low shape that rode the horizon for several hours. The next island came to her like a map, an oval with a single mountain on it, a volcanic cone. That was enough to confirm the location of the ship. Bryheris had not brought his cargo of refugees to Ascal, but to the Sanctuary Isles.

Which meant one of two things. Either he was an ally of the Siofray Mage Dur—or bought by him—or he planned to dump the valueless part of his cargo on one of these barren islands.

Her erratic ability to glimpse probable futures had become even more sporadic after Malart was killed. She had almost no data to work from except the knowledge already in her head and her training in logic—though logic could be a broken reed if not frequently supplemented by observation and information.

Learning the ship's destination almost broke her. Each day she'd congealed into a harder substance until she barely felt hunger or thirst. Certainly all grief was gone; she couldn't remember Malart except as a vague shape. There was nothing left of his warmth, not even the spiky edges of his anger when he felt left out of the bond between her and Faobran.

The Isles were shut away from the mainland. They were as much a prison for those who ran there to find safety as it was the haven they sought. That notion stirred her from her coldness and apathy. "I can't allow it," she thought. "I won't."

[4]

After dropping anchor in a shallow bay, Captain Bryheris strode to the front rail of the quarterdeck and stood looking down at the passengers his crew had rounded up for him.

They were looking restlessly about, muttering and glaring at cocked crossbows in the hands of crew clustered behind him and on yardarms above them.

Bryheris thrust out his hand for the megaphone his First Mate was handing him. He whistled through it, shook it, put it to his mouth, and started talking.

"Some of you may have heard that now and then Ascal captains will act as slavers, given opportunity and a sufficiency of choice. The rumors are wrong. Under those conditions Ascal captains are *always* slavers.

"You and everything you thought you owned are now my property.

"My First Mate and his selection team will be descending to the deck. Anyone who tries to lay hand on them dies instantly. The rest of you, get away from the fool quickly. My men are good shots, but they could possibly miss their targets and take the innocent with the guilty. They will be fined if they do but that won't help the dead.

"Those too old or too young to bring in hard cash at an auction will be left ashore. Be grateful that I am a compassionate man. There is ample water on this island and a sufficiency of birds and fish to support life for a fair number of diligent workers.

"The rest of you will go into slave chains. Family ties mean nothing to me; the only value I see in any of you is your potential for increasing the profit of this voyage. Make a nuisance of yourself and you'll find the ocean deep and convenient.

"This is the only explanation you will get. The only choice you need to make. Cause trouble and you're dead. Remain obedient and you have a chance at life."

[5]

Yasayl was culled into the discard line. She could not immediately figure why Bryheris had given her a cabin if he was going to toss her away, but then came up with a likely enough answer: Because her Gift was unpredictable, the captain had been weighing his decision. More important than that, however, was the fact that after Malart's death, it was more likely than not that there was someone *she* would kill — the assassin. Thus, it was more profitable for Bryheris to protect the rest of his cargo by locking her away while he made his decision than to let her and the assassin hunt each other on deck and likely damage other wares in the process.

She didn't know whether to be pleased or offended that she had finally been judged not worth the slaver's bother, but she was more than a little annoyed because the assassin, whoever she was, would likely be one of the chosen, and the definitive answer to the *why* that still tormented her would be taken beyond her reach.

Bryheris left Yasayl's staff with her because it was old and worn and full of years — and of no value to anyone but her. Abandoning her here on an island, that, however fulsome his words, was a place with just enough vegetation and just enough birds and other food to let her slowly starve to death, was a bitter joke on her and her Seyls, an answer to Corysiam and Faobran's threats — in his mind, a response to all the insults he'd suffered in silence for so many years. Those insults might be products of his imagination, but the satisfaction he was getting from dumping Yasayl on that desert island was very real. She could smell it on him, strong as the stench from a roasted oilfish. He was dropping her there not for profit, but for pleasure, spending his coin on the easy satisfaction of revenge.

The oilfish stink increased as he ordered the other discards onto the island. A revenge on another one of them — no, another revenge on her.

The assassin had been culled as well, whoever she was, and sent to the isle with Yasayl as one last slap for Bryheris's pleasure.

[6]

Yasayl's Gift came alive once more a short time after the *Kelai Maree* dropped below the horizon. As usual, her visions were disjointed, incomplete and difficult to sort, dream images:

Hands not her own pressed to her temples. Then pain, a stabbing pain, a thousand times worse than when she was blinded.

Then clarity, and visions as clear as what she'd seen before coming to rely on the pseudo-sight:

A boy dancing, eyes green and brown.

A wall of water crashing down.

A woman with close-cropped hair — one she'd seen on the boat with her pseudo-sight — crawling and squirming with pleasure before Mirrialta like a newly whelped puppy.

Rada's body, lying broken and lifeless.

Other images fluttered about, like bright scraps from a quiltmaker's bag tossed into the air, with no time to comprehend the intricacy and details of the patterns before they vanished from her Sight: Bauli and a crab; Corysiam and a pot; Faobran in Breith's room; more water washing down, pouring onto the floor.

And reflected in that water, and a dozen other fragments

with water and reflecting pools all around him, a man's face. Dur.

She wasn't certain of all of it, or when or if any of these things would come to pass, but the image of Rada's death gave her some dark satisfaction and more than a hint of certainty. In the end, she managed to patch together a fairly detailed picture of what was likely to happen, at least in the short term.

Dur was coming, and she had best be prepared.

She made her way to a flat rock at the top of a pile of rocks, climbed onto it and sat there with her staff laid flat across her lap.

Hours passed. She grew hungry, but when shame drove the others to offer her a share of their meager gleanings from the nests and sands of the island, she took no food from them. When someone brought her a wooden cup filled with water, she drank and smiled her thanks. And she waited.

[7]

Dur came south for her before the sun set.

Yasayl had had a bit more time to sort her visions and was able to make sense of the ones that tended to linger, the images dealing with the past: Dur had learned of her Gift from a number of sources and meant to use her as he used every female Siofray with a talent or property he needed. She knew his habits well enough and intended to let herself be used—on her terms, not his, insofar as she could manage that. At the moment, she needed him far more than he needed her; to make sure he didn't realize this, she used the time of waiting to prepare a series of jolts for him. Jolts and temptations—glimpses of what she could do for him.

She sat on her meditation stone, using her pseudo-sight to

help pose herself to her best advantage: a gaunt, scarred idol with an ancient staff laid flat across her knees, the heavy robe draped in folds beneath it.

Dur started when he saw her. Yasayl had a flash-vision of another woman, with straight posture and a stick in her hand. A vision plucked from the front of Dur's mind and his past: his mother.

Good, she could use that.

"Cay Yasayl."

"Mage Dur."

"Then it's true."

"Yes."

"I have a proposition for you."

"I know."

"This is . . . difficult . . . to deal with."

"I imagine it might be." She turned her blind stare away from him and gazed out to sea, seeing nothing, the pseudo-sight gone completely now that body and mind were returned to serenity. "You don't know what it is I know, and can't prepare to counter it, and you never will." The corners of her mouth curled upwards in a mirthless, chilly smile. "I will cede you this. Remember that this Gift is less than it appears to be and my ignorance greater than implied."

"Why the warning?"

"I want Radayam dead and her army destroyed."

"And you think I can do that?"

She pressed her lips tight, smiling wider, cheeks taut. "I know you *will* do that."

"Then you accept the proposition?"

"Not yet. I have demands to be met."

"They are?"

"That the folk abandoned here be removed to a more vi-able situation. No one to be left behind when we leave."

"Agreed."

"That your men bring before me the woman who killed my Seyl."

"Why do you think she's among those here?"

"My Gift gave me the face of the killer and another gift has shown me that face here after the *Kelai Maree* departed. Why is she here? Another joke by Bryheris. He was annoyed at her for nearly ruining his plans. He left her here, thinking that I wouldn't know her, won't know that the Death of my Seyl is living here on this island, that I might even make her a friend."

"You want her dead?"

"I care nothing about her." She spoke coldly, the words coming heavy and slow from the stone heart she'd grown in place of her flesh one. "Would you destroy the knife that killed a friend, or would you prefer to deal with the one who wielded that knife? She can live or die as you choose; she is an assassin, therefore presumably healthy and skilled; in other words, useful to you. I want to ask a question and I want to be satisfied with the answer, then she's free of me, and I neither need nor want anything else from her."

[8]

Thador stood stoic and silent, waiting for the death she considered inevitable, hoping only that the woman whose Seyl she'd killed didn't intend to torture her.

The blind woman seemed to see her. "Why?" she said. "Why did you kill him? Why did you leave me untouched and take him?"

The unexpectedness of that question startled Thador. She blinked, swallowed. "Mirrialta," she said. "She wanted him dead. I am her hands, her breath, I am her extension into places she can't come near. I killed him because it would please her. You? You're nothing to her, so you're nothing to me."

"That's it? That's all?"

"Yes."

The blind woman turned to the stocky man beside her. "All right. I'm satisfied. Do with her what you want."

6

Seekings

By the secret calendar of the Watchers, events dating from 8th Seimis, the seventh month of the 739th Glandairic year since the last Settling.

{ 1 }

The late summer afternoon was still and hot in the walled garden behind the little house in the Concubine's Court, which the Emperor had presented to Hudoleth after he'd pronounced the edict that confined her movements to the area within the Palace Walls. A few clouds scudded across the sky, but no wind reached beyond the top branches of the trees. She lived here alone, her only servant a Semmer girl who came every third day to keep the place clean. She had a few of her books and some of her mirrors, instruments snatched up hastily the one time she was allowed to visit her University house; the Niosul had inspected all these and had given reluctant permission for her to keep them.

In the garden, limbs heavy with large purple fruit, plum trees bent gracefully over a square pavement of black basalt flags, the mottled shadow of the leaves dancing across the silver lines of two pentagrams inlaid in the stone. Mirrors were set into the brick of the walls, Mage mirrors, wide as her shoulders, long as she was tall. A place of secrecy and Power.

Hudoleth was tired. The slaughter on the battlefield had sufficiently fascinated the Emperor, distracting him from the vision of renewed youth. Even so he kept watching her, his face wrinkling with indecision, and the questions he asked had little to do with the scenes playing out in the mirror.

In the end he let her go without speaking his desire.

[2]

"Moooaaaahhh!"

The thwack! of a staff connecting with muscle and hide.

"Mwa mwaaa mwa!" Crackle and thud of hooves on the thick cushion of dead leaves.

"Mooommmwaaa. Mwa. Maaaaaa. Mwa. Mwaaaa." Half a dozen other beasts picking up the complaint of a beefer intent on escape and adding their bleats to his.

The discordant blats of the butcherling beefer broke into the rambling, incoherent dream—belly knotted with anxiety, a sour metallic taste in his mouth, Talgryf ran before a shadowy horror that never drew close enough for him to give it its name, ran in endless futility across land that kept changing, sometimes the narrow, twisting streets of the Bothrin, sometimes a confusion of pastures and mountain slopes.

Caught in the paralysis of the suddenly wakened, for a breath or two Gryf couldn't move, then his feet tingled and his nose twitched. He pinched his nostrils to kill the sneeze, rolled onto his stomach and began digging in the straw to uncover the backpack he'd buried there. Out of here, he thought. Got to get out of here before . . .

"Vadzin katch!" A shout in a deep, rasping male voice followed by the crack of a staff against short horns. "Stubborn yeleet, get ye back a-line."

Talgryf went still. It was a small herd, five or six of the beefers, no more. Even so, there'd be more than one drover.

When the noises told him the herd was being bedded down in the paddock behind the sheds, he eased his arm down to his belt and slid his knife from its sheath. Working slowly, careful not to rattle the straw, he cut a slit in the canvas and put his eye to it. One drover was bustling about, close enough to Talgryf's haymow for the man to reach out and pull straw from it to use as tinder. He looped the straw, knotted it into a neat twist that he dropped on the knobby roots of the nearest sundew to wait until he was ready to build a fire.

The drover was a typical land-tied wealman, a stubby brown root with a net of wrinkles etched into his skin, fine black lines that were nearly invisible as the last vestiges of day vanished with the sun. He scuttled about, moving in and out of view, busy as the squirrel he resembled. Cutting wood for the fire. Digging a bake-hole, lining it with grass, tumbling in half a dozen yams, covering them with more grass, tamping the earth down over them. Building a wood pile on the disturbed earth, the straw twist tucked in place, waiting for the spark from the firebox. Hammering iron spits in and around the pile.

When he'd got the fire going, he took a kettle and marched away, heading for the well.

Hastily, Talgryf slid over the straw, cut a second slit in the canvas, put his eye to the opening and scanned the next haymow in the line, where Lyanz and Amhar were sleeping— might be sleeping—unless they'd slipped away and left him. Body tense, brow deeply wrinkled, Gryf scrutinized the taut canvas span by span, hunting for a sign—any sign—that would tell him whether they were there or had abandoned him.

Abandoned—

He ground his teeth, furious and ridiculously hurt by the possibility—

A second later the breath he hadn't been aware of holding exploded out of him.

Near the top of the hay mound, the faded canvas was no longer a uniform curve; it rose in a shallow arc, dropped in an elegant catena to a lesser bulge—could be shoulder and hip. Gryf rubbed at his eyes, strained to see in the thickening darkness, blew out another breath as he thought he found a few additional bumps and hollows. It was enough. Lyanz and Amhar were there. It looked like they were sleeping so soundly they weren't aware of the herd or the drovers.

Gryf dropped his head on his arms, relief rolling in waves through his body. In a few breaths, though, that relief changed to anger. Anger rapidly escalated into hot rage.

Sleeping. Tanew curse him for a fool. We should have been gone from here hours ago.

Gryf switched ends and crawled back to his first view-hole, muttering, sweating, his belly knotting with rage.

No one on watch. Rutting in the straw. Sleeping!

When he was in place, he folded his arms, put his eye back to the slit, wriggling about to find a position that was both comfortable and stable so the rustling of straw wouldn't betray his presence. When he heard the mutter of voices, the crackle from feet kicking through fallen leaves, he went still again, breath catching in his throat, anger temporarily forgotten.

Two small, square brown men—so like the other that they might have been his brother—walked into the ragged circle of firelight. They squatted beside the fire, held their hands to it, the red light touching broad noses, stubble-darkened chins,

calloused palms. The elder of the two tilted his head back
and squinted at the sky. "Comin' t' rain."

"Ah." The second speaker was thin and wiry, young
enough to be a son to either of the others.

As the third drover came into view, holding the kettle away
from him so the water streaming from it would drip on the
ground, the youth jerked his thumb at him. "Rudz, ye not t'
only 'un judgin' so. Eh, Fidd," he called. "Ye dump blankets
in shed?"

Fidd poured some of the water into a battered tin pot, then
hung the kettle on a spit hook. He dropped to a squat, sucked
his teeth as smoke blackened the bottom and sides of the
kettle. "Blachich filt'. Shed? Ya. Comin' t' rain." He felt
around behind him, dragged a shoulder pack into the firelight. "Ye see what were walkin' yesternight?" He turned the
flap back, fished out some grayish anonymous lumps and
dropped them into the pot. "Me, I figger 'twere a sign." He
reached into the pack again, brought out a tangle of wilted
greens. It joined the lumps. A third dip brought out twists of
cornshuck holding a thumbs-worth of powdered seasonings;
these he sprinkled on the mix. He lifted the bail and hung
the pot from one of the spits. "Eh, Rudz? Berg? Ye see ol'
Hag dancin' with t' lightning? It were near t' end of t' mid
watch." He pulled his shirtsleeve over his hand, caught hold
of the bail and shook the pot, slopping the stew against its
sides, blending in the seasonings. "Huh?"

Hag? A chill ran along Talgryf's spine as his stepuncle
Hisoman's face popped into his head. Uncle Hiss. They
called him Hiss for his yellow eyes. Snake eyes. He worked
in the Temple, a lay brother and one of the sweepers who
kept the place clean.

"Bad boy, bad boy, Hag's gonna get you," Hiss'd chant,
then he'd cackle he-he-he. Then he'd waddle after Gryf, his
hands shaped to claws that opened and shut in time with the

cackle. He-he-he. Later, when Gryf went to the Temple for his religious schooling, Uncle Hiss would walk him home and tell him cautionary tales that scared him out of his skin, especially stories about the Hag and the men who served her. Stories of the old days before the first Tyrn drove the Hag and Her followers from Nyddys and built the Temple for Dyf Tanew.

Talgryf forgot anger, hurt and fear and listened intently.

Berg grinned and slapped a hand against his thigh. "Kiss 'n tell, Fidd? Eh? Eh? Give us t' truth, Uncle. Weren't lightning, it were ye out there kickin' sparks."

"Yer a idjit, Bergo. No fool like a young 'un, yeah?" Fidd turned to Rudz, lips stretched in a grin as if he'd made a joke but even Gryf could see the fear in the mud-dark eyes.

Berg snorted and started to answer, but a glance at Rudz silenced him.

"Din't *see* Hag, Fidd. Mid-watch I were sleepin', 'member how hard ye hadda shake?" A square hand rasped over the stubble darkening his jaw. "Me, I thought it were those 'shrooms ye dropped in pot got me in belly. 'Nd bein' so long away from m' woman this season with all the traveling Broon Mothun been doin' and haulin' me with him to carry messages like now and tend his horses. What brung me the dreams, I mean. Hag. Floppin' her dugs at me." Blood reddened his rugged face, though his expression didn't change. "And all."

Berg bounced up and down on his heels, grinning and making clown faces. "Dreams," he said and snickered. "Hot dreams. I . . ."

"Shut y' tater hole 'n fetch t' tinners," Fidd snapped. "And a shovel from t' shed. Be near time to dig out t' yams."

Berg jumped to his feet and stalked off, indignation visible in the set of his shoulders, the stomp of his feet.

Rudz watched a moment, then shook his head. "Yearlin's."

Fidd nodded. "Think they know everthin'." He reached into the pack, felt around a moment, then pulled out a ragged piece of canvas. He used it to lift the pot from the spithook and settle it on the warm dirt beside the fire. Another dip into the pack produced a wooden ladle. He stirred the stew, bent over the pot and sniffed. "Aaaah! Good 'un."

A puff of early night wind blew the aroma from the stew into the view-hole. Talgryf ground his teeth and pushed his fist against his stomach as it rumbled with hunger. Tanew curse you, eat! Finish your business and hit the blankets so we can get out of here.

Rudz grunted. "Big doin's at Kruseel Hall."

It wasn't a question, but . . . Gryf narrowed his eyes, tried to read the old wealman's face. The uncertain light from the dying fire touched Rudz's nose and chin with red, gleamed briefly on his brow and angular cheekbones, left the rest of his face to shadow and turned it into a bizarre mask as expressionless as his voice had been.

Fidd lifted his head, but whatever he meant to say was lost as Berg dropped a shovel on the ground beside him, then bent in an exaggerated bow and handed him three tin plates.

"Yeah," he said, separated out one of the tinners and began ladling stew into it. "Big doin's. Which you know more 'bout nin me."

Rudz nodded. "Butcher ground gonna be busy. Ten Broons come visitin', maybe more. 'N all their women."

"Bergo, take this round to Rudz, eh? Then ye come back for yers. Hm. Twice what we had to the weddin' last year. We be run off our feet, yeah, we get the herd down t' Hall." He handed the second tinner to Berg and began filling his own.

Gryf watched the drovers spoon up the stew, their jaws moving as rhythmically as any cud-chewing beefer. His stomach rumbled again. They were taking forever to finish that meal. "Get a move on or I'll start gnawing on drover haunch," he whispered into the hand covering his mouth.

Fidd ate in silence for several minutes. "Ye got names a which Broons be comin'?"

"Not to know. Put together m' dream and what ye seen an' what I seen last couple a months, I could make a guess." Rudz set the empty tinner on a sundew root and got to his feet. "Hand me up t' shovel, I'll dig yams. Just talk, ye think, or real plannin'?

"Couldn't say." Fidd grinned sourly. "Don't move in them circles." His grin vanished. "Guessin', I'd say close 'nuff to plannin' to start an itch workin' on me neck." He set his plate on the dead leaves beside him and watched as Rudz scraped the coals to one side and began to uncover the yams.

Berg spooned up the last drops of stew, grimaced at his tinner. "Any left?"

"Some. Come round and get for yerself." Fidd got to his feet, stretched and groaned. "Takin' first watch, me. Bergo, mid-watch is yours."

Berg was tilting the stew pot over his tinner; he straightened and dropped the pot. "Ah katch! I hate mid-watch. Unca Fi, do I hafta?"

"T' teeth, ye old 'nuff to act a man. Ye been told. Do it." Fidd glanced at Rudz. "Walk round to paddock with me, eh? Good. Bergo, listen tight. 'Member what I been showin' ye sin' m' sister march ye up to winter graze. I been lettin' ye slide sin' ye was learnin', but now's as good a time as any for ye to do 'stead a lazin' round jus' watchin'. Rudz ha' dug the yams out, we'll take ours, ye take yern. Bury t' skins 'n garbage when you done, if ye put it with t' coals, the hole's already dug. If ye wash t' tinners afore ye fill the hole, ye c'n dump t' dirty water in, use it to kill t' fire. Hmp. Ye seen me do such. Jus' 'member I be seein' what ye did."

Ignoring Berg's sullen scowl, Fidd tossed two of the cooling yams to Rudz, put one in his pocket and juggled the other from hand to hand as he strolled into the darkness beyond the reach of Gryf's view-hole.

The two older men were speaking earnestly and quietly; the broken syllables drifted to Talgryf on the wind. He could guess their general subject. The party assembling at the Kruseel Halstead was a clutch of Haggers. Gryf closed his hands tightly about bunches of straw, his face drawn with worry.

Hag's men. The last few years he'd seen Hagger facemen in Tyst standing on street corners and preaching to clumps of listeners, putting a fair gloss on the image of the Hag — though they called that Well of Vitriol the Great Mother — offering to men soured on the world a justification for their anger and disappointment along with a call to join the followers of the Mother and receive the good things of life that men and circumstance had denied them.

Talgryf had hung round the fringes of the growing crowds that listened to the Haggers, attracted by the words that spoke to his own anger — until his father noticed what was happening and explained to him that this so-called Great Mother was a mask on the face of the Hag.

[3]

Door locked, wards in place, her privacy guaranteed, Hudoleth stripped, carried to the nearest of the pentagrams the ivory tube she'd set in the notch between two branches of a plum tree. Her face pinched and pale with strain, she went to her knees on the stone and dug out the wax plug that stopped one end of the tube.

She upended the tube. What looked like several tangles of silver wires fell beside her. When she shook the biggest tangle out, it became a long tunic made from silver symbols bonded together by tiny silver links. She pulled the tunic over her head and smoothed it down, cool against her skin despite the glare of the sun. She unrolled wide filigree bracelets and clasped them about her arms, slipped the linked power rings onto her fingers, spread out a filigree silver fan with three mirrors set into one face.

She rose to her feet. Narrow hands swaying before her, she turned on her toes, twisting the fan so its mirrors caught the sunlight and danced reflections off the brick of the walls and those Mage mirrors that hung there. Chanting a wordless song that changed imperceptibly into the old tongue of Chusinkayan, the tongue before time, she began the Summoning.

"Oda, Syntayo," she sang, her rich soprano filling the garden.

"Oda Syntayo mai yapuur." Command in the words, the fan held level, slicing through the heat waves rising from the black stone.

"Ida shi anata shi." One hand beckoning, the other holding the fan upright before her face.

"Ida shibar wijiti." The fan danced through a flat figure eight, the other hand darted out, slashed to one side and the other.

"Anata yi ida hanuur,
Anata kai kus ida shuur."

As the last words hung in the air, a shimmer formed in the second pentagram but did not solidify until Hudoleth uttered the final command.

"Doë rhu Syntayo!"

The Syntayo bulged and warped, changing from shapeless light to shapeless cloud rising in a gnarled and knotty column, gray and white with patches of darkness not quite black. The column writhed as she squeezed its name from the chaos within. Though it had no eyes, she could feel it gazing at her and weeping impossible tears, but she was shielded against its pain and waited in patient silence for the captive Wisdom to accept its condition and prepare itself to submit to her demands.

[4]

The conquest of Tilkos was both costly and annoying. Mahara was losing patience, not that he had much to begin with. The Dark Wyrm of the Earth was a primordial force—no matter how many parts the Dragon Rueth cut it into, they continued to regrow, or at least twitch annoyingly and not stay dead.

The same was true of the resistance forces of Tilkos. The Farmyn was their last hope, but like hope, he was maddeningly hard to kill, always springing up again after you did the deed. The royal family of the Farmyn was ordered in a complex pattern of cross-cousin marriage via the matrilineal line, from the days long before Kale had conquered Tilkos and turned it into a satrap, but now that the tree of the royal family was cut down, they were getting to its roots, and those proved to be among the marshfolk, the most ancient line of the Tilk. By the rules as set down by the Dark Wyrm, the Farmyn—the true heir of Tilkos—was the current husband of the royal bride. As for who was the true royal bride, this fact was ascertained by a special caste of Tilk witches, the Bloodrite Witnesses, the midwives of the hillfolk, a fancy way of saying that the old biddies watched as the current chieftain of the moment took some girl's maidenhead, and with it the title of Farmyn and the rulership of the Wyrm of Tilkos.

Every time this happened, the Dark Wyrm began to regenerate, and Mahara had had about enough of that. To that end, he had the midwife brought before him.

She was old and small and dark as a pickled walnut, with

about as many wrinkles. And she was dirty. She seemed to hate him all the more for the grime the war had left on her. Her white habit was smeared with the ash and soot from the catchfires, the dirt that rimed every available surface in Tilk and smeared off at the slightest touch. The occasional snowy crease and the starched peak of her wimple showed the fastidiousness that was her usual mode. "Good Mother," said Mahara from behind his camp desk as she was brought into his tent, "I am glad you do me this honor."

"The honor of Kale is something I find invisible," she spat, then spat literally.

Mahara looked at the blob sitting on the floor of his tent, and decided that he didn't like this woman. Not that it would make any difference in what he was going to do, but it would make it more pleasurable, a small bonus.

"Which of the virgins are the sacred girls of Tilk?"

"Why would I tell you?" asked the midwife. "I keep that secret in my heart. Do you hear me?" She spat again.

Mahara smiled. "I've heard you, and I've seen you spit too. But your heart will tell me all the same."

The old woman began to rail and curse then, peasant threats in some obscure Tilkos dialect Mahara didn't understand and didn't care to. The guards held her secure by each arm as Mahara took out a silver bowl and poured water into it, as well as agents and reagents, the gum of powdered moss and metallic salts. He then took a dagger and trimmed a circle of parchment slightly smaller than the circumference of the bowl. Mahara examined it and the bowl, ignoring the old woman's continued ranting and spitting, until at last he turned to her. "Do you think this bit of parchment will fit into that bowl?"

She paused, the question very obviously not what she was expecting. "I suppose so," she said at last. "Why?"

"This," he said and plunged the knife to the hilt into her heart.

He twisted the knife once and then back, pulling it out like a key from a lock, careful to step aside so the woman's pumping blood wouldn't gout all over him. "Hold her there," he instructed the guards, then held the dagger over the bowl and let the blood drip in.

The heart's blood shimmered on the surface of the gum and water, then swirled and rippled upon it. Mahara made a series of magical passes through the water with the blade of the knife, cutting the surface into a complex pattern, like the sheet of a ledger, then tapped the side of the bowl so it shivered and rang. He then threw in the scrap of parchment and wiped his dagger clean on the dying woman's sleeve.

She looked at him, not quite understanding, but at least not spitting and cursing.

Mahara made a pass over the bowl with the knife, then lifted out the sheet of parchment with the tip of the blade. He examined the patterns left by the blood, the intriguing swirls and characters now marbling the paper. "Hm. Jesmuun of Akrana village and her sisters Inlirre and Frantki. Does this sound familiar?"

The midwife began to curse and struggle then, which only made her bleed faster, then more slowly. Half a minute later, Mahara smelled the stench that meant her sphincters had relaxed and the old woman was finally dead.

Mahara gazed at the marbled parchment disk with pleasure. This would make matters much simpler.

[5]

Rinchay sought and asked and sought and found. Among the dead of the Grass Clan, the Dmar Spyonk and the others. Among the killing fields.

Liar!
You have misled me.
You have misled my Clan.
My Alaeshin is dead
for your perfidy.
I will seek you.
Seek you in dead hearts.
In dead eyes.
In dead mouths and dead tongues.
In the whispers of the insects who kiss the dead
And give them new life.
Mother of Maggots
Your children will betray you
And serve me.

The maggots roiled forth from the corpses at her words, a sea of whiteness, a lively loathsome mass, pale and wrinkled as the skin of a dying concubine who'd used too much arsenic to pale her complexion.

Rinchay Matan raised her arms and let them flow up and around her, their tiny hair-legs tickling her flesh, their tiny mouths licking, sucking, kissing her like a thousand thousand lovers, each shrunk to the size and color of a withered snowberry. They covered her, hissing and whispering with their movements against each pale and wrinkled sibling, crawling and writhing, and she heard in their sliding the voices of her dead kin, the dead of the Grass Clans and their dying God, crying out for revenge.

She opened her mouth to speak, but the maggots only crawled in till she burbled and spat them out, blowing air through her lips and clenched teeth till the vibrations knocked them loose and she could speak freely.

Dead ones.
Eaters of the dead.

My slain kin and children of my enemy.
Show me the fastness of she who spawned you.
Show me the Liar so I may repay her.
With DEATH
DEATH
And DEATH *again.*
The DEATH she has so freely dispensed
I will repay
In kind.
Measure for measure
Like sacks of grain.
Each seed a tear
Or drop of blood
Or maggot.

The maggots roiled and oozed about her, then one by one they clung to her skin, locking their hair-feet and their pincher mouths to her flesh, as they began to pulsate, and pupate. Rinchay felt the fires of growth within them and fed them with her Shaman's fire, as she'd used it to speed grain to growth and mares to foal, to feed Kin and Kind. It was the same here, except that she sped along a thousand times a thousand corruptions and eaters of death. They roiled along her skin, tiny twitchings and internal movements sped up a thousand times till they fairly vibrated within their shells. Then at last, with a sound like grain crackling before a camp-fire, they split, one by one. Though she could not see through her closed eyes, she could feel the life emerge from deathlife, as life was spawned from death before it, and then her sight was that of a thousand times a thousand times a thousand jewels, vista upon vista upon vista viewed through tiny diamond panes, seeing the iridescent wings that covered her in a shawl of dreams, the shiny blue-black carapaces, the barbed black hairs, the silver jeweled eyes.

The maggots were maggots no more. Each fly took a moment to lick and dine on the protein-rich husks of their pupae cases. With each hooked and suckered foot latched into her flesh, the flies began to whirr, and Rinchay poured her force of Revenge, her Revenant Gift, into each tiny wing.

Fear me, Soul Eater.
My eyes are the thousand times a thousand things.
My spies will be everywhere.
Everywhere you have killed.
I will be there.
Everywhere you have lied.
I will come.
I will seek you.
I will find you.
I will repay the Death you have given
A thousand thousand fold.
I will craft a pain
More exquisite
Than any the world has ever known
Or will know.
I will know what you fear
And what you love
And what you seek
And I shall take it all from you.
All.

The flies buzzed their approval of this oath, the whispers of the dead of the Grass Clans, and she felt the approbation of the Death Guides for her design of revenge on the Eater of Souls. Her feet lifted off the ground, and Rinchay flew through the air, covered with a thousand thousand jewels of revenge.

{ 6 }

"Syntayo Ayneeros, I greet you."

The cloud's outer surface crumbled to a fine mist that shivered in the wind of a long sigh. "When one is compelled to appear, the softest of greetings bears thorns." The Wisdom's voice was sepulchral, a basso groan emerging from deep within the cloud. "This one perceives that you have respected established protocol, Mage, and have imbedded the Rule of Three in the Song of Summoning. Ask."

"The reason for this invocation is memory, Syntayo. An inconvenient memory that I can't simply uproot because it would return each time the Rememberer looked at me. I need a barrier to turn aside the thought before it ripens. Spin for me a Lizomo Knot."

The Wisdom recoiled, shuddered, contracted until its cloud stuff was thick and crumbly and it had shrunk to half its former height.

Hudoleth tensed, anger flaring as she felt the Syntayo's fear and its attempt to resist the compulsion of the spell. She hammered the momentary rebellion flat and increased the pressure of her demand.

The Wisdom whimpered and vibrated, currents of darkness twisting through the gray—faster and faster—white—gray—blurring—white—black threads—web—more threads—

In a spot where the threads were packed so closely that only a few glimmers of white broke through, the cloud-surface bulged outward until it formed a node about the size of a hen's egg. The threads quivered, then began to flicker through sinuous patterns, moving faster and faster until the node suddenly broke free to float beside the cloud column.

The Lizomo Knot.

A gesture with the fan brought the knot drifting toward Hudoleth until it reached her pentagram; like a boat that the current of a deep, slow river had pushed against a bank, the knot butted up against the silver line and quivered there.

Hudoleth closed the fan, snapped it open. "Noi otz," she murmured.

A small gray pouch dropped into her free hand.

Whispering the minor incantation that would let the knot pass into the pentagram, she flicked the fan back and forth behind the blob of Pneuma, wafting it across the line-barrier, into the mouth of the pouch. She pulled the drawstrings tight, tied them off, and dropped her prize onto the stone beside her knee. "My deepest appreciation, O Syntayo Ayneeros."

Enveloped in an aura of wry amusement, Ayneeros expanded to its original dimensions and its surface currents slowed until they regained their leisurely grace. "This one would find your gratitude more agreeable, O Mage, if words of dismissal followed immediately after its so graceful expression."

Hudoleth spread her hands, the fan mirrors catching the sunlight and reflecting it into glitters that danced like knife blades in the cloudstuff of the Syntayo. "Alas, O Ayneeros, your wisdom is renowned among your kind and mine, and my need is too great for me to renounce any part of it."

"So it always is, though this one always hopes for a generosity beyond the ordinary. Two requests remain. Ask."

"When it became clear that the Settling had begun, I understood a number of things, one of which was that I would need a secure power center from which I could . . . hmm . . . perform certain acts in order to achieve ends that I found . . . desirable." She folded the fan and ran her fingertips along the power signs of the uppermost vane as if she sought among them for the proper words.

"Unfortunately, at this time the Emperor showed signs of becoming something of a nuisance. He found the notion of bedding a Mage irresistibly enticing." She wrinkled her nose. "I yielded to his desires because it seemed the easier route. I thought that once I was close enough, I could set an aversion in him that would keep him from interfering with me a second time. I did not know then that no spell lasts long when cast on those of his blood." She narrowed her eyes. Though the Syntayo had no mouth, she thought she heard it laughing at her. No matter, she told herself. I hold the whip. Wisdom, fah! It will scream its no-teeth out of its non-mouth if its impudence carries it too far. "I never let go of an insult until it has been repaid not once but a hundredfold. Do you hear me, Ayneeros?"

"I hear, O Mage."

Satisfaction was sweet on her tongue as she tasted the subdued note in its voice. It wasn't truly afraid of her, but it would be wary from now on, using a careful courtesy in all of its responses. She dipped her head to acknowledge its answer and continued her careful explication of her problem. "The second time the Emperor summoned me, I avoided my earlier mistakes. I created succubi to snare his attention and conceal my activities from his Niosul. This proved effective enough, though there were a few small drawbacks." She touched the fan to her lips and sighed.

"This is the Virtue of that act: I acquired a secure, undisturbed place to work."

She waved one of her fans in a graceful arc. "As you see," she said.

"This is the Failing of that act: His family frayspell gift has already begun draining the mystery and allure from the succubi; he is growing bored with them. Within the next few tennights, he will dismiss them.

"As my second request I ask you this, O Syntayo: Having studied the man—the Emperor—and pondered the limits and worth of the frayspell gift, delve into your wisdom and present me with other means of distracting and controlling the Emperor of Chusinkayan—remembering that the Lizomo Knot will be set in place by sundown tomorrow. I will allow four days for this search, and if the answer you bring to me pleases me beyond my expectations, I am prepared to leave you free of my Summonings for one thousand years from the day you give that answer. If the answer is merely adequate, the grace period will be reduced to one hundred years. My word is good; I never promise what I cannot or will not proffer. This you know." Hudoleth lifted the fan and began working stiff muscles as she prepared herself for a temporary dismissal.

"Understood, O Mage." The cloud column wavered and its voice was hesitant. "Will the Mage present her third request at this time? One should not like to lose the happy accidents bestowed by Fortune and her capricious son. Chance will often provide the cleverest resolutions if not the wisest."

Hudoleth frowned, then she nodded. "You convince me, O Syntayo. My third request is the least pressing of the three, yet it might prove the most difficult. There is a youth somewhere on Glandair who is as empty of magic as a newly fired jug is empty of water. Bring me a device that will point to him when I call on it, wherever he is, however far away. I wish to know where this youth is whenever I feel a need to look at him."

The indefinite edges of the Syntayo's pewter gray smoke column fluttered and tore into shreds that floated away, then curled back to reemerge with the column. For several beats the Wisdom didn't speak, then it produced a sound hardly above a whisper. "That is more dangerous than you know, O Mage."

Hudoleth went taut with anger, a crackle of age lines etched into her velvety skin, her eyes stony. "Compliance with this request will serve as evidence of your resolve and will do much to gain for you the full relief from the Summonings, the thousand years that I offered. Consider fully what you do, Ayneero."

[7]

The air was cold, with snow beginning to fall, and the ride was more pleasant for it. The smell of smoke was dulled to a bare whisper, and there were spots where the hooves of their horses were able to make a fresh impression through the new smooth crust to the mud of the road below.

"So what is she like?" the Third Prince asked. "Courtship in Kale is a somewhat more formalized affair." He tapped his wrist with his riding-crop, an echo-whisper of the gestures done with wands at the Court of Kale.

The gesture was slightly suggestive and vaguely lewd, and Mahara smiled, thinking he'd fathomed some of the gist, even if he'd never grasp all the nuances. "Consider it just an affair then. Once you've conquered Tilk, Zulam my friend, you can do away with her. Or at least lock her away."

The Third Prince smiled back, his pale Rhudyar face shining pink behind the falling snow. "You're right. There's always that." He sighed and looked wistfully away. "I've greatly missed Pika Mar."

"She's a fine woman. She'll likely forgive you." Mahara shook his reins. "So long as you're a widower on your return, that is. And you'll still have a spare 'Bride of Tilk' or two if you need to be Farmyn."

The Third Prince laughed. "You don't know Pika. Even if I return a widower, she'll never forget the affair."

Mahara thought back, remembering the night's assignation he'd shared with the Third Prince's favorite and the complex double standard that such women as Pika Mar could have.

"Well, I suppose not." Mahara shared a chuckle, hearing it mix with the *clip-clop-clip!* of the horses' hooves. "I'd suggest bringing her lots of jewels. And once you become Emperor, you'll not have to worry about marriage for alliances."

The Third Prince chuckled. "Rueth's scales, you're right. But that's seeming a long way off at the moment. I'll be content with getting a solid grasp on Tilkos for the time being."

"Or at least Akrana, which seems to be the hidden key."

The village as they came to it was small and grimy with a smell of more ash and wet bleaters. Hardly a place to find the bride for a Prince, yet with war, appearances could be deceiving, and with conquest of Tilkos, they'd already done away with all of the more presentable heirs of the blood of the Dark Wyrm.

Mahara raised a hand, feeling for the Pneuma-traceries etched on the parchment inside his jacket, near his heart, with the heart's blood of the midwife still drying upon them. Back and forth, feeling the flow of the Power leading into the nebulous space where the gods rested, until he found the source. "That one," he said, pointing to one of the smaller hovels.

The Third Prince gestured and his men rode forward and surrounded the house, kicking down the door without any show of ceremony, and emerging a minute later with a group of five. One grown woman, apparently the mother, a grubby half-grown boy, and three girls, ranging from the youngest just above childhood to the eldest on the verge of womanhood, with one middle sister in-between.

"Jesmuun of Akrana?" the Third Prince asked.

Proudly, the eldest of the three girls shook off the guards who held her arms. She was a small, dark Rhudyar, plump despite the privations of the war, with long dark curls. "I am she."

The Third Prince smiled slightly. "I am Zulam, Third

Prince of Kale. I am here for the rulership of Tilk."

Mahara admired the girl's defiance, but only in the way you admired an entertaining actress. Brave, but stupid all the same. "You will never have it."

Mahara felt the god-twitchings about her . . . and the boy. Her cousin, likely, younger than her, pretending to be her brother, but now the Farmyn, heir of the Dark Wyrm, their consummation likely only hours old. "Not from you, at least," Mahara remarked and formed a Mage-strike, twinned, raw Pneuma to sear both the girl and her impromptu husband into ash.

The ash, white as birch bark, fell with the snow, swirling with it, nothing left of either of them but steaming black footprints and the singed hands of the guards who had been holding the boy.

Mahara had been wanting to do that for a long while, ever since the old Farmyn's Wizard had blasted his army with similar fire.

He glanced then to the middle daughter, now the eldest remaining, and felt the god-twitching, now unmoored, move to her. There was a certain delight and a cold savor of revenge in all of this. "If you are clever, and want to spare your little sister, I suggest you cooperate with your new groom."

The mother cried out then, a mindless wail, but Mahara just let the Prince's men knock her unconscious.

The middle sister stood there, then the guards released her, and still she stood, dark hair blowing free from its kerchief amid the whiteness of the snow. "I'm Inlirre."

"You'll do," said the Third Prince. Zulam then turned to Mahara. "Now what?"

Mahara smiled. "The meaning of that little gesture you did with your riding-crop?"

Zulam raised one delicately arched eyebrow. "Oh, *that*? I didn't know we needed to get that fancy."

Mahara chuckled. "Probably not, but it's your wedding night. Go for broke."

Zulam looked at the interior of the dingy hut, then at the girl. "You'll do, as I said. Come along."

He grabbed her by the wrist and led her inside. Inlirre, rather than looking defiant, or apprehensive, simply looked blank, in a state of shock.

Mahara shrugged. If she stayed quiet, she might live a good while longer, since a Tilkos bride along with the favor of the god would do well to unite the troops. That would probably be best.

When he started this campaign, he'd planned to have the forces of Kale hone themselves on the bones of the Tilk, rather than the reverse, but so long as there was a strong army behind them to overtake Faiscar, all was well.

Inlirre, as it turned out, did not stay silent, and Mahara wondered what exactly he'd told Prince Zulam to do to her. But when the Third Prince emerged from the hovel, Mahara could see the god-light shining over him, and knew that part of whatever perversion Mahara had suggested was the more mundane act the Dark Wyrm of Tilkos required.

Mahara raised an eyebrow.

"She did," the Third Prince replied simply.

[8]

Brother Kyo did his best to ignore his tired feet, his sore legs, and even the pain in his fingers where he gripped his walking stick. Maratha monks did not complain, especially when under a vow of silence. Maratha Alaesh did not give anyone a burden that was too great for them to bear.

Even if it sometimes felt like it.

He made his way along the lane, making the blessing sign at a flock of red-capped fletches pecking about the haymows for lost specks of lintengrain. The birds too were Maratha's creatures, even if they would have preferred crumbs of seed cake to blessing signs. Unfortunately, he'd fed his last seed cake to birds and hay-rats three days ago, and now those same birds and hay-rats were beginning to look more than a bit tasty, even despite his vow to forego the flesh of his fellow creatures.

Of course, before his vows he'd eaten those same rats and birds fried in butter, seasoned with powdered musach berries, and it was much easier to forget how delectable some of Marath Alaesh's creatures were when you had a stomach filled with grain-curd and vegetables prepared by the expert hands of the Temple cooks. He made the blessing sign with an extra flourish and frightened the fletches into the air, a whirl of red and black chattering and scolding at him like disapproving aunts, making him feel shame and annoyance, the second of which was a sin, even if it was natural.

He was beginning to wonder if the parables were pipe dreams made up by Temple calligraphers who had inhaled too much blessing incense, as opposed to genuine miracles of Marath Alaesh. In all the stories, monks who gave their last seedcakes to starving wild creatures were soon rewarded, if not with divine feasts from Marath Alaesh himself, then at least with being shown the way to convenient berry bushes or peasants in need of some blessing, ready to fill his alms bowl with their bounty in thanks.

Then again, he could recall none of those stories being set during wartime. The one time he'd followed a flight of wild birds, hoping to find some miraculous handout to quell his growling stomach, he instead found the fletches feasting on — not nuts and grains, nor even worms and grubs — but the eyes and decaying flesh of a group of murdered villagers.

The birds had been a sign, true enough, and he had done his duty to Marath Alaesh and buried the bodies as best he could, making the blessing sign over them and saying the prayers for the dead. Yet every time he'd done that back at the Temple, it was followed by a funerary feast, with moon cakes for the departed souls and lots of extras for the monks and other mourners.

Such thoughts were unworthy, but they were there. You could deny the flesh, but if you denied it too long, it started to complain, and worse yet, fight back. Even when fasting, he had never been this hungry before, or this tired. Back before he had been Brother Kyo, merely Kyodal Kurrin, spoiled scion of a rich house, he'd been given whatever he wanted, and able to take the rest. His looks, his connections and his small penchant for dishonesty had led him to take things other people wouldn't miss simply for the thrill of it, knowing that his father could always buy his way out of any trouble he got into.

Except he never had, and his father was now dead. And his god had commanded that he aid his brother, who was now left alone. Somewhere.

Kyodal still didn't know where Lyanz was, or what aid he needed. He finally decided to commit another act of sacrilege mixed with an impromptu prayer for guidance. Marath Alaesh may have given him a vision to start this journey, but it didn't take a genius to figure out that you were supposed to bury corpses if you found birds pecking them, and not expect fletches to be grateful for seedcakes after being robbed of what they considered a better meal. Small wonder the birds hadn't shown him any berry bushes. And despite other parables, no grateful albeit murdered maidens or other ghosts had come out to feed him, show him the way, or perform other deeds in way of thanks.

Brother Kyo reached into his robe and brought out the icon of Marath Alaesh, which had started him on this quest. The other monks did not know he had taken it, but he had not lost his touch and when you had a direct vision from your god, it was rather hard to think of it as theft.

Or even desecration.

War and the confusion of the Settling no doubt called for different measures. With this thought, Brother Kyo kissed the foot of the icon, drew his arm back underhand, then snapped it forward and bowled it down the lane.

The wooden ball rolled and rolled, then began to bounce and gather speed, and Brother Kyo chased after it, uncertain whether Marath Alaesh had answered his prayer, or was punishing him, or was in his laughing aspect again and had decided to do both—along with testing his faith and his running skill.

Brother Kyo ran and ran, chasing the ball, and on and on, the icon always a few paces ahead of him, and at last, he laughed.

It had been a long time since he had run, or felt the joy of a child's game of Finjin Finjin Catch the Ball, and as he felt that joy again, he felt his hunger slip away, along with his exhaustion and his doubts.

Marath Alaesh bless.

[9]

In the swaying, vertical cloud, currents of darkness began twisting through lighter gray, the agitated whorls and eddies of the Wisdom's Pneuma. Making no allusion to its manifest fear or its earlier protest, it spoke, its voice very soft, almost diffident. "Visualize the boy, O Mage. Show this being the physical appearance of the target. This one has searched and has not found such a person as you describe."

Hudoleth scowled. "You pretend to be as weak as new hatched tadling." She snorted as the smoke column bent and swayed before her. "But I will give the image this once.

Once!" She summoned out of memory the representation Oerfel sent to her when he'd called them all to attack the Watchers and the boy. With a sweep of her hand, she planted the portrait in the mirrors set into the brick walls that closed in the garden — the beautiful, golden youth staring out of the glass with arrogance and defiance.

The afternoon was almost gone, the sun tangled in the branches of a plum tree, its dimmed light glittering off the silver symbols that caged her naked body. Though the flow of Pneuma had driven off everything living inside the walls except her and the Syntayo — if a demon made of smoke could be considered alive — birdsong drifted into the silence, coming from other gardens, other trees. Sweat ran in rivers down her body, slithering from the heavy knot of black hair pinned atop her head, forming in droplets at the end of her lashes, dripping from the tip of her nose, the point of her chin.

As the day died, its weariness filled the garden until Hudoleth drowned as much in fatigue as in sweat. She ignored both. Her will was stronger than her body.

Trembling, shuddering, the cloud column once again produced a calloused area, a round black disc that floated on the surface smoke. If Hudoleth had set the tips of her forefingers together and touched thumb to thumb, she could have enclosed the disc in the circle.

In the beginning the disc was a soft sooty black and looked like a sneeze would blow it into fragments. Whining like a swarm of black biters on a hot summer evening, the disc began a slow gyration, imperceptible at first, then turning faster and faster. The insubstantial smoke hardened as the speed of the turn increased, the opaque substance of the Wisdom's Object growing more and more transparent as it transformed into obsidian, the black volcanic glass smoothing at the end of the spell into a curved mirror.

Opening the pentagram again, the gap protected by traps she'd laid there, Hudoleth held out her hand, her mouth curling into a triumphant smile when the cool disc settled onto her palm. As soon as it touched down, the Hero's image bloomed in the black glass, around him the place where he was.

One hand tucked beneath his cheek, his hair tousled into a fine halo about his face, his mouth pinched into a soft pout, the Hero was curled in a nest of grassy hay, sleeping like a baby. Hudoleth's smile widened and her eyes glittered with satisfaction. "Yes," she whispered. She drew the tip of her forefinger along the curve of the mirror. "Show me a wider view."

She found herself looking down at a ragged line of hay-mows protected from wind and rain by squares of weathered canvas, a pair of sheds and a scatter of squat trees with pale, lacy leaves. "Yesss. A Nyddys Turnout. He's still on the island." She blew the image from the mirror. "I have him. Whenever I'm ready, I can take him. Mahara, you'll never outpace me now. The boy is mine and so are you." She lifted her head and viewed the Syntayo with a relaxed contentment of a sort she hadn't felt since the battle for the boy had begun.

The sun that had once been captured by the branches of a plum tree was now a drop of vermillion trembling on the western wall, draining slowly away. End-of-day shadow pooled inside the garden walls. As Hudoleth moved through the dusk, the glimmers of the silver symbols swam like minnows through the dark waters of a mountain pool.

The cloud column bent into a shallow arc. "This one is weary, O Mage." The Syntayo's substance was so attenuated that at moments it seemed hardly more than a faint grayness painted on the air. "If you desire a swift resolution to such a lengthy study of the Emperor and his frayspell gift, it would be well to dismiss this one so the study may begin."

Once again her head came up, eyes glittering with a sudden rage. Despite its deference, she read that speech as a subtle challenge, almost a slap in the face. Impudence! I'll twist its tail till it shrieks—but not now. Not till I have the last boon in my hands. She softened the glare of her eyes, gathered in her anger and shut it away. "Yes," she murmured. "Let it be done."

The smoke column knotted and twisted, then straightened. The personality of the Wisdom that had more or less inhabited this physical envelope for the past several hours retreated to the core of the column, the effect diminishing until even the Mage would have to strain to perceive it.

Hudoleth closed her eyes, stood very still for several moments, then began to sway. As her movements broadened, the metal tunic with its array of control symbols caught the last, fugitive rays of the sun, the gleams leaping from line to line, silver shimmers lancing through the dusk, the tinkle of the symbols accenting and uplifting them. She danced within the pentagram, using the movements of her body to ease herself into her power, to take hold more firmly of the Wisdom and ensure his return with the one remaining answer.

She sang to the scuff of her bare feet on the stone, the clink of her silver tunic, meaningless sounds that changed gradually into Power words from the ancient tongue spoken when Chusinkayan was born, more than a dozen Settlings before this. "Ja ayara," she sang. "Yah ida hanuur. Ja da, Syntayo. Ja DA!"

The smoke cloud dissolved. In half a breath all evidence of the Syntayo was gone.

[10]

The snow fell in slanting, swaying white curtains, silent, tranquil, settling with steady persistence on the steep slopes of the mountain peaks and on a small lake that filled the blunt end of the almond-shaped valley. Like a straying clot of white-ness, the White Bird dropped down and down until her webbed talons slid gently on land and her ruffled feathers smoothed down. The even smaller finer needles that had whirred and slammed into the flesh between those feathers — ice-needles fragile as shreds of fine glass — smoothed and melted, icy tears blinding the pain.

Cold. So cold.

Water, melting melting melting within her. Ague stirring.

By yestermorn, she'd already stuffed herself — killing a number of the lumbering, plump gylfinri flying back north for this year's breeding, tearing them apart and eating them as she flew. But the hunger was back, like an oil puddle floating in mid-air or riding the pocks the gentle snow made in the water of this high-mountain lake.

The White Bird pedaled her legs, squeezed and stretched her feet to get rid of the numbness. When the worst stiffness had been worked out, she swam in a slow circle, turning herself in the water, searching for shelter from the increasing chill of the air and stone around her. A few clumps of yellow-tip reeds were nearby. These tubers were crunchy with a hint of garlic, a touch of ginger, and the cool bright tang of straw-berry mint.

She blew heavy gusts of wind through her neb-holes and managed an internal grin.

She felt comfortable here — not because of the sheer walls that sheltered the lake from the dwindling winds, nor because the valley was so high and remote that it felt the foot of man no little more than once or twice a year. No. Though she was sunk so deeply into the bird form that memories from her former life were mostly closed off from her mind's eye, this valley and its appendant stream struck unexpected sparks from misty memory, sparks that bloomed into equally unexpected scenes and images that twisted and dissolved the moment she tried to see them more clearly.

Ather's Farm. The stream that had come leaping down the mountainside from the lake in that hollow had been her chief joy; she'd fished the waters, learned to swim in the deeper pools, watched the colonies of tiny durbabas play in other pools. She felt deeply, warmly at home here.

When she'd drifted too near the outlet, she shook herself from her demi-trance and paddled to the southeast side of the lake. The wind came dropping down the mountain slope like a skier crouched low over his boards; it blew harder and harder with each breath she took, lifting her feathers until they performed like miniature sails, moving her faster and faster across the water. Finally, her keelbone jammed into the slushy sand of a hooked spit at the mouth of a cove ringed with conifers. Porfero vines had sent tendrils from tree to tree to build a wall—more than a wall, more like a heavy tapestry, thorny shoots woven between the trunks; those star-shaped thorns were a formidable barrier, protecting many a sleeper from even the largest and hungriest predators that roamed these altitudes.

It took a moment for the White Bird to realize what had happened. The dark water licked with lazy musicality at the sand, the beach's pale lune like a ghostly reflection of a moon no longer drifting across the sky.

Last night had been difficult for her. Most nights were, thanks to the Follower.

Since the White Bird had flown from the farm, she'd felt something trailing her . . . something more like a demon than a man . . . a daimon using the dirt roads wind-winding through the foothills, coming along relentlessly though he never got close enough to touch her. Each night, at varied intervals, she heard him calling to her though she couldn't make out the words. Every night. As if he were a farmboy tossing corn and calling the flocks to eat.

When he got close, he terrified her though she didn't know why. That terror was all the more distressing because she *knew* dimly but beyond doubt that somewhere inside her were answers to all her questions.

She did not want those answers. Instinct warned her that they were packed with grief and fear, pain, rage, and perhaps even death. Her death.

She flew into exhausting flight, flinging herself into the heart of the snow clouds, darting behind the peaks of the mountain range that formed the spine of Nyddys, struggling to widen the gap between them. Nothing worked. The Follower clung like a burr whose barbs were coated with poison. He found her every time as if he had an invisible line tied to her leg.

Her head drooped. She shook it, opening her beak, snapping it shut. When she'd purged the worst of the terror the Follower woke in her, she began the endless task of preening her feathers, redistributing the oils that insulated her from the wet and the cold.

Touch the oil glands above the anal opening.

Use the beak to spread the oil along one feather.

Choose the next feather.

Continue.

Snow drifting down around her, blinding white, thicker and faster as the sun cleared the horizon, a pale round glow muffled by the steady fall of the snow.

Gentle eddies caressing her body, her legs.

Inside her was a hollow dug by hunger, a growing weakness and a grinding ache, but she continued the preening; it was too important to neglect and besides it gave her an almost orgasmic pleasure. The only thing that disturbed her tranquility was the Follower. He was directly east of her, less than a dozen miles away. What worried her more, he'd stopped and presumably made camp. How did he know she had reached the limit of her strength?

Her head lifted with a quick jerk as she heard the hoarse bugling of a male gavaor and the softer whistles from his herd of females and juveniles. With a liquid, fluttering moan, she paddled free of the inlet, snapped her wings open and half-ran, half-flew across the lake water until she was able to power herself into the air.

The herd of gavaor were south of the lake, which meant she had to fly into the face of the gathering storm. Once she was in the air, battling the suck of the snowfall and the battering of the blizzard wind, she had to circle the lake several times before she managed to locate and ease her weary body into a milder airstream. Hunger drove her and the warm, musky odor of the gavaors; her stomach rumbled and her gut knotted as she drove herself eagerly toward the food that waited in tranquil ignorance; even the Follower was forgotten.

The White Bird was an eater of meat and fish, though on occasion she felt a need to tear up an improvised salad—the tender shoots of new-growth cattails, the moist, spicy tubers of yellow-tips or alaooa flowers—or mow down a field of cereal grass to the screaming annoyance of the farmer. Like her diet, her feet suited a blend of waterbird and skykiller, webbed for swimming though her talons were long and her claws strong and sharp enough to pierce the body of a grown man.

Flying as low to the ground as she dared, she peered through the heavy curtain of snow, scanning the slopes for the patches of the black, brown, or brindle coats that would mark the gavaors. Tufts of feathers lifted from her head, shaping themselves into cones so she could hear the faintest sound. Her ear-cones flattened, focused downward in a flash as sounds from below broke through the howl of the wind.

A blatt and a churning.

The crackle of breaking branches.

Distressed whistles, dull thuds, the occasional ding or clatter as hoof horn struck against stone.

A yearling gavaor had stumbled into a brush-filled crack between two boulders and found himself unable to scramble out again. Three larger gavaors were running in agitated circles about him, females from the herd, alarmed and helpless.

The White Bird propelled herself higher, thrusting herself round and round until she could no longer see anything but the whiteness falling around her and hear only dimly the sounds from the struggling calf.

Higher and higher she went, then she plunged downward, her talons spread, ready to strike. She hit with enormous force, breaking the calf's neck as her talons sank into its flesh. Wings beating with desperate speed, the wind they generated buffeting the snow at the other gavaors, driving them away from the calf, she plucked the carcass from the crack and carried it away to the lake. The harsh, mournful barking of the gavaors rode the wind that howled around her.

[11]

Hudoleth grimaced and winced as she dragged the silver tunic over her head; despite her precautions, the sun had burned her skin, transferring the outlines of the symbols from the tunic and armbands to her body; anything that touched her stung painfully. Weariness flowed over her. Her limbs were so heavy, moving them took enormous effort. She looked at the tunic, sighed and dropped it on the stone. The Niosul were the only ones who would recognize what it was, who could touch it with impunity, but they never came here. She lifted aching, heavy arms, stripped off the silver bands and dropped those onto the pile of silver symbols and wire, along with the mirrored fans and her rings. As the last of the Power web fell away, she felt enormously lighter, as if she had stripped away the greater part of her weariness.

Yawning, groaning as her body objected to the stretching, Hudoleth picked up the pouch with the Lizomo Knot and carried it, along with the special scry mirror, into the house.

7

Distractions

By the calendar of the Watchers of Glandair, events dating from the 11th day of Seimis, the seventh month of the 739th Glandairic year since the last Settling.

{ 1 }

Isel suspected, damn him! Not directly, not traceably, but he knew he was being puppeted, and by sorcery as well. Stupid! Oerfel saw it in the man's every last look and glance, from a hundred different angles in a dozen scry mirrors, and knew others did as well. It was cold comfort that the guards and spymasters dismissed this behavior as simply more signs of Isel's growing paranoia. But just because the Tyrn was paranoid didn't mean that he wasn't right, and now that he was aware of Oerfel's manipulations, he'd question every stray thought he had and weigh it with mechanical precision.

The Tyrn peered about with the eyes of a hunted thing, looking at everyone in the palace with grave suspicion. Oerfel was quite glad he'd quit the Tyrn's service. Isel had a sharp enough mind, and even one less apt-witted could inspect his own memories and draw up a fairly narrow list of people who'd been present when he'd had his most disastrous stray thoughts, the Court Secretary near the top of that list.

Of course, Oerfel knew enough of the game of cat's paw to know when and where to spread doubt. A simple trickle of Pneuma was all it took to tamper with the memories of Isel's wife, giving her the recollection of having proposed the mating of Isel's stallion with Broon Tichnor's mare—a fact that she stated when he asked her if she knew who'd put the idea in his head.

As a result, Isel doubted his wife's memories and motives alongside his own. The Tyrna, however, had a strong opinion of the authorship of her own thoughts, or at least a sense of pride, such that she fabricated a whole slew of recollections around that one false memory like an ouzoet weaving blossoms round her nest. Her dutiful sycophants and handmaids then echoed these anamneses, knowing better than to question their mistress even if it meant contradicting the Tyrn.

Isel wondered aloud if he were going mad, as did many others in the palace, outside his hearing.

Despite this pleasant turn of circumstances, Oerfel's headaches were growing worse. Until this point, all the Tyrn had had indications of was conspiracy, standard fare in the walls of any palace. The manipulations of a Mage were another matter entirely, and it would only be so long before Isel realized it would have to be a Mage. The only other Pneuma-workers of note on Nyddys were the Watchers of Cyfareth, and taking a direct hand in the affairs of the Court went against both their vows and centuries of inertia. Also, they would have no discernible motive to kill the daughter of one of their own, and thereby start a blood feud between them and a powerful Broony.

However, as Oerfel knew full well, such a turn of circumstances would greatly profit a secret Mage on Nyddys, to whom both Tyrn and Watchers would be a constant threat.

Stupid. What was I thinking? Out of my mind with head-aches and doolybrew. Oerfel clutched his head and dug his fingertips into his temples, wishing that the pain would sub-side and the Tyrn's suspicions would go away. Except neither would. They'd just keep pounding and pounding till he was left as nothing more than fragments of bone in the crypt for the rats to chew.

Oerfel gritted his teeth against the pain. The migraines would continue, but the suspicions did not have to point to him, nor did his influence upon the Tyrn have to be direct. Just as he now watched the Tyrn in mirrors, peering around corners and through reflections, he could manipulate Isel in-directly, like a malicious dance master directing a turn of a figure just *so*, making it pass down the line to cause the cou-ple at the end to stumble.

Isel was caught in the dance of Court, and while he was supposed to lead and the others to follow, that was not always the way the dance went, especially if one had a willful part-ner. All it took was a nudge from a courtier here and a nod from a handmaid there, and finally a lock of the Tyrna's hair in a bowl of mercury, for Oerfel to kindle a passion for nov-elty in the proud woman's breast. Tyrna Afankaya began to demand dancers, fools, acrobats, and even more exotic pleas-ures, most of which the wary Isel denied, causing a strain on their relationship and increasing paranoia in the Tyrn.

Of course, these divertissements were merely products of the Tyrna's own jaded fancy, with none of Oerfel's hand be-hind them beyond the initial desire. They were merely frills and distractions to cover one item he wanted added to the royal itinerary. . . .

On the fifteenth of Seimis, Oerfel went to the Palace to have lunch with Pontidd, his successor as Secretary, to see how the man was doing, chat about the events of the Court, and subtly suggest one candidate over the others for the position of Court Poet, vacant since Ellar left the post. As Pontidd confided to him, the Tyrn was still railing about that, though as a new wrinkle Tyrn Isel was now secretly claiming that the poet's disappearance and subsequent death were the result of dark sorcery. Apparently, they had been authored by a mysterious Mage no one had ever seen or heard of, who had done this horrid act for no other reason than to spite the Tyrn and drive him mad.

Oerfel nearly dropped his pork bun at this, and had to bite into it quickly to cover his expression. Isel had ascertained more rightly than any other that not only was there a mysterious Nyddys Mage, but that this Mage was also the author of Ellar's death, a fact only that Watcher's freak of a daughter might know, and this only because she had seen him do it right next to her as they stood in the Flow. On the other hand, Isel's interpretation of Oerfel's ultimate motive for the crime was so completely off base as to be ludicrous. Oerfel almost crowed at this unexpected gift, like when he was a boy and old Sasa the candyseller had tossed an extra sweet in the bag just because.

"Shocking, isn't it?" Pontidd inquired.

Oerfel merely nodded, swallowing a dry mouthful of bun, then reached for the pitcher of syruped fizz-water and refilled his glass. He took a drink and gagged the pastry down. "Most shocking," Oerfel agreed and pounded his chest twice to clear it. "These Mages—they seem to have it out for the arts, don't they? Who was that one at Cyfareth, the dramatist?"

Pontidd chewed a jewel-flower canapé for a moment, then reached for another. "Gylas Mardianson," he said at last. "Talented, from what I've heard. At least enough for Cyfareth to bribe Dyf Tanew's censors to look the other way—not that it did Mardianson any good in the end, mind you. But that, of course, *was* the work of a Mage. Just not some secret one from Nyddys. Siofray, and what's more interesting, one of their men." He smacked his lips and cast about the tray for another dainty. "Caused a great stir at the University."

Oerfel nodded sagely. "He has a sister, you know."

Pontidd looked up. "The Mage?"

Oerfel laughed. Not so far as he knew. "No, Mardianson. Actually, several. Though of note, one of them is a poet. Considered her for the post myself, actually, before settling on Ellar Yliarson." Oerfel took another bite of pork bun and gave a chew, doing his best to look introspective.

Pontidd selected a bun of his own and leaned back, tearing it apart with his short fingers. Oerfel missed the Palace cooks already. "Tana Mardiandattar? Hmm, yes. She's a lyricist as well, isn't she? Plays the finger-pipes? That would amuse the Tyrna, with a fringe benefit of pleasing the University without any drain on the Tyrn's coffers." He popped a morsel of bun into his mouth, chewing for a moment, then dusted his fingers on his napkin. "Good idea."

Oerfel smiled. "I thought so."

And so it was arranged. Tana Mardiandattar came to Court. She was pretty and talented, which pleased Tyrna Afankaya, but more important than that, since it pleased Oerfel, she was next oldest sister to the late Gylas Mardianson, more commonly known as Mole, the troublesome Pneuma researcher whom the Siofray Mage had so thoughtfully fried to a cinder. However, while the Siofray Mage had not only done Oerfel the favor of killing that pest, but maiming the Watcher's chit of a daughter in the bargain, he had not gathered up Mardianson's notes on the workings of the Pneuma flow. One of the Mole's tricks had already proved invaluable, his technique of stepping behind the Flow and moving in obliquely. Where there was one trick, there would be more, just what Oerfel needed to give him the edge against Hudoleth and Mahara and that impudent Siofray who'd just stepped into the game.

Oh yes, my darlings. You might know about me now, you may have seen my face, but you don't know the tricks I have up my sleeve, the subtleties I've had to work out over years of hiding my power. And those will lose you the game. . . .

However, even were Oerfel to retake his position as Secretary — and Pontidd would never give that up without a fight — getting Mardianson's notes assembled in Cyfareth and sent to Tyst would be next to impossible if attempted through official channels. Polite requests to University officials would be met with equally polite refusals, and a less polite sweep of the Tyrn's censors across the Halls of Cyfareth would net no more than a handful of fragments, far less than what Oerfel needed. Divinations had revealed the futility of that approach.

No. Like his namesake, Mole had hidden his notes away in holes and tunnels, crammed his secrets into dozens of different heads, and only those who knew him intimately and knew the workings of his mind would be able to ferret them out and gather them all together in one place, revealing Mole's secrets for a master of the Pneuma Flow to put to use.

And so Tana Mardiandattar came to the Tyrn's Court. She recited her poems, sang her songs, and then, when the Tyrna craved more illicit pleasures at the cutting edge of fashion, told her stories of the theater hidden beneath the halls of Cyfareth University where, instead of reproducing histories and god-tales, the students performed wholly new tales unapproved by the priests of Dyf Tanew. Wonderful, marvelous fabrications never heard before, neither by priest nor warrior, nor scholar, nor farmer. Tales written by the dramatists, the new artists, the greatest of whom was her late brother, who had left his last and greatest work unfinished, a heretical comedy called *The Congress of the Little Gods*.

The Tyrna was more than intrigued. She didn't believe the Siofray Mage had killed Mole merely to spite her, but she still took his death as a personal affront. And, with the passion of a rich woman who's been told there's something she can't have, the Tyrna immediately turned the conversation to asking how much it would cost. Tana, the new Court Poet, had jewels pressed into her hands and was told to finish her brother's play herself, or see to it that it was done by another. The Tyrna didn't care which, so long as it would be ready for viewing when she made an official procession to Cyfareth for the Festival of Masks. The Tyrna was willing to court Heresy for the sake of fashion, but she was not so much of a fool as to do it under the noses of the priests of Dyf Tanew. Cyfareth, however, was far enough away to risk it. Were the Tyrna and her entourage to accidentally stumble onto some heretical performance art during the festivities, well then, that would be almost mundane, compared to many events in previous years.

Finishing the play, of course, did the double duty of gathering together the notes of the dead Mole, who'd mixed his observations on the Pneuma Flow with his observations on life and his notes for the theater. Messy and disorganized — Oerfel would never have put up with such work from one of his undersecretaries — but he couldn't fault the end results. *The Congress of the Little Gods*, besides no doubt incorporating much of Mole's final research on the Pneuma, also — obviously — had something to do with the little gods, those pests who were now becoming larger and more troublesome, and whom no one but the Scholars of Cyfareth had ever felt worthy of attention. Likely a mistake, if Mole's previous work was any indication. One of Mole's secrets had already let him rid himself of the Watcher Ellar. Thanks to that act, her own lack of skill, and the handiwork of the Siofray Mage, the Watcher's misbegotten sport of a daughter had crippled her own flesh and taken herself out of the picture.

For the time being, that is. Oerfel had underestimated her power once already. An unacceptable random factor, she would cause trouble again, probably when Oerfel least desired it. Because of that he needed Gylas Mardianson's notes so as to be familiar with the perversions of the Pneuma the Mole's protégée was liable to throw at him.

Besides which, if the Tyrna were to go on procession to Cyfareth, it was highly probable that the Tyrn would go with her, Isel being as paranoid of having her taken from his side as he was of being led into a trap. And trap it would be. After all, if Anrydd and his men were to take the Tyrn, what better time than the Festival of Masks, and what better place to stage the coup than Cyfareth University? With all luck, the University would be in flames and the Tyrn would be dead, making the siege of the capital simple and the damage to the Palace minimal if any.

So many things to attend to. Oerfel adjusted the mirrors and prepared for the latest round of the choosing of the mistress. It had gotten beyond tedious, Isel having set aside his latest mistress with no more ceremony than would be used for firing a kitchen wench who'd burned the toast. Oerfel sighed as he inspected the candidates the spymasters had chosen—two good choices, two poor choices, and two indifferent ones, not as clever as they could be but not quite fools. He spun the glamour about the poor choices, prompting them to quicker answers than they would have had otherwise, and caused the tongues of the clever wenches to stumble, watching Isel as he looked at the women and shrugged.

What he did next, however, shocked Oerfel. The Tyrn tossed a bone die upon the table, looked at the five spots on its upturned face, then, counting from left to right, selected the fifth of the six women. With no more ceremony than that, he took her by the hand and dismissed the rest.

Oerfel felt the sweat pouring down his face as he watched the women leave, and he looked at the one that was left. Not one of the truly clever ones—Tanew be praised!—but not one of the stupid ones either, merely an average girl who was clever enough to play the fool. Oerfel considered killing her, but decided against it. Isel had tossed the die once, he could do it again, and next time he might do better than breaking even.

Clever Isel. Clever boy. Well, you've figured out enough to spite me. Let's just hope your new whore tells you just enough of my plans to drive you mad and nothing more.

[2]

"Haggers," was all Gryf had said when he pulled them from the straw and into the darkness, but his fierce whisper and the glaze of fear on his eyes in the light of the dying campfire were all that Amhar needed to see. She'd pulled Lyanz out as well, with a finger to his lips. They picked up their gear and slipped out of the Turnout, carefully and quietly as mice dodging their way through a tullin's stubblefield.

The young thief didn't speak until they were miles down the road and dawn was approaching, when he simply waved his hand and said, "Folk't worship the Hag."

Amhar wanted a bit more explanation than that. "What do they do?"

Gryf shrugged. "Kill you. Suck your bones clean. Same stuff as the Hag, only not as quick an' with more arguin.' " He glanced back at her and Laz. "I know what's good for us, an' we're steering clear of them. But t'teeth! They'll be all up and down the road, on're way t' Kruseel Halstead. Broons're havin' a meetin' there, and we'll be goin' through Broony lands the whole way, forwards and back."

Laz reached out and took her hand, squeezing it. She faintly squeezed it back, almost on reflex. "Kruseel Halstead?" Laz asked. "Isn't that . . ."

"We'll be going right by it," Gryf responded sourly, "unless . . ."

Amhar saw by the tensing of his muscles that he'd made a decision before he said it, and so followed him off the main road and into the darkness, pulling her lover along with her. Though it looked no different than a dozen other deer trails they'd passed, Gryf had appeared to recognize it, and Amhar thought it best to follow. It wasn't the usual thing for a man to lead, and far less so for one to know what he was doing. But then again, city boy though he was, Talgryf was the closest thing they had to a native guide, and all her Scribe's training told her that the one who knew the trail and the dangers was usually the best choice.

The deertrack wound and bent through the trees of the Broonyland, past patches of snow and dry frost-edged grass glittering in the starlight, then under the branches of a low fir before emerging into a wider path between the trees. It was not so large as the main road, but was far better maintained for all that.

"There's Pneuma work here," Lyanz said, hand going to his swordhilt. "Lots of it."

Amhar sensed it as well. Not so clearly or as quickly as Lyanz, whose emptiness echoed the Pneuma Flow like a stone bell resonating in sympathy, but in the chill of her bones and the prickling on the back of her neck. The Pneuma tensed against her and held, like cobwebs against her face. "We're not welcome here."

Gryf shrugged. "Haven't been welcomed yet is all. This's a Poacher's Path. Broonwardens use them to get around the woods, 'n poachers use 'em to get around the Broonsmen."

The Broonwards were almost suffocating, pressing on her, making her want to step back off the path and get away. "Then why are we here?"

Gryf smiled, a sly smile, like a hunting cat in a Scribe's marginalia. "I've been here before. Been welcomed, an' I know the Warden in these parts. Old Daffo; Da introduced me." He glanced about. "Broonwarden's job isn't t'keep poachers out; 't's to make sure there's enough game for the Broon an' his favorites when they come through." He shrugged again, stepping down the trail with the needles barely crunching beneath his feet. "Warden kin still hunt for himself, 'n sometimes trades that hunting or right to it for good stuff from the city." He gave a nod to their packs. "That's why you'n Laz'r sloggin' some of Ellar's wines, most 'specially that little present he had from the Tyrn. Wine from the Tyrn's own table—that'll buy a lot of looking the other way. An' hopefully a way past Kruseel Halstead."

Amhar looked around herself, at the dark woodlands of the hunting preserve. "So you're saying this is a trading post?"

"Of sorts. But we don't call it that." He looked up and down the trail, then polished the winebottle he'd taken from his pack so it glittered like an amethyst in the starlight. "What this is is a crosstrail, and my da told me that this is where the Broonwardens set their spells. It's like plucking one of the spokes of a spider's web t' get it's attention, but not falling into the trap." He scuffed his boot in the needles. "They'll be around shortly, the Wardens, Old Daffo or one of his lessers. Now put your staff away an' take out your wine 'n let me do the talking. . . ."

[3]

Isel had despaired of ever finding a clever mistress who could tell him what he needed to know, but was thankful that at least he'd found a foolish one who could do the same. Wyling was a daughter of the Bothrin, too pretty for her own good, with no intellect to speak of, but a fine memory for everything new or intriguing, like an ouzoet building her repertoire. But instead of the cries of other birds and animals, Wyling's passion was stories and songs and gossip. Like an ouzoet, she

loved the sound of her own voice and could listen to it forever.

> *"The old dame's men*
> *Came round the bend*
> *To suck the biddy's tits.*
> *The cripple said*
> *He bit them off*
> *But he's just full of . . ."*

Wyling stopped and simpered. "I can't say the next word,
'cause it's nasty, and you're the Tyrn."

"Don't worry," Isel said, caressing her side, "I can fill it in
myself." And indeed he could. Wyling was simple enough to
think it was just a naughty song, but Isel could easily identify
it as an affront from the Haggers. The old dame was none
other than the Creator Hag, and the cripple was Dyf Tanew
himself, whom the Haggers were taking their power back
from. The biddy still has her tits, yes indeed, come get some
Vis.

Isel played a bit with Wyling's, which were prettier than
the Hag's ever were, and considered his options. Tyst was
becoming unsafe. The Haggers were gaining more power in
the city, masking the old biddy with the new name of the
Great Mother, and Anrydd's raids were becoming more and
more problematic. Tanew's teeth! If the god had just done a
proper job of biting the biddy's dugs off the first time, he
wouldn't have to deal with this.

But facts were facts. Wyling sang more masked Heresy in
the form of children's songs about toothless cripples and biddies' nipples, and Isel kissed and sucked hers till she squealed
like the Hag herself. The Heretics might hide their doings
from the spies and even the men on the street, but they
couldn't hide what they said from their children, who'd re-

peat what they'd heard as part of games and songs. Girls like Wyling, who were hardly more than children themselves, would remember those and repeat them.

The capital was unsafe. That was a given. His wife wanted to go to Cyfareth, for the Festival of the Masks. Suspicious, but far more suspicious not to go, and far more dangerous politically. Lauresa Falloranedattar, a Watcher's favorite child, was dead, and the whole court of Broony Mirmyan had done everything short of accusing him outright. Lauresa and a serving maid had both been found murdered in the gardens. A new street ballad told of a jaded Tyrn picking flowers and tossing them away until he made the mistake of plucking a sorcerer's prize lily and stripping away its petals. Ha-ha, how very witty; if the veneer were any thinner, it would be transparent.

Isel had spread speculations back that the culprit was Broon Tichnor's son Chamelly, even though he knew him to be innocent. Street ballads and gossip aside, Fallorane was calling blood feud on Mirmyan, and the only way to calm the situation was to pour Tyrn money on both. Enough money could bury any problem, even though too much would look like an admission of guilt.

Isel was certain that the death was no coincidence. Someone wanted him destroyed, and Cyfareth as well. Anrydd? Possible, but unlikely. Magic took a great deal of scholarship, something his bastard half brother had never shown any inclination for. Then again, his father had had so many bastards it was hard to keep track of all of them.

As a happy coincidence—could anything be a happy coincidence right now?—his wife wished to endow something at the University, she didn't care what, so long as it gave her an excuse to go on procession to Cyfareth for the Festival of Masks and, in a particularly transparent bit of charades, view some scurrilous entertainment authored by the new Court Poet's dead brother. Frivolous, but in all likelihood harmless.

Whoever the Mage was, he or she was unlikely to be doing all this work remotely from Cyfareth, what with all the Watchers. Therefore, if the Mage wished to continue the game, he'd have to somehow join the royal retinue and expose himself. Or herself.

Isel counted the known Mages. Mahara of Kale was quite tied up in their Court and their wars, and Isel's spies assured him that he was no threat to Nyddys except in the general sense. The Watchers spoke of a second Mage in Chusin-kayan, and his informants believed her to be a woman. Now the Siofray Mage, known to be a man. Two men in the open, one woman in hiding. And now a fourth Mage.

And so a procession to Cyfareth, with some endowment for the University as an excuse. Isel thought a moment, then discreetly suggested a memorial garden for the dead Lauresa to his wife.

Afankaya immediately recognized the profit in this. To endow the stables at the University would look like a direct bribe to Fallorane, but to endow the other half of the agriculture department by way of a garden, placing his dead daughter's name on it, would look more like sympathy, or at least like the Tyrny buying off the University's blood feud against Broony Mirmyan, which in the world of politics came to much the same thing. If Chamelly had murdered Lauresa — which he hadn't, but the truth wasn't important in matters like these — Broon Law could do nothing against him, but considerable damage could be done to both the Broons and the Tyrny by a feud with the University. The only fault Broon Tichnor could own up to is that he had failed to protect the daughter of a Scholar, and thus one of the Tyrn's vassals, while she was in his lands. Since Isel had also been present at Broony Mirmyan at the time of the murders, however, he could claim that the responsibility for Lauresa's safety was that of the Tyrny, not the Broony, and hence the need for a memorial garden and an official visit, to give honor to the dead.

To allay suspicions—and feather her own nest—Tyrna Afankaya suggested that the memorial also be made in the name of the Court Poet's dead brother, another shocking death. Gylas Mardianson had been even more of a University pet than Lauresa Falloranedattar, if that were possible. *That* murder could never be pinned on the Tyrny, except in the most general sense. Making the Tyrny memorial to Mardianson as well as Lauresa would be a grand gesture, saying, *Well, people, look—your Tyrn cares for you, but we unfortunately live in insane times. Terrible things can and will happen, including power-mad Mages from other worlds burning men to cinders and everyday psychotics murdering young girls as they stroll through a Broon's gardens. Sorry. The best we can do is mourn and try to get through these troubling times as best we can.*

Of course, it would have to sound better than that. Isel summoned the Court Poet and requested that she put these sentiments into somewhat more eloquent prose, which he might read at the dedication, as well as compose an appropriate dirge or eulogy to deliver herself. The new Court Secretary, Pontidd—could he be the Mage?—was instructed to send letters and funding to Cyfareth, commissioning the memorial garden and seeing that it was ready in time for the dedication.

Isel also instructed Pontidd to draw up the most formal and abbreviated retinue possible. After all, this was a state visit for the purpose of remembering the dead, not an excuse for lavish spectacle—the garden was for that. While they would require a certain number of servants for appearances' sake, he and the Tyrna were not taking one extraneous body. That this procession would coincide with the Festival of Masks was unfortunate, of course, but murder was not designed to go on a convenient schedule. Others might do as they liked, the

Tyrna included, but he himself would be spending the night of the festival at the Temple of Dyf Tanew in Cyfareth, mourning the dead, instead of getting drunk and debauching himself as half the populace would be doing and the other half expected.

With any luck, Afankaya would go off and royally embarrass herself as only a Tyrna could, taking the weight of public scrutiny and scandal off him and onto herself. It was high time his wife took up some of the responsibilities of rulership.

Isel smiled. The hidden Mage may have thrown a corpse at his feet, but he'd just bury it and be glad for the funeral.

[4]

Gryf didn't know if it were Hero's Luck or just Bothrin Planning and he didn't much care which. Old Daffo had materialized in less than an hour, all smiles when he saw Gryf and fine regards for Gryf's da, with sympathies when told of his ill health. But sympathy sweetened the deal. One bottle of wine had bought them passage on the Poacher's Path; a second obtained entrance to Daffo's nearest tack house; and the third one—the one from the Tyrn's own table, or at least his cellars—had gained them a feast worthy of the Tyrn himself.

Tyrn's Luck. That had to be it. And good Bothrin Planning at the same time.

Gryf squeezed his father's notebooks, the most precious thing he had next to his father himself, and guaranteed to outlast him.

Gryf could almost hear his father's comments and his mother's scolding. There were, certainly, better places to have spent such a find as Ellar's put-away bottle of special red— insane collectors of all things related to the Tyrn would slaver like a pack of hounds for the presentation bottle the last Tyrn had given his last Court Poet. One Broon or another would likely find use for it as a memento to hand out as proof of his own largesse — but from a lesser Broon's Gamewarden, such as Old Daffo, who would never have a chance of gaining such a Tyrn-favor except through the rarest of circumstances, it bought hospitality and a load of good will that would last into the next Settling.

If the worlds survived that long.

Gryf penned a note into the margin of his father's third journal, improving the debt-marking for Daffo from moderate to the next best thing to saving a man's life, then carefully lined it out and closed the journal.

Sometimes, as with the wine, you had to spend your Tyrn's Luck all in one place.

The Haggers were one peril, and avoiding them was worth a great deal more than just a bottle of wine, no matter how fine or overrated the vintage. The Broony's Gamewardens were another, one that could not be avoided if you entered the Broonwoods, but unlike the Haggers, the Wardens could be negotiated with. Like the thieves of the Bothrin and the Moneylenders of Tyst, the Wardens kept neat ledgers, if just in their heads.

Gryf nibbled on another marsh-duck leg, made greasy-sweet with a sauce of fatroot and dried summer berries, and made his decision. Time to cash out. Good will wouldn't do him a whole lot of good if they didn't get Laz to the Empty Place.

"More wine?" Gryf asked, reaching into his pocket and producing a small bubbleglass flask. "This also comes from the poet's stores. Herbal bitters for after a fine meal." He extended the vial, letting his thumb and a little duck grease smudge Ellar's warning label.

"Why thanksh you, thief. Yer mush too kind . . ." Old Daffo was drooling duck grease into his plaited gray-streaked beard.

After downing the draught, his pronouncements and anecdotes became even more incomprehensible—but happy—until at last they trailed off into contented snoring.

Ama raised one finely arched eyebrow at this, but Gryf only reached for the roasted nut-and-cheese-stuffed apples that were to be their final course. It was one thing to drug a man, especially an old friend of your father, but another to insult his hospitality, and they needed to give Ellar's infusion time to take full effect.

The apples were excellent, the red skins turned brown and cracked in the hearthfire, oozing tiny star-shaped welanuts and purple-veined Krissen cheese. The best Gryf had ever tasted, with the extra savor of a scam played well. He ripped off a piece of the dark home-baked bread from Daffo's hearth and used it to mop up the last of the dessert-sauce and the duck grease of the meal. It would likely be a long time before they ate this well again.

"Salen leaves," Gryf explained at last, standing up, and wiped his mouth on one sleeve. "He'll be out for hours."

Laz leaned away from Ama, with whom he'd looked about ready to share an after-dinner kiss, and looked puzzled. "Why?"

Gryf shrugged and did his best to ignore Laz and Ama's continued romantics. "We'll be going into the Maze, and that's filled with thieves and spies. Like as not, Mage that's after you paid one or more to look out for you an' Ama both. That means we need cover. Saw a beefer cart out back; not something a Warden'd use, so must be something Daffo took from a poacher for not making an arrest. 'E doesn't need it, and by rights it belongs to his Broon, but 'e'd still want more than we've got in trade to get it."

Laz looked even more appalled. "So you drugged him?"

"Daffo'd do the same t'me if the scam was right. Not taking

anything of his anyway; just borrowing stuff he's borrowing to begin with."

He gestured to their packs and the gifts the Warden had thrown their way for Ellar's bottle. "Take those and nothing else. With a little Bothrin Luck, he'll think the poachers snuck back to liberate their cart while he was still sleeping it off. Without it, I'll owe him a case of Tyrn's wine on the way back. If your Hero's Luck holds, Laz, maybe the Emperor of Chusinkayan can spare some, assuming we run into him."

[5]

Firill sat alone in her room—their room—her desk awash in the scattered remnants of a life: charcoal sketches, Pneuma crystals, costumed figurines with porcelain faces and painted paper masks and everywhere parchment upon parchment, scraps and stacks and sheaves and scrolls and huge loose-leafed folios with stray sheets sticking out of the edges, Mole's countless revisions and production notes. Her shoulders tensed and her head shook. The responsibility was just over-whelming.

But there, on the table before her, was a scrap of parch-ment with a line in Mole's fine script—*Begin at the begin-ning, end at the ending, and all else in-between should fall into place.*

Easy enough advice, so long as you knew where the be-ginning and ending were. But that was what organization was for, something Mole had never paid much attention to. Or, to be more accurate, had paid all too much attention to, believing that one thing was interconnected to another, and both of those in turn applied to a third.

The Congress of the Little Gods: A Comedy was meant to be a masquerade, each actor portraying one of a number of hypothetical little gods who bore a strong resemblance, in turn, to the greater gods, and whose movements and actions in turn illustrated a number of magical concepts and Mole's own speculations about the Pneuma flow. It was, however, incomplete. Only a good third of the lines had been written. And while the story had been carefully outlined to its conclusion, Mole had left a number of minor characters—and a couple of major ones—with their final fate unspecified, and thus ultimately in Firill's hands.

She brushed at a tear on her cheek, then steadied her hands and poured herself a cup of tea. It had gone cold, and wasn't sweetened—and she was out of honey and soursweet— but warming tea and fetching honey weren't going to help her write a play. Neither would tears. Mole might be charred to ash by some foreign Mage, with nothing left to even put in a grave, but a finer testament to his life was right here on her desk. Neither tears nor any further procrastination would get his final work finished and produced.

Neither would sharpening quills or grinding ink. The tullin feathers were sharp enough, and the ink was black and close enough to the right consistency, and all it took was a hand on the page to set words down. So she did, scratching and lining out whenever something didn't sound right, stealing whole lines from things she remembered Mole as having said, or that it seemed likely that he would. *Close enough,* said Little God Mole, *is often exactly what you need. That's what makes Mages so dangerous, you know—most of them couldn't hit the broad side of a barn, except that they're throwing another barn, so they've got room to be sloppy.*

Firill tried to laugh at the irony. Mole had planned the ultimate conceit—the narrator of the congress was a little god named "Mole" who went about making Mole-like commentaries on the various proceedings. The plot of the play concerned the rest of the little gods on a quest to find this mysterious Mole, who they'd heard about but never seen, and knew was important, but didn't know why. The whole situation bore a strong resemblance, in fact, to the Watcher's quest to find the Hero. While on one level the little gods seemed to reflect the greater ones, on another they sounded a great deal like the faculty of Cyfareth University. Certainly the arguments regarding who would be the god in charge of turnip production resembled the fight last year between the rivals for the head of the botany department, down to the line about, "You may know everything there is to know about growing turnips, but you'll never know a thing about what they're good for unless you bite into one."

Firill had added impetus to finish the play, beyond simply finishing Mole's last work. Tyrna Afankaya had heard of Mole's productions and was desirous of seeing the latest, never mind the fact that such things were unofficial, unapproved and underground. Like a mole. Mole said (and whether it was the author or the little god, it was hard to tell), "All the best work gets done underground, behind the scenes, where the daywalkers seldom notice it. Close one tunnel and another opens, for softly, softly go little mole feet, and who knows where they will carry him?"

Who knew indeed? But Mole's sister Tana, now the Court Poet, had asked her to finish the work, and there was no one else who could.

8

Dreams

By the calendar of the Watchers of Glandair, events dating from the 13th day of Seimis, the seventh month of the 739th Glandairic year since the last Settling.

{ 1 }

The White Bird ripped a last gobbet from the calf's flank, flipped it around until she had it properly settled, then forced it down into a belly already crammed with meat. Her eyelids drooping low, her head drawn down between her shoulders, her whole body torpid from the gorging, she crouched on the sand of the inlet and fought the overwhelming need to sleep. A few breaths later an itch from below insinuated itself beneath her feathers, an irritation like ants crawling all over her, biting at her. The Follower. Looking at her. Somehow. She didn't understand it, but she felt his eyes on her, drilling holes in her body.

Using this irritation as a lever, she broke free of the numbness induced by fatigue and overeating, used her beak to lift the remains of her meal from the bloody sand and lumbered clumsily to the thorn fence. Oddly enough the Follower was doing her a favor—helping her to stay awake, helping her to get away from him once more. After she'd hung the carcase high on the porfero thorns, she waddled back, guided by the soft lap-lap as the lake water slapped at the rim of the sand; the snowfall had thickened until it made walls around her and she could no longer see beyond the tip of her beak.

She slid into the water, paddled slowly, cautiously, to the middle of the inlet where she began cleaning away the blood and other fluids from her wings, reapplying oil to her feathers to keep herself from freezing. When at last she got the muck off her feathers, she fluffed them and swam to the tiny island in the middle of the lake. She kicked about in the reeds that grew at the edge of the island until she was in a nest of sorts and protected from drifting. When she felt safe, she drew her neck in so her head was resting on her shoulders and plunged fathoms deep into sleep.

DREAM AMBIENCE: Broad, yellow ocher earthenware crater turning slowly on its side—the design in the belly of the cup was a mix of wide and narrow black lines brushed on and burned into the clay—

The Dream Path begins . . .

The angular outline of a girlchild with tangled black hair blowing about her face, trudged up a game trail that jig-jagged alongside the stream leaping down the steep slopes of the mountain called Brynn Bannog. Weariness showed in the lines of her body; determination to reach her destination was apparent in the somber curve of her mouth.

As she moved into a brighter section of the path, she shook clumps of mud from the paper she carried in one hand, muttered over and over words written there then declaimed those rhythmic phrases into the scratchy shadow around the patches of winter-stripped brush.

(The White Bird moaned in her sleep, coughed, then shuddered as if she were being beaten all over her body by a heavy maul. Or by the constant tik-tik-tik of dream-words spat at her from the musings of the dream-child.)

The Dream-Child's Musings:

The year before she was born, the one that the Nyd-Ifor called *"Dyf Tanew's Sorrow"* because it was so wet and cold, there was a terrible storm, one of the worst in the memory of man. Many older trees were ripped from the ground and tossed aside; one of the largest fell across the stream. Time had scrubbed away the bark and turned the wood soft with rot, but the remnant of the glasfir was still heavy enough to hold back the water.

The durbabas moved into the sunny pool three tendays later, the adults sealing the dam with the twigs, clods of rooty mud and water-polished pebbles.

The girl pushed through a thin patch of brush, smiled as she caught sight of her favorite nesting place. She trotted to the tree's stubby root-mass, then crawled along the thick trunk until she found a soft, sunwarmed spot. She stretched out on it, rested her chin on her fist and watched drowsily for the durbabas to swim from the lacehead reeds or the piles of water-polished pebbles, all the varied hiding places they'd leaped for when they heard her coming.

Durbabas were tiny creatures, hardly the length of her hand—tiny, naked water people with rubbery frog faces, three-fingered hands and webbed duck-feet. They looked like they were made of glass and, unless the sunlight hit the surface of the pool in just the right way, were almost impossible to see. Growing from wrists and ankles, the men had fins as bright and supple as silk ribbons. They spent their days dancing, gambling and teasing the women.

The women ignored them and bustled about the pool, turning over pebbles to find cooterbugs and starworms, crunchy roots and reedroot tumors and a thousand other gifts of the earth that the gods sent for their pleasure and the sweet bellies of their children. The durbaba babies were plump and lively, with tadpole tails instead of legs. Now and then they paused to help their mothers fetch or dig, but mostly the girl saw them immersed in their games — hide-and-seek or follow-the-leader or tag, tickle-me-pink or trail-the-snail or home-first.

The girl sighed, thrust her pointing finger into a pocket.

(The White Bird moved restlessly, seemed about to wake.)

As if she were aware of the soul overwatching her much as she spied on the durbabas, the girl removed her hand quickly from that pocket. The next draw produced a soft, wrinkled apple. The girl bit into it, wrinkled her nose and tossed the remnant of the apple into the pool, scaring the durbabas into hiding.

With a patience uncommon to her, she waited for them to settle again. Up there on her mountain there was no one her age to talk to and she had no kin except a father who was often absent either in mind or body. Or both. All the hours she'd spent watching these tiny folk had turned them into kin — almost, anyway. She wept with them when one of the swimmers died or was hurt, rejoiced with them when they were celebrating a birth or one of their enigmatic festivals — though as yet she did not dare touch or speak to them.

(The White Bird shuddered under the hammer of the powerful emotions released in her. As she fluttered upward toward waking, the scene before her shimmered and faded into nothingness.)

[2]

Ignoring the heat and the tickling of the talisman that grew continually more insistent — like Amhar when she nagged at him in those days back at Urfa House as she was teaching him bare-hand and staff fighting — Breith closed his eyes to slits. Guided by Pneuma probes, he groped toward a vague darkness ahead of him, hoping more than knowing that it was the hedge that fenced a small paddock that he'd glimpsed a few hours ago. Beyond that darkness he could feel a dozen centers of warmth moving about and a dozen paler blotches that went nowhere, just swayed back and forth, bending with the wind. Horses and trees. And, Prophet be blessed, no wealmen. Nothing else alive — except a small raptor of some kind perched in one of those trees and a few rodents digging in the snow.

An hour ago the horse he was leading had picked up a stone and gone lame. Between the storm and the prodding of the talisman, he hadn't noticed this until the beast screamed with pain, lurched and nearly fell. Even after he dismounted and used Pneuma to pry loose the jagged stone, painting over the bruise a thick layer of Pneuma that was supposed to suck away the pain and mend the wound, it took him half an hour — half a freezing, mind-numbing hour — to get a first step from the horse, then a slow, hobbling walk. Since that first step he'd covered less than a quarter of a mile. If this place proved out, at least he'd found shelter for himself and the suffering beast.

Following the curve of the hedge, he turned into the teeth of the wind, huddling his shoulders in the blanket he'd wrapped about himself. Despite heavy boots and thick socks long enough to fold about his toes, his feet were numb from the cold; inside the oversize mittens he'd stolen off a washline his fingers were losing the ability to maintain their grip on anything, especially the thin leather thongs that served as reins. He nearly lost these when the horse jerked his head up and snorted as a sudden gust of wind slammed gouts of snow against them. "Hoo, boy. Haa, boy. Easy now. Lit'l bit more."

The wind carried his voice away, but enough sound must have reached the beast because he dropped his head and went back to lurching painfully over the uneven ground. His elbow pinning the blanket against his ribs, Breith eased his left hand away from his body, held it with the palm flat and facing the hedge; despite the hammering of the wind, he managed to read the ghostly prickle of the hedge thorns and keep to the path he'd chosen. "Prophet Prophet Prophet," he muttered. "There has to be a gate."

Knees trembling, the toes of his boots catching in ruts and brocha holes, he almost missed the sudden cessation of the prickling. He turned, plodded toward the smooth area that had appeared as if it were an answer to his prayer. Smooth meant gate, meant heavy wooden slats pegged to uprights with spaces between them that a weary road walker searching for shelter could crawl through if the Broon or Free Farmer who owned this land were so tightfisted he put padlocks on his paddocks.

Despite his care, Breith misjudged the distance to the gate and jammed his fingers into it. His hands were too numb to feel any pain, though he knew he would later. He didn't think he had broken a bone, but he wouldn't know until he thawed out a little. After some fumbling about he found the latch, a wooden hook and lever arrangement, and tried to lift it. It was frozen solid. "Might as well been padlocked," he muttered. "Comes to the same thing." Behind him his mount caught a whiff of the horses in the paddock and nickered impatiently, then pushed at Breith with his nose. "Patience, patience, ol' horse. I know you're hurting and hungry. Let me . . ."

He leaned against the beams of the gate, closed his eyes and began teasing a fine thread from the turbulent Flow overhead, struggling to create so little disturbance that even the Nyddys Mage wouldn't notice his interference with the Pneuma. Like one of his kinswomen at Urfa House working at the spinning wheel, he pulled the thread down, twisting it tight and smooth, coiled it in neat loops that hung invisibly over his wrist.

The draw seemed to go on forever, but he persevered, knowing he would need a good store of power to ease the horse's lameness while he kept himself alive and intact until the storm blew itself out. Revisiting the Flow unnecessarily was far too dangerous as long as Cymel was locked into the bird form and unable to protect herself from the Mage.

Tease Pneuma free of the Flow, twist it into a thread, loop it with the rest.

Over and over.

The snow thickened around him, the wind howled as it blew past the curve of the paddock hedge and the cold intensified; inside the mittens his fingers were numb and clumsy. The wrist with its burden of Pneuma was the only warm spot on his body, but that warmth made the rest of him ache all the more.

Over and over he pulled the thread, wound the loops— until his brain seemed about to explode out through his ears and his knees about to fold under him.

Over and over.

He sighed finally, broke the connection and let the collected Pneuma sink into his body. "Made it, horse. I'll have this gate open before . . . ah! There we are."

With a crack as loud as that made by a lightning-struck tree, the gate yielded and dug a path through the snow. Whinnying and whuffling, the horse lumbered past him, shoulder slamming into him, almost knocking him from his feet.

Breith sighed and tugged the gate shut. Now he had to catch that idiot beast and strip the gear off him. The fire striker was in his saddle bags along with all the food he'd brought from the Tower and all his blankets; if he didn't want to freeze like that gate, he had to retrieve his supplies. He shivered at the thought, then started trudging toward the largest of the trees, muttering his discontent. "Wears you out . . . slogging through snow up to your waist . . . can't do a cursed thing . . . hands won't bend . . . fingers . . . can't hold onto anything . . . cold . . . always cold. . . ."

The lower branches of the parasol pine hung down around Breith, the hard nubbles of their tips brushing slowly back and forth across the snow, their stubby needles packed so tightly against each other that the wind he hated so much could get through them only in dribs and drabs and icy drafts. The snow blown into these needles added another layer of insulation from the storm intensifying outside the cave-like shelter the tree provided. There was very little snow under Breith's chosen tree, just the drifts that dribbled beneath the hard thorny tips of the branches and through gaps where the needle growth was thinner. The rest of the roughly circular space was carpeted with clumps of limp, wiry, sun-bleached grass. He'd hung the saddle and the rest of the gear over the budding limbs on the heavy trunk and spread his blankets next to the small fire he'd built between two crooked, knotty roots. A kettle of snow was melting over the fire, water for stew and tea.

Fighting off sleep Breith leaned over the fire, its warmth spreading through him until he was so comfortable the thought of moving started a pain worse than a bellyache. He swayed over the fire, steam rising from the water, painting heat across his face, letting himself remember the start of this trek.

After leaving the Tower weighed down with supplies from

Ellar's food store, he'd walked north for three nights, collecting blisters and falling farther and farther behind Cymel. On the fourth day he'd found shelter in a Turnout with horses grazing in a field next to it. When night came he rode north on one of those horses.

That horse's backbone was a punishment for the sin of theft, and by sunrise, for all the other sins he could call to mind. Yet the rapidly increasing urgency of the talisman's tug told him he was closing on the White Bird.

He drew his hand across his face. The triumph of that first night had trickled away as the gap sometimes increased, sometimes diminished, but never vanished. She was scared of him. He didn't know why or how to reassure her. Tonight she was as close as she'd ever been, close enough to start the talisman jigging and slapping at his chest. With a long, weary sigh, he pulled it from inside his shirt.

The clasp with its tangle of black hair flew out of his hand and struggled to escape the leather thong that bound it to his neck. She was directly west of him, only a few miles away. And she seemed to have settled in to wait out the storm. If he ate the hot stew and drank the tea . . . witched one of those horses out in the paddock and got him saddled . . . he just might be able to get close enough to see her despite the snow . . . and drop a Pneuma net over her . . . tie her down . . . find a way to unfold her from that spell. . . .

He shook his head, long light brown hair brushing across his eyes, worked his hands over the pot of water that was on the point of boiling. Just the memory of the cold outside the parasol pine's sheltering dome set new aches in his bones. There was no way he could force himself back into that storm. With a windy, weary sigh, he rubbed his hands together a last time, then cupped them about the hair clasp, the ache inside him as painful as the barbed throbbing in the frozen patches on his face. "Cymel. Why're you acting so stupid?" He tapped the leather clasp against his cracked and crusted lips. "As long as we're on Nyddys, the Mage . . . Gryf said she scared spit outta him, sent him running like his tail was on fire . . . but if he picks up that she's scared of something . . . maybe I should herd her over to Nordomon . . . keep following her . . . pushing at her . . . get her away from this place, this Mage . . . and then it'll be *safe* to run her down and pull her out of this. Safer maybe. If I catch her here on Nyddys . . . don't know . . . can't use large currents here . . . too dangerous . . . and I'll need . . ."

The scratchy sound of boiling water broke through his whispered musings; from beyond the heavy curtain of the downhanging branches a horse whickered, then started pawing through the snow, digging out the sun-cured grass. The suddenness and the ordinariness of the sounds, the pawing horse, the rattling pot, flooded Breith's mouth with saliva. He straightened up, grimaced at the twinges behind his eyes, then began assembling his supper.

[3]

Capturing icy air in cupped feathers, timing her wing beats to the churn of her webbed feet in the dark water, Cymel skimmed across the lake and rose into the gathering night, a shadow in the silent snowfall, tiny flakes spiraling down and down from clouds that hung eerily motionless above the mountain peaks; erratic puffs of a feeble wind shaved wisps away from their towering billows, but the clouds themselves seemed never to change.

She flew north, riding those winter winds in long graceful, hypnotic curves. The Follower was still behind her, clinging like a tick. She moaned softly, the song of the White Bird, a sad lament that mourned not only her own sorrows but the tragedies of the world. The sound merged with the rising, falling moan of the winds so the Follower couldn't possibly hear her, but after a while she grew more afraid and forced herself to match the silence around her.

An hour before moonrise the gap widened between her and the Follower, shrank again as her wings started trembling from fatigue and she had to change from muscular flight to soaring, reading and riding the high winds.

On and on she went, getting as much rest as she could in silent glides, right arc into left arc into right again. On and on till she flew out of the snowfall into heavily overcast skies, suddenly heavier winds that buffeted her and threatened to send her tumbling to the ground.

Squeals and screams broke through the wind sounds—the rattle of rock against rock, the sharp reports of wood splintering. She spiraled lower. An avalanche of boulders and snow tumbled down the mountain below her, cracking open trees, snapping their trunks so they skidded free of their roots, tearing up brush and vines, alternately burying and spitting up a small herd of goats, their hairy, blood-soaked bodies pounded to pulp by those tree trunks, those boulders.

Hunger rumbled in her stomach. For a fleeting moment, she forgot the Follower as she searched out the largest and meatiest of the goats, locking onto it just as the avalanche sucked it under again. Patiently, she waited . . . and waited . . . the avalanche spat the herd out again . . . their matted, blood-drenched white hair blending with the dirty snow.

Cymel clapped her wings shut and plummeted in a deadly stoop.

Talons driven deep into the goat's flesh . . . trees and tumbling brush flashing by her . . . looming suddenly ahead of her . . . no room . . . she couldn't extend her wings to their full length . . . couldn't produce enough power to raise herself and the carcass of the goat . . . until a strange lightness filled her . . . as if the air she drew into her lungs had an extra lift to it . . . so she vaulted suddenly above the rumble of the deadly snow, branches brushing at her wings and sides . . . winter-dormant oaks, the scratchy needles of the conifers . . . fled mindlessly until the sounds and the ugly sights were behind the breast of the mountainsides . . . fled until she found a high, wind-swept ledge above the tree line. . . .

She perched on the up-tilted ledge and began tearing at the carcass of the dead goat, lost in the satisfactions of warm blood and rich red meat.

The moon rose half an hour later, a fat gibbous blur dimly visible through the clouds, remnants of the storm Cymel had left behind her. Gliding northward beneath a leaden sky, starless and foreboding, she twitched and blinked sporadically as life fires popped at her from the darkness below. One here, one there, two or three in close proximity in a tight little arc about a mountain meadow, a scattered cluster, slightly larger, down on the plain, then a modest burst of lives, about thirty of them, packed tightly into an area smaller than last night's lake — a village? — a wider, sparser sprinkle of life in the narrow river bottomland — Free Farms? — and in the northwest a dense concentration of life heats that burned bright as a forest fire — a city?

She rose higher, spiraling up and up till she could see widely spaced, lamplit windows around the edges of that wide yellow shine to the north. *Yes . . . city! And I know that city,* she told herself. *I know its name . . . Dadeny on Dadeny Bay . . . I heard . . . no, learned . . . I learned a poem once. . . .*

The memory was sudden and vivid, a black-haired child trudging up a footpath beside a stream, scowling at a bit of crumpled, muddy paper, muttering over and over the lines written on it, struggling to memorize them. Lines of a poem about a Northlander attack on a port town called Dadeny. In

her mind's ear, she heard clearly the child's voice chanting
lines from that poem —

Sodden the soil	*Streams in full run*
Blood blacks the water	*War's woe is the bane*
Nor charms of the harp	*Nor surcease of wine*
Dulls the hurt of the heart	*At the death. . . ."*

The words faded as another image replaced the first, a tall,
lean man with light brown hair streaked with gray, blue eyes
twinkling behind round spectacles in thin gold frames.

Pain stabbed through her, an ache of memory this time,
not of the body. She could not . . . would not . . . finish the
thought or suffer the image an instant longer. She left the
curving glide through the peaks and raced toward the city as
if the place that had evoked that memory could also exorcize
it and leave her at peace. Peace at last. Wings snapping the
air behind her in rapid, powerful beats, she flew over Dadeny
in a wide circle, the tips of her wings on each back-beat
churning through the low-hanging clouds.

Below her, torches threw patches of light along crooked
streets out near the wharves, picked out sparks on the black
water of the bay, woke sudden darts of brightness from bits
of polished metal that the walkers who filled those streets
wore as ornaments or weapons. It was long past midnight, but
Dadeny's Heart never rested.

Dadeny's Heart. Buying and selling. Cargoes from every
corner of the world, some selling in broad daylight, others in
the slippery, slidery dark of the night. You could buy anything
from anyone in a Dadeny night if you had enough patience
and enough coin. Even slaves — though that was river gossip
and never proved.

She glided through a long-sided circle, a little farther in

from the periphery this time. . . . passing over the homes of daylight merchants where everyone slept and the only lights were gatehouse torches . . . passing over small vegetable farms beyond the darkened homes, the farms that fed Dadeny . . . passing over the light and shadow of the Heart where some of the life fires were dimmed and dreary . . . some with the edge of a killing knife, bright and deadly . . . some with the bittersweet smell of musk, the odor of predators stalking each other.

Heat rose from the torches and from the lanterns carried at the ends of poles, ordinary heat that was cleaner and more comforting than the poisonous fever of the men of the Heart, and this heat wrapped round her like a mother's arms, comforting after the cold and the fear from all those days of flight and fright. Her eyelids drooping low, she rode the updrafts with dreamy pleasure; it was like sleeping in a nest of feather beds, the casing pouching up around her. . . .

A shout from the street.

Men pointed up at her, stood with their necks bent back into a tight arc as they stared at her. Bathed in the rising warmth from the torches until her mind and body had shut down, eyes drooping almost shut, gliding in tight circles, she was dimly aware of what was happening below her, but undisturbed—as if it were one of those dramas that she'd sneaked out to watch when she was living at Cyfareth University . . . entertaining . . . but wholly unconnected with her.

The street emptied swiftly as if the doors along it had sucked the Dadenese inside.

A second later, some of them burst out again, heavy curl-back bows in their hands, quivers tucked under their arms.

Cymel squawked, startled as a searing pain scorched along her side. A second agony bloomed along her neck, driving her out of her pleasure trance.

They were shooting at her.

Standing with legs splayed and braced, they were shooting at her!

She snapped her wings out, fled out over the Bay as fast as she could, more arrows humming after her, clipping bits of feather off her wings and tail.

Thuds, shouts stabbed through the darkness. Arrows whistled by her, clipping away bits of feather, burning along her body.

She risked a quick look back and saw men piling into boats. Coming after her. Fool fool, she thought. What was I thinking? She drove herself harder, faster, climbing into the clouds, heading for the broad mouth of the Bay where it emptied into the Halsianel Sea. They wouldn't follow her there. Taking rowboats onto the Halsianel was even more foolish than exposing herself to men who smelled profit.

When she could no longer hear sounds from her pursuers, she glided downward in a long slant that brought her out of the clouds. The sea below her was dark and nearly invisible, except for phosphorescent lines of white foam repeatedly decomposed by the storm winds into ephemeral gleams rather like a scatter of glowworms across a patio in a late spring night. The incoming tide and those winds drove the rolling breakers high on the precipitous rocks of the seashore. She was *so* tired. Her wings were trembling and a haze thick as window-paper pasted itself across her eyes, blurring into an indecipherable muddle all the details she'd seen moments before.

More than once during her flight north she'd let the fear of the Follower drive her to the edge of exhaustion, but never so far as this. She had to find a perch — and soon — or she'd be sinking into the tossing water below. Ending up as shreds of meat in the bellies of a wreath of eels. Her wings faltered. Fear was icewater flooding through her.

Enough heat remained in the water to birth steady updrafts. Too exhausted to tilt a feather and direct herself toward the shore, she spread her great wings and rode the rising air south along the coast, not caring where she was going, unafraid of the Follower because he couldn't come out on the water; she could relax till she regained the strength to carry her to the land. It was too bad she couldn't stay out here forever, gliding in lazy swoops back and forth along the rugged cliffs of Nyddys's northern shore.

Cymel . . . A whisper from the middle of the wind . . . a name? Yes. Her name? That was the question. Or was it just a sound the wind made? Her head was too fuzzy to puzzle that out. Once again the whisper threaded through the wind, louder this time, more urgent. *Nordomon . . . you have to go there . . . cross the sea . . . now . . .*

The White Bird shuddered and cried out a harsh reverberating denial, at once refusing to acknowledge that any of the demands were addressed to her and that whispers in the dark had any authority to demand anything of anyone. Pinched by fear and prodded by defiance, she cried out once again, scraped up the fragments of energy that lingered in her muscles and fought the wind until she crossed the planted ground and sank clumsily into the brush and tall grass beyond.

Her flight muscles ached, her head swam with fatigue and fear. She was vulnerable on the ground, needing either a wide stretch of water or a long slope downhill to get her off the ground again. The huge, spiky clump of brush surrounding the bald spot where she'd half-crashed, half-settled was a measure of protection, but it was dry—and horribly dangerous because of that. If the Follower found her and wanted to kill her, he wouldn't have to push through the thorns; all he had to do was throw a torch on them and she'd most likely roast in the fire that followed.

She needed meat and water to power her flight, but far

more than that, she needed sleep. And she needed to forget the strangeness of that voice, the compulsion in it that almost trapped her. She opened wide her beak, gave a great but wholly silent shriek. The thick, tall brush with its tangle of little, crooked branches broke the worst of the wind, but her genetic blanket did a better job. She fluffed her feathers to fill them with the insulating air that would hold her body warmth close to her skin, tucked her wings about her and dropped deep deep into a dreamless sleep the moment she felt the first warmth flowing about her.

[4]

Breith swore as the striker broke and sent splinters of flint into his hand; the pain would have been worth it if the feeble flicker he'd produced had caught and started burning strongly, but the tinder was as sodden and cold as he was and smothered every attempt at a fire. And now the cursed striker was reduced to shards.

Reluctantly he released a minute blob of Pneuma, found a dry sliver of painted wood and coaxed it alight.

He'd been brooding over Cymel's terror whenever she felt him near. He was beginning to suspect his use of Pneuma triggered the worst attacks. The other things were valid — she didn't remember him, she knew he was after her, trying to touch her, and all the reasons he'd come up with earlier, but the smell of Pneuma sent her into a panic.

He'd discovered an abandoned shack with walls so full of vertical cracks it was more like a crate than anything meant to be lived in. An ancient chair, daubed with a malodorous varnish that had refused to dry, was broken apart and tossed into a corner, left there, he suspected, because the varnish had also refused to burn. He'd broken its pieces into smaller bits, liberally smearing himself with the varnish, arranged them in good burning pile, dirt-dipped patiently until he'd robbed several vole dens of their fluffy, dry nesting materials that he tore apart and stuffed into his pile, kindling to make the fire actually burn. Now, all he had to have was a match.

9

The House of the Spider

By the calendar of the Watchers of Glandair, events dating from the 1st day of Wythamis, the eighth month of the 739th Glandairic year since the last Settling.

[1]

Lyanz lay in the hay beside Amhar, kissing her, hugging her, loving her. She was hard and warm, and soft in all the right places, and all he needed right now. Gryf, Maratha Alaesh bless him and his for seven generations for having stolen the beefer cart from his friend, the Gamewarden, had said, "If you're gonna roll in the hay and sleep all day in it, you might as well hide in it too."

It made sense. Lyanz knew that he, with his Myndyar looks, was more than a little exotic for the Nyddys Maze, and Amhar, as an Iomardi Scribe, even more so. But Gryf, a skinny half-Rhudyar boy on the edge of manhood, leading two beefers and a cart piled with hay and assorted basketry, didn't warrant a second glance in the Maze. Everyone was smuggling something here, and with winter on, no one much cared if it were wine or carpets or simply an empty load of assorted straw that would be used to cover other goods on the way back from the Trivon Tangle.

And so, for over a week, Lyanz had been able to make his love nest with Ama, curled in the straw like two mice hidden away in a wall for wintertime. Lined with blankets and feath-erquilts — praise Gryf for acquiring these somewhere as well — the nest was as warm as anything and twice as secure, at least in its illusion.

The warmth inside and the cold outside were at once a drug and an aphrodisiac. Lyanz didn't want the moment to end, or to have to remember where he was or what he was supposed to be doing. The sight of the dead Watchers kept coming back again and again. Haunting him. Taunting him. Accusing. Ellar's twisted and broken body. Mela losing her form to feathers and talons. And far beyond all that, his father, his drowned father, looking at him through the murk of the sea and guilt-memory and sneering: "So, this is the Hero, eh? This is the hope of two worlds? A lazy slugabed, lying in the straw with his personal whore while his friend does the work and carts his ass to safety? Pfah! A poor second choice is what you are, Lyanz, and what you'll always be. Would that I hadn't pushed your brother away and been forced to settle for you."

Lyanz squeezed his eyes tight, willing the taunting vision to go away, but even massaged by the hardness of the boards and the smell of the feathers and the rocking of the hay with Amhar there in his arms, he couldn't banish the dream-image.

Amhar's hand came up then, feeling his face, wiping his tears away. "Shh," she whispered, "you're crying. What are you thinking about, Laz?"

He squeezed her tighter. "Just how much I love you. How glad I am that you're here...." A lie, a truth. What she needed to hear, what he needed to say. Anything but the pain of memory.

She kissed him then, full on the mouth, and Lyanz forgot for just a second, just a half a second, transported by the sweetness of her touch. He wanted to forget. It just wasn't fair.

His father was right. He was a poor second choice. If Kyo hadn't left to become a monk, if the other boys hadn't died, he wouldn't have to be the Hero.

Hero—Hah! That was a laugh. He could use a sword well enough, but only because the best teachers on two worlds had been willing to do everything for him, even die. Die to save him, when he hadn't done anything to deserve that.

Ellar's mutilated corpse then appeared, twisted and ash-blackened, silently accusing, another phantom summoned by the darkness amid the hay and the glancing bits of light that came through it with the winter sun slanting through the straw.

He didn't know why it was him, or had to be. *I'm nothing special*, Lyanz thought. *The Watchers said I had no magic, that I was "empty," and that made me special. But all that means is that I can sense magic, feel the echo of the Pneuma when Amhar works it when she fights, sense it in the weavings of the Watchers. I can't do it myself, not even touch it. Why should anyone so ordinary be needed? And why can't I go home even once this is done?*

That was the most awful bit of it—Gryf, his friend; Ama, his lover. They might both love him, be risking everything to try to help him, but they were also trying to kill him, as surely as the Mages were.

Well, not as surely, not quite the same way, but close. The Mages, Ellar had said, just wanted to kill him so they could take the power of the Empty Place for themselves. Ama and the others . . . well, Ellar had tried not to talk about it, but Lyanz had overheard enough of the Watchers' conversations at the Vale to know what was in store for him. Once he made it to the Empty Place, he would somehow, he wasn't sure how, balance the power of the two worlds, complete the time of the Settling, and then . . . cease to be.

Perhaps not exactly. The Watchers had talked about some form of spectral existence, rather like a god, or ghost, but something better and transcendent. So they said. Half of it was myth and theory, the other legend and conjecture, and the third part, the hidden bit left unspoken, Lyanz feared, was that they didn't know what would happen, only that according to all the records, the Hero ceased to exist, at least as such.

Then again, the Mages wanted the Empty Place, and that meant there had to be something to recommend it, likely a great deal of Power and control over the Pneuma, even if he did lose what he was.

Which might have been fine, except that Lyanz didn't want it. Any of it. He wanted Ama, and the ability to walk with her into Kurrin House and show her to his mother, take a little of the regular everyday responsibility that his father's death and his brother's leaving had left in their wake.

Except that wasn't his lot. His lot was to be the "Hero." Whatever that was. The Watchers' writings and speculations about it were maddeningly vague. The Hero must go to the Empty Place to restore the balance of the two worlds. No one could give him any assurances that he would even exist, even as some sort of god-thing, after he had reached his goal, that nothingness-echo that was drawing him, and did whatever it was he was supposed to do.

It might, Lyanz feared, be nothing more than a convenient lie. The whole quest for the Hero might be nothing more than an excuse to get some fool with the right lack of magic to step into a vortex of Pneuma and obliterate himself in exchange for saving both Glandair and Iomard.

But that was the trouble. If both worlds ended, he would still be dead anyway, without even some strange ghost-existence as consolation prize.

And all he wanted was Ama and this one. That shouldn't be too much to ask for anyone. . . .

{ 2 }

Anrydd stood with his men, bespangled with sequins and wearing a codpiece in the shape of a vicious horsehead, a bustle behind him for the horse's rear, with little false legs at his side so that his true legs could serve as the forefeet for the horse. His sword was sheathed with tinsel and golden foil, making it appear a gaudy prop, but its truth would be revealed the moment it struck. The rest of his men were garbed the same way, the merry bandits from a child's tale. They pranced about the fringes of the garden, while inside his half brother Isel and his wife sat in a royal bower listening to a woman read poetry while onlookers wept.

Isel had gone on procession for this? Anrydd could hardly believe it, but then he could hardly believe that the man was his brother. So pale, so weak, and what's more, mad. But at least he hadn't gotten it from their father.

However, now was not the time to strike. An honor guard stood on both sides, and while their swords were as gilded as his own and far less falsely, underneath the gilding they were just as sharp. Isel might have exposed himself, but only so much, and it was only thanks to the Festival of Masks that Anrydd and his men could get this close.

But if they just watched closely enough, an opening should present itself.

[3]

Lyanz dozed, drunk in the stupor of afterglow. Amhar was warm beside him and curled around him, her hair soft between his cheek and the featherquilt, with the rustling of the straw and the swaying of the cart around them. He wanted this moment to go on forever.

Unfortunately Fate, and Talgryf, had other plans. Light suddenly flooded into his and Ama's mouse-nest. "Wake up, children, we've arrived!" Gryf jerked the featherquilt back and there was light, blinding light, and air, and green, green everywhere, as if they'd suddenly been transported into the middle of a giant emerald, held up to the sun.

Lyanz squinted, holding up one arm to shield himself from the glare, but sat up. Ama came with him, not quite as sleepy. A light breeze was blowing, foggy and damp, bringing the scent of salt and mud and the sulfur-stink of decaying plants, and strangely, of sugar and some form of spiceroot, steam from a bake-oven somewhere.

Ama shook her head and rubbed one hand across her face. "Where are we?"

Gryf responded with a chuckle. "The Trivon Tangle. Get that straw out of your hair, Scribe—you look like Hot-to-Trot Maggie at the end of the Beefer Faire."

Amhar raised herself all the way out of the hay, her bow alongside her. "A man would be beaten for speaking that way to a Scribe back in Iomard." She paused. "Maybe here too."

Gryf just snorted and shook the reins. "The way you've got yer skirts hitched up, Ama, looks like you'd be beatin' a lot of them then. But who knows? There's some that'd pay extra for that."

Ama snarled and adjusted her skirt, causing Gryf to chuckle again. "You might want to change your hairstyle too,

Scribe, unless, like I said, you want to attract a few customers."

"Watch your mouth, thief."

Lyanz's eyes began to adjust, and he saw Gryf perched in the driving box of the poacher's gray driftwood cart, shrugging. "Suit y'self, Ama. Just a little advice. Don' hafta take it. We're in the Trivon Tangle is all, an' if y'ain't sellin' somethin', best not to put it on display."

Lyanz licked his lips and glanced about at the towering green Pole Trees and hanging vines. "Are we safe?"

"Safe?" Gryf snorted. "It's the Tangle—'course we're not 'safe.' But if you're wondering if anyone'll care about a blonde Myndyar and an Iomardi Scribe now that we're here? T'teeth! It's a Bog Town, the grandest of all of them. People are used to foreigners, and even more used to masks, if you want to cover yourselves up." Gryf chuckled then and waved one long-fingered hand, picking the pockets of the air. "In fact, you might want to cover yourself too, Laz—you're hanging out."

Lyanz realized then that while he'd gotten to his knees in the cart, his trousers were also hanging down around them, the drawstring long ago done away with. He quickly fumbled about, getting his pants up, looking to see if anyone had noticed. A swatch of yellow-gold amid the green—a girl in a cradle-swing hanging from one of the balcony-arms of a spreading Pole Tree, perched like a weaver bird in her nest, gave him an appreciative glance and a bird trill as the cart trundled past. Lyanz felt his cheeks grow hot, and tried to knot drawstrings that weren't there, in the end simply holding his trousers up with his hands as he got to his feet in the back of the swaying cart.

Amhar glanced fiercely at both him and the girl, then set about pulling straw from her curls and trying to erase the effects of having made love in a haystack for a week. Lyanz then looked over the edge of the cart, down the banks of the raised levee they were riding the crest of, and up at the reaches of the spreading Pole Trees rising from the swamp, and took in what Gryf had called the Trivon Tangle.

It didn't appear much different than any of the other Bog Towns they had passed by, until he realized they were on the outskirts. The houses he was seeing were merely the procession of poorer homes and shops that had set up along the main road, like a receiving line of lesser dignitaries before meeting the Emperor.

As the beefers plodded on, the dwellings became grander and grander, going from small huts with green sod roofs and red selaflowers growing in their windowboxes to stilted houses with wide verandas and isinglass screens to marvelous mansions woven from the Pole Trees themselves, one grafted into another with vines supporting or festooning the rope bridges that went from the roadside to where they stood out in the bog, and with bubbleglass as green as the leaves set into the trunks themselves, done in diamonds between lattices of meticulously grafted twigs and shoots. Sapphire and crystal wintermoths floated above the weed-checked water, occasionally alighting on the snow-edged petals of a swamp lily and unfurling long logic-curled tongues to sip the nectar from the center, like Nikawaid merchants sharing a bowl of scorpion liquor at the close of some intense trade deal.

They then came to the edge of the levee, and the splendor that was the Trivon Tangle became readily apparent. To their right was the Halsianel, as wide and gray as a widow's prospects, with small spots of sunlight shafting down from gaps in the winter clouds. Across from them and to their left were more of the Pole Trees, ancient as the lineage of the Chusinkayan Emperor and just as interlocked, edging both sides of the river as they came down to the sea, with rope bridges and vines and their own spreading branches weaving them together in an ancestry tangle impossible to see the beginning or end of. In between the Pole Trees, in water smooth enough to be the shallows but evidently deeper than it appeared, were ships tied up with vines, the long low smuggling sloops and river barges of the Maze, quaint little junks and fishing boats from up and down the coast, trading ships from Faiscar and Tilkos and Kale, and even the form of a Myndyar merchant ship from Nikawaid, as Lyanz had set sail on so many years ago.

He felt a tear come to his eye, remembering his father, remembering his dream-father's words, and felt renewed guilt that the beauty of the Tangle was something he could never share with him. The Pole Trees and the houses built into them and around them were a wonder. Almost equally marvelous were the stilted lodges, swaying back and forth in the shallowest of the shallows. Lyanz recognized with the Pneuma-echo in his heart that these things were enchanted, or at least the bases of them were, the dwellings built atop loading platforms that Pneuma-work could make to flex their legs and move slowly through the swamp like a wading bird.

Or a water spider.

The House of the Spider. That's where Gryf had said they were going, in the short breaks when he'd slipped them out of the straw to feed them or give them a few minutes in the dark to stretch and relieve themselves. Lyanz, dreaming in the hay with Ama, had imagined a great many things of the Trivon Tangle, but nothing like what he was seeing now.

"The House?" he asked.

Gryf pointed and Lyanz looked to see a platform, larger than any of the others, climbed into a nest between three Pole Trees sharing balcony arms high up to become one, like a water spider bracing itself between three reeds, camouflaged with flotsam and jetsam to appear nothing more than a random dab of mud and dead leaves. But the House of the Spider was more than that, the same as a water spider was more than the collection of muddy leaves it appeared. Ropes came up and down with vines, like a spider's webs, and Lyanz saw that with the arrangement, the house could pick up or drop cargo onto a ship that sailed beneath its trees, or even lower itself onto the deck for the spiderhouse itself to be taken to a new lair.

"That's where we're going?" Ama asked.

Gryf nodded. "That's it. Let's hope they haven't sold us to the Mages already."

[4]

Oerfel soaked a rag in sweetwater and laid it across his eyes. They were so tired. So very tired.

But there was work to be done. He repositioned a mirror, gaining a better vantage on Anrydd and his men, then surveyed Isel and his wife, then Firill in the basement of the Arts building, her face a mask of mixed composure and grief. He believed he could lay a fairly easy finger on her thoughts; her lover was dead, and she was too busy preparing for production of his last work to be able to attend the memorial service.

Of course, the memorial service was a sham, meant more to gild the Tyrn's dignity than to actually mourn the dead, but Oerfel had to admit it was a political masterstroke. He repositioned Isel's mirror and looked at the Tyrn's face. More clever than he first appeared, or at least gaining the cleverness that came with the instincts of a jackal. He'd been waiting all his life for his father to die, and he'd turned that to his own advantage; now the same with the bodies of Lauresa and the Mole.

So many things to pay attention to. So many things happening at once. And all under the nose of the Watchers, what ones were left alive, anyway. Most of those left at Cyfareth were the old and infirm, unable to make it to the slaughter at Caeffordian, or else the young and untrained, students as befit a university. Though the greatest concentration of those seemed to be about Firill, and he watched as she had them place mirrors about the basement of the Arts building, mirrors arranged in very familiar patterns. Oerfel laughed. Dig, dig, dig, little Mole. Gylas Mardianson may not have been a Mage, but he was not above using a Mage's tricks. Oerfel looked at the arrangement of the mirrors, meant to be empowered by a Watchers' meld, if they could find enough Watchers, and the heap of gray velvet that was the Moleskin.

Puppetry. They meant to use the Pneuma Flow for puppetry, having it fill and animate a sack of velvet, which would then dance about and narrate the play, taking the part of the Little God Mole. Oerfel didn't know whether to be shocked at the perversion of power to such frivolous ends or intrigued by the technique. A little of both, actually, but what was more shocking was that the velvet puppet was embroidered with Mage signs. The circle upon the left wrist gave an accurate estimation of the passage of time, and the sigil upon the brow was equally familiar, but a great many more of the signs were new and original. He wished he had the cloth to study right now, but it was folded neatly on the podium in the center of the stage, and most of the signs were obscured. But in a few hours, all would be revealed as part of the performance.

Oerfel also wished he'd thought to bring something to eat, perhaps a bag of the puffed salted grains they sold on the street, but he didn't dare lose a minute of this. He whispered to his mirrors as the students hung their own, tying his to theirs and trickling in a thread of Pneuma Power with one of the Mole's own techniques. Not a full Watcher meld, just a bare touch, with the Pneuma leaping across the gap like a spark jumping from finger to metal after walking on a wool rug.

After all, everyone watching the performance was expected to lend something, and Oerfel didn't see why he had to be the exception. He wanted this performance to be a success as much as anyone, if not more so.

[5]

Isel's gut was clenched in a knot. There was something wrong, he knew it. Everything was going too well. The Procession had gone without a hitch, not even a horse throwing a shoe, and the memorial service was likewise perfect, or at least as perfect as such things could be. Fallorane had collapsed to the ground, weeping, to be comforted by the likewise weeping Court Poet. Isel had had to rub his eyes till they stung to generate the requisite tears.

They were still smarting, though now from the smoke and bitter herbs piled about the feet of Dyf Tanew, the crippled god. Isel stood up at the right places, sat down at the right places, and let priests stuff whatever herbs in his mouth they needed after his tasters had already taken communion and hadn't turned blue and died. His wife had begged off the midnight mass, as conspicuous in her absence as he was in his presence.

It was almost a relief when the bottles were tossed in the door and shattered, vomiting flames across the pews.

Isel reached for his sword. Haggers. They'd be waiting outside the doors with swords of their own, and there was little trouble guessing that they'd be targeting him.

The smoke, however, would soon be choking, with no chance of putting it out. Flaming oil and wood were a dangerous combination, and even a battalion of priests yanking down tapestries and desecrating them wouldn't be able to smother it all. All they were doing was fanning the flames and causing them to spread. One priest's cassock caught fire, and he ran screaming down the aisle.

The preponderance of the Royal Guard, however, had gone with the Tyrna, for what harm could come to one in the Temple of Dyf Tanew? Stupid. The Haggers would slaughter him the moment he got outside the door. Regardless of this, the guards, in brave stupidity, flanked around him and tried to move him to the main entrance. "Clear the way!" He waved toward the doors. "I'll follow."

He didn't. The doors, of course, were barred from the outside, and while the guards had the sense to use one of the nonflaming pews as a battering ram, that would still just be a trivial obstacle to the assassins outside. Isel grabbed a priest by the arm. "Side exit? Where?"

The priest took him behind the altar and down a passage. "This way, sire." Isel followed, ripping the crown from his head and stuffing it into his sleeve. Haggers, damn them. They'd be killing the priests just as easily as him. Then again, the priests didn't have swords. He grabbed the priest by the arm, stopping him for a moment. "Cassock—where?" The man looked blank and dull. Isel shook him until his eyes cleared.

"Here." The priest threw open a wardrobe in the hall and Isel pulled out a cassock about the right size, shrugging it over his head as they ran down the passage. It was the Night of Masks, after all. He'd dispensed with his, so as to show devotion and contrition and whatever else the Gossips might desire, but he'd happily take it all back up if Dyf Tanew wasn't going to stop this.

The priest threw open the side door of the vestry and ran out, only to immediately be gutted. Even the scream was abbreviated.

Isel reached for his sword, only to find the cassock in the

way. The swordsman stepped through the door, grinning beneath a half-mask with the face of the devouring Hag over his own, three rows of teeth shining in the torchlight as blood dripped from his sword to the floor. "Where's the Tyrn, priest?"

Isel grabbed the edge of his trailing sleeve. "Here!" He whipped it toward the swordsman, the crown giving it weight, and caught the man in the side of the head. He dodged aside, knowing where the sword's blow would come, and jumped out, dragging the door shut behind him.

He stood for a moment, his weight on the handle, all that stood between him and the murderer within, then saw another half-masked Hagger wearing the crone's devouring maw over his head, but with the mask pushed up for better vision, her teeth a jagged fillet across his brow. The man smiled. "Isel."

Isel looked at that face, a barbaric version of his own, and a younger version of their father's, like the one he'd worn after he'd bedded a new conquest. "Anrydd."

The man inside hammered on the door, screaming his rage. Isel stood, holding death back with both hands while waiting for it to come from his brother's. "So, is this how you'd imagined it?"

Anrydd laughed. "Not quite. I thought it more likely that you'd get as far as that tree over there, then I'd kill you and take the crown from your head." His eyes flickered with reflected flames. "You don't have it, I see."

Isel smirked, glad to have a moment's malice. "One of my men is wearing it. He's making his way out the front, dressed in my robes."

"I'll have it then."

Isel gave a bitter laugh. "If you can trust your own men. After all, some are in the direct employ of your master. They'll bring it directly to him, so he can wear it as Tyrn after he deposes you as a filthy pretender." The Tyrn tasted the bile in his throat. "Oh yes, I know all about the Mage. Do you, dear brother?"

Anrydd took a step forward, threatening, but Isel made his decision. He released the handle of the door, then turned his back toward it. Almost as if by sorcery, a moment later, Isel saw the sword's point emerge from his chest.

"No!" roared Anrydd.

Isel then felt the pain, and the blood on his lips, and he knew himself for a dead man. "I can deny you this much, half brother," Isel gasped, choking blood, "but the Mage . . . he will deny you more. . . ."

Isel fell to the stone outside, across the body of the murdered priest, and felt the tines of the crown poking into his leg through the fabric of cassock and shirt.

Oh yes, dear brother . . . I can deny you this much. This much, and possibly more. . . .

[6]

Something was deeply, and not very subtly, wrong in the Trivon Tangle. Gryf had spoken the passwords and made the signs that gained them entrance to the House of the Spider, and they were welcomed with all proper pleasantries and inquiries as to the health of his dying father. But while the beefer cart was fenced, and quickly, for far more gold than it was worth, passage by sea could not be bought for money or love of money from any of the captains drinking doolybrew at the tables of the greatest of the Tangle's smuggling houses. Gryf tried wheedling. He tried pleading. He even thought to try extravagant cheques drawn on the accounts of Kurrin House, of which Lyanz was still the ostensible heir.

Nothing.

Talgryf was beginning to contemplate the love angle, but

while Ama might bear a passing resemblance to Hot-to-Trot Maggie, he didn't think the Scribe would go whoring herself even to save two world. Then again, Laz was more than good looking enough, but somehow he didn't think that pimping the Hero was what the Watchers had in mind, even if he sold Ama and Laz together to enterprising captains looking for an exotic threesome.

In any case, sex wasn't love. Sex could also be bought in the Tangle, far more cheaply than the money Gryf had to offer. The trio of Pole Trees the House of the Spider was nested in were in fact the Three Sisters, the most famous (or infamous) Houses of Discretion in all of the Maze. While they didn't have a Hero on their boards, they had just about everything else, along with prices. The going rate for discreet companionship was still generally less than the price for smuggling three people across the Knuckle at the start of winter.

The captains' excuses were always the same, with the overly smooth and apologetic tones of something rehearsed beforehand. The Halsianel was too icy. Winter had come early. The Hag had been seen dancing across the surface of the Knuckle, shaking her withered charms at Dyf Tanew and inviting him to come get a piece of them.

Only the last of these did Gryf even half believe. The Halsianel was no more icy than it usually was this time of year and, in fact, perhaps a bit warmer than it might be. Boats could still go in and out of the harbor mouth, but all he saw enter or leave the Tangle were small junks with their catch of fish.

Tanew's Teeth and the Hag's Dugs both! He'd have to get to the bottom of this, or they were stuck. Laz would never get to the Empty Place.

Gryf saw to it that Laz and Ama were nestled in one of the private bowers of the second of the Three Sisters, which catered to affairs and trysts and those who'd already secured their own companionship. After all, he'd already provided the twosome a cart filled with straw, he might as well give them a private bower with a gilded bath and hope they took advantage of the second. After their week in the cart, they were both as rank as a pinkbelly that had flipped itself out of the river a week back.

Gryf walked down the wooden stair molded into the inside of the Pole Tree, avoided the inquiries of the madams in the lobby, and stepped out through the curtain of teardrop beads to the dock outside.

The night was cool and damp. A short distance away, a crowd of gondoliers stood about gossiping, their discretion masks tilted up atop their heads like visors. Lit dragonreeds dandled from their hands, the tips glowing in the night. Occasionally, the gondoliers sucked on the reeds, exhaling clouds of perfumed smoke.

Gryf tried eavesdropping on their conversations, but the gondoliers were too well trained and too discreet. Things that were said inside the Three Sisters or the House of the Spider were not discussed outside of them, or at least not this close.

One gondolier noticed Gryf's glance and came toward him, her river skirts showing traces of beading and gold brocade. "Pleasant evening, sahib. Would you be needing transportation?" She said this with a practiced obeisance, skirts held wide, head bowed, her discretion mask falling down into place with the motion, displaying the fierce fish-toothed visage of some nameless river god, likely her family patron.

Gryf had been itching to relax into his city self. "That'd depend on the price, good lady."

She smoothed her skirts, calling attention to them again, and Gryf saw they were embroidered with an intricate map of the Tangle. "Expertise does not come cheaply."

"No, it doesn't," Gryf allowed, then set into bargaining.

The woman offered him a few puffs on her dragonreed, and Gryf declined. When they settled on a price they could both live with, Gryf then took the remainder of the smouldering reed and sucked on its perfume-spiced smoke as the woman poled her skiff away from the dock.

The prow was carved into the same fish-toothed deity as her mask and glided through the water with the ease of an ancient god. Laz and Ama would likely have something to say about Pneuma-work, but it wasn't Pneuma-work that got Gryf the price, nor was it magic that taught the gondolier her way through the Tangle, around the poisoned knees of the Pole Trees, and through the swiftest shallows to take him to the Watermarket.

The Trivon Watermarket was second only to the Bothrin of Tyst in the quantity of wares for sale and the quality of goods, and as with all such things, surpassed it in many ways. Most notably, where the Bothrin was based on cobbles and stone, with market stalls to duck about and run behind, the Tangle's Watermarket was a collection of boats moored up in a wide shallows, as smooth and flat as if the Hag had sat Her great behind down there and crushed the Pole Trees flat, leaving nothing but a tangle of roots and knees that were covered with water at all but the lowest tide.

Here and there, spider platforms held the somewhat more permanent stalls, but as with the Bothrin, the best goods were from the small sellers, who spread their blankets in the bottoms of their small shallow boats rather than on the cobbles of the street.

Come night, the whole was lit with candlewood torches, or the clear light and almost intolerable stench of burning oilfish. Gryf puffed on the reed until it was spent, and instructed the gondolier to pole from stall to stall, from old aunties selling home-baked nut tarts to peddlers with boatloads of scrap to boats selling shiv-wood spits with dozens of frog legs, doused with an assortment of sauces and roasted to your liking. He went about, tasting and sampling and picking up the occasional supply. All the while, he listened to the gossip, recalling the sense of the Bothrin and knowing from the sound of it where to slip to and where to slip away from.

At last, Gryf lingered around a boat where crawling mud-pinchers and swamp snails were plunged live into boiling water, their shells turning from azure and green to brilliant crimson and pearl, then smashed with hammers and the meat eaten with shiv-wood tongs and spiced nut butter. It was a delicious meal, and more than that, an excuse to down pints of Trivon glog, guggle-muggle made from fresh cream and doolybrew, with the expected results. Tongues loosened and began to wag at both ends, like a child's wood-and-ribbon toy snake.

Gryf ate lots of mudpinchers, but barely touched the glog, listening instead as the sailors and merchants and drunk market wives told the story: The Hag might have been sighted over the Halsianel, but the far more immediate danger was the fact that the various pirate crews were being impressed or bribed into the navies of whatever nation was closest, and likewise the merchant ships that strayed too close to either end of the Halsianel. A bad time for the smuggling trade, and a worse one for possibly being thought disloyal to the Tyrn or whatever other ruler held sway over your home port, especially the Princes of Kale. Safest bet was to dock early for winter and blame it on that and the Hag if the Tyrn's men or any other strangers came asking round the Tangle.

Gryf downed his glog then, but was mindful of keeping his tongue still. They were trapped here. Trapped in the Trivon Tangle for the winter, by the simple practicality of the smugglers and the machinations of war.

No wonder the Hag was shaking her withered assets all over the Knuckle.

[7]

Afankaya and her ladies entered the theater, robed as maidens from the Festival of the Little Ones, bearing fan-masks painted with cheerful dollfaces, the silk oiled to translucency such that the owner's face could be half-seen beneath the painted features. The owner's faces were yet again painted to look like dolls for an extra surprise once the fan was moved aside. It was a pretty conceit, and all the more pleasant after the endless dreariness of her husband. Sneaking out garbed as little girls on their first day of school seemed the order of the evening. Face-paint and fans would allow a range of vision that masks would not. And Afankaya did not want to miss this for the world.

The Tyrna was vaguely annoyed, however, that Tana, her husband's new Court Poet, had refrained from dressing as part of the doll ensemble, instead taking on the raiment of the Mourning Tyrn from the old tale of the same name. But the Mourning Tyrn, the Doll Tyrna, and her bevy of Doll Maidens — it all had a pleasant symmetry to it, after a fashion, and she supposed that even for the Festival of Masks she couldn't expect Tana Mardiandattar to wear anything out of keeping with her deep and abiding sorrow for the loss of her brother.

Afankaya did her best to not think of the eulogy from that afternoon, which had brought her to tears, not for the loss of Tana's brother, of course, or poor Lauresa, but for the simple beauty of it and the loss of her maternal grandmother years before.

If I die
Take this ring
And remember
A circle is unbroken

What once was
Will be again
A ring that is turned
Will hide its stone
But it is not gone
Only hidden
What once was
Is
And will be
Again

Maudlin sentimentality, but Afankaya felt the tears threaten. Damn Tana's poetry! She'd wanted to go as the Doll Tyrna, not the Creator Hag—a costume all too many of the University students seemed to favor. She took a white kerchief and dabbed at her eyes, catching the worst of it, then turned to the handmaid to her left. "My eyes?"

The girl looked, her own makeup the perfect face of a Doll Princess, her visage different only from the Doll Tyrna's in the hatch-marks of innocence above the eyes and the lack of the stars of rank on her cheeks. "Just a touch, my lady."

Afankaya knew it was more than that, but let the girl quickly get out her powder and makeup brush, borrowing the Tyrna's handkerchief for a moment to remove a smudge. Maudlin sentimentality, that was all. The girl retouched the Tyrna's makeup, then snapped her compact. "Perfect, my lady."

Afankaya nodded, then went back to looking about the theater, stealing glances past the edge of her fan. She would place it totally in her lap once the show began, but it was far more amusing beforehand to play the flirtation of the Night of the Masks.

A woman stepped forward, dressed in a gown of crystal spangles with a long train hooked to her left wrist for gesture and ease of motion. Her hair was braided up and pinned high, arrayed like spokes of a wheel with long silver wands from which depended strands of more crystals, obscuring her face like the fall from the central bowl of a fountain. She curtsied low, the train brushing the floor. "My lady."

Tyrna Afankaya did the schoolgirl's giggle she'd been practicing: "Tee-hee! I am the Doll Tyrna!" Her handmaids tittered in chorus behind her.

"And I," responded the crystal-spangled woman, "portray the Pneuma flow."

The Mourning Tyrn leaned over to Tyrna Afankaya behind her fan. "Firill Gylasleman," Tana said. "The playwright."

The woman bowed her head. "One half the playwright," she corrected, and Afankaya decoded the other half of what Tana had said—*Gylasleman*, the lover of Gylas. Or the widow of Gylas.

The Tyrna looked at the woman's costume. The flow of the Pneuma. Or a fountain of tears. Either interpretation might be correct. On impulse, Afankaya pulled the ring from her finger. "I understand it is the custom here for each viewer to contribute something to the production." She proffered the ring. "For you."

"My lady . . . you have given so much already."

Tyrna Afankaya shrugged. "My jewel box is not yet empty. And you and Tana have lost so much more. As she said today, 'Take this ring and turn it . . .' "

Firill reached out and closed her hand around the ring, with the other cupping the back of the Tyrna's hand as she went down on one knee in a cross between a gesture of obeisance and a clasp of heartfelt thanks. "It shall be worn tonight. . . ."

Afankaya noticed then the ring that Firill wore already, large and beautiful, yes, but made of crystal and silver, barely a step above the stage prop it was meant for. The white gold and sapphire confection Afankaya had given her replaced it magnificently, and the Mourning Tyrn said, "It suits you well, O Pneuma flow." Tana reached into her sleeve then and produced a scroll. "I offer this poem of remembrance."

Firill took it. "If it is the one from this afternoon, I know the place for it."

The Mourning Tyrn nodded, and then there came a chime of bells. "But a minute," said Firill. "We shall start very shortly."

Afankaya waved her fan in a gesture of dismissal, then held it up again as the mask of the Doll Tyrna. "Tee-hee! You may go, O Pneuma Flow!"

Afankaya thought she saw Firill smile, beyond the oiled silk and the fall of crystals. "Another poem. You are too kind, my lady." The crystals tinkled as she departed, and Afankaya heard stringed instruments and woodwinds start up as the playwright departed. The lights were dimmed, the lantern shutters turned so that only pinpricks of light were released, and the tune began, sweet and ethereal, not quite touching on a single melody and all the more intriguing for it.

"In the beginning," spoke a voice.

"There was naught," said another.

"But the Pneuma flow," said a third, and then came silence, all except for the voice of a single flute and a chime of crystal bells. Then all at once, Firill appeared. Or really, her dress did, ten thousand sequins all lit from within with Pneuma-fire, the sapphire ring Afankaya had just given her glowing blue in a sea of white lights.

A single stringed instrument, high and light, joined the flute, and the two began an ethereal interplay as Firill danced, only the crystals and the ring visible. Then a harp joined the flute and strings, and the third voice, an old man's, came from the direction of the harp. "The Pneuma danced between the worlds, between Glandair and Iomard." As he named the worlds, a clash of cymbals punctuated each. To either side of the stage huge ricepaper screens with maps of Glandair and the unseen world of Iomard lit up with phosphorescent fire. "And from Her dance sprang the gods, and from the gods sprang men, and somewhere between it all, no one knows where or when, there sprang forth the little gods!"

With a clash of cymbals and a dazzling explosion of Pneuma-fire, strange creatures and monstrosities burst through the ricepaper screens, glowing purple and blue and pink with the Power of Pneuma and no doubt some phosphorescent alchemical powders, giggling and tee-heeing like a whole classful of Doll Maidens bursting through the doors after the first day of school. One monster, shaped like a large green insect, bounced in front of Tyrna Afankaya. "I am the Little God Bug!" it announced. "What will you give me?"

"I will give you *this!*" Afankaya snapped and tried to slap the impudent actor with her fan, but the Little God Bug, or at least the actor who portrayed him, just grabbed her fan and ran off with it, holding it up before his face and announcing, "Look! Now I am the Doll Tyrna!"

"Who is the Doll Tyrna?" asked other of the little gods, and Afankaya realized that much of the play was extemporaneous and interactive. The little gods sang. The little gods danced. The little gods sawed one of her handmaids in half as part of their quest for the missing Little God Mole, who some of the little gods thought might have been swallowed by the Creator Hag. Not finding a Creator Hag in the audience, they went for the next best thing, the Doll Tyrna, until Tyrna Afankaya volunteered her handmaid in her place, accusing her in a loud tee-heeing voice of being the Mole-eating Creator Hag.

Afankaya had seen women sawn in half years before, on a childhood trip to the markets of Tyst, but here it was made all the more amusing by the actors and the sparks of real Pneuma that flew when the sides of the box were pulled apart. However, as a difference, once they put the box back together, they reached in to give her a hand out, only to have the top half of a woman fall out onto stage, minus the lower torso.

There were gasps, one of them from the Tyrna herself, but then one of the equally shocked little gods picked up the upper torso and shook it around, stuffing falling out of the middle as it was revealed to be a woman-sized doll dressed in the robes of a Doll Princess. A large hamper that had been sitting across the stage all evening began to vibrate and cry, "Let me out!"

The little gods rushed across the stage to the basket, revealing Afankaya's handmaid, unharmed. They then shoved her back in the basket, denouncing her as the Creator Hag, then took out long swords and rammed them through the basket. When they removed the swords and opened the basket, they found nothing more than a bunch of clothes that they began to pitch across the stage. Afankaya's handmaid sat up, rather bewildered, from the forgotten saw cabinet.

Then, suddenly, one of the items they had tossed from the basket, a shapeless sack of gray velvet, stopped in midair, suspended. It slowly inflated, like a balloon, then came to rest on the stage, standing in the form of a comical mole embroidered with an astrologer's sampler of sorcerous patterns. The Little God Mole put its mitten-paws to its lips in a gesture of silence, to both the audience and the handmaid, miming for them not to alert the other little gods, then helped the girl down from the table and quietly led her back to her seat.

Tyrna Afankaya was able to get a good look at the Mole, indeed a puppet animated by sorcery, hollow but for Pneuma shining out of its crystal eyes like stars. A dangerous trick, especially at this time of the Settling, but the theater was more delicious for that. The Little God Mole danced about the room, a magic clown, appearing and disappearing from one place or another as the needs of the plot demanded, the little gods having council meetings to find him and not noticing that he took the part of the servant behind them. Then they spotted him once and led a hue and cry, chasing about the theater to catch him only to have the Mole circle around behind them, joining the posse.

The Tyrna was doubly pleased by her choice of masquerading as the Doll Tyrna, since it made it quite reasonable for her and her handmaids to giggle like schoolgirls and shout, "There he is! There he is!" whenever the Mole sprang up in a new place.

At last, the little gods were ready to admit defeat. They had not found the Mole, though he was right under their noses, and since they could not find him, they had to conclude that he either never existed, or else he was dead. At which point the Mourning Tyrn stood up, Tana the Court Poet, dressed in the black feathered cloak and tullin-beaked mask from the children's tale. "You are wrong, foolish godlets. That which is remembered is not dead. That which is desired cannot die. Look around yourselves and feel the Pneuma flow. Entire worlds are separated by less than a bee's wing. In between those worlds lies every possibility that the mind's eye can imagine." Tana gestured grandly as Firill's dress winked alight again. "The Pneuma awaits. You have merely to turn the ring to reveal the hidden stone."

"How very nice," said a voice then. "Time to die, children."

Tyrna Afankaya looked. There, standing in the stairway from the hall above, stood a man, sword bloody and unsheathed, his face masked with the visage of the Hag, her teeth a jagged slash across his cheeks, her tresses a long nest of matted raffia.

"Go," said the Mourning Tyrn. "You are not welcome here, ancient one."

"I'll tell my self where I'm welcome," said the Hag, and in three steps crossed the room and ran Tana through with the sword.

Afankaya saw the sword, and the blood, and gasped, then calmed herself. It was just another trick, a conjurer's ruse enhanced by the true power of Pneuma. But then she heard the scream of agony, a scream she'd heard before when men had dueled before her, and she knew it was real, though she hoped beyond her certainty that she was wrong.

And then, unreal, the conjurer's velvet bag that was the Mole puppet appeared and interposed itself between Tana and the Hag as the swordsman drew his sword back for another strike. "Try that again with me. . . ." The voice was odd and musical, as if coming from a very far distance.

The Hag's man laughed. "Gladly." He plunged his sword into the Mole puppet, but it did not come out the other side. Instead, it plunged in up to the hilt, as if he'd encountered nothing in the strike but empty air. Around the rift in the fabric shone light as the swordsman fell *through*. Then he was gone.

And the Mole reached to the back of his neck with his now real claws and slit the fabric-fur, pulling forward the mask to reveal a face very like Tana's, a man who could only be her brother, Gylas Mardianson. The murdered Mole. "Life for life, flesh for flesh, 'tis done," he said, then turned around, holding a hand pulsing with Pneuma over the wound in his sister's gut. "Get her a medic!" he cried, then, "Smash the mirrors! All of them! And bar the doors!"

"Mole," breathed the Mourning Tyrn, "you're alive. . . ."

"After my fashion, yes," the Mole said, "though that's more than I can say for you if you don't hold still and let me hold this wound."

Around her came the sound of crashing glass as the lighting mirrors were shattered. The Mole smiled at her. "Tyrna Afankaya, I presume?"

The Tyrna nodded slowly, feeling the chill of shock steal across her cheeks. "Scholar . . . Gylas?"

He nodded in return. "Thank you for your patronage. I don't think the play could have been such a success without it."

{ 8 }

Oerfel watched, hissing as bolts of Pneuma shattered his mirrors, the last at a look from Gylas Mardianson, that damnable Pneuma researcher, somehow come back from the dead, the Mole's last remark, he knew, aimed as much at himself as Tyrna Afankaya.

Oerfel watched the last of the mirrors shatter and cursed, more than half certain he'd seen Mardianson wink. Damn the man! Now that Oerfel had seen the play, he could understand the import of it all. A full Watcher meld—and then some—of the best and brightest Cyfareth had to offer. Plus the Power of a Mage—himself!—funneled into it. Plus little bits of otherwise trivial witchcraft—the blood of an elder sibling, the willing sacrifice of a man's life, the fool swordsman who dropped himself into the rift between worlds where Mole's consciousness had been floating, disembodied, since the Siofray Mage had toasted his body.

Oerfel thought and surmised. Mole's half-step, the oblique way of stepping behind the Flow. Use that in conjunction with the old seer's technique of divorcing the mind and consciousness from the physical form, becoming an independent consciousness in the Pneuma Flow. Not much of a consciousness, honestly—it would take a great deal of cleverness just to keep the mind together, especially over such time—but with plans set into motion before one's death that could lead to one's return . . .

Oh, clever. Very clever.

Oerfel realized, however, that the next gambit was his. Just as he'd revealed his existence to Mahara and Hudoleth when he was powerless without their aid, so had Mole revealed himself to him. Not honestly and forthrightly, no, as Oerfel had with Hudoleth and Mahara, but then again, if he could have snookered those two the way that Mole had just hoodwinked him and Tyrna Afankaya, he would have done it in a heartbeat.

What to make of him, though. A Mage was a Mage because of sheer power, yet a Mage became successful via subtlety. Of the Mages, there was some question who might have the most raw power. Mahara? Possibly. Hudoleth? Certainly in the running. The Siofray Mage? An unknown quantity, but capable of frying a man to ash with a thought. Yet if such Power were all that it took, well then, that freakishly talented Watcher's daughter, Cymel, might very well have outshone even Mahara if the Siofray Mage hadn't burned it all out of her head. Though that happy eventuality was at best wishful thinking. From a realistic standpoint, she'd been wounded, at best. Once she'd had time to heal, she'd probably be back, more dangerous and more troublesome than ever.

Subtlety was something he'd thought he'd had everyone beat at, hands down, Hudoleth included. But now Mole had taken a seat at the table, where before there had only been three Mages, then four Mages, playing against each other and the Watchers' Council of Cyfareth, with the impudent child Cymel occasionally coming in for a hand to disrupt the flow of the game.

Oerfel shuddered. The scope of the game had just become mind-achingly complex.

Mole had taken the prize for subtlety by manipulating Oerfel—him, Oerfel, who had fancied himself the master-manipulator—into helping to orchestrate the ritual that brought his consciousness back from the matrix of the Pneuma Flow. And if he recovered Cymel. . . . Tanew's Teeth! He'd sat there nibbling salted grains like it was a puppet show put on for his amusement. Not only that, but Gylas Mardianson had snookered not a few of the Watchers' best students, and a few Watchers for that matter, into lending him the power for his little trick.

And what was the Watchers' Council going to think of THAT? Ellar had been too paralyzed by pointless vows to do anything but sit by and watch as his wife was murdered. What might they think of someone resurrecting the dead, right there in the heart of Cyfareth University, and billing it as an evening's entertainment, a comedy no less?

Oerfel imagined all the remaining Watchers dying from spontaneous apoplexy and the image gave him brief pleasure. Suffice it to say that while Gylas Mardianson may have been one of their star pupils, he'd quite obviously graduated beyond the scope of the teachings of Cyfareth University. And the Watchers would be opposing him, the same as any Mage, if they weren't mostly dead or scattered.

That, however, was another matter. Oerfel was quite pleased that Anrydd had successfully sacked the University and killed Isel, even though he had not recovered either the crown or Tyrna Afankaya, two tokens that would make it all the easier to secure the Throne.

And Mole had the Tyrna, and likely the crown. Damn! If only Oerfel knew what the man's game was. Every Mage was powered by an aching need, an insatiable hunger. The only drives he'd sensed in the man were a desire to amuse himself and others, as well as a healthy dose of curiosity. Yet since Mardianson had never before done so much as kill one of Hudoleth's sacrificial birds, Oerfel had concluded—most likely falsely—that he didn't have the drive it would take to compete in the Mages' game.

Was it possible for someone to need to be liked so much that they turned the grand game of the Mages into nothing more than a popularity contest? Was there now the bastard Mage of Curiosity or Popularity or some other bizarre childish need competing in the game? Or was Mole to be classed as some new breed of player, not Watcher—since he was certainly not content to just watch—nor Mage either, not having the requisite Power. But with subtlety in such measure, it was necessary to classify him, if just for peace of mind. Oerfel could not abide disorganized files, and the only thing he could stand less were items that were deliberately mislabeled. Like Mole. Harmless Pneuma researcher my ass! Better to call him something else. Master Sorcerer. Mastermind. Archmage. Manipulative sneaky little bastard who should have had the decency to stay dead!

Fact is, Mole, like Cymel, was something new and unclassifiable, and unlike the Mages, he and Cymel could play as a team. She had the power; he had the subtlety. Together, they were more dangerous than any single Mage or even the fractured Watchers' Council.

Oerfel clutched his temples and gritted his teeth. Ignorance truly was bliss. Or at least knowledge of what he was now up against didn't make the game any easier. To tell Hudoleth and Mahara and the Siofray Mage, or to keep this extra dimension of the game between Mole and himself?

It was a game of subtlety now, a true Mage's game. Hudoleth and Mahara knew of him, but did not know his identity, or even his name. Mole knew both, there was very little doubt, as he knew both of Mole. Were he to betray Mole,

Mole would betray him, and they would both fall to the more powerful Mages. An alliance? Not out of the question, but Mole no doubt had his own goals and would not be inclined to share.

And what end was Mole playing toward? Aiding the Hero, or taking the Power of the Empty Place for himself? If the latter what would he do with it?

10

Hudoleth's Troubles

*By the calendar of the Watchers of Glandair, events dating
from the 11th day of Seimis, the seventh month of the 739th
Glandairic year since the last Settling.*

[1]

In the cool of the evening, the Syntayo returned. Hudoleth's
patience was stretched as thin as the skin of her knees against
the courtyard's stones. Yet she maintained the courtly inclination of her head and the demure angle of her mirrored fan.
"The task I set you has detained you beyond my expectations,
O Syntayo Ayneeros. I am hoping that the answer you have
brought me is worth this additional delay, for much wisdom
is useful only as it is timely."

The Syntayo sighed, a breath like the creaking of the fruit-
laden branches of the plum trees above. "So very true, O
Mage. Yet wisdom becomes more useful as it is complete.
Weighing the halves of the equation, it is only now that I felt
it proper to appear and present you with an answer that this
one dares but hope might be to your liking."

Hudoleth straightened, rubbing her knees where the

chains of the power-suit had pressed. "Please do not delay any further, O Syntayo. I am most eager for the answer . . . as I am certain you are eager to be released from my second question and your third service."

The Wisdom shimmered, like the air above an alcohol lamp. "That is so, O Mage, and as such, here is your answer: The Emperor is not to be touched with magic, at least not by yourself in this present time. The frayspell gift is too powerful and too subtle. It could be destroyed, but at great cost, even to a Mage such as yourself, and certainly not without alerting the Niosul and thus the Emperor. The Emperor's family gift is but a small fire of Pneuma, yet a bright one, burning like a coal in the ashes, smouldering, yet slowly kindling all other magics that it touches. The charms of your succubi are all but spent. He will tire of them in a few days' time, and it will require greater and greater magics for you to amuse him in this manner."

Hudoleth's lip curled in distaste. "This is the wisdom you bring me, O Syntayo? This message of despair and futility?"

The Syntayo shimmered, laughing in its strange way, but added, "Yes, O Mage Hudoleth. I bring you a message of futility in your current course of action. The coal that burns with magic cannot be held long with tongs of wood. However, wooden tongs may hold tongs of metal, which may in turn hold the coal."

"And if the coal heats the metal, which in turn burns the wood?" Hudoleth inquired.

The Syntayo breathed out its wispy laughter. "What does it matter, so long as the hand maneuvering the metal tongs positions the coal to her liking?"

Hudoleth rolled her eyes; this was the problem in dealing with spirits—always too pleased with their own cleverness. "I tire of speaking in riddles, O Syntayo. Please be kind enough to reveal your wisdom in plain words so I may properly appraise its worth."

"Of course, O Mage," breathed the Syntayo. "I speak of one simple gambit, with two possible variations. The first could be accomplished with relative speed, gaining the Mage the desired goal in the short term, that of a return to the University and her studies and privacy there, yet this variation would by its very nature introduce complications into the Mage's later life. The second would be more costly in the short term, both in time and investment, but in the long term would, in the opinion of this humble spirit, profit the Mage greatly, and could even, if worked carefully, subvert the frayspell Gift by setting its Power against itself, or even put the Power of the frayspell into the service of the Mage."

Hudoleth nodded, even though she still did not hold the answer. "I must admit I am intrigued, Syntayo. Tell me of this gambit, beginning with the simpler form."

The translucent spirit floated in the air, the branches of the plum tree behind it distorted by its substance, like an image viewed through rippled glass. "The first gambit is quite simple and apparent after an examination of the facts and mortal nature, O Mage Hudoleth. The Emperor is of middle age, bordering on old. While the Lizomo Knot has turned aside his remembrance of the renewal of your youth, the attractions of youth are still there, though by the same token, so is the flattery of the wisdom of age. Were he to take a new bride or concubine who would be a match for him in temperament, yet younger so as to be dependent upon his experience and thus flattering to him—an attraction that neither you nor your succubi could provide, yours being an illusion spun from lies and flattery, as opposed to an enticement with a crystal of truth at its heart. However, once such were arranged, while the Emperor would still feel quite se-

cure in his hold over you, his new paramour would fear you
as a rival and so would put all her cleverness and wiles to
working against you. Not to destroy you, for being a clever
young woman she would rightly fear the retribution of a
Mage were any drastic action to be taken, but to simply use
her newfound influence with the Emperor to have you sent
back to the University, using her wiles thereafter to keep you
out of fashion and off of any guest lists to courtly functions."
The Syntayo shimmered, not quite a laugh, but a giggle, like
an impudent schoolgirl. "This whole matter would be given
added urgency were she to carry the Emperor's child, for she
would then fear both for her beauty and for what effect the
presence of a Mage might have on her firstborn."

While Hudoleth had many problems with the spirit's attitude, she could find no flaws with the Syntayo's reasoning. A
clever rival for the Emperor's affections—which she wanted
no part of in the first place—would do much to keep her
away from Court, and more than that, could manipulate the
Emperor with no use of magic whatsoever. And were that
rival to get with child, well, that would indeed give added
impetus, allowing her to leave the Court in a matter of
months.

But still, a complicated matter on the whole. "And this you
say is the simplest arrangement of the gambit, O Syntayo?
What of the second, the more elaborate?"

The Syntayo shimmered. "The second depends upon a
small fact this humble spirit was able to discover after long
study of the history of the Emperor's family—the sole weakness in the frayspell gift: The royal family of Chusinkayan are
not immune to their own magics. A careful study of history
as well as the scent upon the bones of the ancestors will bear
this out. However, aside from the frayspell, none of the current generation are sorcerously gifted, let alone Mages, and
so the weakness does not apply. Manipulating any of the

royal family against the Emperor would be impossible or unprofitable, for many reasons, depending on the individual in question, and ultimately futile since the time it would take to school such a one in the ways of magic would be a poor investment. None are inclined to sorcery, and even those who might have a shred of aptitude would not have the slightest interest. However, I speak only of the current generation, and it might be possible to ensorcel the Emperor by means of one as yet unborn. Indeed, were this individual one who combined your flesh with that of the royal line of Chusinkayan, then that child would be as susceptible to your magics as the Emperor would be to his or hers — or even to yours, were you to take the child's will for your own and use its body as a sheath by which to slip your own magics past the Power of the frayspell gift."

The Syntayo shimmered, another schoolgirl's giggle. "That, of course, is only the magical advantage of such a child. In the mundane world, the chains of affection that rein a child to each parent can be tugged both ways. Even before such a child could be used to work magic, it could be used to manipulate the Emperor with bonds that have little to do with the workings of Pneuma. Indeed, if it were male, such a child might even become Emperor in due time, leaving the Mage in a highly advantageous position."

An Imperial bastard, that's what the spirit was saying, and not just any Imperial bastard — hers. The thrice-damned Syntayo was coyly winking at the suggestion that she get herself knocked up by the old lecher, then take at least a dozen years fighting it out among the other Imperial wives and concubines to get her child to the Throne. As if her only path to power lay through the door of the Imperial bedchamber!

And yet . . . there was a certain excruciating logic to all of it. The Emperor desired her for her beauty as much as her power. If she were the crone she'd seen in the mirror, all the horses in the royal stables wouldn't be able to drag him to the bedchamber, even without the frayspell gift. But with a child of her body to snare his heart, and her face to snare another organ entirely, it might be possible. Or, as the simpler option, she could just let him be caught by another woman and her child, that other woman becoming the rival who would send her from the Court, just as she wished, though in the long term that would become quite a problem, since the Syntayo intimated that whoever that new favorite might be would become, if not Empress herself, then at very least mother to the next Emperor of Chusinkayan, the beloved of Sugreta. And having the dowager of the Empire as an enemy would be more than inconvenient, even if she were to seize the prize in the Empty Place, since an Empress could cause troubles for even a god.

This matter bore considering. The Syntayo's logic was good, even if it left certain realities unspoken. Perhaps, with enough care and delicacy, she might gain the best of both of the gambit's foldings.

There came a sighing from the silver circle opposite her. "This one is tired, O Mage, and hopes you will consider this one's services at an end, hoping beyond all hopes that the answer is beyond your expectations and this one will be free from summonses for the thousand years you promised. However, if the answer is merely adequate, this one will understand if the period of grace is only one hundred, though begs the Mage to say otherwise."

Hudoleth inclined her head and gestured with her spangled fan. "The wisdom you have shown is sound, O Syntayo, and more than adequate, but not the facile and easy answer I had hoped for. Which is to say, my expectations have been met, but not exceeded, and as such, I would not feel right granting you the full thousand years." Hudoleth touched the fan to her lips, tapping it for a moment. "However, I believe

I will split the difference and grant you a grace period of five hundred years. Would that be acceptable to you, O Wise Syntayo?"

"The full thousand would be even more desirable, O Mage."

"Yet not deserved. All that are owed you, O Syntayo, are the simple hundred. Do not test my generosity as you have already tested my patience."

The spirit sighed. "Five hundred years are more than generous, O Mage, and this one accepts your beneficence, regretting as it does that it could not have given you a more munificent and prompt answer to your inquiry."

Hudoleth bowed. "Then perhaps the revered Syntayo might keep that in mind for the questions I may ask it in five hundred years' time." She waved her fan in dismissal, chanting the words of the banishment: "Ja ayara. Yah ida hanuur. Ja da, Syntayo, aya! Syntayo, ayara. Ja da, Syntayo. En no Konofa, ja da!"

The air shimmered and the Syntayo was gone. Hudoleth folded her fan and tapped it against her lips, considering the wisdom of the Wisdom and the possibilities it had presented.

[2]

Despite the fact that the boat was seaworthy, small enough for three people to sail, large enough to cross the Halsianel Sea despite this, and poor enough that pirates and the Prince's sailors wouldn't give them a second glance, Laz and Amhar still complained. Mostly about the smell.

Gryf spat over the side in disgust. "So it smells like fish guts. T'teeth! Whad'ya expect? The Tyrn's own gilded barge?" He sputtered in exasperation. "Next time I'll steal that, and I won't hav'ta watch you two under a blanket pretend that yer not doing the dance of the slowworm."

"You're putrid," said Amhar.

"No, you are," Gryf shot back. "Next time I pack for the Tyrna, I'll remember to take extra mooncloths."

She hit him then, and Laz took longer to stop her than he should, being a friend. But he hadn't been much of that for a while, too busy being Ama's lover. "Do y'have yer men in the Domains wash 'em f'ya too?"

She hit him again, and this time with the boom. Gryf cried out as he was knocked overboard and went flailing in the sea as the boat raced off across the Halsianel. He screamed, getting a mouthful of water, and began to beat at the sea, the long fingers of the Hag starting to drag him under. He wondered if this would be the end for him, and if they were going to stop, or just leave him for the eels.

Problem was, even if they wanted to, Laz and Ama weren't as good at steering a boat as he was, for all that Laz had been on them before. But Gryf had been at the docks in Tyst, and at the taverns where the sailors came, and he'd been hearing the nautical talk since he was small, and so knew the meaning of tack and jibe, and from knowing the meaning to making the moves was just a long while of practice.

And all Laz and Ama had been practicing was the sex, which they'd been without since Ama's moontime had come upon her.

But swimming was another thing that Gryf had never tried, and unlike sailing, there was no forgiveness for not knowing how. The water began to fill his mouth and creep for his lungs, and he swore, the Old Hag was dragging him down to her dark garden, when suddenly she grabbed him around the throat and pulled him *up*.

His head broke the water and Gryf coughed and sputtered, struggling with the Hag and her claws around his neck.

"Quit fighting me, you idiot, or I'll let you go."

The Hag spoke with Amhar's voice, which wasn't entirely

inappropriate, especially since it was her moontime, but after she punched him in the ribs, he realized it was Amhar.

"Sorry. Now let me save your life already."

Amhar, as part of her Scribe's training, had been taught how to swim, and more than that, how to swim with a drowning man. With the crook of her arm around his neck, she dragged him back to the boat, then swam round to the other side and pulled herself in to counterbalance while Laz held Gryf and talked to him. "Sorry. Oh, Gryf, I'm so sorry, I didn't . . ." Then Amhar was in and Lyanz had the weight on the other side of the boat so that he could pull Gryf in without falling in himself.

Gryf was sputtering water as Ama and Laz pounded it from him until he signaled that he'd had enough and he held onto the mast while he coughed the last out. He turned round and looked at the two. "Y'know," he said, "in th'Bothrin, when summun saves summun's life, there's a big debt. But now . . ."

Amhar and Lyanz both looked at the floor of the boat with looks of shame. And at each other with longing.

[3]

It took two days of discreet inquiries and boring tea ceremonies to search her out, and another four to arrange a meeting that would not invite suspicion, but at last Hudoleth found her: Padmila, the daughter of the lily, whom the Emperor had bedded the night of the Festival of Fair Words three years before, the first year of Hudoleth's incarceration within the palace. She'd almost blotted the girl out of her mind, annoyed as she was at the continued impositions of the damnable Imperial Personage. Hudoleth was doubly annoyed at herself since the lily's daughter could have extricated her from this difficulty years ago if she hadn't been so prideful. Foolishness. The Emperor was like a spoiled child, pleased with the gift of a pretty toy but expecting a prettier and more marvelous toy every day thereafter. All it would take to content him would be the pleasure and familiarity of an old and comfortable plaything he'd long ago set aside and forgotten. Such as the daughter of the lily.

Of course, it appeared that the lily had given birth to a singrit, a gawky wading bird, for the girl was even taller and thinner than Hudoleth remembered, and like a singrit, she was not terribly lovely in her body, but beautiful in her movements, standing hesitantly before the door of Hudoleth's apartments, a smudged note on Hudoleth's personal stationary in her hand. "Scholar Hudoleth," she said, "to what do I owe the honor of this invitation?"

Hudoleth smiled, seeing the angle of the girl's head and the suspicious look in her eye; both signs of strong intelligence and an intuitive mind—fine qualities in a future Empress. However, Padmila was a flower of the Court, and as such, would only be able to interpret matters within her necessarily limited purview. "I have a proposition for you," Hudoleth said simply, inclining her head. "But come, let us not speak of this on the doorsill. Come inside and let me offer you tea."

The girl nodded, entering, and Hudoleth shut the door behind her as Padmila walked down the flight of steps into the gilded main chamber of the apartments the Emperor had presented her with. Her eyes started at the opulence, yet her lips remained closed, demurely refraining from comment.

"The Imperial Personage favors me," Hudoleth remarked, joining her, then added, "at least, for the moment . . ." She touched a pillar, letting a flame of Pneuma lick up it, lighting the gilded veining with a subtle fire and causing jewels in the dome to wink like whores in a teahouse. A student of magic would have recognized it immediately as a gaudy trick, an unforgivably garish at that, but to one unschooled in the manipulations of Pneuma, it had its desired effect: Padmila gaped in awe. Hudoleth knew that she'd kindled a fire of desperate envy and longing in the girl's breast.

Hudoleth lifted the hem of her reception gown and swept past her. "Spiderwort, moonflower, or plain?" she inquired, opening a drawer of her tea chest and startling Padmila back to reality as she let the flames of the envy-fire wink out. At least the magical ones. "Or do you prefer goldflake? I have half a cake from the Emperor's last visit, and his servants always bring more."

Goldflake, of course, was the Imperial blend, the compressed green cakes covered with gold leaf and stamped with the Imperial chop, with more flakes of dream-thin metal pressed in with the concentrated tea. The blend was reserved, upon pain of death, solely for the use of the Emperor and those he chose to favor with the Imperial pot during Court functions. And, of course, the Emperor's wives and mistresses. The remains of a cake of it was almost payment for an assignation.

Padmila looked quite crestfallen. "It has been years since I have tasted it."

Hudoleth smiled. "Then it is high time you tasted it again." She took out the cake and carefully shaved off slivers with a silver knife, warming and washing the pot by hand as she set about the duties of hostess. "Please, by all means, make yourself comfortable. I won't be but a moment."

Out of the corner of her eye, she watched as the girl sat down, bringing out a pad and pencil, and began to sketch with swift sure strokes. An artist as well as a poet. Intriguing. Hudoleth was sure more than ever that she had made the right choice for this gambit, but simply went about her task of the moment, carving apple slices and arranging them into an attractive fan and selecting cakes and wafers from their lacquer chest with an eye toward conveying a message of friendship rather than the opulence of an Imperial mistress. The goldflake was more than sufficient for that.

At last it had steeped sufficiently. Hudoleth took the tray to the low table and set out the delicacies as Padmila gave the last flourish to her sketch, then turned it around. "My gift to you," said Padmila, presenting a startling likeness of Hudoleth, and very flattering at that. "I am sorry it is so humble, but I know not what else to give such a noble Scholar as yourself." The undertone said, *What do you give the witch who has everything?* Mixed with that a threat. Image magic was always potent, and while the girl hadn't a whiff of a Pneuma-talent about her, she was clever enough to know the stories, and would therefore know that her sketches would be of use to any witch or Wizard foolish enough to work against Hudoleth. Magics of this sort were often contracted to sorcerers outside the walls of the Palace, and as such, many nobles never left it for fear of ensorcelments left waiting for them just outside the range of the Niosul.

"My thanks," said Hudoleth, taking the portrait. "I shall treasure it always." Which she would, actually. Portrait magic worked both ways, and could be used to affect the artist almost as easily as the subject. And when the subject was a Mage . . .

"You are too kind, Padmila. You do not know what this means to me." Hudoleth smiled, holding the portrait to her breast. "But let me go put it in my workroom so I may contemplate it later."

So saying, Hudoleth did, setting it in its proper position among her birds and mirrors, retrieving as she did a basket of plums, including one particular plum, carefully and specially prepared. The ritual had involved a drop of the Emperor's seed, caught beneath her fingernail during one night's assignation, her own menstrual blood, and an egg torn from the body of a mother tickbird before she laid it in an ouzoet's nest, forcing the silly ouzo to raise the ticklet as her own. Chants and sorcery had combined her blood with the Emperor's seed, the charm of renewal restoring her own to viability, then introduced them to the tickbird's egg, around it wrapping the flesh of a plum, full and sweet and bursting with juices.

Hudoleth set that one at the top of the pile, then returned, placing the plums on a table to her left, out of Padmila's reach, a simple and elegant second course for their meal. She then arranged the skirts of her reception robe and poured the tea, turning the talk to Court pleasantries and matters of little consequence, at least so far as she was concerned, though evidently they meant the world to Padmila. An Emperor's one-time mistress who had not conceived a bastard was an uncertain quantity; she no longer had the cachet of her virginity to recommend her to other men, and while there were enough Imperial presents to make up for that lack as part of a dowry, there was also a very strong possibility that she might be barren—and for another man to get a child on her, whether as mistress, wife, or concubine, would be to intimate the scandalous possibility that the Emperor had become sterile. Moreover, the girl, as Hudoleth had found in her research, was too well connected to be banished from Court or sent to a far province, though not so well connected that she couldn't simply be relegated to the hell of the unfashionable, excluded from all Imperial functions save those that required the maximum number of warm bodies to present a spectacle, and given the most modest lodgings that the Palace could offer, making her a mere step above a serving maid.

Oh yes, she had desire. Hudoleth saw it in her eyes. Desire strong enough to make her willing to take on a Mage. But in the silly and meaningless game of Court politics, something Hudoleth wished she could just concede immediately. But that, unfortunately, was not the way the game was played.

Hudoleth lifted her cup to her lips, taking a long sip of the bright green flavor that was goldflake, and composed her words carefully. "Yet we have been talking of mere pleasantries, and there is something more important I wish to discuss. I have a proposition for you, Padmila. One that I hope you will be open to." She watched the flecks of gold dancing in her cup like lanterns reflected in a stream, calming herself so she could speak the most believable lie she could. "I am afraid, you see, that I may soon lose the Imperial Favor. Oh, not all at once, mind you, but by degrees, slowly. The Imperial Personage is . . . how do I say this without sounding disloyal? Well, let me simply say that the Beloved of Sugreta is a complex man, with his mind on many things, and it is a difficult task for even a woman with sorcery at her command to keep his attentions for long. I have spun fire spirits into flesh and he has had his fill of them, and he has tasted what I have to offer as well. And, were he to grow sufficiently bored, he might even send me away from Court—after all, I do not have the connections of family that you have, Padmila." She patted the girl's knee in a sisterly fashion. "But were I to have a compatriot and advocate here, speaking for me, then I would never find the Favor too far from my hand." Hudoleth took her hand back and raised the cup of tea to her lips, curious as to what the response to this lie might be.

Padmila inclined her head. "I believe I follow what you are saying, Scholar Hudoleth. But why do you come to me? Many women in the Court are much more liable to attract the eye of the Emperor, compared to one such as I, who has already felt the touch of . . . the Imperial Favor . . . yet now has lost almost all hope of finding it again."

Hudoleth was dumbstruck, but hid it as best she could. This silly little singritling was actually in *love* with the Imperial Personage. Even in his youth he could not have been such a stallion as to warrant *that*.

Then again, the Emperor had been Padmila's first, and only. Combine three years of privation with a schoolgirl crush and you could create a driving desire that even a Mage could respect. Hudoleth could hardly believe her luck—this would make it all *so* much easier—and she was ready to let the Syntayo have the full thousand years of reprieve so long as she didn't have to tell him about it.

Padmila valiantly kept tears from crashing down, most likely having cried them all years before, after Hudoleth's first use of her as decoy. "I do not think the Imperial Personage even gives me a second glance, especially when compared to all the fresh new flowers of the Court."

Hudoleth patted the girl's knee again, and gave it a squeeze in consolation. "That is so. Yet all of those women would also seek to have me set aside. I believe that if an old favorite were reintroduced at the right moment, we could, as an act of sisterhood, keep the attentions of the Emperor far longer than either of us might individually." She set her teacup on the table with a definitive tap of porcelain, then leaned back and steepled her fingers. "In fact, I believe the Emperor may visit tonight."

Padmila paused and swallowed. "Here?"

Hudoleth gestured to each side, with a wave of her silver-edged nails. "Or perhaps not. The Beloved of Sugreta, as I said, is a complex man." Or, to be more accurate, an easily distracted one. There was more than half a chance he would not take the bait as she had laid it—mention of a desire to see him away from the prying eyes of Court, made with a wave of the hand and a flutter of lashes—for like a mog-kitten, he was prone to chasing after butterflies and trailing robes. But it was still a fair bet.

"Even so, I expect him." Hudoleth reached one hand languidly down to the specially prepared plum. "Would you care for a bit of fruit? These are quite sweet and juicy, grown right here in my private garden. I'm afraid we've finished the last of the tea."

Padmila nodded, her mouth no doubt gone as dry as a well beneath a witch's curse, and Hudoleth tossed the plum to her. She caught it, biting into it, and the bright juices dribbled down her chin, till afrighted that she might spoil what looked like her one good robe (and not very fine at that), she stuffed the plum whole into her mouth.

Hudoleth gestured, sealing the spell, and Padmila swallowed on reflex, the plum, the blood, the tickbird's egg and the Emperor's seed at the center. "Oh dear," said Hudoleth, "did you swallow the whole thing?" Padmila nodded and Hudoleth whisked the cloth from under the teapot, quickly wiping Padmila's face with the tea-damp linen. "My, my. You seem a girl of amazing talents. I'm quite surprised that the Son of Heaven set you aside."

Never mind the fact that the virtues of a girl who could swallow whole plums would be lost if all you had was a shriveled prune. "Well," said Hudoleth conspiratorially, "maybe not surprised."

Padmila blushed and managed a giggle, and Hudoleth joined her, feeling like a schoolgirl or a Syntayo overly pleased with its own cleverness. But she felt the laugh was well deserved.

[4]

Brother Kyo walked with the Myndyar army, searching each face for the face of his lost brother. When last he had seen him, Laz was still a boy not yet full grown. He would be a man now.

Kyodal did not know whether Lyanz would be taller than him, or shorter, or a mirror of his own form in all but subtleties. The onset of manhood was an odd thing, taking one boy months and others years, early for some and late for others, with no set schedule except for a family, and even then, having many exceptions. Though Lyanz had been a tall boy for his age, just as Kyodal had been, he could have sprouted up to far greater height, or stayed where he was, or gone anywhere in-between. Would he have a beard yet? Would he shave? Would he have gone bald as a youth, as one of their uncles had, or have slightly thinning hair as Kyodal had himself before shaving it all off and joining the Maratha Order, making the foregoing of vanity a vanity in and of itself?

It was often hard to fathom the visions of Marath Alaesh, but Brother Kyo believed he fathomed this one. Though a monk, Kyodal Kurrin knew he was still a child of a rich trading house, and his own vows of poverty governed neither his father, now dead, nor his mother, who had always been an extravagant woman, and would not be above letting word fall to some of the elder monks that she preferred her eldest son to remain with his duties at the Temple, safe and sound during wartime, rather than go to tend the wounded of the Myndyar army, as so many other brothers and sisters of the Maratha Order had gone off to do.

Family was family, and while Marath Alaesh frowned on many things, He smiled on others, and one of them was a mother's love for her child. Even if Marath Alaesh knew best.

It was a simple scroll to pen: After the death of their father, Lyanz had likely either joined or been conscripted into the Myndyar army. One monk alone at the Temple polishing icons made no difference except for his own safety. Whereas one monk out in the field tending to the wounded would save many sons and many brothers.

Possibly even his own.

A hundred times it seemed he found Lyanz, and a hundred times he was wrong. Sometimes his heart broke with sorrow that he was wrong, when he noticed a look, a glance, a laugh or other passing resemblance that reminded him of the boy he had helped raise, taught to climb trees and sing songs and peep at the maids when they shed their shifts in the wash-house. Sometimes his heart surged with joy, and a terrible guilt, when he saw a face among the dead, or dying, or horribly wounded and thanked Marath Alaesh in his heart that it was not his brother.

It was an unworthy thought, but Brother Kyodal did his best to tend each man as if he were Lyanz himself, washing their wounds, placing the steamed cloths fresh with tea and healing herbs to the Pneuma-burns, making the gestures of the final rites, and closing each eye with a kiss and a blessing sign.

Each time, they thanked him. Voices rough, voices soft. Deep with manhood, or light as a boy's. Brother Kyodal realized that he didn't even know now what Lyanz's voice would sound like. It would have changed. It must have changed. Yet he was always surprised by how little relation the tone of the voices had to the men who held them. A huge man thick with muscle could have a voice light and high as a girl's, while the wisp-bearded boy next to him had a rich basso tone deep as a Temple gong.

Brother Kyo couldn't even use his. His vows were upon him, of silence and patient works. He wondered if his voice had changed at all over the years, and if he would even recognize it. Or would it be like his memory of Lyanz, faded and perfected with fondness to something that bore no resemblance to the cruelties of reality?

Kyodal wept as he failed to save another man's life, wishing he had spent more time in the classes in the healing arts rather than praying at the Temple and polishing icons. But he was practicing now, and if his prayers and polishing had led him here, then it was as Marath Alaesh wished it and he could not protest. Not without breaking his vows.

Once he had reached the army, the ball icon had become lost. Brother Kyo did not know if its purpose had been served, or if it had just passed into the hands of one who needed it more. It was miraculous, but so many things in this time of the Settling were. War magics abounded as well, terrible things darker than the darkest imaginings of the Dark Gods. Burns that festered with living fire. Worms that spat acid and burrowed into flesh. Poisoned incense, pink as a courtesan's blush, that brought sleep with a scent of rosepetals and a choking fever from which the mind seldom returned, and never returned intact.

Only men could be that misguided, or stray that far from the way of peace.

Brother Kyo continued his work, and was rewarded, or at least broke even: The next man lived to thank him, at least for the moment, staggering off to join his comrades, promising to bring Brother Kyo a bowl of steamed grain. Kyodal made the blessing sign and felt the tears for those he had not saved begin to flow down his cheeks. His silence would not let him give voice to his pain, not one word or wail, and at last he folded himself into a ball and rocked back and forth in the meditation posture of Marath Alaesh, waiting for the next who would need him, hoping for the strength to go find them himself, praying that his brother Lyanz would not be among the dead and the dying, and that their mother would have at least one of her sons come back to her.

Filial piety was not a sin. Since he could not pray for himself, he prayed for their mother.

[5]

The combined forces of Kale and Tilkos behind them, Mahara rode in the Third Prince's palanquin, watching as the mist-smoke of their Serpent gods moved on either side.

Rueth, winged Dragon-Serpent of Kale, rode the winds to their left over the Halsianel, rippling and resplendent as the green and gold pennants and puffed sails of the Royal Navy of Kale streaming below. While to their right, over the main force of the army, the Dark Wyrm of Tilkos undulated across the sky, Its opalescent eyes blazing, ocher-flame dripping from Its mouth. Enemies now made allies through war and conquest and magics as old as man and woman both.

The same might be true and would be true of Cypresta, Goddess of the Merchant Skirts, rising above and behind the Faiscar capital of the same name with all the bland composure of a market woman seated at her stall, ready for a very hard bargain with two extremely difficult customers. She rose high into the air, the vanes of her golden crown alight with jewels, an image formed of light and mist and reflections from the gilded spires of Her city. Trade bangles of silver and gold adorned each arm, glittering with the metal of rooftops and railings. Diamond plugs twinkled in each ear, winking like the windowpanes, and feather charms hung in Her hair, fluttering like the flocks of wild colo who nested in Her eaves. Above and between these hung either the sun faded in the mist, or else Her right eye squinting through a jeweler's loupe magnifying that eye thrice as great, giving her visage a glare as fierce as the jewel-eyed serpents facing her.

Yet even this was not the most awesome vista of Cypresta. Below her ample bosom and her scapulary of coral and pearls were the Merchant Skirts for which she was famed, a patchwork composed of hundreds upon hundreds of pockets, each a different color, each holding a different secret, a different treasure, a different price. Indeed, the lower edge of Cypresta's skirts mixed with and became indistinguishable from the houses and shops of Her city, the gaily painted buildings forming checks and diamonds, row upon row up the hill, with streets like beaded trim. Mahara could not be certain whether the crest of the hilltop were the city's peak or the goddess's knees, or whether there might be any significant difference between the two. Balanced at the summit was a gilded colonnade that was either the façade of Cypresta's grand trade hall, or the edge of the deity's personal accounts ledger, her hands laid atop it, cool as a market woman ready to make a deal.

She was going to deal now, or die.

In mimicry of their goddess behind them, or perhaps the other way around, the Merchants' Council of Cypresta had set up a long table and benches on the bluff overlooking the Halsianel, shaded with an awning of elegant patchwork silks and gilded bunting, looking for all the world like the judges' booth from some market fair held outside the city walls. Indeed, Mahara suspected that this was exactly what the raised dais and pavilion were from, too fine to have been scrimped together for a war parlay, too gay to be truly appropriate for a peace settlement.

The Faiscar Merchants were decked out like their goddess, arrayed with jewels both real and paste, their guards in matching livery in their Guild colors, rich velvets and fine satins slashed with snippets of dyed fur and reptile skin. Faced with both the Dragon of Kale and the Dread Wyrm of Tilkos, some seemed to realize that this might be a *faux pas*, and Mahara saw one woman remove her rich golden serpent-skin gloves and place them in her belt pouch, leaving her hands unadorned save for liver spots and elegantly painted and jeweled nails.

The Third Prince gestured and the Royal Palanquin of Kale was set down before the table, becoming, as it was designed, a small portable pavilion. The Prince's slaves, all dark Rhudyar like Mahara himself, scurried about, putting up blocks and making it level so that neither Zulam nor Mahara, nor either Inlirre or her sister, had to touch the Cypresta's ground.

The Third Prince had thought it best to bring his new bride with him, for show if nothing else. Since the death of her elder sister, she had hardly spoken a word. Mahara was unsure if this were shock or reticence, since the youngest sister, Frantki, who'd been brought along as equal parts protection and threat, had never ceased to shut up. That one seemed cut from the same mold as the dead Jesmuun, with the same defiant tilt to the head, though at least she had the sense to keep her constant chatter down to a continuous whisper. Mahara paid it no more mind than the buzzing of beetles in the grass.

He wondered if killing the eldest sister had been a miscalculation, but didn't think so. The type that had pride would always try to plot against you, no matter how pathetically, and once her maidenhead was shed, she was as useless as a seed-cherry whose stone has been stolen. Good riddance, with the added benefit of it helping to keep her younger sister in line.

The next youngest sister, at least.

Though essentially nothing more than a farm girl, Inlirre had polished up nicely as a child bride, wearing gauds and silks they'd looted from Kar Markaz, likely the stash of a few courtesans and royal mistresses. Such women generally had the best clothes, dream princesses often looking the part better than the true ones, and though Inlirre had likely never dreamed of having such finery to call her own, she betrayed no illusions about her true role. Indeed, the girl had the glazed look of a beefer calf, washed and smoothed in a buttermilk bath with a blue ribbon tied around her neck preparatory to being brought before the judges' bench. The same judges would praise her one day, then eat her the next, once the fair was over and their only use for the fair calf was a platter of thin-shaved *carpaccio* drizzled with nut oil and vinegar to snack on in between courses of wine and pickled fruit.

The Merchants of Cypresta did, indeed, look very much like the judges at a fair. Mahara wondered how good their judgment would be, and if he would need to kill any to make a point. Possibly none. Cypresta, the goddess, had a hard and practical look about Her, and so did Her townsfolk, at least the ones selected to face them.

One man rose at the end of the Merchants' table, wearing a green velvet doublet with matching emerald lip and ear-plugs. Gilded hooks tied with fine green feathers looped through the flesh of his eyebrows, giving him a perpetually surprised expression. Mahara didn't know whether these were markings of his Guild or fashion accoutrements, though he suspected that if the man were thrown off the side of a boat and dragged across the Bay of Cypresta, he'd come up with at least five pinkbellies on his face.

"I am Swindeho, of the Fishermen's Guild, Ranking Guild of Cypresta." Beneath the gauds and feathers, the man was too young to be the ranking Merchant. Mahara guessed that, at best, Swindeho was the Guildmaster's spoiled son or ne'er-do-well nephew. All of the Merchants at the bench looked too young or too old, and therefore expendable, though there was likely enough wisdom and audacity between the two extremes to beat a hard bargain. "I, Swindeho, welcome you to this parlay table, in hopes of finding an amicable settlement to our anticipated difficulties."

"I am Zulam, Third Prince of Kale and Farmyn of Tilkos," said the Third Prince, easily sliding back into courtly attitudes and graces, "and this is my new bride, Princess Inlirre of High Tilk, who has brought me her forces and god as dowry." He gestured with his riding-crop, making a few high Rhudyar flourishes that likely the Cyprestan Merchants found just as incomprehensible as Mahara did himself. "What are these difficulties of which you speak?"

The old woman with the liver-spotted hands and painted nails chuckled lightly. "Trouble to our economy, dear Prince. I am Zhala of the Moneychanger's Guild. Were our fair city forced to accommodate so large a dowry," She waved her nails to the assorted forces and the Fleet of Kale, making the colors flash like beetle wings, "I fear we would have great difficulty making the transaction."

"Are you barring us from your city, then?"

Swindeho shook his head faintly, the motion something Mahara would have missed if not for the way it made the feathers on his eyebrows bob. "Never would we do such a thing, good Prince. As Cypresta Herself has commanded, 'Let the rivers run free and the harbor be open, so that the fish may come and go as they please, bringing their bounty with them.'"

Zhala waved her beetle-jeweled nails to the fleet again. "It's just that such bounty, if dealt with improperly, is rather like spawning season for pinkbelly in a flood year. Messy, smelly, with an unfortunate propensity for dead flesh to be left out to rot in the sun." She steepled her fingers before her in a respectful obeisance and smiled demurely. "Speaking meta-phorically of course."

Zulam laughed, tapping his riding-crop down his forearm as punctuation. "Do you surrender then?"

"As always," said Zhala, glancing to the Merchants on ei-ther side of her, "we simply seek an accommodation. Once we understand your needs, Cypresta will do what She can to see that these needs are filled, in the most profitable manner for us all. After all, prosperity is based on return customers. Cypresta never wishes a customer to leave unsatisfied."

Mahara glanced to the goddess Cypresta, then to Inlirre with her courtesan's gown, and noted a certain similarity.

The Third Prince smiled. "Kale happens to be expanding its markets, and is looking for new acquisitions. We have re-affirmed our rights in Tilkos and are now looking toward Cypresta as a logical and necessary expansion along our way to controlling Nikawaid."

Some of the Merchants seemed to choke at this, far more plain speaking than they were doubtless used to, but Zhala, the old bargainer, and Swindeho, the young one, only smiled and retained bland expressions respectively. "Ambitious plans such as these," remarked Zhala evenly, "require much planning and forethought. Given your recent difficulties securing your market share in Tilkos, I anticipate that if you wish your goals in Nikawaid to come to fruition in the most timely and profitable manner, you will need support and financial backing without the unpleasantness of market irregularities. This Cypresta can provide."

"You are speaking of an alliance."

Zhala nodded slightly. "I speak of a business partnership. We of Cypresta are favorably impressed by Kale's business plans, and while we can only speak for Cypresta Herself—and not the hinterlands of Faiscar, independent by ancient treaty—we believe that a merger would be of profit for us both."

"You would submit yourself to the Princes of Kale?"

"Cypresta has no royalty," Zhala demurred. "We are simply Merchants. However, as Merchants, we are quite used to and content with dealing with royalty in the style to which they are accustomed, so long as we maintain our rights to control our own commerce and accounts."

The Third Prince chuckled. "War is costly, you know."

Swindeho laughed back. "All investments require some risk. The greater the risk, the greater the profit."

"Generally speaking," Zhala added, then to Swindeho, "If you are to quote the proverbs, quote them fully." Then back to the Third Prince. "Though young Swindeho here is right, in this case. It will be costly to back you, but a good risk. Opposing you would be equally costly, with no chance of profit for Cypresta. But if we secure our ancient rights as Merchants of Cypresta, then I believe that a formal alliance with Kale would be a good thing for us both."

Prince Zulam smiled and nodded. "Agreed. And the hinterlands and other cities of Faiscar?"

"They are independent," said Swindeho, "and as such will have to be negotiated with separately."

Zhala waved her beetle nails again. "Though Cypresta, of course, will make an advisory proclamation."

"Of course," said the Third Prince.

Zhala took out a ledger. "Shall I draw up the documents?"

"Please do."

In the sky above, the goddess Cypresta mimicked Her servant Zhala's motions.

[6]

Rinchay wove a nest in the grass, made from mud and twigs and the living roots of the plains. She felt the power of the earth and wove it in, making a shield, a screen, a shelter . . . a hunter's blind she could watch the world from, while it didn't see her. Sword-edged reotho leaves stood over her head, the tall plumes of their blossoms dripping carrion-scented honey, attracting flies, drunk for the intoxicating rot. They fell into her nest, buzzing orgasmically, and she listened. Listened to the whispers. Listened to the dead.

They told her the news of the world outside: The Mother of Lies was installed in the Royal Palace of Chusinkayan, concubine and counselor to its withered Emperor, thrice accursed be his line and may all his heirs be stillborn. The Liar's name was Hudoleth. She was a Mage, masquerading as one of the Scholars of Kingakun University.

The Liar hated her place at court, the flies buzzed, whispering with their death tongues the gossip and rumors of the Palace, the thoughts and speculations of its courtiers and servants, showing Rinchay a thousand faceted visions of her enemy and those who surrounded her. The tale they told was a simple one, reflected in the Liar's every frown and pout and sadistic smile—she wished to escape. Wished to escape the finery and artificiality of Chusinkayan's Court. But why, and to what end?

The Liar was cruel—Rinchay knew this—and heartless as the Revenant Shaman was now herself. But the heartlessness of the Mother of Lies was more an emptiness, an emptiness in her soul that longed to be filled, and which the Pneuma accommodated, making her a Mage.

Rinchay knew this because the flies did not only visit the Palace of Chusinkayan. They visited markets and universities, farms and villages, and battlefields everywhere. Priests and Scholars alike whispered of the Power of a Mage, of their malice and insatiable hunger. While the wiser ones suspected that there was a Mage in Chusinkayan, one behind the bloodshed of the wars, they did not know who, or to what end.

Fools. More fools. More fools such as I.

Rinchay listened to the buzzings of the flies. She learned of Mahara, the Mage of Kale, and his war on the other half of the continent. He was working toward something there, as ruthlessly and cruelly as the Liar was on Rinchay's half. The Shaman saw the pain he caused, the suffering, the misery, the mothers with their sons torn from their arms, the sons with their mothers slaughtered before them. The faces were different, dark Rhudyar and light, gaudy Faiscar and humble slave, but the misery was the same. Rinchay knew it as she knew her own, for it was the same.

Fools. More fools.

She pitied them, but did not have time for them. Her time, and her revenge, were for the Liar alone. If their gods cared, and the dead did as well, vengeance might also be visited on Mahara, though by other hands than hers.

Mahara, however, was interesting for another reason. He was working toward something, and more directly and honestly than the Liar ever would, though he was cruel and ruthless all the same. By studying him, Rinchay could gain a better understanding of what the Liar sought and attempted to hide with her illusions and veils and masks. With bone pins and skins and maps of the world beyond the world of the Grass Clans—her world no longer—Rinchay saw that Mahara was forcing the armies of Kale north, just as the Liar manipulated the Emperor to send forth the armies of Chusinkayan. The Dmar Spyonk had not even been the Liar's true enemy, just something the Mage found inconveniently in her way, something she could simply flick aside, like a farm girl snapping her finger at a fly.

Fool.

The flies were everywhere, and saw everything. They saw that the Palace of Chusinkayan was well guarded, with Niosul women in gray veils who could sniff out the faintest traces of magic, like trained sows snuffling about for fungus, even wrinkling their veiled noses at the infinitesimal whiff of Pneuma upon Rinchay's flies. Any attempts of Rinchay's to inveigle herself into the Court of Chusinkayan and kill the Liar there would be met with opposition and failure.

Yet the Shaman did not need to meet the Liar in her lair to craft a suitable revenge. Or even wait on the stoop for her to emerge.

There was something the Liar wanted, something the Whore of Untruths desired beyond all reason. Rinchay Matan knew with the coldness of steel and dead bones in her heart that the best way to destroy the Liar and to make her pay for her outrages and Heresy was to find the thing the Liar sought and destroy it before the Mage's eyes, or else destroy the Liar herself within sight of her prize, letting her know that it would be something forever denied her, in this world and the next.

Rinchay listened to the buzzing of the flies, and the roiling of the maggots about her feet, and breathed on them, reinvigorating the dying ones and hatching the new ones into life. "Go, my Alaeshin. There is much still we do not know. Find out more and we shall have our Revenge. . . ."

11

Prophecy

By the calendar of the Domains of Iomard, the 26th Ekhtos, the
eighth month of the Iomardi year 6536, the 723rd year since
the last Corruption.

[1]

When they had reached Darcport, the land Dur had claimed
for his people, he saw to it that the blind Seer was attended
to. Yasayl was settled into a neat little house with a boy called
Urs to serve as her eyes, and a pair of housemaids to care for
her. He allowed a few days to give her time and privacy to
arrange things to her liking and for him to compose himself
for their next meeting. But in the end, he could postpone it
no further.

Dur entered the house to the smell of ghadidis blossoms,
the ugly green flower with the wonderfully sweet perfume.
They were arrayed about the room in vases, their mottled
blooms like moldy confections, and the couches were strewn
with soft blankets and furs. "I see you have made yourself at
home, Cay Yasayl."

The blind woman smiled from the corner she had chosen

for herself. "As much of a home as it can be without my Seyl or my sisterwife. But that fault is not yours, Mage Dur." Though they bore little physical resemblance, he was reluctantly impressed by a fugitive reminder of his mother, a likeness of the spirit, an indomitable will that the two women shared. She patted the cushion next to her. "Come, sit, we must talk. May I have my servants bring you refreshments? Perhaps a glass of tafia tea with melon juice?"

Dur paused, remembering his mother, and how he used to beg her for that treat, even when not in season. "There is no need to show off, Seer." He bristled, the memory a small and private thing he'd shared with no one. "I am quite confident in your abilities as it stands."

She shrugged. "As I said, my Gift is both more and less than it seems. I have visions, often jumbled and seemingly unrelated. One was of a little boy asking his mother for that treat. I knew it was you, and it resonated, for my own son, Breith, is also fond of tafia tea, though he prefers his with tantana syrup as opposed to simple melon juice. I prefer mine plain." She turned her head, her scarred eyes looking to another part of the room, as if seeing something else there, and for all Dur knew, she was. "Your mother . . . though my vision of her was short, I understand her. I too am mother to a Sighted boy, and I too have done and will do all I can in my power to save him from the hands of fanatics such as Radayam." She paused, holding a finger, crooked, to her lower lip. "Had circumstances been kinder to you, Mage Dur, you might have been a man much like my Seyl, Malart."

"Your Seyl is dead."

She nodded. "And we are alive. Both of us scarred and bitter. War seldom favors the kind or the gentle, does it?" She patted the cushion again. "Will you sit? And will you have any tea? I am about to ask for a glass for myself and it's as easy for the servants to bring two as to bring one."

There was an echo of his mother in her mannerisms, and it wasn't the sort that came from an actress playing off her visions. "Yes then, Cay Yasayl. That would be pleasant." He found a seat on the couch on the end opposite her.

She raised a hand to the corner where one of the house-maids and the boy Urs stood ready for her needs, yet silent. "Two glasses of tafia tea, both plain, and a small pitcher of melon juice." She turned back to him. "As I said, my visions are often incomplete, and I believe you'd rather pour to your own taste."

Dur regarded her for a long moment, taking the tea silently as the maid brought it, nodding his thanks and for her dismissal. He watched as the boy Urs placed the other glass in Yasayl's hands, signaling to her his proximity with a touch on her arm. "Have you had any other visions of interest?"

"Of course." She took a sip of tea as the boy sat down on the floor beside her. "But before then, perhaps we might discuss a bit of who you are, specifically, what makes a Mage a Mage, as opposed to a mere Sighted male."

"There would be training," Dur said, pouring a large measure of melon juice into his glass, the yellow juice clouding the tea. "Large amounts of it. As well as dedication."

"And desire." The blind Seer let the last word linger, taking a sip of her tea, then handing it to the boy to hold. "Desire is what makes a Mage, gives him his power. Or her. There's a woman in the other world named Hudoleth whose desire burns just as brightly as yours, Dur, if not brighter, as does that of Mahara and the mysterious Nyddys Mage. However, of the four working their wills in these wars, one is different, and I'm not speaking of Hudoleth. I am speaking of you, Dur. All three of the other Mages have desires that, so far as I can see, are turned inward, personal and selfish. Yours is different. What is it that you want, Dur? What is it that you want most of all?"

Dur set down the pitcher and took a drink from his glass of tea. What was it that he wanted? He wore it like a heart upon his sleeve. "Freedom. Not just for myself, but for my people."

"For my son, Breith?" asked Yasayl. "And my Seyl, Malart, had he lived? And for who else? Women as well as poor defenseless men and boys?"

"The women and the Lynborn have everything," Dur said. "You did not live as I did, a Daroc boy in fear of the knife."

"I lived in an enlightened town," Yasayl said sweetly. "Were I to fall into the hands of Radayam, she would kill me, either for being a cripple or for possessing a Gift the Prophet didn't see fit to speak of, which therefore must be 'impure.' I wonder sometimes which she would feel is the greater crime? And women are being killed by Radayam for no greater crime than being of mixed blood, just as much in fear of their lives as you with your mismatched eyes and your gift of the Sight."

Dur thought a moment. "Yes, them as well," he said. "They are as much mine as the others."

Yasayl sighed. "What would you say," she asked, "if I told you that your dreams of freedom were doomed to failure? That while you will kill Radayam—that I have truly seen— and may bring down Mirrialta, in the end the grand constructs of Mages are but castles built of sand, crumbling to nothing the moment that the Mage dies?"

She was trying to anger him, and doing a very good job of it. Dur set down the glass before it shattered in his hand. "I am willing to die to free my people," he bit out. "They must be free."

"Yes," said Yasayl, "we are in agreement on that fact. And likewise with the fact that you are willing to die, something that sets you apart from the other three Mages. Death is not an acceptable part of any of their plans. It is, however, an acceptable part of mine."

Dur looked at her, looking so much like his mother in demeanor and attitude, not to mention strength of will. "You are willing to die to save my people?"

"If I have to," said Yasayl. "It's not a pleasant option, but then few things are pleasant in this war. I would have died to save my Seyl, Malart, but he is now gone and it is too late for that. I would still be willing to die to save my son, Breith, my daughter, Bauli, and my sisterwife, Faobran. Die to save the rest of your people? Well, if I were truly that willing, then we'd have a fifth Mage in the equation, which we do not. However, I'm willing to die to save what I love, and you, as I have foreseen, are the best means to saving them. I myself am doomed, as are you, unless we take one option I have foreseen. In which case we are still doomed, but our deaths will be more meaningful than our lives."

"And what have you foreseen?"

She waved a languid hand in the air. "Death. Heresy. Change. It's all rather a muddle, but I know how to make it clearer. Are you familiar with the Parable of the Braysha Boy?"

Dur bristled. "The Prophet's excuse to kill all Sighted males, or at least to geld them and burn the Sight out of their heads? Yes, I'm quite familiar with *that*."

Yasayl shook her head. "I don't think you are. At least not from an objective standpoint. Look at the tale and what do you see? A Sighted boy, yes, but a somewhat cruel and immature one, using his Gift to smack field mice, and a rather high-handed woman with more Power than him who doesn't like what she sees and so does something about it, making rather grand pronouncements after the fact about why she did what she did, with people misinterpreting the story ever since."

Dur paused, picking up his tea and took a delicate sip. "Well that's a rather novel interpretation of the Scriptures."

Yasayl smiled. "If Radayam wants to kill me, I might as well add Heresy to the charges. The fact is, I have Looked and Seen, and I know that the Prophet was simply a woman. Nothing more, nothing less. However, she was a woman with a great deal of Power—as much or more than any of you Mages—and a unique perspective on how to use it. Rather than building for the present and herself, she built for the future and others. She, like you, was willing to die for what she believed in." Yasayl sighed, then reached out and patted the back of his hand with a touch like his mother used to use. "What I am saying, Dur, is what your people need is not a Mage, but a Prophet. And, in due time, a Martyr. Your cause will only outlive your death if you die before you would otherwise. I have foreseen this."

Dur took his hand back. "How can I believe you?"

"I knew you would say that," she said, "and I know there is only one way for me to convince you. And I'm willing to die to do so, so long as you promise to save my son and my wife and my young daughter. Will you?"

Dur nodded, then realized he was facing a blind woman. "If you can convince me, yes."

"You will convince yourself," Yasayl said. "What I am offering you is my Gift. I know you have taken other women and force-grown their Gifts to serve your own ends; and while I can neither approve of nor forgive that crime, I can understand it, and had I to do the same to save those I love, well then . . ." She shook her head, as if not liking what she saw. "It is of no importance. What is important is that if you use your rites upon my Gift, I believe it will allow both of us to see the future clearly. While I will die, you will know what must be done to set matters right. You will become the second Prophet, and unlike the works of a Mage, what you build will last." She reached for her glass of tea, and the boy, Urs, put it in her hands. She took a long drink, then gave it back to him. "I am ready now if you are."

Dur looked at her, so like his mother with her weathered face and her scarred hands and her great and indomitable spirit. "I do not want to do this."

"Want and need are two entirely different things," Yasayl shot back. "Cymel did not *want* you to use her for a Bridge, yet your *need* was greater, or at least you thought it was, and that's what makes you a Mage. Save your qualms of conscience for your past deeds; I'm willing, and that's more than I can say for my son's friend Cymel."

Dur felt a flash of anger. "Very well then, Seer. I will. But remember—you asked."

"I know," said Yasayl, "though I didn't believe this when I first saw it either."

Dur placed his hands upon her head and tugged upon the Pneuma, letting it flow into her Gift and back into him, growing and expanding. And then he *Saw.*

[2]

Radayam sat in her tent as the Scribe stood before her. "I have sad news, O leader of the Pure. Amna Sinder and her sisterwife have left with their Scribes for the Riverines."

Radayam looked at the papers on her camp desk, touching her document seal with one finger. "That is the third this week. Do you know what might have motivated them?"

The Scribe sighed. "The sister to Amna's sisterwife once gave birth to a Sighted male, and Amna's wife is wide around the middle."

It was bitter, but Radayam understood. "And Amna listened to the blandishments of Faobran of Urfa House rather than the exhortations of the Prophet." She looked up. "How much have her forces swelled by the defection of the Impure and the Unfaithful?"

"By no less than fifty-three Scribes, and more than twice that in Darocs and Lynborn attendants." The Scribe pushed a stray strand of golden hair back from her face and a long and uncomfortable silence stretched between them. "Do you require anything further, O Leader of the Pure?"

Radayam waved her hand in dismissal. "No, nothing. Only privacy."

The Scribe bowed her head and left, slipping silently out the tent flap, and Radayam rose and followed her path to the entrance, buttoning it shut then sliding a thin wand of brass through the loops of twined sinew so none might enter save through cutting a new flap.

So much impurity. So much faithfulness. "O Prophet, forgive me. I have been too soft." She clenched her fists, driving her nails into her palms until the flesh peeled, then went to the chest in the corner, falling hard on her knees before it, feeling the rocks bite into them from beneath the canvas floor. The pain was great, but not great enough. She opened her palms and then the chest, taking forth the chain flail and rope of thorns and the stone that she used to pound her forehead. "Impure!" she cried, "Impure!" then rent her robes and cast them to the ground, whipping the barbed rope across one shoulder and the chains across the other, from time to time picking up the stone and smashing it with both hands against her forehead until the skin cracked and bled and she saw the dancing white stars of pain and dizziness. But not the white light of the Prophet's Peace.

She continued to flagellate herself until she could no longer stand or kneel, and at last fell to her side, bleeding from her many cuts and abrasions, her head pounding with the pain like a band of ridos in full gallop. She had been too soft, too vain, and the pain itself was merely another vanity.

"Proud woman," she whispered through split lips, "you think yourself so holy, and that in itself is a vice."

She reached for the stone again, holding it in her hand, over the rope of thorns welded to her palm like a barbed rosary, but was unable to lift either, her limbs paralyzed with exhaustion. "Prophet, forgive me," she prayed, "forgive me my weakness and take me into the white light of your heart."

But the Prophet did not, and all that came for her was the darkness of unconsciousness.

[3]

The way the great Houses of Valla Murloch were built and positioned, there was a good forty degrees of arc along the north end of the city, running from the ocean shore across the river and into the hills beyond. Defensible, but not impenetrable. Urtha House was better situated than most, and had become a center of the dead and the dying. Faobran had found herself thrust into the position of leader of the resistance, from the simple fact that she'd been resisting the influence of the Domains longer than any other.

But the defenses were crumbling. Radayam's Pneuma-bolts had toppled buildings and shattered tiles throughout the city, and those who hadn't been vaporized outright had been struck by the falling debris or wounded in the clash with the Army of Purification as it stormed through the breach. Thankfully, those same tottering buildings could be collapsed on the invaders. At a great price of blood and pain, the army had been driven back.

Faobran walked along the audience hall that had become a hospital, watching Scribes and healers tend to the fallen. About the only thing that helped was the fact that Radayam's fanaticism had led her to turn her Inquisitors on her own ranks, leading to defections of Scribes with a trace of foreign blood or Sighted males in their line or simply a bad taste in their mouth for the continued cry of "Purity!"

Yet something prickled and itched at the back of her mind, and she wondered how her loved ones fared, and strangely, which of them she missed more and what things she longed for most. Malart's kind touch, Breith's impudence, or just the love hidden behind Yasa's sharp tongue? Yasayl would tell her when to worry and when not to, and have some choice words on the usefulness thereof. She could almost hear her right now, but couldn't quite make out the words, except to know that they were fond and disapproving at the same time.

Carefully, Faobran picked her way back across the hall, waving off inquiries from needy Scribes, and took herself upstairs to her son's room, which had become something of a sanctuary for her since her own chambers had become makeshift council rooms. But Breith's small room was too tiny to be of use for families, and too far up the stairs to be right for the wounded. She had been able to keep it untouched, as much from practicality as design.

Breith's wooden ships were there, and his toys, along with clothes tossed aside with one shirt neatly folded atop them to disguise the disorder. She smiled. His scrying bowl was there as well, on the table that had grown too short for him. She filled the basin with water, waving across it with a tug at the Pneuma, hoping to see his face or Malart's or Yasayl's.

The water silvered, then changed to black. Two eyes formed, green and brown, but the face around them was unfamiliar. A Daroc man, weathered and tanned, with his hair tied back in braids.

"Faobran," said the man.

She touched the side of the bowl. "You are neither my Seyl nor my son to speak to me so informally. Who are you?"

The man grimaced. "Someone you won't like, but you need anyway. At least if you want a world for your son to return to." He took a breath, then said quickly, "Malart is dead. Yasayl too."

Faobran didn't doubt the man for speaking her fears, but clutched both sides of the bowl, causing the vision to ripple. "How?"

"An assassin killed Malart; I have her, for what it's worth. Yasayl died at my hands." He bit his lip. "She was very brave."

Faobran was ready to dash the bowl to the floor, but then the man held up a hand. "Fori, no! Listen to me! Listen to me if you want even one hope of saving Breith's skin, and your own in the bargain!"

She stopped, hearing herself addressed by the familiar nickname of lovers or family, and took her hands away from the bowl, resting them, palms flat, on the table. "What are you?"

The man touched his temple, rubbing it. "I was the Mage Dur. Now? I suppose I'm the Prophet Dur. Your sisterwife gave me her Sight, and I suppose there's something different with a gift when it's freely given instead of taken, because it's with me still. Not as clear as the first visions, but she died for those. But the visions I have now show me that you can help me and I can help you. I see the past, I see the future, and I know most of what she knew."

Faobran hissed between her teeth. "You couldn't."

He grimaced. "I do. Even if I'd prefer not to."

"Why should I believe you?"

He shrugged. "Because, Fori, you'll die if you don't." There was no trace of Yasayl's inflection anymore, none of the familiarity that gave her pause, but there was a directness and an honesty to him all the same.

She took a deep breath, as much to steel her nerves as to give her a moment to think, but at last let it out along with what felt like all the warmth in her heart and half her blood. She was glad for the support of the table and the hard wood beneath her hands. "Very well. What do you propose?"

He nodded briefly. "Your position in Valla Murloch is indefensible. Radayam will complete the invasion in less than a week. Let her. Before that, I will extend the Chaos Storm as far south from the Sanctuary Isles as I can, giving you and your allies cover to flee by boat for Darcport. There we can regroup our forces, and then retake the Riverines and then the Domains."

"And if I refuse?"

"My victory will be that much harder, and you will be hung from daka the tree before your House in five days' time." He shrugged again. "If you don't trust me, trust your sisterwife. Yasayl saw it before, and I'm seeing it now."

Faobran steeled her hands against the table. "I see. Is there anything else I should know?"

He paused, contemplative. "Bring as many Scribes as you can. And if you have any gelded males from the Domains, bring them as well." The vision then vanished, and Faobran stopped herself before she dashed the bowl across the room.

After all, a general was calm. A general was rational.

With great deliberateness, she tipped the bowl on its face, spilling the water across the table, then slammed the door behind her.

[4]

Urs held the other boy by the hand, leading him through the fog and up the rocky path to the cave. "Dun' worry. 'T'snot much farther."

"You said he wants me? I'm of no use to anyone."

Urs looked around at the other boy, taller than him, gangling, and a bit older, his hair off-brown with a mix of Lynborn blood. And gelded, though all that showed of this was the height and the mismatched eyes and the angry brand across his cheek that marked him as impure, the ideograph of the dead mouse from the Braysha teaching tale. "Yeah, 'e wanted *you*." Not specifically, though. Mage Dur had only said he wanted a gelded male, the younger the better, and that Urs was to bring him to the Cave of the Stone Candles.

The Mage was now not even called the Mage, at least to his face. He had taken on the name of Prophet, and for that crime alone the Army of Intolerance would come for him, even if they had to swim to the Isles.

"I'm useless . . ." the boy said. It was obvious that when the Seers had burnt out his Sight, they'd burned a bit more of his mind just to make sure. He stood in the fog and shivered, then sat down abruptly on a rock and began to cry. "I ran, I tried to run, but they caught me . . . and their knives. . . . Cay Rada said she'd whip the evil out of me. . . ."

Urs saw the scars on the boy's arms, and on his neck where the shirt pulled down when he leaned over. "When I ran the next time, they didn't care . . ."

Urs sat down next to him, trying to give him some comfort, and watched the boy flinch at the touch. " 'not useless. Prophet wouldn'a ask f'ya if he didn' want you." Urs realized he didn't even know the boy's name.

The boy cried, and Urs held him in the fog, wishing there were a Daroc magic that could help him. But Daroc magic was slow and subtle. Unless it were the magic of Mage Dur.

"Chilly out here, ain't it?"

Urs looked around, only to see the Mage—no, the Prophet Dur—behind him, emerging from the fog. But aside from his green and brown eyes and the red signs painted on his skin, he didn't look any different from a dozen different Daroc men Urs knew. "Yes'm," Urs said. "Um, I mean, 'sir.' "

"You're Daroc-born, aren't you?"

Urs nodded, swallowing. "Born and bred."

The Mage smile, his mismatched eyes laughing. "Same

here." He looked at the crying boy. "How 'bout you?"

The boy looked up. "I'm useless. . . ."

The Prophet grinned. "Don't think I've ever heard of that tribe. How 'bout your parents?"

The boy swallowed. "My da was Daroc. My mum's Lynborn, but her brother was Sighted, so no Lynborn wanted to be her Seyl."

"Lynborn then," the Prophet concluded. "Well, I'll try not to hold it against you. After all, you've got more reason than I do to hate Radayam. Come on, and you too." He looked to Urs, and Urs helped the other boy to his feet and led him into the cave.

It was lit, but the candles were red stone, pools of wax or oil atop them with wicks floating in the middle. And in the center of the cave was a black pool, dark as ink from a Scribe's pen. The air inside was hot and muggy, with a salt smell, like walking through a fog of blood.

"Take off his clothes," the Prophet told Urs, then to the boy, "You stand there, before the pool."

The boy did, and as Urs helped him off with his clothes, the rest of his scars were revealed, bright pink weals and red cicatrices down his back, the marks of scourges and chains, attempts to instill him with "Purity," and below his manhood, a deep red scar from an operation done with the same knives that gelded the herd animals and riding beasts.

The Prophet Dur raised an eyebrow, then shrugged, picking up a small clay pot of red paint and a brush, beginning to paint the boy with designs like the ones that adorned his own skin, from time to time consulting a book of ancient writing and adding a flourish here or a scroll there or a completely new sigil on some portion of the child's anatomy.

Urs didn't ask, and neither did the boy. The Prophet at last tapped the handle of the brush to his teeth, surveying his handiwork, then shrugged and threw it back in the paint jar.

" 'L'have t'do. T'bad I can't consult with the Mage in Chusinkayan, but Mages don't generally share their secrets until after they're dead, and don't have time to kill her right now." He smiled, a quick smile of mischief. Urs didn't know if he were joking, and wasn't certain if the Prophet knew himself.

"You're Urs, right?" the Prophet asked.

Urs nodded.

"Good. Come here. You're just the right age."

Not certain what would happen, but more afraid to disobey than obey, Urs went to the Prophet, who took his left hand by the wrist, then took out a long knife and pinked the tip of Urs' next-smallest finger, the second from the left, letting drops of blood fall into the pool, one, two, three. Then the Prophet said, "Enough," and took his hand away, allowing Urs to put the cut finger into his mouth and suck the wound dry. "Over there." The Prophet waved the knife, indicating a pile of blankets and jugs in the corner of the cave, and Urs stepped aside to watch. The blankets stank of pee and vomit. Urs chose to stand instead, leaning on one of the stone candles.

The Prophet Dur began to sing, his voice echoing from the ceiling of the cavern and causing the pool to ripple and the flames atop the stone candles to dance. "Ja inta, robeosa. Ja intai kentra! Sa ifrandi kendta. Sa ila, sa ila, mach da!" Around the boy the Prophet danced, cutting grooves onto his arms and the boy's, then at last taking the knife, lifting the boy's manhood, and ripping open the scar where he'd been gelded.

Blood poured down, like a woman's first flow, and the Prophet Dur brandished the knife. "Ja inta! Ja inta! Se robeal mach lantra ach da!" The cavern crackled with Pneuma and a light grew from the pool, then suffused the boy and his reflection as the Prophet danced behind them and the boy began to dance as well, mimicking the Prophet's movements but a foot behind him, like a puppet on strings but with the sinewed litheness of a dancer.

The Prophet fell silent and the boy began to sing. "Ja inta la charmadc. La krin fela nach la! Se inroni penliana. Ke firandi mach ma!" The glow spread from the pool, and the Prophet, concentrating on the boy, now stood behind him, his hands upraised, truly like a puppeteer as the boy continued to dance and sing with the same possessed grace, his voice becoming sweeter and lighter. "La fina ra kronti no lisa cha machti. Hei fina le lina trach mandi noch ta!"

One by one, the scars opened and erased, blood pouring forth, then flowing in, leaving smooth unbroken skin behind them, as the boy became smaller, and younger, then the brand across his cheek sizzled alight with fire, then was gone. Then the Prophet Dur placed his hands upon the boy's head, glowing with Pneuma, and the boy screamed, the pain an agony of memory that thrummed through the cavern and spoke to the soul, a cry without words, the Pneuma light blazing out his eyes and mouth.

And then nothing, except the flow of blood trickling back up his legs, like red yarn being gathered up into a ball. Or rather, two of them, and then the skin sealed over and all was unmarked and unscarred as the rest.

The Prophet lowered his hands and the Pneuma light faded. He looked pale and drained and years older, but his eyes glowed with the fierce joy of triumph. "The Rite of Renewal," he said to Urs, "it is done. Go find another like him, and we will work it again."

He looked to the boy. "Now tell me your name, now that you are no longer 'useless'."

[5]

The ships were not built for the sea, nor for so many people, but Mage Dur had kept good on his promise. The wind was sweet and fair and fast, the currents pulling the river barges along at unimaginable speeds upon the open sea — a suicide ploy in any other situation, but to stay in Valla Murloch was suicide itself. She didn't need Yasayl's or Dur's visions to tell her that, even if Faobran said they were one and the same.

"So what's it like where we're going, Aunt Cory?" Her niece, Bauli, hugged close to her, leaning upon the railing and watching Mage-tossed waves dance.

Corysiam sighed. "I don't know, dear. It's a town, in the north, so it will be colder. But it will be much *much* safer. Much safer than Valla Murloch."

"Mum said there's a Mage there, and you said he was bad. But if he's bad, why're we going there?" Bauli looked up at her then, her face very much like Malart's except for the eyes, a pale blue like Yasayl's would have been had the Seer's not been scarred over. "The Daroc kids say he's good though, and that he's like the Prophet, 'cept I thought you said there was no way a Mage could be good, and Mum said he killed Mam, and I'm scared." She hugged Corysiam tighter. "An' Mum said someone killed Da too, an' where's Breith . . . and . . . and . . . you're not going to leave, are you?"

Corysiam hugged Bauli back, then dried her tears. "Hush, dear. Hush. Remember, you're seven; you're not a baby anymore. And girls don't cry."

"But I don't understand!" Bauli wailed. "If he's a bad Mage, why are we going to him, 'an if he's a good Mage, then why'd he kill Mam?"

Corysiam was at a loss for words. She smiled, wiping away Bauli's tears and doing her best to comfort her while she tried to reconcile the refugees' words of praise for their benefactor—including the Daroc's heretical hero worship of the Prophet Dur—with the brutal man who had mind-raped Cymel and later killed Yasayl.

What was she to make of Dur? Monster or Savior? The two images did not fit together, but as Yasayl had often said, war seldom favored the kind or the gentle. How was what Dur had done to Cymel any less terrible than what Radayam and her brand of fanatic had been doing to innocent boys for millennia?

Dur had done it out of need, not out of a twisted belief in what was Pure. That was it, plain and simple. Or as simple as it was going to get.

She looked at Bauli. "I'm sorry. It's complicated. The simplest I can put it is that people like Radayam do things, not because they need to do it, but because they *think* they need to do it, and people like Dur do what they do because they want to survive."

Bauli looked at her for a long moment. "Simpler?"

Corysiam sighed, exasperated. "Rada wants to cut your brother's balls off, and Dur wants to kill her for trying. And Dur's done some bad things, but he did them because he's trying to save his skin. That simple enough?"

Bauli bit her lip. "Is that why he killed Mam?"

Corysiam sputtered and waved her hand, giving up. "I suppose so. Faobran said that Dur said that Yasa told him to kill her, and if he were going to come up with a lie, I think he would have come up with a better one. Anyway, it sounds just like something your mam would say."

Bauli nodded. "Like when she killed the mog-kitten an' I cried for days. But when the healin' Scribe came, she said the blood was crawlin' with baby henta worms, an' if Mam Yasa hadn't squished it with her staff, we would've all been dead." Bauli looked out at the water, moving along outside the boat at preternatural speed. "I guess it's okay then. But I'm still going to miss her."

Corysiam sighed and leaned on the rail. "Me too."

"Is it still okay if I don't like Dur anyway when I meet him?"

"*Yes.*"

Corysiam sighed then, feeling as if she'd sparred a duel with Amhar, not just had a conversation with her seven-year-old niece. Had Dur not mind-raped Cymel, and thereby escaped Glandair, these people would not have been saved. Faobran, Bauli and the rest would now be dead unless shunted across the worlds, and Corysiam could never Bridge that many. At most one or two, more if they were small, and that was why she was on the largest and most overcrowded of boats with the mothers and crying infants. Were the boat to founder, she could at least save some of the children, including her niece . . . whom she would take first, even if a dozen infants died in her place.

Such was the coin of war and the bitter price of necessity. She could step between the worlds whenever she wished, but how different for one who could not? Hearing the talk of the Daroc made her look at herself, for while the need of a Mage was an evil thing, what if that philosophy were in itself evil?

Where there was a hole, the Pneuma flowed to fill it. The Daroc around her all had a need, a hunger, focused on this Mage, who embodied their need more strongly than any one of them individually. And from that need he had crafted their salvation, along with that of Faobran, Bauli, and the other folk of the Riverines, Daroc and the Lynborn alike.

Or he could just be an ordinary Mage toying on the hopes of one and all, saying what he needed to say and doing what he needed to do to craft an army to take the world of Glandair for himself. But faced with fanatics like Radayam, who would kill all who didn't agree with her view of a perfect world, throwing in one's lot with Dur was an easy choice.

Corysiam sighed and hugged Bauli, watching the ship move fast across a sea at once tempest-tossed and smooth as the waters of a reflecting pool, their fleet in the eye of the Pneuma storm extended south from the Sanctuary Isles. Truly, war seldom favored the kind or the gentle, and even when it did, they were protected by the violence of those without such virtues. Like the calm in the eye of the storm. To save these children, it was necessary to trust Dur.

But pardoning and forgiving were entirely different matters. Just because they were taking Dur's offer of Sanctuary didn't mean they had to like it. Or him.

[6]

Thador had been left shackled and chained in the hold of the ship, with two casks of water, a small barrel of ship's biscuits, and a salted eel so old and dry that even the rats wouldn't touch it unless she hit them with it. She'd killed three so far, pretending that they were her jailor. But the stocky man was wise in the ways of assassins, or busy with other matters. He had left her here to rot until she starved to death or went mad from the solitude and darkness and the rocking of the ship and her own filth.

She had lost track of time. It could be more than a week and less than a month. Her menses had only come once, but starvation could stave it off an indefinite amount, and she'd carefully rationed her biscuits and the bits of rat and the all important water, even to the point of drinking her own urine to keep the moisture and salt. She'd hardly touched the eel except to kill rats.

When the light appeared, she was almost blind, but still trained enough and honed with the rehearsals of dreams and imagination to hurl the eel with deadly accuracy. Or what would have been deadly accuracy had not a shield of burning Pneuma been interposed between herself and the light, vaporizing her weapon in an instant, leaving the air filled with the stink of salted fish and lye. Thador screamed and threw feces and rat bones, which vaporized as well, not improving the scent.

"Are you through, assassin?" asked the voice that she knew to be that of the stocky man.

"Kill me!" she screamed. "Kill me or release me! I don't care which! Just let me out of this stinking hole!" Her voice cracked with disuse, harsh upon her ears, yet the man in the door only stood there, safe behind his shield of Pneuma-light.

"I think," he said slowly, "that I will do something of both. I see you are loyal to Mirrialta, a loyalty that neither coin nor torture will buy, and so I won't attempt to do the impossible, or even the difficult. My energies are sorely taxed at the moment, and all I believe I need do is make a suggestion, and a small binding. . . ."

With these words, the Pneuma-light reached out tendrils that slowly enmeshed her, as creeping and inexorable as spikeroot vines, sliding their force underneath her shackles and rags till she could neither move nor hope to move. The barbed edges of the tendrils grabbed her eyelids by the lashes on both sides, pulling them open so she could not help but see even if she rolled her eyes back in her head.

The man came forward then, dressed now in the ceremonial gown of a Scribe. For a moment Thador did not recognize him, as he looked not so much older, as wiser, wasted and haggard. Yet his eyes were still the same, green and brown and angry, and he looked into her own, placing a hand on each temple and sending tendrils of Pneuma deep into her mind until she writhed inside her skin trying to escape. But the clutch inside soon became as firm as without, and he spoke to her, his words speaking more to her memories and fantasies than to her present mind.

"And then, Thador," Mistress Mirrialta said, "after you have killed that freak Malart—Prophet grant that he'd been strangled at birth instead!—you will make your way back to the Army of Purification where you will deal with my sisterwife. Radayam should just be ready to start her assault on the Riverines, and I want her to die, ideally in a great and grand manner such that I, Mirrialta, can play the role of the weeping widow and quickly step into the power vacuum left by my sisterwife's passing; but if you just have to hold her head down in a chamber pot, oh well, it's the result that counts. She'll be dead, and that's my main objective in this game. You will do this secretly, of course, to all but Radayam—as she dies, I want her to know whose was the hand who wielded the knife—then make your way back to me. But if there is even the slightest chance that you will be apprehended, you know what you must do."

"That will never happen, my lady," Thador remembered herself saying.

Mirrialta smiled. "That *must* never happen. I depend upon you, Thador, and you know as well as I do that Radayam's Seers and Scribes can look into your mind and twist what is there. Why, you might even be made to strike against me!"

"That is impossible."

"I know, my sweet," Mirrialta said, and leaned over, kissing Thador full upon the lips, long and slow with a hint and a promise of things to come once Thador accomplished her mission. . . .

Time then moved forward, as in a dream state. Thador forgot what the stocky man wanted, if he wanted anything, save to leave her another box of crackers and cask of water and let her rot another month. This time they were careless—the cask was seamed with nails and copper, not pegs and rope like the first. Once she had broken it apart, the nails gave her something to pick the locks of the manacles, and the manacles gave her something to leverage the fine strips of copper once she worked them through the cracks of the door and caught the tops of the pins on the outside.

Then it was out and over the side, swimming to another vessel where she stole a small rowboat, taking that south to where she remembered—how long ago was it?—that oyster divers moored their small sailcraft off the shoals. She traded one craft for another while the woman who owned it was down holding her breath, then set off down the coast, eating a lunch of raw oysters that tasted like the manna of the Prophet and the blood-sweet kisses of Mirrialta.

12

Satisfaction

By the calendar of the Watchers of Glandair, events dating from the 16th day of Seimis, the eighth month of the 739th Glandairic year since the last Settling, and on into Wythamis. And a small interlude in Iomard. . . .

[1]

The Emperor's visit came and went, and the Emperor came and went, and then so did the days and the weeks until Padmila was round as a ripe plum with the Emperor's child, which, incidentally, was also Hudoleth's child, and not the girl's, except in the way that a silly ouzoet could claim to be the mother of a tickbird. The Niosul sniffed about, of course, smelling the reek of Pneuma about Hudoleth's quarters, but as they hadn't been willing to turn Padmila upside-down and stick their veiled noses up her skirts, the fact of the girl's pregnancy was cause for polite smiles and nothing more.

In spite of how well the first stage of the gambit had gone, Hudoleth was furious at the time this little charade was taking and had taken and the degree to which Padmila was enjoying herself. This was her unfortunate miscalculation since becoming one of the Emperor's two favorite concubines meant that she became roommates with Padmila, with a grander suite of rooms, yes, and lavish gifts, but no privacy to work her magics save locking herself in the bathing chamber for an unconscionable amount of time — especially when sharing the suite with an irrational pregnant woman who'd once even jimmied the door into the bathing chamber, then vomited into Hudoleth's scrying bowl. Though thankfully, the girl was irrational enough that she'd bought the tale of a ritual she'd interrupted and the powders and reagents merely being Hudoleth's personal beauty secrets (which they were, but not in the way she was thinking).

However, Hudoleth's anger and frustration at this state of affairs was more than enough for the girl to misinterpret as jealous rage. "Stay away from me," Padmila said. "I am sorry you have not conceived, but do not envy me that which I have." The daughter of the lily turned her back to her, facing the courtyard. "Perhaps one day you will have a child of your own."

Hudoleth looked at the round, full swell of the girl's belly. *Sooner than you think, my dear little ouzoet.* Yet delicious as the irony was, she'd happily trade irony for privacy. But she only said, "Do not forget that you would not have that which you are so proud of if it were not for *me*. And don't be so proud yet — nothing is so certain that it is written in the Book of Fate."

Padmila glanced back, hands over her belly. "What do you mean?"

"I mean," Hudoleth said with icy clarity, "that things can happen. Conceiving a child is one thing. Carrying it is another, and bearing it is yet a third. And this, after all, is your first." Hudoleth gestured, pointing a silver-framed nail to the girl's belly. "You have no way of knowing whether it will be born alive, or even human."

Padmila shrieked as if goosed with a cherry twig. "Keep your fingers away, witch! Do not even look at me!"

Hudoleth feigned an attitude of shocked anguish, but couldn't help but grin slightly. "But . . . no! I did not ever mean such a thing! That is the Emperor's child! It would be treason to even think—But no, I'm certain the child will be straight of limb, strong and well favored in all ways. . . ." As certain as one could be with sorcery, at least. There were always pitfalls—the child might be born with tickbird feathers—but it wasn't likely. Hudoleth's divinations (at least before Padmila had vomited on them) had indicated that all was going as to plan. "Please, take my assurances, everything should go perfectly. . . ."

"You had better pray that that will be so, sorceress. If it isn't . . ."

"Of course," Hudoleth said quickly. "A thousand pardons for my even suggesting such a terrible possibility. Oh! Padmila, please, don't cry—I—I must remove myself. I do not wish to see you become overwrought!"

Hudoleth rushed from the apartment, covering her sleeve to suppress a fit of giggles. That had gone almost too well. She wondered if she should immediately seek out the Emperor and ask to be removed from Court, or let Padmila do it first, but decided to give the move to the girl. In Court politics, the one who moved first generally won, and after all, Hudoleth was playing to lose, at least in the short term. As such, she went strolling in the orchards, a public place for private contemplation. The citrus trees were still laden with fruit, their limbs hanging heavy with white or green or yellow-pink orbs. Hudoleth passed through them, finding one of the tangerine trees, still bright with orange fruit left on the tree over winter, regreening and gaining sweetness with every season until now warmed by the bright sun of Wythamis. Hudoleth picked one and peeled it with her nails, watching the white inner rind come away from the little sectioned ball. How she missed her sorcery, and strangely enough, classes. The school year was now into force and students would just be taking their finals, giving her an extra space of privacy to herself, something that never occurred about the palace, especially since she began sharing quarters with Padmila.

The Syntayo's little gambit had also taken her away from the war, and that, no doubt, would cost her. But it was necessary. She ate one section and then another, savoring the sharp tang. The fruit, like her plans, was not quite ripe, but satisfying all the same.

Hudoleth's only regret was that she hadn't fed Padmila another plum to give the little bitch twins. Padmila deserved to suffer, if just for her whining and morning sickness and her girlish flights of insecurity. By all the twisted organs of the various little gods, she should have ensorceled the whole basketful of plums and force-fed them to her till she puffed up like a wood-borer Empress.

But that, of course, would give away the greater game. Let Padmila and the Emperor win for a space, giving her the consolation prize she wanted, namely banishment from Court. Once Hudoleth had used that extra time to kill the Hero and take the prize in the Empty Place, she could turn the Emperor's frayspell gift inside-out and turn his little whore into even more of a bloated sow than she already was. Padmila wanted fertility? Well, she could certainly have it.

Hudoleth scattered the tangerine rinds on the immaculately raked dirt of the orchards and wiped her nails clean on a linen cloth she'd tucked in her sleeve, taking a moment to suck the last of the white pith out from under one nail. She took out the mirror the Syntayo had forged for her from its essence, inspecting for a moment her high cheekbones and smooth brows as might any lady of the Court, then breathed upon the obsidian and polished it with the edge of her sleeve, speaking a word in the ancient language of Chusinkayan under her breath.

The surface cleared. Hudoleth observed the scene as if reflected from a high vantage point, the beautiful youth and a red-haired girl lying in the grass by the side of a sandy road, as impassioned for each other as that little rutting sow for the Emperor. Hudoleth considered a spell of fertility to slow their journey, then thought better of it; such magics, when done over a distance, would leave traces that even an asthmatic Niosul could sniff. Besides which, casting fertility spells in an orchard, while appropriate to the resonance of the Pneuma, could cause unfortunate complications, especially if the Emperor wanted a last-minute tryst before banishing her.

But a spell of passion, however, was easily done. Hudoleth merely whispered the words of the old language, breathing out a fog of Pneuma onto the black glass, then watched the Hero and his woman grab each other with renewed energy, doing their best to let nature work its own spell of fertility. She kissed the mirror and laughed.

"You are amusing yourself I see, Hudoleth," said a voice. She whirled, only to find the Emperor standing behind her, Niosul hiding like the smoke of smudge pots under the branches of the tangerines. "Do your visions please you?"

Hudoleth quickly tucked the mirror away in her sleeve. "Not so much as your presence, O Son of Heaven."

"Your words are as fair as your face, Scholar." The Emperor inclined his head. "But come, walk with me. We have matters to discuss."

Hudoleth nodded. "Of course."

The Emperor offered her his hand and they walked down the artificially rustic nonpaths of the Imperial orchard. "Padmila is most upset," the Emperor said at last. "I attribute that to morning sickness." It was a soft word, but with a slight barb. Hudoleth knew he in fact blamed her, and inwardly she rejoiced. "However, women in her condition — especially young ones — can be quite demanding. Even of an Emperor." He stopped and looked at her gravely. "Padmila is very dear to me, Hudoleth, and I'm certain she will see reason again in time. But until that point, I believe I will arrange a house for you outside the Palace Walls, close enough that I can visit it for an afternoon's hunt, but far enough away to give the daughter of the lily the peace she needs at the moment."

Hudoleth gritted her teeth, steeling herself. No magic. Not even a whiff of Pneuma to set off the Niosul. "My lord," she said, "please, let it not be so. Could you not send Padmila —"

The Emperor held up a hand abruptly, silencing her. "You overstep yourself, Scholar, and have not the excuse Padmila does." He looked her up and down. "I believe, however, that other arrangements are in order. You will go back to the University, take up your former life there, and if and when I have need of you, you will be summoned to the house outside the Palace Walls."

Hudoleth bowed her head, letting the fall of her hair hide her smile. "Of course, Your Imperial Majesty. I —"

The Emperor patted her on the arm. "Let us speak no more on this. You may go to your rooms and have servants pack what belongings you wish to take with you. In fact, pack all of them. Padmila will need the space for her child, and after what she said . . . well, I can't have you two squabbling."

"Your Imperial Majesty is infinite in his wisdom." Hudoleth bowed. "If I may be excused, I will go and arrange matters as you have said."

"You are," said the Emperor. It was the hardest bit of acting Hudoleth had ever done to drag her feet dejectedly rather than skipping down the rows of the orchard.

[2]

There was celebration in Tyst, and pomp, but Anrydd enjoyed none of it. The wine and sweetmeats were like ashes and gall in his mouth, for he knew they were not served for him.

Oerfel sat in the corner and watched. Watched as he made his speeches. Watched as he took his crown. Not the old crown—lost and no doubt stolen by one of his men, or hidden by the Mage for his own purposes—but a new crown specially fashioned for the occasion, fashioned the same way as the false words he had publicly asked retired clerk Oerfel to write for him on the day of his ascension, words speaking of how a new crown was needed for a new Tyrn, et cetera.

Tyrna Afankaya had been lost as well, vanished in the siege of Cyfareth. Anrydd was fairly certain that the Mage had watched as he'd performed in bed with the woman they'd selected to be the new Tyrna. Certainly his mind had prickled during the act, and he'd wondered if the old sorcerer were spanking off to it, since looking into a Mage's mirror was the closest that one such as he would ever come to a beautiful young woman.

But Anrydd had learned to wear the mask well, the mask taken from the face of his dead father. Folks in the palace swore it was almost as if he'd flayed the skin off and grafted it over his own but thirty years younger. The old Tyrn had laughed? Anrydd laughed. The old Tyrn had made rousing speeches? Anrydd made rousing speeches. Drinking and whoring? Anrydd did those too, with far better flair than his pale half brother Isel ever had, damn him.

Isel had taken his secrets to the grave with him. Or at least to the bottom of the river. Anrydd had personally seen his body tossed, sans head, over the bridge outside Cyfareth Uni-

286 · *Jo Clayton and Kevin Andrew Murphy* ·

versity and watched it sink to the bottom of the river. Isel had watched as well, or at least his head had, and had ridden back atop a pike to the capital with him, Anrydd's trophy and his proof.

After all, if you couldn't have Tyrna or crown, the dead Tyrn's head still did fairly well to back up your claims of rulership.

Anrydd eyed Oerfel, sitting quietly in the corner of the grand balcony, out of sight, as Anrydd mouthed another prettily written speech, regarding the wars in Chusinkayan and Kale, and seeing as how the victor would then turn his attentions to Nyddys, Nyddys should take a preemptive action and strike both while they were at their weakest and their hatred for each other was strong. The crowd in the square below applauded, as much because he had a sword and a severed head held up for all to see as for any real approval of his plans. But that was all it took—Nyddys was off to war and the armies were setting sail, taking their ships and going to secure the mainland.

Anrydd didn't know what Oerfel's game was, but trusted his dead brother enough to know they were both being played for the fool. Oerfel had probably secreted the crown and Tyrna away for himself and was just waiting for the right moment to kill Anrydd then place himself as Emperor of all Nordomon. After all, even if you were bald and bony, having all three tokens of power tended to back up your claims, especially if you marched back to Nyddys with a triumphant army behind you or simply set up housekeeping in one of the other Imperial Courts. Chusinkayan, maybe, or perhaps Kale, or some spot between the three where you could set up a fashionable new Court to consolidate your power.

Of course, Oerfel wasn't the bastard son of the old Tyrn, but if someone who'd been Scribe to the Court for that long couldn't forge a patent to the nobility, then something was seriously wrong with the world. Aside from the things that obviously were.

Anrydd waved his sword, finished with a last few of Oerfel's carefully prepared words, and listened to the crowd roar with approval and bloodlust. Anrydd merely smiled and wore the mask of the conquering hero. After all, if he conquered Chusinkayan and Kale, it would be rather hard for anyone to claim that he was a pretender to the Throne. Even if they did manage to arrive with the Tyrna and the crown, and he still had his head.

[3]

They landed in a hidden cove on the coast of Faiscar, near the smugglers' town of Lo Phreomo, which Gryf had marked on his maps. After Laz and Ama spent too long behind the dunes "gathering driftwood"—and complaining about sand afterwards—they ate a meal of badly cooked fish, then began the trek inland.

The land was filled with danger and heat. Where there once were prosperous mining and timber towns, now there were only burned-out houses and feral bands of men who preyed on anything that was too weak to fight. Amhar killed three with her arrows, and Gryf killed two with his crossbow.

It was not the first time he'd killed, but it was the first time he'd been able to look at the bodies close hand. They looked like the Faiscarese who came to Tyst, one like Hertys, the baker, who'd given Gryf day-old Faiscar sweetrolls as a child.

Amhar and Lyanz were untouched by this. Amhar because she was a woman of Iomard, who felt, even if she didn't say it, that men were beneath her, and the folk of Glandair, with the exception of certain Heroes, were portions of the Corruption. Lyanz because he was born of rich merchants, and expected to see people die outside his walls every day. Seeing it up close was just unpleasant, not frightening.

Gryf shuddered with each death. He'd been hungry, he'd been chased, and he'd been frightened, and he knew the instincts that took over anyone, man or woman, in those circumstances. Lyanz and Amhar had the consolation of having each other, and knowing they were both people who mattered. Amhar was a Scribe of Iomard. Lyanz was *the* Hero, the one who came about only once in a millennium to save two worlds.

Gryf was a thief from the streets of Tyst. If he died tomorrow, only his family would shed a tear, or even remember for more than a day. In a war, no one would remember him at all.

That was the fate of these folk, the Faiscarese. They didn't matter, and so they died, or lived on as cannibals and scavengers.

And Laz and Ama didn't understand. They never could.

[4]

Mole took a deep breath. "Tyrna Afankaya," he said with as much control as he could muster, "I've just come back from the dead. The only thing I can think to do for a fitting encore is help to save the world. Both of them, in fact. Tending to your comfort doesn't even rank close."

The Tyrna, now dressed like a barge woman in a costume hastily ransacked from the University basement, sat on the crate at the edge of the raft and looked, for all the world, like a Tyrna dressed as a barge woman. "Scholar Gylas," she began, "I must remind you of your proper place in the scheme of things. You are a Scholar. I am a noble. . . ."

"And I suck last teat behind you, or so the Haggers say," Mole agreed. "However, right now, we're performing a little charade to save all our lives and I'm the master of this stage —

and you're a barge woman. And barge women get off their ass, get on their feet, and pole."

"I have poled," said Tyrna Afankaya, showing her blistered hands. "I've poled upriver. I've poled downriver. I've poled up and downriver again. I've poled past bleaters and eidergeese and farms. I've poled past towns and villages. I've poled past burning cities that I don't think are anywhere on Nordomon, let alone Nyddys, and I don't think we're on the same continent anymore, let alone the same world."

Mole applauded, briefly and sarcastically. "Your grasp of the situation is admirable, Tyrna Afankaya. We are not on Nyddys anymore, let alone Nordomon, since by my calculations, we're somewhere in Glandair right now. And unless we pole upriver as fast as we can, we may be staying here for a very long while."

"You're joking, Scholar Gylas."

"No," he said simply, "unfortunately I'm not. We're in Glandair, somewhere in the Domains. Where they take a very dim view of foreigners, including Tyrnas."

She turned a bit pale, looking at the countryside around them, the low hills and oddly built farmhouses. "The Settling . . . we came here by accident?"

Mole shook his head. "No, we came here on purpose. When you spend your time behind the Flow, you get an understanding of how it settles, the way it eddies and shifts, and when the river shallows out and flows from one world to the other. I'm not an Iomardi Scribe with the talent to Walk or Bridge the worlds, but I've managed to learn something of how they interact. So we're making our way to the Empty Place by the best shortcuts I can find, following the spiral of the Flow like water flowing down a drain to the Empty Place." Mole smiled for punctuation. "So get off your ass and pole."

Tyrna Afankaya was obviously not used to losing arguments, even when presented with insurmountable evidence. "I don't see you poling."

Mole continued to smile. "That's because I'm not the Hero. I don't have a natural affinity for the Empty Place drawing me there; all I have is some very hard-won knowledge about the way the Pneuma flows and a pretty good guess of where the Empty Place is likely to be. Besides which, we have actually been traveling through Nyddys on occasion, so we have to keep the charade going for anyone who *does* observe us. And right now, I'm playing the part of your lazy-assed husband who has nothing better to do than sit around keeping the Pneuma-shields in place so certain Mages, Scribes, usurpers, bandits, and whatever other major or minor players out there who know about us don't scry us out and fry us. Been there, done that, trust me but it's not pleasant."

Still smiling, he formed a Pneuma-bolt with his left hand, small, just enough to sting, and aimed it at the Tyrna's behind. She yelped and stood up. "And I've left the role of Scholar as well. The Watchers' Council sits around and doesn't do much of anything, and I never took their vows to begin with. Not that they'd take me now." He mimed readying another stinger and was gratified to see Tyrna Afankaya pick up a pole and at least play the part of an inept, unenthusiastic barge woman.

It was better than nothing. Her handmaids, at least, had easily taken on the role of barge folk who'd made the mistake of coming downriver to Cyfareth on the same night that Anrydd had staged a coup and were doing their level best to pole their way as far back upriver as they could, away from Tyst and war and press gangs, though some of them, like the Tyrna, had no doubt begun to suspect they were not in Nyddys anymore. By the time she finished whispering with them, they'd no doubt be up to speed the same as the apprentice Watchers and students.

Firill came over and massaged his neck, easing the tension of keeping his form intact. "Nicely done."

"Thank you. Being annoyed at that woman helps me remember what it's like to be alive."

"Let me give you another reminder," said Firill and gave him a kiss, long and deep. Mole almost melted in her embrace but left a part of his consciousness aside to keep his shape stable. The realization that all life was Pneuma and all Pneuma was life, while a gratifying justification of certain theories, was another matter to deal with.

Right now he was as real as a little god materialized, or a sinta blossom or mera moth, those flowers and insects that bloomed only on the walls of temples or the parched land of wizard's duels because they were, in essence, the expression of the life of the Pneuma flow and the reality behind all the gods, little and great.

Mole was drawing upon that reality right now, fighting against the current the same way the raft was, at the moment, poling up the banks against the flow of the river. It was possible, but taxing, and took every ounce of strength and concentration, especially since the time of the Settling meant that all Pneuma in both worlds, including that within the Gods, was being sucked out into the place in-between, ready to flow through the Empty Place and enter the Hero . . . or whatever Mage put himself in his place.

Mole wondered if he dared, and what he would do with the power if he had it. Rule two worlds? Walk the earth as a god? Marry Firill, settle down, and raise a family?

He came up for air from their kiss and licked his lips. "Better than I remember it."

Firill smiled. "That's because I missed you."

"Thanks, but much as I want another one like that, I don't think I want to die again first." Mole hugged her, patted her once on the bottom, then went to survey the other side of the raft while she supervised this one. Too many people, of course, but some of them were the best students of Pneuma in the University, and their makeshift band was holding together like a rogue Watcher Meld, which was what in essence it was. It wasn't as if the Watchers' Council was in any shape to object.

Objectives. That was the trouble. Find the Hero or just get to the Empty Place? If you did one, you did the other. Aid the Hero or take the part of a Mage and take the power for yourself? Pray to the Gods for deliverance, or realize the Gods were in the same boat you were in, so to speak, in just as much danger from the imbalance in the worlds? Pray to yourself, the Little God Mole, created from a memory and a ritual and the Pneuma-born contents of a dead scholar's consciousness?

So many questions made it hard to think. Mole scratched his head with the claws he kept forgetting to unmake. Little wonder that the Watchers had decided to sit on their hands and do nothing. But they were all dead. Mole had already been down that path once before and didn't care to take it again, instructive as it had been on the workings of the Pneuma flow.

He was . . . well, he was Mole, and whether he was a resurrected man or a new god was a matter for scholarly debate, which was something he didn't really feel like now, especially since he didn't feel like either. What to do, what to do. . . .

[5]

The Drums that hung about the walls of his tent sang and pounded, pa-pum, pa-pum, tapping the beat like market women in the privacy of an inner court. It was a tune for dancing. Mahara strained to make out the rhythm as the Mage Drums continued to play in a ring, one then the other, pounding without the beat of human hands, each with the power of a murdered Mage. Zehirl the Great. Muedafi Keyn. Faraza. Burgu. Hasrem Rell. Sitoon Kaa. Their tattooed skins vibrated with the force of the Pneuma, beating like the hearts of the Mages who once wore them.

The echo of the Drums' vibrations set off a sound inside his skull, like a bell that chimes in sympathy with another when the sister-note is struck. Mahara began to understand the purpose of the Mage Drums. It was to speak to the Pneuma, the core inside of each, but no one but a Mage would have a deep enough well, a great yawning emptiness inside, to make it echo and resonate within.

Without knowing quite what he was doing, Mahara pulled the long iron pin from his hair and began to scrape it across his skin, across the surface of his palm and down the inner side of his right arm where no sigils were marked, then the same across the left. The Drums sounded, echoing within him, until at last they fell into silence and it was done.

Mahara opened his eyes and gazed upon the blood pouring down his arms, at the ruin of his flesh, and felt the Pneuma pouring from him and into him, from the Mage Drums and into the empty well inside. Then he realized what he had crafted—a map of Glandair on the right arm and of Iomard on the left, stretched out and elongated, with the Pneuma flow pulsing between the two. When he held his arms forth and palms up, the Pneuma threads were stretched taught as a drumskin, blank like the Chaos Drums the Watchers of Cyfareth had used to find their Hero. Yet he had one as well now, the last Drum of Chaos, the silent one, and he knew the drum's purpose as well. It was a map that charted the Pneuma flow between the two worlds. And there, at the crook of his right wrist, was the spot where no Pneuma flowed and all did, the Empty Place, marked like a map by the needle gouged into his bleeding flesh.

He knew where it was. He'd found the place they were all working toward. And while it lay deep within the territory the bitch Hudoleth had taken with her armies, she hadn't moved there yet. With army against army, he could push her back, and take it for himself. The needle in his skin burned with the pain of certainty. A fly buzzed around his head, attracted by the blood. Mahara did not care to kill it. He had no one to share his joy with, and a fly worked as well as any. "Tell her," he whispered to it, "tell that bitch Hudoleth that I have found the Empty Place and it will be mine and mine alone!" Then he laughed, long, low and rich, and threw wide his tent flaps, shooing the fly outside. His laughter was echoed only by the silence of the drums.

[6]

The wind whipped across the dry hills of Faiscar, blowing clouds of ash with it. Most were spent, burnt to empty whiteness, but occasionally the flakes were lit, glowing tinder bright, mixed with a plume of smoke or a swirl of sparks from the stump of some tree left filled with coals like a catchfire, fanned ablaze to spark new fires of anything that would burn.

Anything. Lyanz had seen the bodies, twisted in their death agonies, shrunken like crickets, their blackened hands twisted into hooked claws. Crickets the size of men, though there were no other insects about. The air was too dry, the wind too hot, the ashen hills too barren to support flies or maggots. But larger scavengers that could range in, birds and beasts, did, and had, leaving the bodies even further mangled, often no more than gnawed bones.

Corpses lay strewn about the ridge above them, victims of a War Wizard, remnants of some garrison of Faiscar resistance or soldiers from Tilkos or Kale, legacies of the army's passage like the war-rent earth and the stumps glowing like buckets of coals.

Lyanz swatted out a bit of stinging ash that landed on his forearm, the spark biting like a dying pincer beetle. In the hollow of his heart, he felt it. "Enchantment there," he said, "some Wizard left war magics on that."

Gryf snorted. " 'S there anythin' they di'n'? T'teeth! You'd think—"

"Be quiet," Amhar snapped, "I need to listen. . . ."

Gryf fell silent and Lyanz strained his ears. The Watchers had trained him well, but the Scribe was even better trained. She, after all, had been in combat. He'd only practiced, seen it, watched it, as others fought and died to protect him. Back at the Vale of Caeffordian, where Ellar and the others had given their lives to save him, their Hero.

Some Hero.

"Nothing," Amhar said at last. "Just coals, and the whispers of old Pnuema-workings."

Gryf shrugged, but still glanced about warily as Amhar led them up and around, passing upwind of the enspelled stump and around other Pneuma hot-spots that Lyanz could sense as well. Her peregrinations led them in a winding track up the hill, past the twisted attitudes of the corpses, and into a trap.

Gryf was the first to cry out, the first to give warning as half of the corpses sat up, the illusion dissolving, the fire-blacked stick figures revealed in truth to be a large band of stick-thin men, smeared with soot and camouflaged with Pneuma-workings subtle in their very weakness.

But only half the corpses sat up. Lyanz felt sick in the pit of his stomach. There was very little difference when you came down to it between a starved man covered with ashes and the corpse he'd been eating. Except there was less meat on the bones of the second, and more meat in the teeth of the first.

Lyanz dropped his pack and his sword was out on reflex, flashing, still unnaturally bright, unused save in practice. Gryf's cleverness and Amhar's expertise had kept him from anything more. Until now.

But the movements were there, and the man before him was weak and slow and did not dance away as Amhar would have, as would have the other Hero candidates back at the Vale. And Lyanz's blade was steel, slicing straight through the man's meager stomach.

Lyanz watched the cannibal fall and die. Watched a man fall and die. A man he'd killed. But before he'd had time to reflect on it, there was another, and another, like demons from a child's puppet theater, nothing real, nothing to feel guilt about. Just things to slice and slice.

It became a dance. A dance of death. He and Amhar going back to back, he with his sword, she with her staff, death on both sides of them. Gryf, who'd had experience with dirty battles in the Bothrin Market of Tyst, just leapt about and ran, tumbling, throwing ashes into one man's eyes, shooting another with a crossbow, using a well-tossed dagger to stab a third who came too close.

Was this what it meant to be a Hero? All the books Lyanz had read as a child had spoken of Heroes facing proud warlords, like Anrydd of Nyddys. Shameful mercenaries like the ones who had attacked the Vale.

Bloodthirsty soldiers . . .

The bloodthirst here was literal. These men were starving. Had nothing to eat or drink save each other and the dead. Had attacked, likely not as some bid of the Mages to kill him, but just out of the sheer madness of starvation. The Hero Band had food in their packs, and the way that one of the men was dragging away Lyanz's dropped bundle assured Lyanz of what these men truly wanted.

What was a Hero? A Hero saved lives. Was meant to save two worlds. If that was him, he might as well start with these men right here.

If they were still men. But the way that one had dragged away that pack assured him that at least some of them still hungered for something other than his blood.

Lyanz took another life, then shouted an order. "Amhar — Walk!"

"What?" she cried. "Where? Are you mad? And why?"

"Go to Corysiam," Lyanz shouted, his sword clashing against another man's. "Get her to Bridge food here. Water. Supplies."

These men were only men, and to a Scribe, that meant lower than beasts. But Amhar had spent enough time on Glandair to understand things being different, and as a Scribe, she was also used to taking orders. "Get Gryf to watch your back!" Then Lyanz felt the empty hollow behind him and the sucking in of the Pneuma as Amhar Walked between worlds.

There was little time to speculate after this. The dance of men became like a flip-book of greasy stick figures drawn with a charcoal pencil and drops of blood. He did not know why they still came, why they still attacked, did not speak the Faiscar dialect they screamed, did not understand.

His mind didn't, but his body did. His muscles were fresh and taut, conditioned and perfectly toned, and he moved in the dance, taking one life then another, in the back of his mind trying to salve his conscience with the Watchers' story that if he died, these men were all were doomed anyway, so he had to survive.

Then Amhar was back, brushing aside the next man ready

to set upon him. "Run!" she screamed. "Run!"

He felt it then, a pulse in the Pneuma flow, as another woman–*not* Corysiam–Walked between worlds, followed by another and another.

They had no bundles of food, nor swords either. Just hands clenched for Pneuma-strikes. But Lyanz suspected that these were lay sisters or some other sort of Scribe than Amhar, for they were unprepared for an assault by a ragged band of cannibals, being mobbed by sheer numbers who saw them unarmed and so thought them defenseless.

Lyanz, however, could also follow an order. Had done so with his father, and with the Watchers at the Vale. He ran, pausing only to snag Gryf's dropped pack, his and Amhar's already carried away.

They ran and ran, past the ashes and away from the screams, at last pausing to look back only when they had reached the crest of the next hill.

Gryf shielded his eyes. "Dunno your friends, Amhar," he panted, "but I think th' saved us."

"They're not my friends," the Scribe responded, her voice a mixture of fire and ice. "Those were some of Radayam's Scribes. Valla Murloch's been invaded."

There was a moment for that to sink in. "Cory?" Gryf asked then.

"Corysiam," Amhar stressed the full name, "wasn't there." She paused, her tones still running hot and cold, warming for the next: "I hope she survived." She gave a cool look to the far hill where the cannibal band was possibly eating, possibly doing other things, to the women who'd followed her. "Which is more than I can say for Rada's Scribes."

Gryf shrugged and turned. "Well, Hero's Luck anyway that th' followed y'here."

"Yes." Lyanz looked at the blood on the blade of his sword. "Hero's Luck."

Hero's Luck always. Someone else dying to save him.

[7]

Hudoleth returned to the University, alone at last with her birds and mirrors.

It was not as pleasant as she'd imagined.

After a long and relaxing bath, tea with honey, and a simple and happy time unpacking, dusting off curios and putting her home back to rights, Hudoleth set the magic room in order, killed five colos, and began a long bit of scrying without intrusions from Niosul or vomiting pregnant women.

The mirrors revealed new problems.

Oerfel of Nyddys was readying an invasion force to strike the mainland, taking the role of counselor to his new puppet Tyrn. Mahara of Kale still had the Third Prince by the ear and had managed to take the armies of Kale forward in several decisive battles against the armies of Chusinkayan. But worse, instead of taking the ground they'd gained and digging in fortifications, the armies of Kale were progressing across Tilkos at a rapid speed, following a course that seemed to offer little tactical advantage against the battered armies of Chusinkayan, but made perfect sense if he had another objective.

He'd found the Empty Place.

Hudoleth raged and strangled three more birds, which did little to improve her mood. Neither did casting their blood in the scrying bowl and adjusting the mirrors, taking out her web of power, and beginning the long invocations to bind spirits to hobble the armies of Kale with every plague and pestilence she could imagine, knowing that, with Mahara and his War Wizards, her efforts would be reduced to mere dyspepsia and flatulence. Enough, however, to allow the remnants of the Chusinkayan army time to intercept their foes and engage them, delaying them long enough for the Nyddys invasion force to catch them in a pincer grip and make them fight a rearguard action.

However, by observing the movements of Mahara, and viewing the progress of the Hero in the Syntayo's black mirror, she was able to triangulate with a map and find a good approximation of where the Empty Place was likely to be. Mahara didn't have the subtlety to go by a circuitous route, and the Hero was drawn to it, like filings to a magnet. Which gave her a chance of getting there first, with whatever forces she could call to hand.

If she worked quickly. Hudoleth gazed in the mirror, and while she did not yet see the face of the Hag looking back at her, she now saw the face of a haggard woman well past middle age, her long black hair streaked with gray. She'd been at the work for days, drawing deep on her energies and sucking power from the charms of youth. She hardly even recognized herself now. Ancestors! She hadn't time to work the Rite of Renewal, not with so many other things to do!

A plot began to hatch in Hudoleth's mind, fierce and hungry, like a tullin chick fresh from the egg. She paused and looked in the mirror and slowly, ever so slowly, smiled, seeing the gray-haired woman smile back. "Perhaps you can be of use, old woman. Perhaps you can be of use after all. . . ."

Mahara and Oerfel were both ensconced with their armies. Leading the charge, yes, but fettered by their own guards. She, having spent more than a year as plaything to the Emperor, had not had time to give herself a fine position at the fighting front. Even if she were to manipulate the generals into drafting sorcerers from the University to help with the war effort—in which case she'd almost be certainly called—there was still a strong chance that the Beloved of Sugreta, or one familiar with his needs, would station her at a place well behind the front lines, far from the charge that would lead to the Empty Place.

It wouldn't do. Not now, not at this time.

But there was a way she could travel with the army of Chusinkayan, unseen and unquestioned, with even the Emperor's Niosul unable to sniff out the slightest whiff of anything untoward. Hudoleth turned the mirror back toward herself. While she shuddered inwardly at the crow's feet about her eyes and the strands of gray among the black, she also recognized the possibilities. "Yes, old woman, you're going to serve me well. Very well indeed."

With that, Hudoleth took up the sharpest of her knives and sawed away at the streaked hair, then got out a razor and shaved the rest of it off, as well as her still beautiful gull wing eyebrows. Once she had the power of the Empty Place, she would have her beauty back tenfold. Tenfold, and more. The Hag had been threatening her for long enough. Time for the old bitch to earn her keep!

Lampblack from the side of a crucible worked to grime her face while still keeping it free of actual dirt. A brush with a jumble of cosmetics served for the assorted filth of the road, though she decided to forgo the perfume—a day in the heat would be enough to obtain *that*. She then took up her humblest yellow robe and put it on. After a moment with the pinking shears to artfully fray the sleeves and a soft-tipped brush to grime the knees with a few more cosmetics, she stood back and took a look in the mirror.

She didn't recognize the woman who stood there. If she saw her on the road, she wouldn't give her a second glance, or anything else save perhaps a string of coppers for her begging bowl. "And how does this evening find you, good Sister? Enjoying the pleasant weather?" She didn't respond for a moment, composing her features into the most humble and serene expression she knew, placing a finger across her lips. Then she took it away and laughed. "Ah, I understand. You've taken a vow of silence. I forget. But then those are common among Maratha nuns, aren't they?"

Carefully then, Hudoleth took a long-handled basket and packed her smallest vials of powder and reagents, using scarves and silken cloths to cushion the Syntayo's mirror, her scrying bowl, and the scroll tube that held her power web. She tucked this all under a cloth she'd bought from a farm-wife so long ago that the original red was faded to rose pastel and the edges were softer than cobwebs, almost as translucent and brittle. Then with this, a moneypouch around her neck, a pair of humble sandals, and a cage of sweetly singing birds, she set out upon the road.

After all, it was the place of a Maratha nun to tend to the dead and wounded of Chusinkayan. As such, she would gain welcome wherever she went and swift passage through the ranks of the army.

13

Quest for the White Bird

By the calendar of the Watchers of Glandair, events dating from the 16th day of Wythamis, the tenth month of the 739th Glandairic year since the last Settling.

[1]

The tug of the clasp on the strands of hair grew stronger and stronger, as did the weight of fatigue in his muscles. So long. It had been so long. The last horse had gone lame the day before, and rather than watch it die, he'd let it loose to graze and heal itself. With luck, it would find its way back to the farmer he'd borrowed it from, with a fine saddle as price of rental. Without luck, it would freeze to death. Breith didn't care to speculate which.

Yet in the forest before him, there was the smell of smoke. A friendly smell, mixed with bacon and apples and pickled cono leaves. At last he came to the farmhouse, if it could be called a farmhouse—as long as one of the Riverine trading houses and almost as wide. Cross-beams of gnarled ginger-wood stuck out at angles at the ends, carved with the faces of animals, their eyes blazing with Pneuma-light. They were either guardian spirits or ancestral gods, probably some combination of both.

He nearly ran to the door, seeing the flakes of snow more than feeling them, his skin so cold once he left the protective canopy of the trees that he only felt the pressure where they landed on his skin. They were the heavy thick kind, like bits of white colodown, each with a freezing drop of water at the center, catching and clinging to the infinitesimally greater warmth of his body and coating him in white head to toe before he moved more than a few feet, wading through the drifts outside the long lodge.

He paused on the stoop, hollowed out between walls of snow on each side, and stowed the pendulum bob of Cymel's braid charm beneath the overhang of his sweater and snow-crusted parka, his mittened hand refusing to let go for a moment, almost frozen rigid. Some strands of hair had iced to the mitten's leather, but at last it melted, sending a trickle of chill water and the frigid touch of the charm nestled against his belly, just under the lip of his frozen trousers.

The door was ornamented with more of the fantastic animals, their bodies carved into lithesome knots and wild shapes, hounds and stags and pinkbellies interlaced with bears and hunting birds. The top and bottom of the door were reinforced with iron chased with gold leaf, as were portions of the carved animals. And in the center, with the most amused expression, was a gilt wooden otter, the stone between its paws meant to bang the brass river clam on its chest when its rope tail was pulled.

Breith pulled, and the otter lifted its rock and struck the shell gong. Once, twice, thrice, and before Breith could pull the tail again, the door was jerked open.

The girl who opened the door was young and pretty, about halfway in age between Breith and his sister Bauli, who would be seven by now. This girl was dressed in white linen trimmed with fur and scarlet embroidery. Her mouth was half-open, looking as if she'd been expecting someone else, but she composed her features, smoothed her apron, and asked, "Who calls upon the Den of the Otter on this cold and wintry afternoon?"

Breith sighed. "A cold and weary traveler, hoping for shelter and news."

The girl paused, obviously unsure what to say once she'd given the formal address. "Um . . . just a minute." She half-closed the door and leaned her head inside, but her voice was still quite clear: "Ma! It's a stranger!"

There was a sound of rapid footfalls and a moment later a woman and an old man were standing in the doorframe over the young girl. The woman surveyed him a moment, then said, "The Den of the Otter bids you welcome. My name is Kureq, wife of the Hunter. Come in from the cold and warm yourself by our fire."

"My thanks," said Breith and accepted the invitation.

The Den of the Otter was warm inside, humid with the smell of drying furs and the rich stew that had drawn him here. Otterpelts and bearskins lined the hall and piled the backs of chairs and benches woven of interlaced branches and carved into the shapes of the same fanciful animals that had adorned the door and roofbeams and ones even more imaginative, tiny deer with the paws of mog-kittens and seals with wings and antlers. Two old women sat embroidering similar designs in gold and scarlet thread in the corner near the firepit, while another tended a huge stew pot from which came the tantalizing smell. Young women and boys had just paused setting the table to gaze at the stranger in the entryway, as did the children playing on the floor.

"My name is Breith," he said, taking his hat from his head

by the expedient of pulling it down over his face so as to not have to undo the frozen laces. "I've come north in quest of a White Bird."

The old man behind him laughed. "Better keep those mittens on then. Bit one of Fuirneil's fingers clean off."

Kureq turned to him. "Hush, Grandfather!" then to Breith, "You must pardon the old man. He sometimes forgets what year it is and imagines things. We know of no white birds save the snow colo, and they are too small and drowsy to do more than peck at grain." She said this last loudly so that everyone in the hall heard it, including the grandfather, who looked to Breith like a man who remembered not only what day it was, but everything else, except for when to mind his tongue.

With a gentle hand on his shoulder, Kureq led Breith away, telling her daughter, who was named Loakh, to help him off with his wet furs and see they were taken to the drying room, and see that he was treated to every courtesy (save being told the location of the White Bird).

Once unmittened, Breith kept hold on Cymel's clasp, and felt the talisman tugging in his hand, even though it was no longer suspended in the air. She was close. Very close. But the twinned sirens' calls of food and warmth were very seductive, and Breith decided to heed them. Were he to warm himself with Pneuma, or use it to snare a snow coney, the ripple in the flow would alert Cymel and she would take flight again. Instead, he waited while the Hunter and his men returned—equally as close-lipped as Kureq once she whispered in her husband's ear—then ate the rich stew, which tasted even better than it smelled, with dried apples and tubers and honey-cured bacon and venison sausage, mixed with roots and onions and carefully dried summer herbs. The wine was equally rich, a melomel brewed with equal portion of honey and some fruit called ahniaberry.

"Ahniaberry," repeated Breith, looking at the rich amber color of his wine in the carved antler cup, "I've heard of that somewhere before. . . ."

"Not likely," said Kureqon, the Hunter. "Ahniavines grow only along the streambanks here by the Den of the Otter, and only bear fruit for a few days in autumn, and that doesn't last. Unless you brew it with honey from the ahnia's spring flowers, as my clever wife here does."

"No, I'm certain I've heard of it somewhere before . . . ahn-iaberry . . ." said Breith, repeating the name, then had the memory come back to him, helped by the fumes of the wine. "I know! I remember Tandrak telling me of that. He said that fresh from the vine, they were the sweetest thing he'd ever tasted. Sweeter even than Rhonao's lips, though those lasted longer."

Breith leaned back into the pleasant fugue of wine and memory, recalling one of his friends, the mutes in Ascal, a world away, until suddenly a voice said, "I am Rhonao."

Breith opened his eyes to look down the table to see a woman, young still, but holding a baby at her breast and with a man beside her. "I am Rhonao," she repeated, "and I was Tandrak's . . . intended. Seven years ago he disappeared on a hunt, the night the strange fog came up from the streambed and odd birds flew through the forest. Tell me, have you seen him? Is he . . ." The words trailed off ominously, and in pain, and Breith watched a tear run down the woman's cheek as she choked out a single word: ". . . well?"

Breith did not know how to tell her that her lover, lost in the fog, had slipped between worlds into Ascal, where he even now lived as a slave, castrated and mute. He could not, would not tell her that. News of Tandrak's life, even if twisted into something idyllic and happy, would prompt feelings of anger and abandonment, for he knew that Tandrak loved Rhonoa still, and it was obvious that the woman's new husband was

having trouble living up to Rhonoa's shining memory, polished by tears and longing. The truth of Tandrak's situation
would be even more cruel, for he was certain that Rhonoa
was the type of woman who would quest to free him, even if
it meant crossing worlds and blackmailing half the sorcerers
and slavers from here to Ascal.

So he settled for the only possible truth. A lie. "I'm sorry,"
Breith said softly, "Tandrak is dead. I was present when he
died, speaking of you and the ahniaberries." Breith swallowed
and looked at the dregs of his wine, hating his disloyalty to
his lost friend, but knowing that Tandrak would never want
Rhonoa to suffer. "Actually, his last words were that he wished
he could kiss you once more with the taste of ahniaberries
on your lips."

A long silence at the table was broken only by the baby's
slurping, and then another woman leaned forward and looked
down the length. "I was his mother," she said, and her eyes
were wet with tears. "Tell me — how did my son die?"

"Bravely," Breith said, taking another swallow of wine, as
much to quench his dry throat as to give himself a moment
to think. Tandrak had been a hunter, and now tended the
great cats of the ladies of Ascal, training them to catch coneys
or ground colo for their mistresses' amusement when he was
not being used as a whipping boy for his mistress's pleasure.
How to turn that into something brave?

Breith looked to Rhonoa, and her baby, and came upon a
device. "Tandrak fell between the worlds. On the other side
of the Pneuma flow, you may have heard of the world of
Iomard. That is where Tandrak slipped to when the fog rose
up from the streambed, taking him to the continent of Ascal."
Breith took a sip of wine, wondering how to gild and sugar
the truth so as to not make Tandrak's mother cry out in horror. "In Ascal, there are many great lords and ladies. It is a
land of merchants and traders, and for their amusement, they

often have trained animals. Tandrak, with his training as a hunter, was able to secure service in the retinue of a great lady, tending to her hunting cats and beasts, which allowed him coin and shelter to live without aid of kin or family while still able to travel the land and seek Wizards and Scribes to ask them about passage to the world of his birth."

Tandrak's mother swallowed. "And his death?"

Breith swallowed as well. "I'm sorry to tell of this. One of the nurses in the lady's household was careless, and a young child made her way into the pen where lived the fiercest of the hunting cats, which Tandrak had not yet broken to the mistress's will. In rescuing the child, Tandrak was grievously injured, and died of fever three days later." Breith took a deep swallow of wine, but even the ahniaberries and honey together weren't sweet enough to cover the bitterness of the lie. "I had taken employment in that lady's household, and so I knew him, and heard his words as he died." Another swallow, and then the truth, "He had many friends among the servants there."

Tandrak's mother was crying, and so was the man beside her and the younger man beside him. But Rhonoa had dried her tears, and was simply bouncing her baby at her breast. "I thank you for having told us your story. We've long wondered what had happened to Tandrak." She put a hand on her husband's and squeezed it. "After the plates are cleared away, I would like to speak with you more. Tandrak was very dear to me, and I would like to . . ." She choked. ". . . hear more of his words."

"Of course," Breith said hoarsely.

The plates were cleared aside, and there was singing and games, while Breith was given a chair by the fire that seemed reserved for honored guests, with antlers carved to resemble wood and wood carved to resemble antlers, the whole covered in a trader's fortune of otterskins and gold leaf. Then Rhonoa came and sat down between him and the hearth, still nursing her baby. "So tell me," she said softly, "what truly happened to Tandrak?"

The fire cracked and popped, as if protesting the words of his lies, and Breith said, "I told you."

She gave a bittersweet smile and rocked the baby. "You told me that my intended longed to kiss me again, with the taste of ahniaberries on my lips. While it is true that he was fond of ahniaberries, and my kisses, they were two things he never got together." She looked at him with a wry smile. "I've never been able to stand ahnia. Too damned sweet." She grimaced then. "In fact, I told him more than once, I refused to kiss him if he had the taste of them on *his* lips." She looked at him for a long while. "So, what became of my Tandrak?"

Breith looked at her, still wishing to spare her pain. "You are better off not knowing."

She looked down at her baby and rocked him for a long while, then looked up with tears in her eyes, dark as river water on a moonless night. "That, I can tell, is the truth." She bit her lip, then uncovered the baby a bit. "I named him Tandrak. My husband protested, but it is a mother's right."

Breith bit his lip. "You really are better off not knowing."

She shook her head. "I'm not. But he is." She looked back at the baby, Tandrak, and made gurgling cooing noises for a long moment before covering him back up and rocking him against her breast beside the firelight. "It will be easier for him to know that he is named after a brave man who died saving a child than whatever evil fate truly befell my love. And so for his sake, I will not ask again." She looked at Breith a long moment, then licked her lips and said, "But one other thing, and answer me truthfully: Why do you seek the White Bird?"

Breith could not lie to this woman anymore. "The White Bird is my lost love, Cymel. She was injured by a Mage from my world and took the form of the bird to escape from her pain. I hope to find her to call her back to herself."

Rhonoa looked at him, dark-eyed, and nodded slowly. "It is a more extraordinary tale than the one you told at the table, but the most extraordinary tales are often true, and so I believe you."

"Thank you."

"Don't thank me yet," she said. "I'm telling you the bitter truth, from my lips to your ears, with no ahniaberry or honey to sweeten it. The hunters of this den plan to kill the bird and mount its skin above the fire, especially Fuirneil and Kureqon. Fuirneil lost a finger and half an ear to it, and Kureqon will have a large dent where he sits for the rest of his life." She smiled the same bittersweet smile. "They take the matter quite personally."

Breith sighed. "Then what should I do?"

Rhonoa rocked the baby for a long while, her figure bobbing in and out of the firelight and making the shadows flicker across Breith's face, but at last she said, "I will tell them that you are a trapper like they are, and that you have special snares in your pack, ones that you must set alone as a matter of lodge honor. You plan to trap the bird, but will need help tracking it and subduing it once you have it ensnared, and so will come back to camp to get them when you are through, so long as they lead you to the beast's lair."

"That is not the truth."

Rhonoa smiled. "You've done enough lying for one evening. Leave it to someone else." She stood and placed a hand on his shoulder, then leaned down and gave him a kiss on the cheek. "I wish you and your love the best of luck."

She left then, off to tell the hunters lies they would believe in place of a truth that they wouldn't, and Breith realized the word she had used, and he had said earlier: love. He loved Cymel.

[2]

Fuirneil and Kureqon led the way, pointing out spots where they had sighted the White Bird, and showing off the scars of their battle with the beast—Fuirneil, at least. Kureqon, as lead Hunter of the Den, did not speak of his injury, though the other hunters did, in whispers behind his back, or slightly veiled punning references such as "Be careful that the bird does not take you from behind!" and "It is a huge and terrible beast! Why, I have heard it once carried off an ass in its beak!"

Such words made it all the more clear why Kureqon even more than Fuirneil hated the White Bird and wanted her dead, even if that took foreign help. But with the hunter's skill at tracking, and the subtle tug of the talisman, they were able to find the White Bird nested high in a mountain valley beside a small round lake.

"Be careful," Fuirneil warned, "there's no sneaking up on the creature; its eyes see even when you think it's asleep."

Breith nodded. "Thank you. But I will need time alone here to lay my snares. Go farther back down in the valley and lay a signal fire; I'll come and get you when I am done."

The hunters smiled and nodded, looking toward him and his packs with the gleam of curiosity, but at last left him by himself. Breith was glad. He knew they wanted the White Bird for the stew pot and the feather bed, while as for himself, he had begun to wonder . . . the ham the folk of the otter ate was very plentiful and sweet, but he had as of yet seen no pigs in these woods, either wild or tame . . .

But that was possibly paranoia speaking. Tandrak had said nothing of his folk being cannibals (though that was a secret he would likely keep even from the other mutes) and Rhonoa had been more than kind. Time, simply, to lay his snares, which consisted of nothing at all, save himself. Mela had flown because she was chased; all he needed to do was leave himself where she might find him.

He looked about the area and found a nice solid bit of cliff to rest his back against, then settled in to wait. The mountain folk would be watching, perhaps all night. He hoped that they would run out of patience before he ran out of time.

A light dusting of graupel began to fall, snowflakes rimed with hoarfrost, halfway to hail, like barley pearls or tiny balls of crystal blown by the wind. They made a rattling, rasping sound as they bounced off the oilskin sheet thrown over his blankets. It was colder here, higher in the mountains, and the air was thinner, but the chill made it easier to stay warm within the cocoon of the blankets. Breith watched as long as he could, but at last his weariness betrayed him and sleep overtook him before the night was half over.

[3]

Rinchay Matan sat in her house of grass, listening to the buzzings of the flies, feeding herself as they did on the carrion nectar of the reotho plumes and the bodies of their fallen siblings.

Flies buzzed about her and crawled on her face, jeweled and jiggling like a bevy of courtesans sharing the latest gossip, each jostling the other for her attention, whispering a secret it had seen from the wall, a conversation it had overheard. The Liar had left her lair at Court, returning to the University of Kingakun. The Liar had been cast out by the Emperor. The Emperor's new concubine, Padmila, hated the Liar with a passion only Rinchay could rival, and had sent her away for the protection of her unborn child.

With the fervor of a mother who had seen her own children dead, Rinchay Matan applauded this. Would that she had been so wise.

The flies whispered more secrets, flashed stolen glimpses across the facets of their eyes. Rinchay pieced together a thousand vistas of her enemy, seen from above and below and behind. She knew the taste of the Liar's sweat, the nectar of the Mage's blood, the sweet poison of her cosmetics and perfumes. Lies. Illusions. Artifice.

Rinchay hated the Liar all the more.

Soul Eater, you have stolen my family. Soul Eater, you have stolen my children, the flesh of my body, and the flesh of theirs. You have wrought nothing but death, and feed on nothing but life. Leech. Tick. Vampire. Succubus.

The last was likely the closest to the truth. The vistas of the flies' eyes showed the Liar's age to wax and wane like the moon or a drunkard's resolution. Sometimes she was young and fair, a bit of fresh silk spun over a trapdoor spider's nest. Sometimes she was old and withered, a crone who had never given life, only taken it, with shrunken breasts that had never known children. But now she appeared to be middle-aged, and had chosen to wear half-the-truth as the mask of half-the-lie. A woman of older youth had left the palace, painted younger with the white powders and blushes of Court. That same woman had arrived at the University, viewed through a thousand faceted vistas.

Rinchay had been unable to see inside the house at the University, ringed round as it was with the spells of paranoia and fastidiousness that didn't allow even the smallest vermin to enter, let alone leave. But the flies of the gardens still saw what emerged from that house of death: a woman of half-middle-age, painted with the colors of dirt and the scents of poison, her hair and eyebrows shaved to appear as one of the mendicant nuns who sometimes wandered up from the Myndyar lands. But the bones were the same, and so was the scent of her sweat.

Liar. I've seen your lie and I am not fooled.

The Soul Eater walked up the paths of the University with determination and purpose, carrying a cage of birds squawking in fear of their lives, knowing that their escape from the house of death was no escape at all, merely a way to postpone their murders until the Liar found them convenient.

Rinchay had a brief urge to fly to Kingakun, confront the Whore of Untruths with what she had done, the enormity of the Mage's crimes. But the Liar wouldn't care.

Rinchay knew she must wait until she knew where the Liar was going.

Half a day passed and the answer came in the form of a dying fly, flown all the way from Mahara. Rinchay cradled it in her hands, breathing life back into it, and stared into its faceted eyes, seeing what it had seen.

A map. The Mage Mahara had carved a map into his own skin and the flow of his Pneuma the same as she did with her own hides and bone pins in the manner of the Grass Clans. She took a charcoal stick and traced the memories of the fly, comparing the result to her own maps and correcting them. Here the Finger Lakes. There the mountains of Kingakun. And high above, in the northern Grasslands of Nikawaid where the Dmar Spyonk had often gone to breed their ponies, a place of great significance, marked by an iron pin in the Mage Mahara's flesh.

Rinchay pierced the matching spot on her own map with one of her own bone pins, letting the light shine through the hole in a legend that would neither fade nor bleed, then listened to the memories of the dying fly, hearing the words that the mocking Mage had confided in it: *Tell her . . . tell that bitch Hudoleth that I have found the Empty Place and it will be mine and mine alone. . . .*

The fly also remembered Mahara's laugh, rich and cruel, and Rinchay joined it with one of her own. No, Mahara. No. This Empty Place, whatever it is, will not be yours alone. It will be mine as well, and I will use it to lure the Liar to her death. . . .

There came a weakness in her limbs then, a sense of satisfaction, but Rinchay knew it to be false and premature. No. There is still much that we must do before we can rest, before blood is repaid with blood. She rolled up the map and stood, parting the grass and the carrion plumes with a wave of her hand.

"Come to me, my Alaeshin. We set forth one last time. For Peace. For Justice. For Revenge. . . ."

The flies came to her then, landing on her, covering her with a carapace of shimmering sequins and jewels of hematite and lacquered jet. She gave back her Power as a Shaman, as the Revenant of the Grass Clans, and they lifted her into the air, taking her to the place that Mahara had been so kind as to find for her—She, as her dead god would have it, was closer to it than either of the Mages, Mahara or the Liar.

[4]

Breith half-woke, half-slept, still wrapped in the bonds of exhaustion and comfort, when something lifted him, then gave him a small, sharp shake. This action repeated until at last Breith could no longer ignore it, or the cold of the night air against his chest.

He opened his eyes to see the White Bird crouching over him, his blanket clutched in one webbed talon. She gripped his loose shirt in her beak and started once again to shake him. As if in a dream, he set his hand on the elegant curve of the beak and whispered, "I'm awake. What's happening?"

The bird shifted away from him, spread her wings, then

turned her head over her shoulders and smoothed her beak along her back feathers, an obvious invitation for him to climb atop her.

"Mela?" he whispered, coming out of the grip of sleep and not quite believing.

She made an impatient sound deep in her throat and Breith grinned. He clambered atop her, pulling the blanket with him against the cold. She had already collected the rest of his gear and strung it about herself. He took a moment to secure the blanket to the pack strap about her neck, forming a cape or a reversed bib under which he might shelter, then said, "I'm ready."

The White Bird ran forward, launching herself from the smaller cliff below them, then with a flap of unfolding wings, they were in the air, spiraling upward. Breith hung on desperately, sliding about. Time and again he was all too near falling, and one time did fall, the only thing saving him being the pack and blanket tied about the White Bird's neck.

She flew higher then, arching back so that he fell against her chest, then leveled out, making him fall back and lose his grip, only to be caught by the blanket, the back of which she'd grabbed in her talons, as if it were a baby sling pulled tight against her feathers. Breith tried not to move, afraid that the knot about her neck might slip. At last she settled down into an easy glide.

They landed with a thud and a bump and a flurry of snow, Breith's rear in the blanket being the first thing to touch ground, causing the White Bird to tumble end over end until the already strained pack strap broke. They both lay tumbled about in the fields of new fallen snow in the next valley, the White Bird looking up from the drift she was in with a perturbed expression in her eyes.

Breith laughed, more from relief at being alive than anything else.

The White Bird gave him a reproachful glance.

Breith struggled to sit up. "Well, don't blame me. I'm not the one with the wings." He then glanced at the jagged holes in the crust of melt-ice over the powder snow below, and the odd angles where the bird's wings would be. "Are you all right?"

The White Bird looked back at herself, at the holes in the rime of crystal atop the pure whiteness, and the confusion between white feathers and white snow, then began to thrash and struggle. Breith's heart leapt into his throat, but after a long moment, the White Bird at last stood awkwardly and shook her feathers clean before folding her wings with an icy dignity.

Breith looked around, to see the holes in the crust of rime where the possessions had flown from his open pack. "We'd better make camp before we freeze to death. Or at least I freeze to death. I don't have feathers, you know."

The White Bird held up one snow-covered foot, as if to point out that she didn't have moccasins.

Breith looked around. "The overhang under that cliff over there would be a good place."

The White Bird turned her sidelong glance to the cliff, then ruffled her feathers, as if to say that while she didn't know about "good," she could at least agree with "better." With great deliberateness and careful strides, she made her way not toward the shelter, but to the nearest hole in the ice crust, a long jagged rip in the expanse of crystal. She stabbed her beak in and a moment later pulled it back out with a sheet of frost hanging from the hook on the tip—the blanket, as coated with snow as they were themselves.

Breith struggled over, helping her to pull the blanket from the drift, then shook it and shook it until the snow fell free and he could lay it out over the top of the crust, a square of brown homespun on an expanse of white.

The White Bird watched this, then made her way up the slope to the next hole in the snowcrust, a small one. A stab of her beak brought up one of his lost mittens, and she flipped it to him as a fisherman would throw a fish onto the bank.

Breith missed the catch, his icy hands too stiff and slow, but the mitten landed atop the blanket with a scattering of snow. A second later, its mate did as well. With stiff fingers, Breith took them by the ends and beat them together until the loose snow flew out the cuffs. It would not do to have it melt around his fingers. He then forced them inside. It was no comfort, they were as cold as the snow, but he knew they would soon be warm enough. More than that, they were protection against the snow, which could scrape away flesh as easily as sand, and far more terribly for he would not feel it when it cut.

The White Bird was farther up the slope, where there were more holes in the crust. Breith could not help but laugh to see her stick her head down in the holes in the snow and fish out one possession or another—a twist of rope, or a sausage—just as a wading bird would spear frogs and crabs, flipping her treasures back to him and the blanket with an expert flick of her beak.

She could not recover everything this way, but they still gathered most of his gear. Once Breith had folded the blanket into a bundle, they made their way to the overhang, Breith struggling through the drifts, the White Bird wading with icy dignity mixed with uncertain flying hops when the snow became too deep. She was a waterbird, and was unable to get the sort of running start her form needed to truly become airborne in these conditions. Nevertheless, they still made it to the cave, half-frozen, but still glad to be alive.

Breith set his gear down in the driest place, then turned to the White Bird. "Can I set up some Wards, or are you going to take off at the first whiff of Pneuma?"

The White Bird eyed him uneasily as he began to reach out, but she was as trapped as he was in the shelter, both by the semi-paralysis of the cold and by the impossibility of taking flight or even running away. Instead, she just moved to the back of the overhang, crouching down in the deepest crack of the stone like a frightened child attempting to hide in the corner of a prison-home she could not escape.

Breith wanted to be kind, to whisper words of soft reassurance, but knew it would be better to simply turn his back and allow her the false comfort of not being observed, to let her feel that her hiding place, no matter how pathetic, was secure.

Kindness and cruelty were often intertwined. Cymel, as the White Bird, might fear the Pneuma, but that fear would not destroy her, whereas the cold would, as would the Mages who would sniff out the use of Pneuma unless he was very very careful.

Breith went to the mouth of the cavelet and teased forth a strand of the Pneuma. He heard a weak cry from the White Bird as he did this, but she stayed put in the far reaches of the cave. Tease and pull, tease and pull. It was like gathering hanks of loose fleece snagged on thornbushes and brambles after a flock of bleaters had been by. But the careful gathering of stray strands of the Pneuma was slow and soft. He hoped it would not send the White Bird into a panic, and hoped even more that it would not alert the Mages to their presence. So he pulled forth another and another, then began to twist them together, weaving together a webwork of glamour such that any who tried to scry out this cave would see nothing more than a sheer cliff wall all the way to the ground, sleeted over with snow and ice.

After a moment's thought, he turned the illusion inward as well, so that the White Bird, when she took her head from beneath her wing, would see the same glacial wall, keeping her trapped, yet safe. O Prophet, grant that neither Cymel nor the Mages saw through the illusion!

Breith then slipped outside the false icewall. The cave might be sanctuary right now, but without warmth, it would soon become a crypt. The icy landscape, while cold, was not quite barren. Not far away, a lone needle-pine stood dead, the main trunk sticking up as bare and straight as a ship's mast on the river before Urtha House. A simple bolt of Pneuma would shatter it, give him and Cymel the firewood that they needed, but such a display of power would set off a signal flare that even the blindest Mage would see.

Instead, Breith teased out another strand of Pneuma, spider thin, and formed a thread and sent it out, drifting with the wind until it touched the crown of the tree. A flick of the wrist and it looped itself around, anchoring itself, fine as the babystrand of a spiderling. Breith anchored the thread to an ice-rimmed boulder. Again, a second spiderweb, then another and another, layer upon layer. It was exhausting work, but necessary, forming at last a braid of twisted strands leading from the boulder to the crown of the dead tree. Breith then sent a touch of heat up the Pneuma thread and caused it to contract, like a ribbon of unwashed wool thrown into boiling water, becoming thicker as it grew shorter, pulling the dead tree farther over and over until it shattered with a report as loud as the loudest Pneuma-strike.

Yet loud as it was to the ears, to the Pneuma it was silent. Breith gathered up as much dry wood and kindling as he could, bringing it back through the wall of illusion and into the cave in several trips. A small fire vortex was all it took to start a cheery blaze. He and the White Bird were able to settle down before it, he to dry his boots and mittens and other clothes, she to dry her feathers.

Breith lay curled up against her side, her feathers tickling him, smelling pleasantly of rosewater and autumn leaves. He felt comfortable and happy. Deeply happy, though Cymel didn't know how to regain her human form and he didn't know enough to help her. He talked most of the night, filling the spaces between the silences, telling her everything that had happened to him since they had last spoken. He could not be certain, but he thought she understood him, or at least most of what he said.

Eventually, Breith drifted off to sleep, curled up against the soft feathers of the White Bird on one side and the warmth of the fire on the other, the crackle of the logs and the sighing of the snow outside forming a lull-a-bye as powerful as a Scribemother's chant.

Dreamscape:

Breith opened his eyes, felt his talons beneath him, then watched as a girlchild, the Cymel-of-years-past, opened the door of the mews and tossed red gobbets of meat to him. He caught one then held it in his talon, ripping at it, gobbling the flesh, and hearing the child sing, realizing on some level that he was within a dream of Mela's memories. "Tullin, tullin, dark and sullen," the dreamchild sang, and Breith wanted to speak, but could do no more than let out a hoarse screech. "Hoo-hoo, here's more for you . . ." sang the child, thrusting more raw meat at him, a bit of coneyflesh, then stroking his feathers with the edge of her finger, making him ruffle them up so she could scratch where the nit-lice bit and lay their eggs.

Then, before he could do anything, he felt the hood being jerked over his eyes and he fell back into sleep, into the bird-form her dream had given him. "I had the strangest dream," she whispered to him, "I dreamed I was a bird—isn't that odd? And I flew about for months, hunting. Strange, isn't it?"

Breith didn't know what to say, yes or no, and couldn't answer but then tumbled through the dream darkness into a circle of light, where Cymel lay, human, older, a dream-woman on a bed of white. And Breith felt the feathers fall from him as he regained his form and his tongue. "Oh, Mela . . ." Her flesh was soft beneath his hands, as smooth and lustrous as oiled silk. "I thought I had lost you. . . ."

"I thought I'd lost you too," the dream-Mela spoke. "Don't leave me. Don't ever leave me again. . . ."

They then fell together, and did what came naturally, what Breith had dreamed of doing time and again. . . .

Breith woke, and their bodies had already done what they could not. Cymel had her form again and they were making love in firelight and a bed of soft white feathers. Breith felt the softness of her flesh, and the tenderness of her touch as she clutched his back as he moved within her, until at last, spent, he lay down atop her and kissed her neck.

"Mole, oh Mole," Cymel breathed in Breith's ear, "Oh yes . . . oh yes. . . ."

Breith eased himself from his lover's arms, pulled a blanket around himself, and went to stand at the front of the cave where the snowfall had turned to freezing rain and beat down around him.

He'd been angry and afraid before. He'd been filled with spite and other ugliness and ashamed of himself afterward. But he had never before been simply hurt like this.

14

The Twisting of Mirrialta's Knife

By the calendar of the Domains of Iomard, the 27th Ekhtos, the eighth month of the Iomardi year 6536, the 723rd year since the last Corruption.

[1]

Radayam picked over her food. It was bland and tasteless, exactly the way it was supposed to be, with nothing to tempt the flesh to sin. Rada found she still didn't care for it. She poked her sticks at a piece of limp cono leaf, boiled until it was almost the same color as the soggy grains beside. Perhaps a fast? Vanity. Were she, leader of the faithful, to stop eating, it would start a fashion among her followers, who would grow faint with hunger when they should be ready for the ugliness of war.

That was the trouble. So much vanity. So much faithlessness. Even from herself. Virtue, in the absence of vice, was becoming vice itself.

The conquest of the Riverines was almost too easy. In fact, it was too easy. Almost everyone with a trace of Heresy upon them — Sighted males, foreigners, and the products of the impure marriages with both—had packed up and left during the unnatural Mage-spawned storm. And then the place was left open to them.

What were left were Darocs with no trace of mix, Lynborn with families as old as the Riverines and strong ties to the Domains, and the few sick and crippled of impure birth who could not stand the hardships of a sea voyage. These Radayam had helped to cleanse herself, while they spat upon her and called her murderess or gazed upon her with silent crying eyes.

Faobran had left them behind to torment her, Radayam was sure. Her Scribes and spies came forth and told her the obvious, that a half-blind mudpig could still see: Faobran of Urtha House had formed an alliance with the Daroc Mage Dur—Prophet forgive them for not burning his Sight and gelding and branding the Braysha child when they had a chance! But that one spoiled grain had flown far from the sheath, and carelessness and neglect had watered it until it reaped this bitter harvest.

But it was no matter. Dur, for all his blindness and impiety—rumors were that he was even calling himself a second Prophet!—was doing the Prophet's work nevertheless. The Tainted were being separated from the Pure. All the easier now for the Army of the Faithful to cleanse the land of blight.

The door opened and the servant came in to take away the food, the woman hooded in the robes of a penitent—the least punishment prescribed for those who had rejoined the Faithful from the Heresy of the Riverines. "Cay Radayam . . . you have not touched your food. . . ."

Radayam shook her head and pushed the tray away. "No, I am not hungry. As the Prophet said, 'Only a glutton eats when the body has no need.'" She stood and went to the window, looking out at the view of the river that the Heretic

Faobran and her family had for so many years. "The fresh air is enough for me."

"No matter," said the servant, shutting the door behind her and throwing back her hood. "I bring you a message from Mirrialta."

Radayam looked upon the woman's face — thin and intense with close-cropped hair and the look of hunger — and while it was even more so than when she saw it last, having become almost a caricature of itself, she recognized it nonetheless. "Thador. I remember you. What is my bride's — " She stopped abruptly, her voice cut off by the knife that appeared in her throat.

Thador crossed the room to her in two steps, twisting the blade and causing the blood to spray. "It would have been more pleasant for you, old woman, if you had just eaten the meal." She smiled, her teeth blackened and her eyes mad. "Do you know how much trouble it is to procure tasteless poison for tasteless food?"

Radayam did not answer, only reached up, clutching for the knife, but failing that, grabbed the speaker talisman that hung about her neck as a pendant, pulling free the Pneuma locked inside it and sending it forth as a great call throughout the Flow, letting her sister Scribes know the identity of her attacker and the hand behind the knife. Mirrialta! She had seen the hunger in the woman's eyes, but had judged her a scavenger content to pick over the scraps of war, not willing to force a matter to a close on her own.

Thador snarled like a hunting cat, but at the sound of footsteps heading toward the door grabbed the knife, slashing it free, and leapt from the balcony of Urtha House and into the river below, while Radayam went to her knees, gasping out her life's blood.

[2]

Darcport looked nothing like Valla Murloch. It was small and muddy, with little houses and hastily constructed shelters, barely more than camps. But it wasn't on fire or being invaded by the Army of Purification, so Bauli decided she liked it anyway.

She also liked the fact that Mum Fori had made it safe on her ship with the Scribes who weren't Bridges, and was there to take her from Aunt Cory as they walked down the plank to the beach and into the crowd of people waiting for them. Mum hugged her and swung her around, but not nearly long enough, since she then had to set her on the ground and hold her by one hand while she and Aunt Cory talked about the journey and politics and many things that Bauli either knew about already, or found completely boring or obvious, or all three together, and were nowhere near as important as where they were now.

The beach in Darcport was covered with round rocks, which was nicer than the mud of the riverbanks in Valla Murloch. Little green crabs scuttled about sideways between them and snapped their pincers and blew bubbles at you when you came near.

"Careful," said a boy, "th' pinch hard."

Bauli looked at him. He was a little bit older than her, with dark hair. A Daroc boy.

"If y'wanna catch 'em, y'gotta use a stick. Like this." He picked up a twig of driftwood and demonstrated, poking it under a rock until an irate crab latched on, which he then jerked out and held up in the air, dangling from one claw.

"Urs, put the crab down." A Daroc man with long braided hair stood next to him, dressed like a Scribe, except he was a man.

Urs did and the crab scuttled away. "Yes, Prophet."

Bauli added it up before Mum Fori did, since she was still talking politics with Aunt Cory. "You killed my mam." Then she kicked him in the shins, as hard as she could.

"Bauli!" screamed Mum Faobran and Aunt Cory as one, grabbing her back and pulling her behind themselves, though Bauli wanted to watch.

The Prophet—Mage Dur stood there, a grimace of pain across his face, but at last swallowed it and composed himself. "I s'pose I deserved that . . ." he gulped out, then, to Mum Fori, "Cay Faobran was remarkably direct and to the point about her feelings. I see your daughter's inherited the trait."

Aunt Cory almost giggled, but looked scared and clutched Bauli's arm with a hand as tight as one of the crab's pincers. But Mum Fori only nodded solemnly and said, "Indeed. Do you fault her?"

The Prophet-Mage gave a pained grin. "No, but my shin-bones are of a different opinion. She'll make a fine ruler one day, once she learns to temper that honesty with judgment."

Mum Fori nodded. "Do you speak hope or prophecy?"

He shrugged. "Little of both, I think. I'm not as used to visions as your wife was. But unless you want your daughter to kick me in the shins again, I think it would be best for my boy, Urs, here to take her to the house I've prepared for you while we walk on the beach and discuss matters of state." He grimaced again, and Bauli liked the way he did it, even while she still hated the man. "Or limp as the case might be."

Mum Fori looked at Bauli, and began to open her mouth, but the Prophet-Mage added, "I can promise you that you will see her again, safe, and that she and Urs will be as safe as any two children can be by themselves. Beyond that I can make no assurances."

Mum Fori smiled sourly, like she did when a merchant forced to buy an item for more than it was worth because she needed it anyway. She nodded. "Very well. Bauli, I expect to see you well behaved when I see you next. And clean. Urs, see that you take good care of my daughter. She's the only one I have."

Urs nodded. "Yes, Cay Fori." Aunt Cory then released Bauli in the direction of Urs and she and Mum walked down the beach with the limping Prophet-Mage.

Urs looked at her and scowled. "Y' shouldn'a done that."

"Why?" said Bauli. "He killed my mam."

"She asked fer it," Urs said. "Not like y'just did—kickin' a Mage in the shins—but direct. With words 'n everythin'."

Bauli confronted the boy, drawing herself up to her full height and getting in his chest. "What did she say? What did Mam Yasa tell him?"

Urs blew bubbles like a frightened crab. "She—she said she didn' wanna die, but she would t'save you an' yer mum and' yer brother, Broak—Braith—Brundo—somethin' like that—an' that if Dur killed her, he'd believe her, and he'd be able to save all of you like he's done us Daroc." He looked at the rocks then and shuffled his feet. "Sh'also told me t'tell you she loved you, 'cause sh'said she saw us 'ere, on the beach, an' for ya t'stop teasing the crabs—it's not nice—and you'd never know if they had worms like the mog-kitten. Sh'said that y'd know what that meant."

Bauli did and started crying, feeling like a baby, and hating that a boy was seeing her like this. But she still hugged him, because at least he was older than her. A little at least. "I just miss her . . ."

"I know," Urs said, "I do too. But Dur didn't wanna. He just had'ta."

"I wish he hadn't," Bauli said.

But Mum Yasa had said that while you don't always get what you wish for, it's sometimes better in the long run that you didn't. Even if that still didn't make you feel any better.

[3]

Mirrialta enjoyed her Seyl, Bruyd, and saw to it that he enjoyed learning the pleasures to which she was accustomed. Radayam had a novel assortment of whips and other instruments of pain. While she no doubt used them for the mortification of the flesh and chastising the wicked, vice was always closely married to virtue. Mirrialta was fairly certain that the old woman enjoyed it on some perverse level she'd never admit to herself.

Ah well. Mirrialta punished Bruyd for every crime he committed and every one she imagined, and a few he imagined himself. It was pleasant to find a mate to whom she was well suited, and even more pleasant breaking him to her will. He would do anything for her save that which was physically impossible. And even then he would try.

Mirrialta wondered when she would conceive and when the old biddy would get herself killed. Ideally the first before the second. It was looked at as bad form, if not quite Heresy, for the bride to conceive in the nine-month period of mourning after the death of the wife. But to do it afterward would leave concerns as to the validity of the heir, for once the period of mourning was over, the challenges to rulership of the House could begin if there were no heir already present. Indeed, more than one bride had found herself in uncomfortable circumstances merely from having a pregnancy run late.

Mirrialta finished with Bruyd and left him suspended while she picked out a robe for the morning and went out to fetch some water. That was the trouble with her practices — they required privacy — and until such time as Rada was well and truly dead and she were in control of the House, Mirrialta could not trust the servants. And it would be a long while before Bruyd was fit to be seen in public.

Outside the doors to her chambers she found Thador, looking half-drowned, beaten, and starved to death, which no doubt she'd enjoyed, at least now that she'd survived. She bowed low, touching her head to the floor. "Mistress Mirrialta, I have done as you asked. They are both dead."

Mirrialta paused. "Both? But I only wanted you to kill— Oh well, it's no matter. With Yasa dead too, Fori will suffer all the more, once she gets the news."

Thador shook her head. "No, Mistress Mirrialta. I have killed Malart, but I left the blind woman alive to suffer, as you instructed. And I have also killed *her*."

Mirrialta raised an eyebrow, trying to remember someone else who had annoyed her. "Which 'her'?"

Thador leaned close and whispered fiercely, "Cay Rada, your wife." She looked about the hall, then added, "It was not easy either. She didn't have any public spectacles, and didn't take the poison, so I had to do it with a knife. But she knew it was you who gave the order."

Mirrialta felt as if ice water had been poured down her back. All her plots. All her plans. . . .

Then she grabbed Thador by the arm and shook her. "Is this your idea of a joke?"

Thador shook her head, wide-eyed. "No, Mistress. I was only doing what you told me. . . ."

"Come in here," Mirrialta hissed, dragging her inside the room where Bruyd was still suspended from the harness of chastisement. She undid the straps with a knife, then dragged him to the door and shoved him outside, leaving him to take out the gag on his own. "Go fetch us breakfast! And take your time! I don't want to see you back here for at least an hour!"

He nodded—silently, though that was no surprise—and hobbled off down the hall. Mirrialta was even more angry that she didn't have time to enjoy the spectacle. She turned to Thador and brandished the knife, slamming the door behind her. "On your knees. Now! And tell me everything. As softly as you can. . . ."

Thador went down on her knees, tears beginning to pour down her face, her will well and truly broken. "Mistress," she said in a hoarse whisper, "I only did the tasks as you set them down: To kill Malart, leaving the blind woman and Cay Faobran alive to suffer, and then to kill Cay Radayam, your wife, letting her know it was you who sent me to do your bidding, for I am nothing but your hands and your will. . . ."

Mirrialta heard it clearly, for all that Thador said it in a hoarse whisper, and she could also hear the beating of her own heart as her plans unraveled. "When did I tell you this . . . ?"

Thador shook her head, as if confused, and said, "I do not recall the exact date, Mistress, but it was before I left for my journey. Due to difficulties accomplishing the first mission, I was imprisoned for a long while, so I was unable to kill Cay Radayam until after she had achieved the Riverines, but I still followed your orders as best I could." She simpered. "Have I not done well?"

Mirrialta wanted to stick the knife into her throat right then and there, but the woman was a trained killer and would probably fight back. So Mirrialta instead chose guile and wiles, the tricks she had best at her disposal. "You have done well, my pet," she said, placing a hand on the side of Thador's head, grown shaggy since she saw her last. "Go to the bed and place yourself in the harness, and I will see to it that you're taken care of."

And so she did, and so Mirrialta did as well.

When Bruyd returned with the breakfast, Mirrialta took it from him, placed it on the table, then pointed to the body. "You—put that in a sack, then take it out and bury it in the garden. Plant a tree over it so it will not be disturbed."

Mirrialta smiled then. Time Bruyd started earning his keep.

[4]

Faobran sat in the house Dur had appointed for them, in the place Yasa had died, and smelled the scent of her sisterwife still in the air. She was gone, and Faobran had never had time to say even a proper good-bye. The same with Malart, who did not even have a grave apart from the sea.

Dur had had Yasayl buried in the garden of this house, her grave planted with ghadidis bulbs — Yasa's favorite. Faobran didn't know whether to thank him or to curse him.

Corysiam entered then. "You have spoken with Dur?"

Faobran nodded. "Yes. And we are in agreement. He has left with most of the Scribes, as well as the Sighted males he has somehow . . . revitalized. . . . They and his Daroc army will strike the Riverines by land and by sea. I will remain behind here in Darcport to . . . administrate."

Corysiam nodded. "I see. Or rather, I don't. Why?"

Faobran waved her hand. "I don't know. When Yasa's sight passed to Dur, some of her stubbornness did as well. Or Dur already had a measure to match hers to begin with." She waved one hand and shook her head, pressing her fingers to her forehead at the end. "He says he's going to die, and I'm not certain if I'm glad. I should be, after all, but then I see what he's done for these people, and that's why he wants me here. He wants someone as Regent until Urs comes of age."

"Urs?"

Faobran shrugged. "Dur says he sees Urs ruling Darcport once he grows to be a man. What's more, he sees him as Seyl to Bauli, and says she's not going to take another wife."

Corysiam gave a bitter chuckle. "So now that he's gone

from Mage to Prophet-Mage, he wants to add Matchmaker to his titles?"

With a sigh, Faobran waved her hand again. "I suppose so. I learned to never question Yasa when she got in certain moods; Dur is exactly the same. Thank the Prophet he's not saying similar things about us; but then I'd know he was lying. Like Yasa's, this vision is vague enough to be in the realm of possibility, and clear enough that I can see the reality. Plus Yasa always said that Bauli would take a Seyl from outside the Riverines. We always assumed it would be a Lynborn of the Domains, but a Daroc from the Domains moved to Darcport still fits the vision neatly enough."

Corysiam sighed. "You have not spoken of whether I am to take any role in this."

Faobran shook her head. "No. Dur said that you should go to Glandair this afternoon, that you'll be needed there, by the Hero. He said you'd be able to find him."

Corysiam paused. "I will," she said, and vanished.

{ · 15 · }

The Silence of Kyodal

*By the calendar of the Watchers of Glandair, events dating
from the 5th day of Soramis, the tenth month of the 739th
Glandairic year since the last Settling.*

{ 1 }

Corysiam stepped across to Ellar's Farm, only to find it oc-
cupied—and not by the Hero and companions, as Malart had
reported. A wealman and his woman were lying there in Ellar's bed, looking even more shocked to see her than she was
to see them.

She quickly stepped back to the house in Darcport. Fool.
Just because Lyanz and the rest were *supposed* to be there
didn't mean they *would* be. It seemed an age ago that Malart
told her of his conversation with Breith. And Malart was now
dead. Any of a dozen things could have happened in the
other world, and obviously, at least one of them had. She cast
about, scrying Glandair, looking for a trace of the Hero.

It was like looking for a glass bead in a pool of water. He
was empty, hollow, *not*. She then changed the focus of her
search, looking for Amhar instead.

It took a long while, but at last she found her apprentice, in the mountains between Faiscar and Tilkos, passing in and out of Sight behind the nothingness that was Lyanz. Amhar held a flaming branch and was brandishing it against . . . something . . . Corysiam couldn't be quite sure what it was. No matter. Corysiam had her bow and her sword, and she was ready to use them.

She stepped between the worlds and joined the fight beside Amhar, sword unsheathed, only to see the attackers melt into the darkness beyond the firelight and flow away, too small to be men, too upright to be beasts, too solid to be shadows.

"What was that?"

Gryf was the first to answer. "Saw a marketwitch in Tyst once do tricks wi' th' firelight 'n shadows 'n puppets. Said if y' weren't careful with the spells, the shadows would come to life 'n sneak away from th' puppets 'n get folk in th' dead'a night." He licked his lips. "That's what I think 'tis."

Amhar was tired and pale, pushed beyond the bounds of exhaustion. "I don't know," she answered, resting the branch on the ground as the Pneuma-flames began to fall to cinders, her energies spent. "It's war magic, whatever it is. The sorcerers of Chusinkayan and Kale have unloaded their bags of tricks into these mountains, and some of the tricks have taken on a life of their own."

Lyanz spoke at last. "No. I saw them." He stood there in the firelight, lit from below, looking more beautiful than ever. "Those are men. Or at least they were, once."

"Before the magic," Amhar added.

Corysiam looked around. They were in a high mountain pass — defensible, with weapons. The darkness beyond the pass scuttled and chittered with the things that may have once been men, but were now something much worse.

Lyanz and Gryf had their swords, and Amhar had her staff,

but they'd long ago run out of arrows for Amhar and bolts for Gryf's crossbow. Corysiam unshouldered her own quiver and passed it to her apprentice. "You hold them off a bit longer. I'll be back with supplies." Then she stepped back, not to the house in Darcport, but to the storerooms of the garrison in Valla Murloch.

She knew where the arsenal was kept. If she came in from the back, only another Walker stepping from Glandair could get there before she stepped out. She grabbed one armful of quivers by passing her arm through their straps, then used the other hand to grab two cases of crossbow bolts and another crossbow, and then she stepped back away from Iomard.

In the bare minute that she'd stepped out, the shadow things had crept back, testing the defenses, but found that the arrows from Corysiam's quiver were sharp even if they came from Amhar's bow. Corysiam readied her own bow, dropping all but one quiver to the ground, then spoke the words to gather Pneuma to the tip and light it tinder bright. The bowstring sang as it flew past her ear, and then the arrow hit the spot of darkness that was blacker than the night around it.

The lurking horror hissed, illuminated from within like one of Gryf's marketplace shadowpuppets made three-dimensional, a mockery of life cut from the leather of a dead man's shrunken skin and lit inside with a hellish flame. And then it vanished, taken back to the underworld or burnt into ash, Corysiam didn't know which.

She touched Gryf's bolts, speaking the words again, and the same with the bolts of the crossbow Lyanz took up, hoping that Amhar would have enough Pneuma reserves to summon her own flames.

She did not, but the next volley of arrows and bolts was still sufficient. Two more shadow mockeries perished or vanished. One bolt went wild, trailing into the darkness with fulgent figures blacker than the night fleeing from its progress.

Once the battle was done, and Pneuma fires were kindled about the rocks to light the pass and guard it from the horrors' return, Corysiam turned to Amhar. "Why didn't you come fetch me sooner? I'm a Bridge; I could have spared you this."

Amhar looked back at her, incredulous. "Well begging your pardon, Scribe Corysiam, I *tried*. But the last time I went back, Valla Murloch was crawling with Inquisitors and Radayam's army. That was a narrow escape as well, and I decided I'd do a better job of helping with the Hero's Quest by staying here with Lyanz."

Corysiam nodded, acknowledging the fact. In the panicked rush to evacuate the Riverines, the idea of notifying the Hero and Companions of the change in circumstances had also slipped past her. She raised an eyebrow. "It's not as if you told me you were leaving Ellar's Tower."

"There wasn't time," Amhar shot back.

"Ditto."

Gryf snorted in disgust. "Are you two world-walkin' women gonna stand there and bitch at each other 'bout who fergot to tell who what, or is one of ya gonna fetch us some food?"

Corysiam and Amhar both stopped. It was unheard of for a man to talk to a Scribe like that, in that tone. But that was in Iomard, and this was Glandair, and more than that, Gryf was right. "That would be me," Corysiam said, and, making sure to scry the location out beforehand, she Walked to the kitchen of Urtha House and grabbed a loaf, a kitchen mitt, and a cauldron, with a wink to the Daroc cook, who would know better than to tell. A missing pot and mitt, after all, were much easier to explain than the appearance of a Heretic Scribe in her old house.

Corysiam set the pot on the ground and almost sat down beside it, her legs ready to fold up from the Walking and the Bridging. She decided to feign hunger rather than weakness, and sat. "Well, let's see what's for dinner. . . ." She lifted the lid with the mitt and revealed a hearty pot of stew, the recipe the same as it always had been in Urtha House, perhaps a little blander to please the puritanical tastes of Radayam's faithful.

Corysiam passed the loaf around. They each tore loose chunks of bread to sop the stew up with, as she began to listen to the tales of their wanderings. The grim and savage story made Corysiam ashamed that she hadn't come sooner. With a Bridge to help with supplies, much of what the Hero Band has suffered simply would not have happened.

"And Breith and Cymel? Where are they?"

Amhar and Lyanz looked silently at each other, holding hands in the Pneuma-light. Gryf spoke: "Cymel changed inta a big bird back at the Vale 'n chased the Mages away, then took us to the Tower, where Breith was. Then she got spooked, so he went off to chase her down, 'n left me to light a fire under their butts and get him t'the Empty Place."

Lyanz looked perfect and innocent, too beautiful to be real, while Amhar merely nodded and did not make eye contact. Corysiam frowned. "Well done, Gryf. Now, let's hope we can finish what you've started.

[2]

Brother Kyo stood upon the battlefield and made the Blessing Sign over a fallen soldier. He could not tell whether this one was Myndyar or foreign, his bones twisted like a fungus by some Wizard's warspell, but all benefitted from the Peace of Marath Alaesh, which knew no borders or allegiances, save what the Temple needed to survive.

A bit away he saw a Sister of his Order bearing a basket and a cage of singing birds, pausing over the bodies of the dead to offer some prayer of her own making or taking the moment to offer the dying a taste of libations from a flask she took from the basket. He wondered for a moment if she were from a Temple from the hinterlands, who did service to Marath Alaesh in ways different from his own, but then she came closer and he paused. Her look was right, and her robe was humble, but the whole had the appearance of artifice, as if her sleeves had been frayed by the bite of a seamstress's shears and the fine dirt upon her face were only a veneer of powders upon the pampered skin of a lady of the Court.

She made her way along the rows, birds singing, and Kyodal wondered if that's what she was. Truly, many of the nuns of Marath had started their service as a small devotion, taking up the habit as a way of working charity as well as stepping outside of the rigid bounds of ceremony and precedence, only to find that the humble life agreed with them. He himself had done so once, beginning life as the son of a rich Merchant who wished to have only a few days of solitude outside of the strict eye of his father, only to find that the work of the Temple was a far greater calling than the trade of a Merchant and the monk's path was the one that Marath Alaesh intended him to walk.

Yet something was wrong all the same. Ladies of the Court who escaped in the habit of a nun kept their long hair carefully pinned up under a humble wimple and rice-beater's hat, while this woman had the faint down upon her scalp of one who had shaved her head but days ago. She did not have the bearing of one who was penitent, stepping over the dead and the dying with care, yes, and a pleasant smile for one and all, but more the look of a noblewoman tending her garden of flowers than a nun offering comfort to those fallen in battle. The words of her prayers were strange as well, in the ancient language of the Dreamtime, which only the most scholarly of monks knew.

Yet he recognized the lilting syllables, even if not the precise words. "Lo sodelu . . . quihok, olh! . . . On virtesan . . .

Mynd ha kifa . . . Sa wetara kre fi na se boluch . . ." She walked by him, with a smile and a nod as he placed his finger to his lips to indicate he was a silent Brother, and he made the Blessing Sign for one who followed the same path. She returned it with as elegant a flourish as the most revered of the lamas, as if she had spent several lifetimes practicing the calligraphy of the gesture and could now place her hands in the sacred mudhras as easily as breathing. She offered the flask which she had just used to give a drink to a dying soldier.

Kyodal paused, and his eyes caught the light in the soldier's eyes as he died, a bit too quickly. Brother Kyodal then raised his hands and demurred, gesturing that the drink should be offered to those who were in greater need of it. The nun insisted, holding it out to him, and Kyodal did not wish to arouse her suspicions by refusing her hospitality or to reveal that he knew she was not a Sister or a penitent lady of the Court, but a murderess.

After another polite gesture of refusal, Kyodal took the flask from the woman, carefully holding his thumb over its mouth as he mimed tossing back a swig and swallowing. Then, with the best acting he could muster, he handed back the flask and fell down in a swoon, willing his body to go into the death trance of deep meditation or as close as he could manage.

The nun leaned down and turned him over, checking his pupils then testing his thready pulse, while Kyodal urged his heart to calm, calm, beat slower, as if drifting off to sleep and then the sleep that mimicked death. At last the nun was satisfied. "Blessings on you, Brother," she said, laughing, then added in the beautiful and sinister poetry of the Dreamtime, "Loch na trin da vi quam pirdre . . ."

Kyodal felt his thumb burn at the words, the thumb that hat touched the liquid in the flask. Yet he continued to lie there in the death trance until he heard the false nun's singing grow fainter and fainter. Only when the words were the faintest strains of evil music did he dare to open his eyes slowly and move his head by degrees until he could see what the murderess intended.

She had moved to the top of a small rise, overlooking the battlefield. She had shed her robe, replacing it with a dancer's web of silver laces and spangles, mirrored fans in both hands and a festival mask of silver lace crowning her head. She danced with the same wicked fluidity that she gestured and sang, a dance from the Dreamtime, yet harsh and dissonant. The sound of her words drifted down to his ears and cloyed while burning, like honey laced with pepper and poison. "Ai lo trono, so le veda, han tralanet'th oh ch'ma nan phargar-erüm . . ."

Then Brother Kyo saw the work of this magic. With a cry of dying birds, and a trill from the sorceress, a wind sprang up, a dark wind, smelling of autumn and must and mold and cellars left untended for long years allowing the rot and decay to collect and ferment until the whole scent was nothing natural, but something foul and unclean, foul enough to wake the dead.

And wake they did. The soldier next to him, though his throat was gashed from side to side and an arrow was sunk deep into his back, stood up, looking to the sorceress with a sightless stare. Around the battlefield the same happened again and again, wherever the sorceress had given her foul blessing and placed her sacrament upon the lips of the dead. "Ankhard fer des t'el h'dan fehl, meichaent hat'rthe. . . ."

Brother Kyo's thumb burned and he wiped it in the blood-soaked dirt of the killing field, watching the mud writhe at the touch and the crushed grass spring up again in mockery of life until he made the Blessing Sign of Marath over both. But Kyodal knew he could not oppose this sorceress, even if he were to break his vows and take a direct hand in the affairs of state and war, for this, he realized, was exactly what this was. The sorceress had taken the dead of Chusinkayan and the dead of her enemies and forged a new army, one that would fight and kill and not tire or hunger or give any complaint, save to the noses of the living and the belief in all that was pure and holy.

Brother Kyo stood, and joined the army of the dead, watching as the corpses raised a palanquin from a fallen general and stood as flesh steps for the sorceress to rise to her throne, bearing her aloft and marching north with her, on their lips the foul chant of the Dreamtime:

> *"Ah, n' o sotha*
> *La no tra*
> *Kyan pha quo'lo*
> *Khan n'nt se*
> *Pa ra nestehleu*
> *Pheleeum ned lefs'kik*
> *Semsem'pradk equuls*
> *De nachzek nü!"*

Kyodal fell into step, mouthing the words after a few repetitions but giving them no voice. The dead neither noticed nor cared so far as he could tell; his performance was merely for the benefit of the sorceress, Marath bring her peace.

Were he a less peaceful man, Brother Kyo would do his best to kill her where she stood. But Marath had commanded that he not interfere in the arts of war or politics, nor keep another from following the course of their road, even if it led down the most wicked of paths. All he was allowed to do was defend himself, with no more force than was necessary.

Kyodal wondered if his road might allow him to bring that

defense around full circle, so that the karma of the sorceress's actions would confront her in the passage of this life and not the next.

Brother Kyo did not know. But with the peace of Marath, all things were possible. . . .

[3]

"I'm sorry, Breith. It's just . . ." How to say it? What to say? That she loved Mole? That when he was killed, something broke in her, followed almost immediately by the Mage Dur burning her brain? And after what Siofray Mage had done, she could never look at an odd-eyed man without remembering *that*.

It wasn't fair, of course. Breith had done nothing to hurt her, hadn't smacked so much as a fieldmouse, and it wasn't fair to throw the story of the Braysha boy and all its baggage in his face. But still there was the look. And the memory.

It didn't help that she loved Breith too, but in a different way. And not just as a friend either.

It was just so complicated. . . . She wished she could speak to Mole. He was older and so much more experienced.

Except he was dead, and even if he weren't, she knew it wouldn't last with him forever—he was linked with Firill, no matter how many lovers he took on the side. But Cymel had wanted her first time to be with him, just to know how good it could be.

Not that it was bad with Breith. But more than half of that was the Pneuma and dreams working their will and her body seeking a way to remake its natural form.

"Breith, please, wait. . . ."

He stood in the lip of the cave, in the freezing rain, and didn't move when she touched him, not flinching away, but not turning toward her either, his skin cold and wet. But at last he let her draw him inside, toward the dying coals of the fire. "*Please*, just sit down. . . ."

He did. The white down she'd shed during the transformation rose up in a cloud when they sat, then settled all over them. Cymel tried not to giggle at how silly Breith looked now, knowing that she must look the same, as if they'd just had a fight with a torn pillow. "I love you, Breith. It's just that . . ."

He looked at her, his eyes green and brown. Like Dur's eyes, yes, but more like his own.

But she'd always seen Dur's that way, green and brown. For almost all of the years that she'd known Breith, his eyes had been brown alone, without the leaf green that to her had always signaled danger. And pain.

"Please, just sit and listen. . . . I—I loved Mole, but he's dead now, and I love you too. I've always wanted to be with you, but Mole . . . I don't know, he taught me so much. About myself, about the Flow . . . and I always imagined him being my first. When it happened, I was dreaming. And you were him."

Breith sat there in the firelight, tears in his eyes. "I was only dreaming about you. . . ."

Cymel hugged him, and—thankfully—he did not refuse her touch. "I know. And that's why I love you. And I'm sorry."

Breith reached over to his clothes, tossed aside in the pile of feathers and blankets, and took out one of her woven leather hairclasps, mixed with a few strands of matted hair. He held it out to her without comment.

Cymel took the clasp, emptying it of the torn braidlet, then gathered her hair back into a ponytail and knotted it together. It felt complete somehow, like a part of her coming back. "I've lost its mate. I think that must be a feather now, along with my clothes."

"What are we going to do?"

"About clothes? Nothing." Cymel understood the working now, and did the steps of Mole's dance inside her head, drinking enough Pneuma from the Flow to work the transformation, letting arms stretch into pinions and mouth distend into beak, but not so much that she lost herself to it.

She didn't think it would happen again. Time as the White Bird had healed her mind, stretching the scars upon the skin of the Pneuma until it felt like it always did, but greater. Dur had forced her Sight to grow before its time, but now the pain of the stretching was done, and the agony of healing had passed. Her Sight had matured. And she could feel the power of the Pneuma ready inside her.

"We need to find Lyanz," she said, feeling strange to be consciously speaking with a human voice while in the shape of a bird. "It's more important than ever that we get him to the Empty Place. I was just in the flow, and I felt where it was going. . . ."

And something else. A familiar ripple. A step in the Dance. No, not the Nyddys Mage, for all that he'd learned to copy the steps as well. No, it was a familiar pattern, one she recognized, like the movements of a friend across a crowded room.

"Quickly," she said. "Get your gear and get on. We have to go."

"What's the hurry?" asked Breith.

Cymel fell silent then. Not knowing how to tell him. What to tell him.

The dance she had felt, the ripple in the current. That was Mole.

Softly, softly go little mole feet, and who knows where they would carry him.

{ 4 }

"Is there any strategic advantage in this?" Prince Zulam looked at the map pinned to the table in Mahara's tent, a copy of the new scarification on the Mage's forearms. "If there is, I don't see it."

Mahara cursed himself for being less than adept at Court politics, or simple outright lies. "There is one. Trust me." He decided to push the envelope. "Have I led you wrong thus far?"

The Third Prince's eyes slid over to Inlirre, his bride, and her sister Frantki in the corner of the tent, then back. He raised one eyebrow.

"Well, admittedly, she's no Pika Mar. But who is? And would you really want to have brought that lovely flower of the Court out here?"

The Third Prince was about to reply when Mahara noticed something that made his blood boil—Frantki, again. On her knee she had an image of the goddess Cypresta, patchwork skirts and all. She was dandling the goddess by her arms and jouncing her on one knee to make her dance for her expressionless sister.

"What are you doing?" Mahara snarled, snatching the icon from her.

Frantki looked up, almost as frightened as her sister, then asked softly, "Playing with a dolly?"

"This is not a doll." Mahara shook the idol, making Her wooden arms rattle, then slammed Her down on the war table, alongside the enameled icon of the Dragon Rueth and a painted wood-and-ribbon snake that had been pressed into service to symbolize the Dark Wyrm of Tilkos. "This is an image of the goddess Cypresta."

"She's a coinpurse," Frantki added helpfully.

"What!?"

The girl pointed a hesitant finger at the smiling embroidered icon. "You just lift up her skirts."

Mahara, with great deliberation, did as the girl instructed. Underneath the goddess's skirts was not only a silver catch which opened in a lewd pun, but an embroidered legend: *Souvenir of Cypresta.*

He smiled then, a deadly smile. Trust the Faiscarese to do something like that. When he had asked for an image for his war table, they had given him a joke, and not a very sly one, except for their smiling expressions and their enviable ability to not betray any humor.

Mahara was wondering if they'd put anything inside, another trinket or present or pun, but the idea of putting his finger up their goddess only made him despise the Cyprestans even more. "How . . ." What was he supposed to say? Quaint? Typical? Annoying?

He threw the coinpurse at Frantki, and unfortunately she caught it, rather than it smacking her in the face.

He hoped he could kill her soon. He was growing tired of this charade. But it was necessary if he was to have the strength he needed to face Hudoleth.

"There's great profit in it. Trust me on this, Zulam. Prince Zulam, I mean. There's a place in northern Nikawaid that holds great strategic importance, and we need to get there first, before Hudoleth's forces."

"Who's Hudoleth?" asked Frantki.

Mahara glared at her, but she'd asked the question that the Third Prince didn't have the sense or the bravery to ask. At least directly. Instead, he just raised his eyebrow and left his young sister-in-law's question hanging.

Mahara sighed. It really didn't matter much at this point. "The Emperor of Chusinkayan's secret general."

"Hudoleth is a pretty name," remarked Frantki. "She sounds like a girl."

Mahara would take great pleasure in killing Zulam's little sister-in-law. "She is. Any other questions?"

The Third Prince grimaced. "Why haven't you mentioned this Hudoleth to me yet?"

Mahara tried to come up with a reason that might placate Zulam. Because he'd only recently become aware of her? Because it was dangerous for the Prince to know? Because the knowledge didn't fit in with Mahara's plans.

Frantki hugged her new doll. "Well if everybody knew, it wouldn't be a secret, now would it?"

Mahara gave her a sharp look, at the same time as the Third Prince.

"No . . ." said Prince Zulam slowly, "I suppose it wouldn't." Then to Mahara, "It's better that she doesn't know that we know?"

Actually, it wouldn't make a fig of difference, but Mahara was grateful for the explanation all the same. "Indeed." He smiled to Frantki, both thanks and warning. "Then it is agreed then? We go to this place in northern Nikawaid?"

The Third Prince nodded, while Franki simply pushed her luck. "What's so special about this place?"

Mahara hated her again. "If everyone knew, then it wouldn't be special, now would it?" On a whim, he threw her the Dread Wyrm of Tilkos, which had the look of a child's toy as well. "Trust me — you'll find out when we get there. Agreed?"

The Third Prince nodded. "Agreed."

Mahara smiled at Frantki. It appeared he had bought her silence, or at least she'd finally learned to take a hint. He swept out of the tent, leaving her to discover the lewd but obvious blasphemy of stuffing the Wyrm in Cypresta's moneymaker.

[5]

They had landed in Cypresta and taken it, but that wasn't much of a triumph. The city had already been overrun by refugees from Tilkos, then looted by the armies of Kale, with almost all of the able-bodied men already impressed into the military. The Faiscarese took another invasion as simply a sign of the times. A few maintained the pretense of doing business as usual, writing things down in ledgers as loans or penning meaningless treaties, while others went about their normal lives, or as close to their normal lives as they could pretend, catering to Anrydd's army as they did to all who had come before. Like rats and colos, they survived, and didn't mind too much if their fellows were killed or driven out.

Anrydd was declared the Liberator of Cypresta, using the same banners, he thought, that had been used for the invasion of the Third Prince of Kale, and no doubt some city festival before that.

Oerfel was darkly amused, as he rode in the back of the Anrydd's racing chariot through the winding Cyprestan streets. "It goes well, does it not, my Tyrn? But remember: All glory is fleeting." Then he smiled, as if he knew some private joke, and an exception to the rule that gave him pleasure.

I know something you don't know too, old man, Anrydd thought. *You don't know that I'm not the puppet Tyrn you think. I wear the mask so well that it fools even you. And the first chance I get, you're dead. Tyrny counselors die all the time, and no one cares. Why should anyone care about you?*

I'm just waiting for the right moment. After all, if I kill you now, I'm only Tyrn of Nyddys. If I wait and let you play your game, I may end up Emperor of all Nordomon. And wouldn't that be a trick for the bastard son of the old Tyrn?

Anrydd silently thanked Isel as well for the information. *We'll beat him soon enough, brother.*

It was amazing how much your opinion of a person could improve once you killed them. Once he was Emperor, he thought it might be good to put up a statue to wise Counselor Oerfel and his late unlamented half brother, Isel. It was always nice to show the family tree.

But Oerfel still had his plans and his uses. He informed Anrydd that the two other Mages were marching for some place to the north, and tactics be damned, they were going to march that way too.

Anrydd gave the orders, letting his generals invent their own explanations. The march for the north of Nordomon was on. After all, the wise new Tyrn had led them this far; he no doubt had something else up his sleeve as well.

Anrydd wondered what it was, and how he could take it from Oerfel.

[6]

Breith still loved Cymel, and wanted to forgive her. But it would have been easier to forgive and forget had Mole stayed conveniently dead.

Prophet's tears, what a thought. But pain had a way of saying what the heart felt, and when the heart was bruised, it said hurtful things.

Mole had come back from the dead. Sweet messengers, even the Prophet hadn't managed that trick. And what was he supposed to do to top that? Save the world? That job was already taken by Lyanz.

All Breith had done was trek across half of the world to save the woman he loved. Shouldn't that be enough?

Her feathers were soft under his fingers. He sat upright in a better harness, rigged to be somewhere between a saddle and a basket swing like he and his father had used when sailing up and down the Siamsa. The three corners of the canvas were made into a diaper of sorts, hooked in the middle with a ring from one of the packs, and that fastened to the line that held to the mast. Or the reins around Cymel's neck as the case might be. Even if he fell, he'd be suspended and safe.

But the wind blew in his hair and made his eyes tear. Breith took a moment to mold a piece of clear Pneuma into bubble patches to go over his eyes, like his father had showed him how to do when he wanted to see clearly underwater. The trick worked in the air as well.

On they flew, and on. Across the Halsianel Sea, and over Faiscar, getting a fine view of the countryside below, and the devastation. Huge plots of forest were burned, or burning. The Grasslands were stained red with blood, or black with soot, or both.

One patch of black and red was moving. What Breith thought at first was a column of soldiers moving with black mail trimmed with gold, red plumes, and green pennants, was revealed to be nothing less than a huge serpent or dragon, crawling across the land. Its neck had a ruff of scarlet vanes, its scales were emerald and gold, and its tiny legs with wicked ebon claws rasped against the soil as it slithered along the earth.

Breith clutched Cymel's feathers tighter. "What by all the holy names of the Prophet is *that*?"

Cymel hissed and flew higher. "Rueth, the Serpent God of Kale!" she cried, shouting not so much in awe or horror as urgency, as she flapped her wings and strained her neck, rising higher so that the crowned serpent couldn't reach them unless it coiled and leapt.

Of course, it was a god. For all Breith knew, it could fly.

They flew past one dream serpent only to find another—

a great wyrm, easily half again as long as the Dragon Rueth and twice as thick, slithering legless across the fields, a chthonic god with a spreading hood and fangs that dripped ocher fire, eyes blazing like the sun focused through a lens of crystal, burning to the flashpoint. Riding on the back of the wyrm, as nonchalant as a lady out for a festival morning's ride, was a woman composed of ethereal light, almost half as tall as the serpent was long, counting her spired crown, her skirts checked like a harlequin and flashing with jewels.

Breith didn't even know what he was seeing, but Mela thankfully provided the explanation: "The Dread Wyrm of Tilkos and Cypresta, Faiscar Goddess of Commerce."

"An alliance?"

"Let's hope so."

Breith agreed. He didn't even want to think of the possibilities of an affair. Cymel flew on, and Breith was glad, but then she reversed course, flapping about in a wide arc to avoid the Wyrm and the Lady astride him.

"What are you doing?" Breith shouted. "The dragon's back there!"

"I know," she said, "but Mole . . . oh, drat! Who knows where they'll carry them indeed! He's in Iomard now!"

Breith clutched her feathers tighter. "What?" Not only had Mole come back from the dead, but he'd discovered how to Walk, and as a man? From Glandair no less? It was hardly fair.

At that moment the world changed, as Cymel suddenly Bridged them from one world to the other.

He didn't comment, didn't have to. Cymel had not only healed the damage that Dur had caused, but kept the capacity she'd been forced to acquire. Breith didn't have much time to think about this, because below them was the object of their quest, or at least part of it: a raft floating down a river with people on it, hardly an army but certainly a sizable crew.

Cymel merely ducked and banked, then came in for a water landing, gliding down upon the water, holding out her wings at the end to brake, sending a huge plume of spray over everyone on the back of the raft.

"Cymel," said a man in neat gray clothes with close-cropped black hair and tiny spectacles over slightly beady eyes. Mole. "How nice to see you."

"You're alive!" She scrambled aboard the raft with her webbed talons while Breith struggled to stay atop her and not pitch head-first onto the deck. "You're alive!"

Mole smiled a secret smile and adjusted his spectacles. "After a fashion. I won't say I wasn't changed by it, and I won't say for the better, except so far as the Pneuma-working goes. But then it looks as though you've been through a rather painful learning experience as well. Or have you done so well at your lessons that you learned how to shapeshift just so you could make an entrance?"

Cymel abruptly changed from Cymel the White Bird to Cymel the woman, and Breith *did* fall onto the deck, tangled with Cymel, still naked, with the harness around her neck. Mole helped to cut her free. Breith noted that he had sharp black claws that shifted back to fingers once they'd done their job, all except for the nails, which were still black and slightly elongated.

And then they embraced, and Breith felt a blush of shame stealing across his cheeks, for while Cymel appeared to still long for Mole, his appraisal of her naked beauty was merely one of dry appreciation and a certain amount of brotherly concern. He called for someone to bring her a blanket, as much to dry her as to protect her modesty. Mole loved Cymel, the way that Breith himself loved Bauli, someone you wanted to help and protect and take joy in as they learned to walk, following in your footsteps and maybe one day even running past you.

He could forgive Mole, for he could see nothing the man had done to lead her on save be himself, yet he could not entirely forgive Cymel. That pained him worse than all the scourges of all the Inquisitors of all the Domains put together.

16

The Prophet's Peace

By the calendar of the Domains of Iomard, the 29th Ekhtos, the
eighth month of the Iomardi year 6536, the 723rd year since
the last Corruption.

[1]

It hurt to breathe, and she could not speak, yet Radayam's
surgeons informed her that the sole reason the wound had
not proved fatal was because of the scar tissue she had built
up from her constant flagellation. If it had not been for that,
Thador's knife would have killed her, and even so it most
likely would in the end.

But the Prophet provided. Her body had taken alternate
routes through splits and scars once Pneuma patches were
applied and the flow of blood was stanched.

Praise the Prophet and all glory to Her in the highest. Rada
had been praying for a sign to renew her faith, and this was
it. The mortification of her flesh had not brought her into
the white light of the Prophet's Peace, but demanding that
or expecting it would be sheer vanity. The Prophet's Peace
came through the Grace of the Prophet alone. In this case,

her devotions had allowed her to build up the resilience that had spared her life, if just long enough to work the Prophet's will in this time of the Corruption.

Her allies were already en route to apprehend the treacherous Mirrialta—Prophet be praised that that wicked woman's assassin had not fulfilled her task; Prophet forgive her that it took such an act for Radayam to realize the woman's duplicity. She had known that her Bride didn't like her, but she hadn't realized that she'd taken a viper to her breast, and a stupid one besides. Mirrialta was no doubt mad, and would need to be culled for that reason alone, along with her perfidious servant.

Their Seyl, he could wait. She would have to see if Bruyd were infected by Mirrialta's Corruption and complicit in her plans, in which case he would have to be culled as well, or simply ignorant, in which case he would need to be chastised and do penance.

After all, it was the Seyl's duty to look after the well-being of both mates, but the Wife always took precedence over the Bride, and if forced to side with one against the other, that is the choice he must always take.

Would that all men would know the Prophet's will as well as that. It was a simple thing, truly. Yet it was so difficult for some, especially those born with the Braysha taint upon them.

She prayed to the Prophet that Dur would see the error of his ways and his folly, but she knew that was not to be. He'd already gone beyond Heresy, almost into inventing a whole new breed of sin. There had been no False Prophets in the millennium that the Scribes had been keeping accurate records, or at least none of any power to be reckoned with. In the spotty histories before that, she was quite certain that there had been no others. The only true Prophet had led the people out of darkness, had shown them the True Way of purity and faith.

If only the folk of the Riverines had obeyed Her will to begin with, there would not be so much pain. Radayam could hardly bear what she had had to do since she had come to rule over this cesspool of impurity and perversion. It had been a constant struggle to winnow the wheat from the chaff, to cast out that which was unclean and keep what was Pure and Holy.

It was difficult. To kill a grown woman was one thing, but to kill a babe was another. Yet the Prophet had commanded that all children be given a chance to birth, for they might still be found to be Pure by some miracle; and as the Prophet had said in the tale of the Harlot of Tiolan, "Even a woman who mates with fifty beasts and their shepherd may still give birth to the shepherd's child."

It was one thing to read of the harsh justice administered to those who broke with the Prophet's will, another to mete it out. Here in Valla Murloch, she had captured pureblooded women who bore in their bellies the children of unclean foreign seed, which of course would have to be put down the moment they emerged to breathe the Prophet's air. Some of these women had even had to be roped to beds until it was time for them to give birth, and she could hear their screams still.

But Radayam was as merciful as the Scriptures allowed her to be; the pain of childbirth coupled with the pain of seeing a child die was enough chastisement for a lifetime.

If the Domains had just done a proper job and tested Dur before his eyes turned and he knew himself to be Sighted, they would have been spared all this, not only a Mage and a Sighted male of great power, but a man who was a hero to the Daroc, to whom the Heresy of the Riverines was not enough.

Radayam read over the reports and inspected the schedules, knowing the Mage Dur would be coming with his fleet this afternoon, letting the winds of the Chaos Reefs do his work for him. She fully expected to die in the attack, and was certain that the Prophet had spared her life only because she was needed. "My thanks, my Lady," she said, "I am naught but your humble servant."

The Prophet's Peace did not descend upon her, but the simple peace of resignation did. Her work would soon be done here, her responsibilities ready to be taken up by other hands.

She only hoped that her passing would be the passing of Dur as well.

[2]

The Chaos Shoals flew before Dur and before the ships of the Army of Independence, whipping the waves into a fury and forming a mass of water that would do more damage than the invasion force alone. He'd talked it over with Cay Faobran. The city could be rebuilt; tumbled stones could be used to build new buildings as well as old. The only trouble was the toll of death that would be levied on the folk of the Riverines who had been left behind, but there was a harsh reality to numbers, and Dur saw the future clearly. There would be fewer dead this way than any other. For the people to be free, many would have to pay with their lives.

He was ready with his own, when the time came.

But the Army of Independence was as strong and overwhelming as the wall of water moving before them. Independence of the Daroc from the Lynborn, independence of the Riverines from the Domains, independence of men from the oppression of women, the right of men to keep their Sight and to simply be as nature intended, without the cruelty of the gelding laws or the harsh judgment of the old Prophet.

After all, there was a new Prophet now, and the time had come for the cruelty of the first to end.

Smaller waves washed behind them and beside them, breaking over the bow as they flew within the storm. Dur had behind him his bright boys, those youths with the green and brown eyes, many of whom had once been older, some much older. Dur was feeling the weight of their lost years. He had not aged so much as he had withered; the Rite of Renewal had drained the vitality from him, but in its place, he had gained a great peace.

He knew he was going to die. Yasayl had shown him that, as clearly as a hand raised before his face. The time and the method of his demise differed only in a matter of weeks, a few variations on a theme, and a matter of legacy. If his Power were to outlast him, he had to give it away, to keep the torch of the Pneuma burning along with his thoughts and ideas. What better way to pass on that Power than to give these men back what had been taken from them?

The Scribes of the Riverines, a welcome addition to the force, had formed a meld with their male counterparts, teaching the untrained the Power of the Sight, and harnessing in turn the youth and vitality and wild gifts that the Sighted males of Iomard possessed. And that, with his Power as Mage and Prophet, is what drove the storm before them and built the wave that would assault Valla Murloch.

{ 3 }

The shoals of the Chaos Reefs had shifted, driven before the Mage-born storm of the Heretic Dur. Radayam stood in the marketplace of Valla Murloch, melded with her sister Scribes and Seers, forming the shield of Pneuma that kept the worst of the force from the city, but could not keep the storm from destroying the fringes, or stop the whistle and howl that was the force of the Braysha Storm as they had come to call it.

It was a wild force, casual in its cruelty but not mindless, like the Braysha boy hammering the innocent fieldmice until the Prophet put a stop to his evil and marked him for what he was. The Braysha Storm howled in defiance, hurling trees and stones, and even bodies of herdbeasts and people who had been caught outside the city wall, against the shields of Pneuma that the Scribes of the Pure had erected. Radayam watched as a small boat plucked from its moorings smashed high against the wall of the shield, and felt the blow against the mindforce of the Meld.

But nothing could prepare her for what came next. There was a groaning and a crying. Beyond the mist of the Pneuma wall, she saw the Bay drain dry, like a basin spilled with nothing left but mud at the bottom. And then the water returned with more, a giant wave that crested over the Pneuma dome and slammed down against it with its full terrifying force. Radayam felt the mindscreams as her sister Scribes to the farthest periphery of the Meld crumpled and died, the light of their Sight snuffed out along with their minds and lives. Yet though flattened, the shield still held.

Until the second wave of the attack. Water, as the Prophet said, is the most powerful of all forces, for while fire consumes and is done, and earth and air must be given impetus to return, water when forced up seeks swiftly to return back. The deflected blow of the tidal wave only increased its force, sending it inland and bringing it back, with the outer walls of the city leading its assault, while a Pneuma-bolt of great power struck the dome from the Bay side.

It was like a cyst lanced with a pin while being squeezed. The Pneuma wall crushed flat, adding to the force of the wave's blow. Valla Murloch was no more. Around her Radayam felt the Scribes of her circle die, one by one, protecting her. The irony was bitter. The same failed tactics that had allowed her army to take the jewel of the Riverines had now been turned against her. The Heretic had won. She was left there, tottering and crippled, her body unable to stand without support and her mind on the edge of shock.

"O Prophet," she cried, beginning to sob, "where are You in our hour of need?"

[4]

The devastation of Valla Murloch was terrible but not utter. That was the force of water—it destroyed quickly, but not totally, and preserved the lives of the lucky and the strong. Even so, Dur wept to see it, remembering it from a hundred angles from Yasa's visions, the Sight-gift that she had used in place of the sight of normal men and women. Here there had been a man who sold stew made from groundfruit, herd beef, and spice; there had been the perfume (and poison) seller who had lost her baby to a carelessness with the wares, and had drunk them herself not a week after. Yasa had been unable to stop that, for her visions were sporadic. She saw the second tragedy, but not the first, and even if she could have stopped the second, it was only a matter of *when* and not *if*.

The sight was a terrible curse as well as a terrible blessing, and Dur would be glad when he was rid of it. Which, in a perverse way, Yasa had been as well.

I know, she had thought as she died, *that this Gift will bring you as much joy as it has brought me. And so I wish you good luck and good fortune. You will need it to survive long enough to do what you will and must do.*

Dur felt Yasa's tears welling up along with his own as he saw what she never could, the death of the city she loved. But with its death would come its rebirth, and with his death would come the salvation of two worlds. This was as it must be, for it was time for the Pneuma to be returned to the Flow from its greatest repositories, and in Iomard, as Mage and Prophet, he had the most there was.

But not all, and not what he needed. To Bridge the gaps between worlds, and to return the Pneuma to the flow, it was necessary to have one who had been born to the task, and so he went to Radayam.

She stood in the market square, if you could call it standing. The assassin's dagger had weakened her severely, at least physically, but her mental state was as sharp as ever. Like himself, she had now become resigned to her death. He could see it in her eyes.

Around her lay the Scribes and Seers of the Army of Purification, their bodies lying at mad angles, their muscles thrown into fits and convulsions as they had died. Cay Rada, whom they had died to spare, leaned against the base of the statue of the Prophet in the market square, dry like the bodies around her, surrounded by a zone barren of water, for the ground was covered with a thick layer of Pneuma, coalesced from what was left of the shield that had covered the city, like a bubble popped and contracted into a single viscous pool.

Rada was drawing it into herself, praying and preparing, Dur knew, for one final assault, one blaze of glory.

"Stop, Rada," Dur said, speaking as much with Yasa's voice as with his own, the blind woman having rehearsed and foreseen these lines at least as many times as he had. She knew that even if she would not be here, her gift would, and what she had foreseen would come to pass.

"Why should I stop, Braysha boy?" Rada cried back. "Who are you to speak to me, you Heretic who profanes the Prophet's Peace?"

Dur drew himself up. "I speak to you because it is you who is the Braysha child and not I. It is you who have no couth and no kindness, as the Prophet spoke. It is you who does what she can merely because *she can*."

"Lies!" she cried. "I do only the will of the Prophet!"

"Are you a Prophet then yourself, Holy Rada? Or are you just a Braysha girl, to match the Braysha boy, crushing the fieldmice because it fits your whim, choosing who lives and who dies simply because it fits your belief, the same way that the Braysha boy killed the mice merely because he could and they did not please him, did not fit into his vision of the way the world should be?"

"I did not!" she cried. "My work has been the Prophet's work, and I have only done as She commanded!"

"Or you interpreted," Dur shot back. "The Prophet did not command that those with the Sight be killed or gelded, or that their Sight should be taken from them, only that they be marked so they might be watched. The Prophet did not command that babes be strangled at birth, only that those who are not wanted should not be born. I have seen you do these things, and more, all because you thought it was right and holy."

"And are you any better?" she cried. "You, a Mage who calls himself Prophet, corrupting and profaning all he touches and living against the Prophet's will."

"I live only against the will of the Domains," Dur said, "and those such as you. I am a Prophet because I have the Gift of Prophesy; it was given to me by Cay Yasayl, a woman whom you would have killed for her Gift trod too close to that of the original Prophet."

"Lies!" screamed Rada, hurling a great bolt of Pneuma at him. "Lies! You are not the Prophet and you never shall be! I have felt Her, I have touched Her, and I live only to do Her will and to feel the Blessing of Her Peace!"

Dur caught each bolt as Rada threw it, and sucked them into himself, into the emptiness that was the heart of a Mage, the eternal Hunger that could never be sated and could never be filled, and therefore was able to hold almost as much Pneuma as two worlds could hold. With each bolt, he came a step closer toward her. His Scribes and his Messengers stood behind him, the wise women and the bright boys who would record this moment and take it throughout the land, bearing the new message of Peace.

At last he stood before her, as he had before Yasa, and Cymel, and other women before them. And he said, "The world is Corrupt because there is no balance. The Pneuma of the worlds must be returned. Yours and mine, but most of all, mine. We must do this thing if the worlds are to survive, Iomard and Glandair both."

She paused then, having no Pneuma left to spend and only raining down physical blows on his chest, a feeble dying woman flailing with her left arm alone. "What do you mean? What do you mean!"

"I mean that I must give up what is mine, if it is to return to the world and to last. Men must be born with the Sight as much and as frequently as women. It is a matter of balance. We wield more Power because we are fewer. But I cannot say whether that will happen. I need your permission if it is to have any meaning."

"I deny you," she said. "I deny you till my dying breath."

"Is that the will of the Prophet, or your own?"

Radayam paused, searching his face as tears ran down her own. "I believe it is the will of the Prophet," she said at last, "but I can never say for certain, for I am not Her. I will not presume, as you have. But since you will kill me anyway, then I will say that if it is the will of the Prophet—my Prophet, and not you—then you have my permission, for as much as it is worth. I am nothing without the will of the Prophet, and while I will happily deny you, I will not deny

Her. If She changes Her mind in the matter of the Braysha boy, then that is Her will."

"I believe it is," said Dur, "and now we shall both find out, for I will die as well."

Rada nodded. "It is a matter of Faith."

With that, Dur placed his hands about her head, reaching deep inside the core of her mind and speaking the words from the Dreamtime, the words that unlocked the power within that allowed the women of Iomard to Bridge between the worlds. But while she Bridged, he held on, anchoring her in this world and pouring his Power into her, and out of her, letting it release back into the void between the worlds.

That was the essence of being a Prophet. Placing one's Faith in the will of the Pneuma Flow, letting the balance right itself between worlds. His vision of a better world would come about only if he did this thing, giving up all that he was so that the world might be renewed. Or so he saw.

"A matter of Faith," Dur echoed, and with that, he died, and the last of his and Radayam's energy poured into the emptiness between worlds.

17

The Empty Place

*By the calendar of the Watchers of Glandair, events dating
from the 8th day of Soramis, the tenth month of the 739th
Glandairic year since the last Settling.*

[1]

Cymel sat on the raft, unsure and uncertain, not knowing
whom to talk to or whom to trust, and knowing that this was
not the place for it, but somewhere had to be. And crying,
for while Mole was here, and he'd survived just as she had,
he loved Firill and always had. And even if she were to make
love to him, for him it would not change who he was. Deep,
yes. Remembered, yes. But not a major moment in his life.

And then there was Breith, looking at her with tears in his
green and brown eyes. She knew how much she had hurt
him, and how much he loved her still. And she still loved
him, but she didn't exactly desire him.

"So, dear, what's the problem?"

Cymel sniffed and rubbed her nose, looking up at a
woman dressed in the brown plaid of a barge woman, like
the ones who'd sailed on the river from Cyfareth near her

house. On her fingers were jewels and the soiled hem of a satin petticoat peeked out from beneath the roughspun over-skirt.

"Mind if I sit down?" she asked as she did so. "If I ask you about your problems, it will help me to sort out mine."

"Your problems couldn't be anywhere near as complicated as mine," Cymel said, sniffing.

"Let's make a wager," the woman said, "if your problems are more complicated than mine, I'll give you one of my rings, and if mine are more complicated than yours, you'll do the poling for me on this raft and tell your friend Mole that I've earned more than a five-minute break. Fair enough?"

Cymel nodded and sniffed. "Okay."

"Good," said the woman. "My name is Afankaya and I'm the Tyrna of Tyst. Or was until the usurper Anrydd laid waste to the University, killed my husband, and would have either killed me or carried me off as the spoils of war—I'm not certain which—had it not been for your friend Mole. But rather than reward him with gold or jewels like any sensible Wizard, I'm expected to dress like a barge woman and pole until I blister my hands. Which is all part of saving the world, he says. Even if it's performed as a history, I'd rather it be something a bit more spectacular than 'Afankaya, who poled a barge to save the world before fading into obscurity' or else 'killed by the supporters of Anrydd while part of an unsuccessful bid to retake the Throne.' I can name you *one* Tyrna of Tyst who reigned through conquest, by dint of poisoning her father and shifting blame onto her uncles so she could rule while they bickered among themselves. So I'm looking for a man to marry to make me Tyrna again, because I've tried hiding out as a barge woman. Trust me, but I'm not cut out for the job." She smiled. "Can you top that?"

Cymel bit her lip. "I'm in love with Mole, but Breith's in love with me. And when Mole was killed, I was hurt so badly that I turned into a bird to escape from the pain, and Breith came here from Iomard and tracked me across half the world to make me remember who I was. Then we made love, but I was dreaming I was with Mole, so I said his name instead of Breith's. And now Mole's here, alive, but he's with Firill, and he treats me like I'm his little sister, and . . ."

Afankaya snorted. "Well, when you put it that way . . ." She paused for a moment. "Hmp! But if you take out the business with the dying and coming back from the dead and turning into birds and so forth, it all sounds pretty ordinary. So let's split the difference and say we've both won. You can have one of my rings, and I get to have a break for more than five minutes while I give you a bit of advice. Fair enough?"

"I suppose," said Cymel.

"Good," said Afankaya and plucked off a ring of gold entwined with rubies that would have bought a small house. "Now," she said, passing it to Cymel, "trust me, but I've seen this sort of thing at Court before, and I've *met* Scholar Gylas. You're much better off in the long run with someone like Breith, who I take to be the young man you flew in here with, than with Mole—unless you're looking for a casual fling, but that's not the sort of thing most young women want in their first relationship. Affairs are something for *after* you're married, when you can blame your actions on the dullness or inadequacy of your husband. Mole and Firill have both assuredly spoken for each other, even if they both have flings on the side."

"Then what should I do about Breith?"

Afankaya waved her hand. "Well, assuming you still want him, you go to him, you kiss him, you cry a lot, you say you're sorry, you apologize, you be honest about everything *save* what you've fantasized about doing with Mole. If that fails, you have sex with him again, and you make a point of saying *his* name this time, several times, and loudly."

"Oh," said Cymel, and slipped the ring on her finger. It was pretty and sparkly and she would have enjoyed it more if she didn't have an idea how much it was worth. "I never thought a Tyrna would speak like you."

Tyrna Afankaya smiled. "In public, we don't. In private, however, it's another matter. If I'm going to play barge woman, I might as well be frank. After all, I'm too tired and sore to be anything else." She laughed then. "So, know any eligible bachelors who might like to be Tyrn of Nyddys and would like a frank, slightly experienced Tyrna?"

Cymel shook her head, and laughed herself as Mole came over. "Um . . . she wants to take a longer break."

Mole raised an eyebrow. "Longer? I hadn't realized there were that many hours in a day now. But then we're on Io-mardi time." He grinned then. "But it's you I want, Cymel."

Her heart skipped a beat, but then she realized that he wasn't speaking of her as her, Cymel, but as Cymel the sorceress or whatever title got stuck on her with her mixed Scribe-Watcher gifts. "What for?"

Mole continued to grin. "You're a Bridge, and your friend Breith has some fairly potent Iomardi gifts himself. I'd say if you joined the rest of us in a Watcher meld we could not only *predict* where the next Settling between worlds will oc-cur, but actually cause it, and in the right direction as well. Which means if all things are favorable, we should be able to join up with the Hero Band and give them a shortcut to the Empty Place."

Cymel blinked. "Do you think it will work?"

Mole still grinned. "I think it's worth a try." Then to the Tyrna: "And if it does, you shouldn't have to do any more poling."

{ 2 }

The Shaman rested in her cradle of earth, Rinchay Matan no longer, now vengeance given form. Around her she felt the pulse of life of the beetles and worms, the roots of the plants dug deep into the earth forming a net, protecting her from the weight of the earth around. Beyond the life of the beetles and plants, a great sea of death. The Liar now mocked life as she did the gods. In the sea, Rinchay could only sense two lights. One old and darkened, sustained upon the lives of others—the Liar—and the other a distance away, young and bright, but shadowed, like a candle within a lantern of smoked glass.

Rinchay wondered whom the second light might belong to, and what the bearer's purpose might be.

But it did not matter. If they were there to aid the Liar, then they too would die; and if they quested for the same vengeance as did she, then they would celebrate together after the Liar's defeat. She rose to ground level then, hiding just under the edge of the mat woven from the living roots of the grass of the plains.

The Liar would die. The Liar would *pay*.

The Lie would be over. . . .

{ 3 }

Hudoleth led her Army of the Dead to the border of what could only be the Empty Place. In the middle of the sea of waving grass that was the northern plains, there was a hollow. In the center of that hollow, the grass was flattened down in a spiral, like a whorl of fur on a herdbeast's withers. Though she was not yet there, Hudoleth could sense the Pneuma, see it circling, a spiral of Power, ready, waiting, incipient, yet ripe for the picking.

Yet she was not alone. Off to one side, at a slight angle, a match for her Army of the Dead, was an Army of the Half-Dead, Mahara's warriors, pushed in a ceaseless and sleepless march to be here before her. Mahara himself sat astride a roan horse, dark as his Rhudyar skin, with another man and two girls on horses alongside him, the three of them looking not much better than the soldiers.

Hudoleth smiled. Though the corpses about her might smell a bit, they were loyal and tireless. Mahara had no doubt only taken the most insane, the most dogged, and the most terrified to get him this far. A power of life and blood to match a power of death and decay. It was fitting, somehow.

She saluted as he approached with his army. They had honed and strengthened their forces through months and months of battle; and while he—mistakenly—thought he had defeated her, she was here to prove him wrong, personally and one-on-one.

Hudoleth waved her hands and the undead servants carrying her palanquin set it down. "Ia e no hono triolanth, nocht zim! Ha vasa ma linde se-fa k'nima!" She touched one then the next of them in turn, drawing forth the Pneuma that animated them and took strength from their deaths and the Pneuma-collecting hollow they were in the life of the world. They fell, like the stalks of grass in the Empty Place, one after the other in a sea about her. One lone soldier took a moment longer to fall than the others, but there was no trouble. The Power she had given them with her powders and chants had been recalled, and Hudoleth stood ready to do battle.

Across the field, she saw Mahara raise his hands and give a similar chant, and his half-dead soldiers became fully dead as well, their life and vigor sucked into the emptiness inside of Mahara just as Hudoleth had recalled the Pneuma she had stored and ripened within the dead men's husks. He touched the man beside him with a sorrowful expression, then that man fell dead, and his horse as well, bumping into the girl beside him and her horse in turn, allowing Mahara to draw forth the essence of both of those as well. The second girl launched herself from her horse, landing headlong in the grass, struggling toward Hudoleth in her rush to get away. While she avoided the arcing death of her own horse, and Mahara's roan toppling as he alighted, the Mage of Kale simply laughed, reaching out a finger of Pneuma, and sucked her lifeforce into himself. Mahara knew as well as she did that the battle now was one on one, Hudoleth against Mahara, and only the strongest would win.

Hudoleth raised her hand, flipping out the mirrored fans of her web of Power, and watched Mahara rend his shirt and bare the tattoos and scars of his own magery. And then they circled in a dance of war, each daring the other to risk the first blow.

[4]

Gryf was the first to see it, but he didn't believe it. One moment the river beside them was empty, the next a large raft appeared, like something sprung up in a street conjurer's trick in the Bothrin. Except this was full size, the type that barge folk took down the river to Tyst, and it was crowded with them too. Plus Breith and Cymel.

Breith waved. "Hi there. Care for a ride?"

After shadowbeasts, soldiers, and even cannibals, it was not something Gryf expected. He turned to Lyanz. " 'M I seein' what I think I'm seein', or am I drunk a' doolybrew and no one's tol' me?"

Lyanz blinked and kept his arm around Amhar. "I think I'm seeing it too."

Corysiam's reaction was somewhat different, one part shock, another part indignation. "You *Bridged* a *raft?*"

A man dressed in neat gray velvet embroidered with silver thread standing next to Breith called, "Not precisely *Bridged*, but it's the same thing in theory. But I'm certain we'll have ample time to discuss theories of the Flow once we help the Hero save a couple worlds. Now care to come aboard?"

Corysiam was still holding her ground. "I'm a Bridge and my apprentice here is a Walker."

The neatly dressed man brightened. "Splendid! That should speed things up considerably. Why, we may even have time to save *both* worlds!"

Gryf didn't know who Cymel and Breith's friend was, but he liked him already.

[5]

Mahara danced about Hudoleth, testing her defenses, testing, ready for her to make the first move, or take advantage of an opening. Her moves were careful and precise, like a dancer, and Mahara knew she was older than he, and now she looked the fact. She had been a power even when his old master was a young Mage.

But the old had their weaknesses as well as the young, and one of those weaknesses was the inability to take risks. Mahara did so, forming a Pneuma-bolt and sending it at Hudoleth so that it scorched the grass. She deflected it with a wave of her left fan. The battle had been joined, and Mahara dealt with the razor edge of Power she tossed with the same motion, Pneuma-knives flying from the edge of the fan.

He put up his hand, erecting a Pneuma wall of sheer might, a demonstration of his power, that would have stopped a blow that might level cities. But Hudoleth's sorcery was old and subtle, and the wall that could have withstood almost any assault shattered at the touch of Hudoleth's knives, like a diamond touched by a jeweler's chisel, shearing apart along the planes of the crystal.

But what was shield could be weapon just as easily, and Mahara sent the chunks of shattered Pneuma hurtling toward Hudoleth, whose delicate sorceries could not stop their sheer Power. Stopping it might have been impossible, but blunting it was another matter. Hudoleth waved her fans and sent forth twin sprays of energy, turning the boulders into a fine flurry of pellets and pieces that hailed down around her, scratching her skin.

Yet she only smiled and began to twirl and wave her fans, summoning up a whirlwind that picked up the dust and bits and began to spin them around into a razorwind that flew toward him, slicing the grass from its roots as it came. Mahara erected another bulwark against this, but the Pneuma-wind sanded away his defenses, the bulk of the particles concentrated in one band, buzzing like a jadecutter's wheel. Closer the cutting sand came, and closer, yet before it could come close enough for Mahara to find a way to turn its force back against Hudoleth, a huge mass of water and a wooden platform suddenly appeared in the fields to the right of the Empty Place.

The Hero had arrived. Mahara looked to Hudoleth and she nodded, the razorwind dropping as Mahara allowed his bulwark to melt and pulled the Power back into himself. They could continue their battle *after* they had killed the Hero.

{ 6 }

Oerfel stood next to Anrydd, their forces attacking Mahara's somewhere far to the south. Nothing like fine Nyddys horseflesh; when Mahara broke away from the rest of his forces with a small battalion of his men in a forced march, Oerfel knew he was making for the Empty Place. All that was needed was a lens of Pneuma to enhance his vision to that of a tullin, a shield of no-see made with the same bending of the light, and Anrydd to drive the small racing chariot he'd brought with them from Nyddys. Then, while Mahara and Hudoleth feinted and peacocked at each other with their vain magics, he could simply slip forward and take the Empty Place—after Anrydd had drawn its teeth, of course. The boy was close behind him, as loyal as a vicious dog about to be killed for its master's pleasure.

Suddenly, an entire battalion of folk appeared, most linked in some sort of Watcher Meld. Those who were armed seemed armed to the teeth. The Watcher students who'd escaped Cyfareth, and Iomardi Scribes—he'd bet even money on it—and the sorcerer Mole, and the girl Cymel. And the Hero, golden as a phoenix and twice as splendid and beautiful. And. . . . He focused his lenses, not quite believing what he was seeing. Tyrna Afankaya and her handmaids?

The last was so ludicrous as to be almost a joke, but if Mole and Cymel were here, all bets were off. Oerfel was suddenly very uneasy about his calculations. Cymel was the wild card—she held the most Power of the new group in the game—but Mole had the most craft and subtlety. Bridging in an entire company from Iomard at the last moment, and what's more, it looked like a theatrical company—well, that took balls. And more than a little ingenuity to boot. But Cymel was still the farthest from the Place, and still the least likely to disrupt what was happening.

And then there was the other one who'd come early so as to get box seats for the show. When Oerfel had arrived moments ahead of Mahara and Hudoleth's charge, he hadn't quite believed it, but there, to the left of the Empty Place, was a woman, waiting, carefully disguised beneath a flap of grass and Pneuma mixed with a little leaves and dirt, sitting in her trap door like a spider, and waiting for someone. Oerfel hadn't the faintest idea who she was, but she obviously had enough Power to find the Empty Place before anyone else, and enough wits to get here. A Shaman of some sort, and her purpose here was clearly to kill a Mage, maybe two of them, or just let them kill each other and take the Empty Place herself. Oerfel was grimly amused by the possibilities. Clever woman. He too meant to stand back and wait his chance. If that passionate primitive forestalled him, well, give her thanks and kill her quick.

Oerfel chuckled. "So many possibilities, eh Anrydd?"

The boy stood beside him like a statue. Or a vicious dog standing at attention, waiting for its master's command to attack.

"That's right, boy, stay quiet. Stay quiet and wait for the right moment to strike. . . ."

{ 7 }

Hudoleth danced through the grass, calculating and gathering her Pneuma for a strike at the Hero, leaving enough in reserve that she would be ready with a second attack on Mahara. By unspoken pact, they'd discontinued their duel long enough to deal with this new threat. The Hero was fresh and ready for the battle, and there was no telling what Powers Fate might have placed in his hands.

And then there was another, come early and clever. The Nyddys Mage, here with his puppet Tyrn, Anrydd, and a chariot, hidden behind a shield of magical subtlety. Hudoleth would not have noticed them if she had not been standing at the right angle and seen chariot tracks pointing to nothingness, then scryed about and between and seen who was hiding inside. No strength for the battle at hand, but strength enough to play the jackal and take down herself or Mahara once they were weakened from taking the other.

A movement from the puppet Tyrn, a hand to his sword, caught her eye. She turned back, but not quickly enough. She had let a hole creep into her defenses, and another hidden player in this game had revealed herself.

Hudoleth had only a moment to get an impression—skins, furs, antlers and bells—and a woman's face grimed with dirt and streaked with tears. A Shaman. A Shaman of the Grass Clans.

The same moment, her spear struck, and Hudoleth fell, pierced through the heart.

"The Liar must die!" cried the woman. "The Liar is dead!"

[8]

Anrydd stood scowling beside Oerfel. He could stand the mask no longer. He hadn't the patience for this game. Disgust sent his belly roiling whenever he had to stand near the man. Driving his chariot here like a servant, then being spoken to like an idiot child or a dog. His fingers twitched and closed about the hilt of his sword, his hand acting of its own volition, striking without thought. He was startled for a moment by a cry across the grass of "Liar!" and "Liar!" again. The Mage Hudoleth was suddenly dead, and Oerfel had shifted focus onto Mahara, raising his hands to strike while the third Mage stood gloating over his good fortune.

Anrydd's sword was up and into its dance, swift and shining, taking Oerfel's head so sweetly the Mage was dead before he could say a word, before his mind could comprehend the futility of all his convoluted planning and plotting.

"I believe that was the right moment, old man," Anrydd said and spat. Oerfel did not respond.

Anrydd suddenly realized then that three Mages—*Mages!*—

coveted whatever it was that lay inside the bounds of that piece of land in front of him. Perhaps a magic so powerful that nothing could stand before it. Why else would they bother? Being Tyrn was proving to be more boredom than pleasure. What if he were Emperor of the whole world? Whatever magic the Mages wanted would most likely be sufficient to give him that.

He was not the fastest racer in Tyst for nothing. A short sprint forward and he was there, on the edge of the flattened grass, of the place that was apparently empty but so precious to those with so much Power, and therefore precious to him.

He took a step forward. Tendrils of invisible force touched him then, caressed him, like the fingers of a skilled courtesan. But that courtesan could be none other than the Hag, for what entered him was so terrible that he could not even comprehend it. He screamed hoarsely and ran away from there as fast as his legs could move, faster than any race he had ever run in his life.

He ran and ran, until his heart gave way and he died alone in the middle of the grass.

[9]

Mahara watched Oerfel die, then saw his puppet Tyrn enter the Empty Place, then scream and run. His mind had been unable to comprehend the sheer Power, Mahara was sure. The only ones who ever could would be a Mage, who'd paid the price of that Power, or the Hero for whom it was fated. But Fate could be changed and Heroes could die. And Mages could take their birthright from them before they had a chance. He ran for the Empty Place, determined to reach it before Lyanz.

Suddenly, out of thin air, a girl stood before him, one hand out to stop him, a Walker Bridging the distance by stepping forward and back to Iomard. Inconsequential. He brushed her arm aside with contemptuous ease—or, rather, he meant to, but the slender arm didn't move. He was thrown back like a panicked horse running into a stone wall. Then he was lifted into the air and slammed back down against the ground—again and again so there was not an intact bone in his body. Still alive, still conscious, he struggled to get away from her. . . .

"Mela!"

It was a sound from out beyond the pain wall. He didn't understand it, didn't try, pain was all.

Pain more pain dull pain sharp pain. . . .

Then pain was gone.

The blurring in his eyes was gone for a moment.

Her face was calm and stony; there was no pity in it for him. "You killed my father."

She lifted the arm that had stopped him, the Pneuma coiling about the rosy-tipped fingers. He couldn't see any longer. Then he couldn't breathe. Then he was as dead as Anrydd.

[10]

Brother Kyo watched as the sorceress died, watched as the woman who had killed her sat down and began to weep. He stood then from among the dead men where he had lain to hide and watch, and went forward to where the woman sat. He placed a hand of comfort upon her back, but she did not respond, only kept chanting her mantra, rocking back and forth, as in a sing-song she said, "The Liar is dead . . . The Liar is dead. . . ."

He could do nothing for her, give her no comfort save by his sheer presence.

Yet beside them was the body of the sorceress, spangled with mirrors and silver chains. On a chain around her neck was one mirror, greater than all the others, black glass amid the silver, and in it was reflected, not his face, but the face of his brother, Lyanz. His brother who had taken his place in the family business when he had gone off to become a monk. His brother whom he had thought lost in the war, who Marath Alaesh had commanded he find and aid.

How Lyanz had grown since Kyom had seen him last, standing tall and golden, a perfect specimen of manhood. Brother Kyo wept for not having seen him grow. For while he heard the Shaman's continued repetition of "Liar," he knew in his heart of hearts that this one mirror showed the Truth.

{ 11 }

Breith caught hold of Cymel, pulled her against himself and held her tightly even when she struggled. She pushed at him, then her arms trembled, went weak. Her breath was a sob, then she was leaning into his chest, sobbing away her grief and rage, and all the ugliness that had seized hold of her when she started to torture the Mage and not simply kill him.

{ 12 }

Amhar held Lyanz's hand, and felt herself beginning to weep. "Must you go?"

Lyanz squeezed her hand back. "I have to. I can feel it. It's *calling* me. That's not quite the right word, but that's what it is." He kissed her then, quickly, then not so quickly, until he heard Gryf snorting in disgust.

He looked back at his friend. "Do you mind?" He leaned forward and gave Amhar one more kiss, not as long as the last, but still lingering. "Don't worry," he said. "I'll be back."

Their fingers parted and he took three steps forward, still

looking toward her, then turned away and ran for the hollow in the Grasslands, as if afraid he would change his mind if he looked back. Then he reached the edge of standing grass and crossed over.

The moment Lyanz crossed the boundary and passed into the Empty Place, he stopped, shook his head as if he had a buzzing in his ears, took a few more steps, then cried out in astonishment.

With a Roar that was not in the ears but in the mind, the Empty Place was filled.

[13]

Mole stood and watched as the Hero took his place, saw the Pneuma of two worlds gather and collect, beginning to fill the man, heard the sound in his ears resonating through his body that was not quite a body, and watched the reactions of the others.

Cymel gave a small cry. Breith fell to his knees. Amhar looked frantically around, her sword out and ready. Gryf stared, puzzled, while Afankaya and her handmaids merely stood and watched, as if this were a spectacle they'd paid to see. Firill and the students in the Meld stood transfixed, their minds as one.

Mole whispered in Firill's ear then: "I can't promise I'll be back, but I'll certainly try."

He knew he wasn't supposed to, but he'd never have another opportunity like this again. He'd never forgive himself if he didn't at least *try*.

Softly, softly, go little mole feet, and who knows where they will carry him. . . .

[14]

Kyodal heard his brother before he saw him, then saw him enter the Empty Place, and be filled by that which was there. Brother Kyo set down the mirror and made his decision. His vow of silence was only until it was crucial that he must speak.

"Brother, wait . . ."

The light from the Empty Place began to grow. Corysiam shaded her eyes, then began hastily herding the younger Companions and Mole's company away from the boundary.

They sat on the grassy slope with the Shaman a short distance away and watched as Lyanz changed. That which filled the Empty Place was flowing into him. His clothes burned away and he began to grow—his body changing from flesh to a form of colored light. His head thrown back, his expression was a terrible mix of agony and joy, his mouth wide open as if screaming, but they could hear no sound.

Two others then entered the Empty Place, Cymel's friend, Mole, and a monk. Mole shifted and changed, becoming more animal than man, while the monk merely had an expression of radiant peace upon his features.

Yet Lyanz continued to grow, and at last he stood with his head in the sky, his arms outflung, his fingers spread. From the tips of his fingers golden light rayed out across the grass and across the plain superimposed on the grass, Iomard wholly visible and present, just as Glandair was visible and present, each interpenetrating the other. The Mole and the monk circled the Hero like moons, smaller satellites in orbit around the greater body.

The Hero continued to empty out the magic force that he had drawn into himself, letting it flow back into the worlds he'd taken it from.

The membrane between the worlds thickened.

The easy visibility was gone.

And, abruptly, the Hero was gone as well, along with the Mole and the monk.

Melted into the ambient air like a summer fog.

Glandair & Iomard

[1]

Gryf snorted. "Well, guess that's all. Thank-you, Gryf, nice fer y'ta help." Not that it wasn't amazing, but more than that, it was completely like Lyanz to do something like that—go off, become a god, leave his friends behind. Including Amhar, who was still sobbing.

Corysiam was talking to her, and hopefully everything would sort itself out as best as it could.

Not that that was likely. Cymel's friend Mole had disappeared as well, turning into his namesake, and with him gone, Gryf didn't see anyone around who knew enough about magic to get them all somewhere worth going. Like Tyst, for example. Corysiam had been going on about how impossible it was to Bridge a raft with a couple dozen people when Mole had gotten Cymel and Cory to link their Powers in some peculiar way and make the trick work anyway, not that any of them understood what they were doing. And by the time those two Bridged everyone else back and forth to where they wanted to get to, their heads would probably explode. Which meant they were going to be here for a while, and they might as well see to finding some shelter, the shack on the raft being the best example. Gryf thought it might be a good idea to stake himself out some bunk space while there were still places.

There was a terrible stink near the raft. When Gryf got there, he saw what it was: They'd been dragging a corpse the whole time, snagged on the timbers of the underside by the sleeves of its long cassock. When they'd run aground, the corpse had come with them. It was bloated and ripe and the flies were buzzing it, and to top that off, it didn't have a head.

Gryf began to turn away, but then the glint of gold caught his eye, and he remembered what every good thief in the maze knew: Corpses in the sewers were likely to be noblemen. While more disgusting and smelly than drunks, they tended to pay better when you rolled them, and not complain nearly as much.

So Gryf went closer, covering his mouth against the smell, and saw the golden tines poking through the sleeves of the cassock. "Huh, whassis?" Gryf asked, then used his sword to cut the trailing sleeve free of the corpse and take it to one side where he could inspect his prize better.

And what a prize it was. Nothing less than the Royal Crown of Nyddys.

Tyrn's Luck, pure and simple. Gryf was certain of that. Every thief in Tyst knew what the crown looked like, how many jewels it had, and how many were liable to be paste, considering the number of times enterprising thieves had managed to get hold of it and swap one of them out while no one was looking. But it was still easily worth several men's lives.

More than ample reward for everything he'd been through. If no one were going to thank him, he'd thank himself. Tyrn's Luck and Bothrin Planning both. Gryf wiped it off and polished it, then, having nowhere better to put it, put it on his head. It was a trifle large, but still fit well enough all things considered.

He wore it back to the group. "So, whaddya think? Is it me?"

Coming after what had just happened, a gold crown was a bit of a letdown, but at least one person was still impressed. "That's the Royal Crown of Nyddys!" The woman who stood up and said it was young enough and pretty, Gryf supposed, but looked like she'd just been put through worse than everyone together.

"Good eye."

She stamped forward then, getting in his face as if she had every right to be there. "I'm Tyrna Afankaya!"

Gryf snorted. "Yeah, right. And I'm the Tyrn."

She gave him a look up and down. "You very well may be. Can you swing that thing?"

"The crown?"

She rolled her eyes and snorted back. "No, idiot, your sword."

Gryf puffed out his chest. "Sure can. Y'won't believe what've fought with this."

"I've seen a lot lately, I probably would, but I don't much care," she replied. "All I need right now is one man, and he's not liable to put up much of a fight. Come with me."

Gryf had nothing better to do at the moment, and so followed Afankaya, who he guessed was probably actually the Tyrna. Her rings were a match for the crown and probably had less paste in them. She led the way across the Grassland, following a path that someone had left before, until they came to the body of someone who looked an awful lot like the old Tyrn, but younger and dead.

"Anrydd the Usurper," Afankaya explained. "I spotted him from the rise up there. Now whack his head off and let's get on with it."

"What? Whack his head off?"

"Yes," she said. "What, are you blind, or just stupid? Now whack his head off and let's get on with this, unless you want to carry the whole body."

"Why?"

She put her hands on her hips, regarding him like his mother after he'd tried to pick a lock with a piece of cheese. "Because, if you intend to keep that crown, you need a couple of things. One of them is a wife with a royal pedigree, which is why I'm here, and the other is the head of the old Tyrn, which is right there, so you might as well take it. You could take the rest of him, but it's not nearly as easy to carry for festivals. Coming back at the head of an army is usually good too. We should be able to find one around here without a commander, and I'm used to commanding and know most of the palace guards, so we should be able to get a creditable entourage."

Gryf was not slow on the uptake, but this was more surprising than everything else that had happened that day. "You sayin' y'wanna marry me?"

" 'Want' doesn't come into the equation. 'Need' is a better word." She looked at him, hands on hips. "I need a man who fits certain qualifications, the main one being that he's got the crown. Being friends with some powerful sorcerers is also useful, and I believed you're covered on that ground. Plus, by your accent, I can tell that you're Tystan, and what's more, from the Bothrin Markets. Well, I'm Tystan too, so we have that much in common, and as for the streets, my husband's father had so many bastards that no one will raise an eyebrow at you claiming to be one of them. Plus as someone from the markets, you'll have an ear to the people, and a certain amount of popularity there, something my husband and I never had, but I've been told it would be useful. I'm willing to try anything once."

Gryf shrugged and grinned. " 'Sound like my kin'a woman. 'Name's Talgryf, Gryf for short."

"Afankaya," she replied. "*Tyrna* Afankaya to anyone except my husband. Now, don't you have some beheading to do?"

Gryf continued to grin. Tyrn's Luck, pure and simple, or Hero's Luck now that the Hero didn't need it anymore.

The Royal Crown of Nyddys, and the right to wear it. Not a bad way to say thanks. *Thanks, Laz*, he thought to his friend, wherever he was now, *I appreciate it.*

His new wife stood there, hands on hips, tapping her foot. "Well?" she asked. "Beheading?"

Gryf grinned even wider. "Sure thing, Afankaya."

Tyrn's Luck, pure and simple.

[2]

Mirrialta did not see them come for her, did not see the Sisters who called themselves the Messengers of the True Prophet. After that, she did not see anything at all.

While she slept, they sewed her eyes shut with coarse thread. Sewed her lips shut as well. Sewed her hands behind her back one to the other with the fingers crushed and broken so that the whole would heal into a twisted mass. Her legs they cut off, and her womanhood they sewed shut as well. Then they burned her brain so she could not use the Sight, like the worst punishments reserved for a Sighted male who forced himself upon a woman, for whom mere death was not enough.

But she heard them. She heard them quite well. Heard

them as they called her "Liar" and "Oathbreaker" and "Deceiver." "Mistress of the Assassin" was also common, as were "False Bride" and "Dur's Whore." They scourged her as they did this, whether to purify her soul or amuse themselves in the same way such a process would have amused Mirrialta, had she been on the other end, she never could tell.

But I did not send the assassin, Mirrialta thought. *I did not send Thador. I don't know who did.*

She never did know, and that was the worst torture of all.

[3]

Breith and Cymel made their way back to Cyfareth with Firill and the rest of the students, as well as Amhar. Since the time of the Settling, they found that the Pneuma was harder to draw upon and their magic was somewhat diminished, to the point where Corysiam could no longer Bridge, only Walk, and Amhar could not Walk at all.

The Pneuma had returned to the world, and with it the flowers and Pneuma-born butterflies, as well as the gods, and the little gods.

There was a new little god at the University, one they could only call Mole, or Little Mole to distinguish him from their friend. Little Mole was small and black, with sharp claws and a sharp wit, and a tendency to appear, scribble cryptic notations in students' books, then run off somewhere else and spy on people.

"I suppose it's penance enough," Mole said, and sighed, "but I never would have forgiven myself had I not gone."

"Never forgive! Never forgive!" chanted Little God Mole, dancing about the room.

Mole sighed again. "But at least I've returned to regular physical flesh."

"Flesh! Flesh!" cried the Little God Mole, popping up out of a hole in the floor and stabbing his claws into Mole's leg to make him jump.

Mole kicked at him and he disappeared. "Can you imagine having all of your worst personality traits given form to follow you around?"

Cymel laughed. "I'm beginning to get an idea." She looked around, at Mole, and at Lyanz, sitting on the couch holding hands with Amhar, the golden boy looking as beautiful and substantial as ever, if not greater and grander.

Lyanz laughed as well. "I believe that was my brother's idea of a joke. The Maratha Monks are known for their humor."

"And?" asked Breith.

Lyanz shrugged. "They believe that in the next life, you'll be confronted by your sins in this one. Since this is Mole's next life, I think Kyodal decided to let him deal with his sins now."

"Sins!" echoed the Little God Mole, purring and rubbing up against Firill's leg.

"And what else?"

Lyanz sighed. "I'm not really cut out to be a god. That much Power, that much responsibility. . . . I mean, I pretty much made a botch of being the Hero. I wouldn't have made it if it weren't for everyone else. And while maybe the worlds need a Hero to restore the Balance, I think they need a Saint to keep it. And that's my brother."

Mole waved his hand. "It makes sense if you look at it. Neither of us are really ready to give up earthly pleasures, and besides which, there were countless decoy heroes for the true Hero. What if the Hero were merely a ploy of the gods to get the Saint into position to take His place among them?"

The Little God Mole appeared on the edge of the black-

board and began to sketch complex mathematical and theatrical diagrams, and when they looked, began scratching his
nails on the slate till everyone held their ears.

"Well," said Mole at last, "it's only a theory."

Rinchay Matan, once Shaman of the Dmar Spyonk, sat
and rocked, chanting her mantra. "The Liar is dead. The Liar
is dead." Seasons came and went, grasses growing over her,
and successive repetitions wove the spell, transmuting hollow
pain to finality, and with it, the phrase: "The Lie is over."

Anger that had once borne maggots melted like hoarfrost
in the sun, passing through its changes till it became grief.
The tears began to flow down her cheeks, one for each of
the fallen souls of the Grass Clans, for each of the Alaeshin,
for each of the Odyggas, the Death Guides, who had poured
their own loss and need for vengeance into her.

And for Kamkajar, the Merciful and All-Mighty, the Parter
of Seasons, god of her clan-now-gone.

Rinchay wept, the tears flowing out of her, the grief transmuting to acceptance and the tears to crystal, pearls of
Pneuma like barleycorns. Seeds.

Rinchay spread her skirts to catch their fall, knowing what
she must do, her final task. She took the silver sickle-knife from
her belt and cut her right wrist in a long, low cut, deep enough
to well the heartblood, shallow enough to give her time.

Seeds must be watered, and she had no more tears.

She stood, rising up past the parched grass, skirts become
sacks, filled with the souls of her clan and her borrowed Power,
Power that she now would repay, with interest. Her clan had
died for her when the Liar deceived her into betraying the Shaman's Shawl. It was only fitting that she die in turn.

She was nothing without them, a dry husk. Even if the
world had not ended as the other folk who had been here
had spoken, her own world had ended a long while ago.

A hand into the grain, a flick of her right wrist across the fields as she walked, scattering Pneuma-pearls and droplets of blood in a spray of red and white across the gold of the dry grass that still lay trampled from the battle seasons past, salted with blood till little would grow. Trampled and forgotten like the souls of the Grass Clans. She was the only one who remembered, and again she cast them forth, again she set them free.

Again and again. They rained down like tiny hailstones, like pearls of graupel hitting the grass in a late winter storm, not quite turned to spring, slowly melting in the sun.

She had thought the tears were gone, but new ones came, water from a hidden reservoir. Her own. And with it came song:

Hear me, my Alaeshin,
souls of my clan,
souls of my Guides,
I am nothing without you.
An empty husk for your corn.
A rind for your seeds.
A calabash filled with your grain.
What I took,
I give back.
What I held,
I release.
I am death,
bearing life
in my heart.
Borrowed life.
I give you back what you gave me,
and what little I can repay:
my love
and my dreams. . . .

Rinchay sang the last word as she fell to her knees, her skirts falling straight and the last of the Pneuma grains falling with them and her tears and her blood.

And her love and dreams.

Fingers clenching the earth, she watched the seeds take root, graincorns sinking into the soil, putting up small shoots and leaves, fine tendrils rising and twining, growing up straight and rising higher and higher into the sky, into the clouds that dappled the skies of the Grasslands until they branched out, taking a recognizable form: Kamkajar, the Parter of Seasons, arms outstretched.

His golden hand on the right, ready to scatter the seeds of life as Rinchay had just done for him, gestured to his Alaeshin rising up in a row from the fields where Rinchay had walked.

And in his black left hand, his scythe, the black edge of flaked obsidian, swept down in an arc.

Rinchay hardly felt it when it touched her, but then Kamkajar leaned down to her, offering her his golden right hand. After a pause, she took it and he raised her up to his level, a measure of the Pneuma Power she had returned to him flowing back into her.

A very large measure.

It was an odd thing to be looking eye to eye with a god, but his eyes, black and gold like his hands, were laughing. *Welcome, Rinchay. Rinchay the Redeemed,* his mindvoice echoed in her skull. She still didn't quite understand, but then she saw her body lying broken and bloodless on the ground, trailing from the tip of Kamkajar's scythe. Rinchay looked to her god and he took the rag that had been her body, drawing it out and twisting it until it became a fringed triangle of leather, of spirit, which he draped about her shoulders, knotting the fringes in the front of the shawl into a bride's knot. *My consort.*

But I am nothing, Rinchay thought back.

And I would be nothing without your dreams, Shaman. Your dreams and your love.

Again, Kamkajar offered her his golden right hand. *My thanks,* she thought as she took it, *I only gave what I had.*

It was more than any other could give. And it was more than enough.